# FOR THE LOVED AND LOST

## THE TUCKER CLAN SAGA
### Book 3

ETHAN WARRENER

*For Lydia*

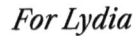

# Contents

# Characters

The Hollands

Mr. Phil Holland- Gunsmith

Mrs. Leah Holland- Phil's second wife, blood mother of Clive and Margaret

Ella Holland- The gunsmith's daughter, a couple years past marrying age with a shy disposition to account for it

Clive and Margaret Holland- Ella's younger half-siblings


Bill Puckett- The Powderman


The Taylor Boys

Amos Taylor- The clan's golden boy, a promising young man, Phil's apprentice guncrank

Harvey Taylor- The eldest of the boys, apprenticing at his father's smithy

Dale Taylor- The youngest of the boys, still shy of apprenticing age (Deceased)


The Drifter- Omar Walking


Mr. Elvin McDaniel- The Watchman

Ralph McDaniel- The Watchman's son and apprentice, a bookish kid (Missing, presumed dead)

Mr. Sam Chambers- The clan Schoolmaster and Middlespeaker

The Brodys
Old Man Brody- The clan patriarch, few call him by his given name, "Salvador"
Mr. Job Brody- Local farmer and crack shot
Ricky Brody- Job's eldest son (Assimilated by an American neurocaster)
Mr. Arnold Brody- The clan butcher
Mrs. Charlotte Brody- Arnold's wife
Becky Brody- Arnold and Charlotte's eldest daughter
Reverend Oliver Brody- The spiritual leader of the clan

The Fillmores
Mr. Rick Fillmore- Hunter and trapper
Victor Fillmore- Rick's son, of the same profession
Mrs. Sophie Fillmore- Victor's new bride, daughter to Bill Puckett and close friend to Ella and Becky

Dr. Jacob Bernhard- The clan physician
Mrs. Helen Bernhard- The doctor's wife and the clan nurse

Mr. Shane Bunton- The carpenter
Nigel Bunton- Shane's son
Mr. Alfred Bunton- Shane's brother

Bert Daly- The town good-for-nothing, a real ornery cuss (Deceased)
Melissa Daly- A young woman with an unsavory reputation before her marriage to Bert

The Grierson Settlement
Johnny Grierson- Head of the settlement, a mean, one-eyed son-of-a-gun

ETHAN WARRENER

Edward Grierson- Johnny's cousin
The Coles- One of the prominent settlement families

Families tending the outlying farms
The Newells- To the south (Many deceased following a Greeenbrier
    raid)
The Hadleys- To the south-west
The Job Brodys- To the north
The Craines- To the west

Other Clansmen of Note
Deek Evans
Clyde McDaniel
Joe Garmen
The Finches

Prominent Junkers
Cora Compton- The Junker Middlespeaker
Mayce Salazar- The Archivist
Jody Perkins- The archival apprentice

The Americans
Colonel Selina Armstrong- Commander of the American garrison at
New Ashburn
Captain Royce Carlson- Leader of the protection force sent to watch
over the Tucker clan
Lieutenant William Chitman- Leader of scouting expeditions
Lieutenant Harlow- Overseer of conscripted labor
Jarvis- Role unknown

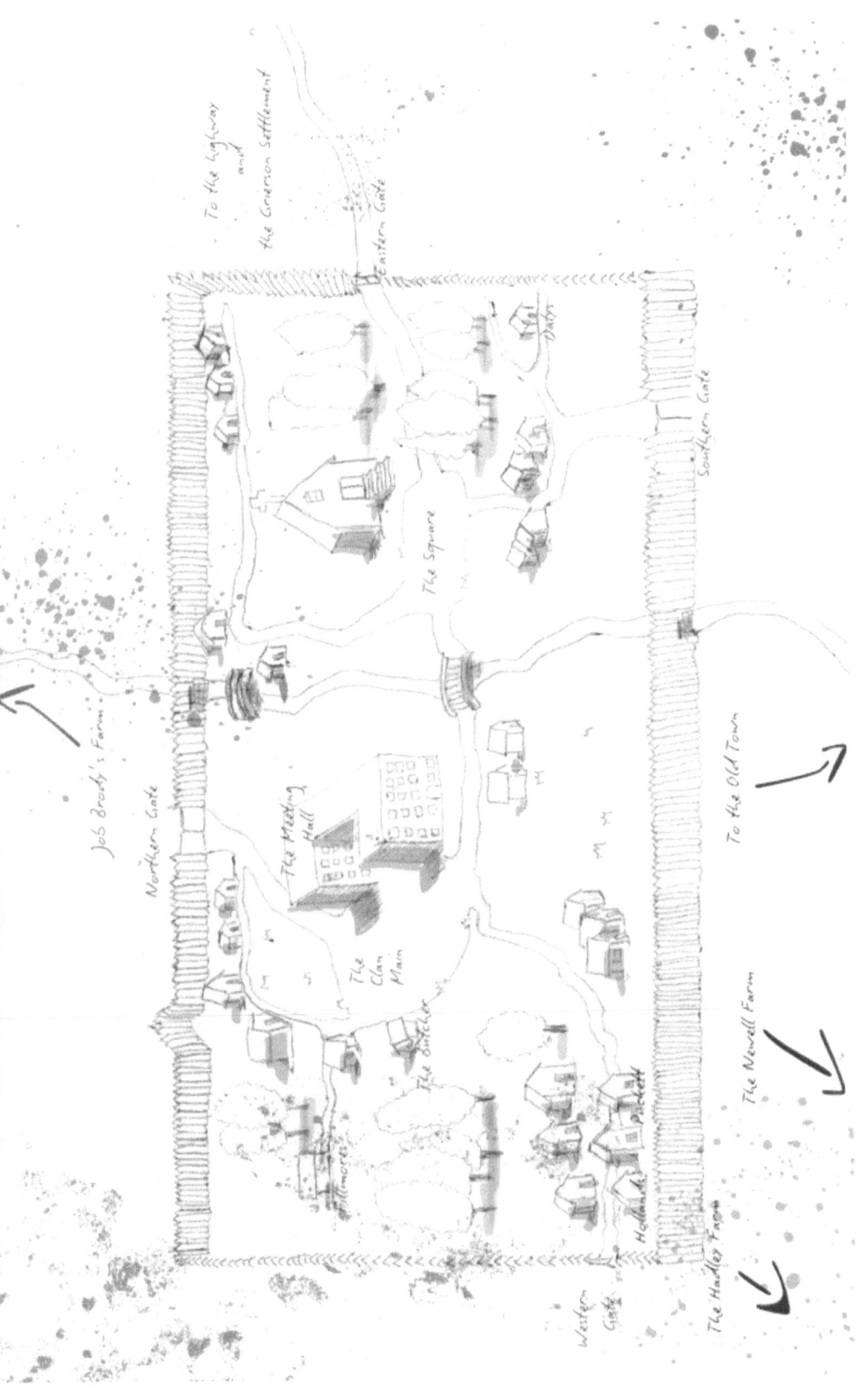

# Chapter 1: The Slow Death

3 Years Ago

*The birdsongs take their time coming back in the wake of the screevler's death cries. The two Tucker siblings don't move from the bubbling brook where they crouch, the older garbed in a tattered base-ball cap and hemp shirt with bib coveralls, the younger in a flaxen skirt and synthetic fiber t-shirt. The older is a man with the confidence of youth and the aptitude to almost match it. The younger is a girl barely old enough for marrying but plenty old enough for womanhood to destroy whatever confidence she might have had as a child. Her breath catches when he suggests the screams might have come from a trap the Tuckers hadn't set.*

*"I'm gonna go check it out."*

*She objects but doesn't move. It's not enough to hold him back, not nearly. The young man primes his black powder muzzle loader and steals into the forest. The sister's low breath rustles the dead leaves underneath her as she waits.*

*The birds sing their frivolous songs, and the brook continues to bubble steadily away. The young woman waits and peers through the leaves for any sign of movement, but she does not move. A pair of squirrels skitter up the side of a tree in a furtive chase.*

*The birdsongs cut short again as a human scream of pain pierces the woods, about as far off as the unbred shriek had been. The young woman holds her breath without meaning to. Another cry rends the air, a cry she recognizes. Flutterings of agonized words she cannot make out echo through the dell, followed by the murmur of a fading whimper and a sob. The young woman's lip bleeds under her teeth as she waits in vain for her brother to return.*

*After a time, the birds continue their silly little songs, and the brook bubbles carelessly away. Neither heed the young woman's tears.*

New Ashburn

Ella didn't know how long she had been in this cell. It was so dark that she couldn't see her hand in front of her face.

The first day had stretched for a lifetime. By the time her captors had brought food to her—some boiled pottage—she'd felt like she would go crazy cooped up in the dark. They had moved her back into an empty storage room in the main building since then, and the passage of several scant mealtimes had told her days had passed. The food she got was tasteless and insufficient, even with her doing nothing but pacing the three steps afforded her between the walls of her enclosure.

What she felt after the first few days—it must have been days—might have been called boredom, but the word didn't seem to fit whatever this experience was. It was a ponderous, awful thing, hitting her in waves, attacking her head, crawling under her skin, waking her when she slept, confusing and mocking her. She started imagining bugs invading her cell, perhaps attracted by the stench of her bucket, but then staying to get into her hair and under her clothes. She scratched herself all over, trying to get the creepy-crawlies off of her. But whenever the door opened, the room was still empty.

In the first day or two, and sometimes off and on as the days passed, she prayed God would save her, that He would let this cup pass from her, that everyone would be all right when she got back, that she would go back at all. There was nothing to do but wait and pray. She wasn't sure what she was waiting for, but she knew what to pray for. She had plenty. She prayed for the safety of the other captives, the slaves calling themselves Sylvanians, for Sophie and her babies, for Becky and Amos and Omar and Clive and Margaret and her pa. She prayed for Leah, who'd always tried to be as good a stepmom to Ella as she was a mom to Clive and Margaret. She prayed for Johnny Grierson and that hardened heart of his, and for Melissa Daly, bless her soul. She even prayed the Americans would see the error of their wicked ways and repent.

And she prayed often for herself. She prayed that she would have courage, that she would always do the right thing and follow the Lord's will, and that she could get out of this situation with her skin and mind whole. She prayed that the vile men here would never look at her that way again, or better yet, that she wouldn't have to see them again. And as long as God was freely answering prayers, if it wasn't too much to ask, perhaps a handsome young man could ride in and rescue her.

Who was she kidding?

Tucker Territory

Becky leaned up against the split-rail fence to stare out across the narrow meadow at the rusty yellow leaves of the paw-paw grove she used to raid for fruit this time of year, at the oaks still holding onto their green color but not their acorns, and at the scarlet staghorn sumac growing below the dappled canopy. At the bottom of the slopes, scattered honey locust trees burst forth with a golden display that masked the vicious clusters of thorns growing from their trunks. The burrs on the chestnut trees were opening, and soon they would drop bushel upon bushel of nuts. The hills stretching beyond flaunted an array of tawny reds flickering like a low fire in the light of the waning day.

Town folks were apt, in simpler times, to set their hogs and goats loose in this hollow. The forage from the seed pods, the fruit, the berries, the nuts, all of it would sustain them on through the winter, human and animal both. A cornucopia of plenty lay within her sight and just beyond her reach, and this split-rail fence was as far as she could go. Sorghum cutting time was about took up. Her pa would have brought out old Shooshie, harness the mule up to the sorghum mill's crank arm, and set the crushing cylinders turning while folks brought in the cane they'd grown outside the clan walls. In simpler times, they would have cooked the juice on down to molasses all day, the air filled with the aroma of warm spice, young folks spinning the sugar into taffy and playing flirty games like candy-breakin'. A boy would take one end of a long chaw of taffy clamped between his teeth and challenge a girl he fancied to bite off the other end, with the winner choosing their next partner. Becky'd nearly got her first kiss that a-way, and if the Americans had let the Tuckers carry on with their lives at all, she'd have likely got a smooch this year from Amos Taylor. All of those expectations, the little looking-forwards, which on their own meant nothing but taken together meant everything, had vanished in the face of the Americans' power, just like Amos himself.

A breeze rattled the tall, dry bluestem and switchgrass growing up in the open spaces and tugged at the fraying patches in her baggy sweatpants, pulling at her as if to remind her not to tarry. Not with an American soldier breathing down her neck. The wind was not yet cold, but Becky still had to rub the gooseflesh rising on her arms. She ignored the wind. No hurry would move her along before she was good and ready. There was nothing in town for her to do. The Americans had shut down everything. No work, no play, no front porch meetings, no kitchen conversations. Nothing.

All for their safety, Captain Royce Carlson had told them. As a gesture of his deep commitment to the Tuckers' wellbeing and safety, he'd set himself up on a rocking chair on a section of boardwalk out near the clan main, where he pretended to make himself available for hearing the concerns of any party. But no one was allowed to approach him. Actually, no *Tuckers* were allowed to approach him. He sat on his wooden throne while the soldiers came and went as they pleased, talking in muffled voices, sometimes laughing, sometimes pointing at this or that passerby. More than a few times, soldiers had pointed at her with smiles that reminded her of her standoff with the Greenbriers at the Newell homestead this last May.

*I like it when they play coy. Come on, honey, talk dirty to me.*

Becky's fingernails dug into the wood grain of the fence. She dared not turn from where she stood facing the hollow, lest the American guarding her see the scowl on her face. The elders ought never have signed that treaty. The thought galled her even as it came to her, seeing as how her best friend's father had been saved through the treaty. But Phil Holland, having recovered from his infection thanks to American-supplied antibiotics, would now be sent off to die in the Americans' war against some people Becky had never heard of. The Americans would steal away Becky and her father, and her uncles and aunts and cousins, and even her grandfather, just as they had already stolen away her cousin Ricky, and Bill Puckett, and Melissa Daly and her toddling son, and Omar Walking. And Ella.

Becky fought back the angry tears welling up in her eyes. They never should have signed that treaty. Better to have started shooting, even against the Americans' absurd firepower, than submit to this. Now it was too late. The Americans had locked away the watchman two months now, and no one had seen the schoolmaster for nearly as long. Not that the schoolmaster would have made any difference; he'd gone over so completely to the Americans' side, he might as well have been one of them. About a month ago, they had taken the reverend and locked the clan down as if they'd been in the middle of a pigman siege. The Americans had rounded up all the Tuckers' guns, their arrows, even their spears and matchets. Everything but their knitting needles had disappeared into the bowels of the clan meetinghouse, which had become the sole domain of the Americans. Last and worst of all, Amos Taylor had gone in after the guns and never come out. The Americans had vanished him, too, the bright young man who seemed to succeed wherever set his gaze, whom Becky couldn't keep from admiring no matter how foolhardy he could be. She cursed her weakness. The Americans had proved too powerful a challenge even for him, and Becky did not know if he were dead or alive. She suspected the former, though it seized her heart to think it. The four-story building that had swallowed Amos along with everything else loomed over the town now, not as a bulwark, not as a citadel, but as one more reminder of the Americans' control: their fortress, their storehouse, their armory, their prison.

All for the Tuckers' good, Carlson and his thugs had reminded her time upon time. Wouldn't want any accidents to happen. Have to keep you safe from the "geemoes." Keeping the peace.

Becky stared out at the colorful foliage and listened to the lazy stridulation of the meadow katydids droning their way to coming winter. A year ago, she would have beheld the arcadian swale below and thought of nature stretching tired limbs for a long winter nap. She would have felt the satisfied exhaustion of a field worker coming in from a day well spent, smells of sanded wood and worn leather on the wind, ready to prop up one's feet and contemplate the flurries of fallen leaves brought on by a mellow weathering.

Now a ponderous death knell rang over it all, a swan song. The faint sweetness in the air was that of over-ripeness, of the first sign of rot.

She would never see this place again. Rumor had it the Americans were ready to move out with the Tucker "conscripts" tomorrow. She was a survivor by nature, but she had no illusions about what the Americans intended for her or the others. They were here to break up the Tucker clan, to pull them up by the root, remove them from the land, and shatter every bond that held them together.

"I wish you were here, Ella," Becky whispered to herself.

New Ashburn

Jody Perkins woke to the sounds of men suffering the agonies of the damned. The sound of men burning stalked the edges of her mind, sounds which receded as she swam up from the somnolent depths of dreams which were not wholly dreams. Her hand went up to touch the burn on the side of her face. The marring she'd received from the leachate chemicals still itched sometimes, sometimes more than itched, etching her face to the bone, sizzling her brain. She couldn't tell if it was from permanent nerve damage or the same mind-shackles that filled her ears with the sounds of burning slaves—prisoners.

She wondered if it weren't a mercy that Colonel Armstrong had ordered the injured slaves—prisoners, she reminded herself—hung. Or was it merely to save resources and keep Bill Puckett on track?

A wail carried through the cool night air outside her cramped quarters in Bill Puckett's new slap-dash office. The screams hadn't been mere dreams, nor memories. One casualty of the disaster in Bill's factory remained alive, and that casualty was a child. The cries belonged to little Earnest Daly, and though slow healing had taken the edge off those first gut-wrenching shrieks, Jody knew she wouldn't sleep any more tonight even if the cries stopped immediately.

She got up and walked outside, then down the outdoor stairs running down the side of what was once some sort of garage and now served as Mr. Puckett's new office. Past the shuttered workshops stood New Ashburn's inner gate guarding the path up to the clan's citadel, once a weather station and now Colonel Armstrong's headquarters. It watched her, cold and imposing—her people's citadel, now an ever-watching tower. She shook her head at the bad dreams still clinging to her. She had no cause to fear Armstrong. She'd done nothing wrong. She'd been a valuable asset to the Americans. She *was* an American. Everyone here except the Sylvanian prisoners of war were citizens of the New American Federation, but... it looked more and more like two kinds of Americans peopled these parts, and only one kind was allowed into Armstrong's sanctum. The only exceptions had been Mister Ricky Brody and Miss Ella Holland, and they had gone in chains. These past few weeks had taxed Jody to the point of distraction, even without taking into account the disastrous fire at the factory. She touched a hand to the puckered skin on one side of her face and chewed her lip. She understood there was a war on, but she'd never seen any fighting. The front was more than a hundred miles away. Why did there have to be such strict military control? Couldn't Armstrong work something out with the powdermaker?

Jody turned to Mr. Puckett's new office. He would likely be sleeping down there, not even stretched out on the mattress the slaves—prisoners—had dragged in on the floor for him. No, he'd be in there with his head rested on the table, a pile of half-done notes and figures scattered in front of him, a whole mess Jody would try to organize in her vain struggle to standardize his mercurial approach to chemistry. He'd been driving himself as hard as his workers, trying to get the factory back up and running again, trying to appease Colonel Armstrong, trying to cobble together some semblance of a functioning formula after Miss Holland had destroyed or hidden Mr. Puckett's originals. Maybe he hoped he could get Miss Holland back, though after several weeks in the Americans' citadel, and considering what the Colonel had already done to those she'd deemed seditious, Jody didn't hold out hope for it. Ricky Brody had emerged from American captivity, but he hadn't sabotaged Colonel Armstrong's nitrogel production, and even then, he'd come out... different.

Bill wasn't in his office, and the wails were coming from further off, in the direction of the western gate. Jody Perkins followed the sound of the cries down the lane, past empty workshops and smithies, until a group of figures resolved themselves down by the factory. A susurrus of hushed voices rose now to the level of hearing in between little Earnest's exhausted cries and whimpers. As she approached, she distinguished first the voices, then the forms, of Bill Puckett, Omar Walking, and Melissa Daly—the three Tuckers not taken up by Colonel Armstrong's disciplinary purge. The three of them had drawn closer together since Miss Ella and Mister Ricky had been detained, meeting often to commiserate, Jody supposed, or in this case to tend to Earnest's healing burns. The child's cries and whimpers obscured their words until Jody had drawn close.

"Can't hardly do anything with Captain Harlow breathing down my—" Mr. Puckett stopped at the sound of Jody's footsteps. "Who's that?"

"It's me. Earnest woke me up."

"We can't be giving him the ether no more. Doctor's worried it'll hurt him," Mr. Puckett said.

"We got him past the worst of it," Mrs. Daly said, perhaps to remind herself it wasn't as bad as it could be. "Now it's up to the willow tea and snuggles to do the trick."

"Can..." Jody stepped forward. "Can I hold him?"

Mrs. Daly sighed. "If he'll let you, I reckon you can."

Jody had worked with them long enough for Earnest to recognize her voice as that of "the paint lady." She lifted him up, close to her face, close to her own burns, and Earnest quieted as if he knew Jody understood his hurt. "I reckon he'll heal up nice."

"But he never shoulda been anywhere near the factory," Bill said the thousandth time since the accident. "When I get this going again, 'Lissa, I'm a-gonna put you on kid duty all day. No more of this juggling three jobs at once."

"But she's your apprentice," Jody said. "The way Colonel Armstrong is right now, I don't reckon she'll allow for any unnecessary tasks. Maybe I could..." She shrugged, patting Earnest on the back.

"Watch him?" Bill said. "But you're working for me, too. I like your gumption, but—"

"Actually," Omar Walking, the steel-cut apprentice who rarely fraternized with even his own clansmen, spoke up for the first time. "That might not be a bad idea. Keep Earnest out of our hair while we get this mess at the factory cleaned up. Armstrong doesn't have to know about this, as long as she gets her nitrogel, right?"

Bill and Omar exchanged a look that went on longer than Jody expected. "Yeah, I guess that could work," the powdermaker said. "Thanks for the help, Miss Perkins. Just keep him cared for and out of trouble, well away from the factory, okay?"

Melissa Daly, Bill's half-breed apprentice, stepped forward to place a hand on the unbandaged side of Earnest's face in motherly affection. "I'll help you put him back to bed now that he's settled."

Jody went along without resistance, but she left with her mind more unsettled than when she first woke up. They were trying to get her out of the way. Of what, she did not know and had no desire to speculate.

Bill Puckett frowned down from his slapdash open-air office at the scrawny kid struggling to bear up the weight of the clay he carried into the blistering heat of the kilns. Most of the kilns were in full swing, firing fresh bricks for building materials and roasting iron pyrite to free up gaseous sulfur oxides. A couple kilns were down for maintenance, with slaves chipping away at the deposits of impurities building up on the output flues.

Copper likely crusted up in those deposits, a valuable mineral in its own right, but Bill didn't have the time or inclination to worry about how to extract anything useful from the waste economically. He might have passed such profitable information along to the junkers, but he hadn't the time or inclination to update them on anything other than necessities lately. And even though his mind habitually registered things like temperature control and brick output and sulfide extraction efficiency, he had neither the time nor inclination to do any more than delegate with a wave of his hand.

His eyes followed the scrawny kid.

If this were a pigman siege, and all the boy had to do was sit on his hands and wait, then he probably had enough calories in his diet to keep him healthy. But this wasn't a pigman siege. The guards around the work camp weren't looking out for unbreds; they were looking in to keep the slaves going and the quotas up. And the kid slipping on the footpath wasn't sitting on his hands; he was toiling fourteen hours a day, pulling clay from the riverbank down yonder in the rapidly cooling fall temperatures and hauling it back to the searing heat of the brick production facilities. The kid's cheeks were going hollow, his eyes sinking back into their sockets, the exact shape of his skull coming through his tightening skin more clearly with each passing day. And all the slaves were in that boat since Armstrong had cut the rations in half to feed the ever-growing numbers of Americans coming through New Ashburn. One of the older prisoners hadn't woken this morning, and

11

Bill had seen two Ashburnite thugs dragging the body out to the woods to leave in a trash heap somewhere.

And he still hadn't seen any sign of Ella since they'd dragged her up to the citadel up the hill.

Ricky Brody had showed up again, but Ricky didn't act like Ricky any-more. He slept in the barracks with the New Asbhurnite thugs and came out dressed in the same American army fatigues as the New Ashburnite thugs. He rarely spoke and rarely came around to see Bill, except to pass along the next quota or demand from Armstrong. He rarely even spoke to Bill, but instead to Bill's handler, Lieutenant Harlow. Ricky had become another one of Armstrong's lackeys. When Bill complained, he only shrugged and said, "Armstrong gives the orders." It meant—if it wasn't clear enough to Bill already—that he was not in charge, even of his own apprentices.

A cry and a ruckus brought Bill out of his reverie. He turned to the ladder leading down from his office to see the kid again, this time coming back from the brick kilns, and not of his own will. Lieutenant Harlow was dragging him along by the ear, an American autopistol slung into a holster under his other arm.

"What the hell is going on?" Bill scrambled down the ladder to the work floor.

The American soldier turned back with a glance that said Bill was no longer important enough to warrant an explanation, but he gave one anyway. "I'm taking him up to see Armstrong. I'm to report any insubordination directly to her."

"Colonel Armstrong has plenty on her plate without having to worry about a runt acting out. Give 'im to me." Bill reached out and grabbed the kid by the wrist and jerked him back away from Harlow. "What're you up to, you rascal? Tryin' to throw off my through-put? Tryin' to slack off?" He boxed the boy's ear, which the boy took with physical passivity, even if his eyes stared back with hate.

"I have to take him to Armstrong," Harlow said persistently.

"I'm having a hard enough time meeting my quotas without workers keeling over and getting hauled off to the colonel. You wanna help, you can take his place at the kilns while he's gone."

Lieutenant Harlow's face was blank, unreadable, so absent the sheen of civility he once wore that Bill's hair prickled on the back of his neck. "Fine," he said finally. "I'm still reporting this to Armstrong."

Once the lieutenant was gone, Bill turned back to the kid and shook him by his raggedy collar. "Listen here, you little shit, I won't have you—" He darted a glance over his shoulder, then grabbed the kid by the face to meet his eyes and hissed at him, nose-to-nose. "*Not. Yet.*"

Bill waited just long enough for the kid's scowl to unravel in confusion before pushing him away as if disgusted. "I'm moving you to help with the laundry. See if you like dousing your hands in a vat of soiled American uniforms better than kiln-work. Tell the foreman I sent you."

The boy's confused stare only grew. Bill's flyspeck twitch of a wink sent him on his way.

# Chapter 2: The Mind-Body Problem

T ucker Territory

Royce cut into an apple as big as his fist and examined the white flesh inside for pests. A farmer south of town had cultivated a decent little apple orchard, a rare thing even in civilized areas. With the clan confined to the inside of the walls and the autumn apple harvest coming in, his men had found it productive to patrol that direction daily.

Standing at attention down from the Tucker's meeting-room stage, Lieutenant Chitman waited without touching the bushel of apples in front of him, even if his gaze did wander towards it. The deep recon expedition, so soon after having run errands all the way out to New Ashburn and then further on toward D.C., had left him leaner coming back than going out, Royce thought. Hauling even one proxy off-road over these mountains had to be a pain in the ass.

"God, this apple is spliced," Royce said, savoring the mellow flavor of the fruit. "What have you got?" He asked with his mouth half full.

"No direct sign of the Pied Piper or any of his proxies."

"So he's moved on?"

Chitman shook his head. "He's around. We've found steadily increasing modified spoor the further south we go. I kept expecting to run into a pigman swarm or something, but about three days out, it became clear whatever geemo force concentration is building, they're evading us. Massed complex behavior indicates influence from a broad neurocaster network."

"But he's still too weak to make a move."

"Or he was trying to lead the patrol into a trap. We estimated several hundred pigmen before we turned back."

"We can deal with a few hundred geemoes. I can't deal with a super-critical neuronet."

"I can't offer direct evidence of that either way, but if he'd transitioned already, I don't see why he'd bother remaining in the region."

"He's either waiting to make a play for the Tucker neurocasters, or he wants to intercept any of ours we'd send out here to assimilate them."

"Or both."

Royce Carlson nodded. "Or both. But it seems obvious to me he's still too weak to make a move either way."

"There's a problem, though."

"What's that?"

"I read your debriefing from the Tucker kid. The one you caught sneaking into the meetinghouse. The number of pigman carcasses scattered around the clan corroborates what he said. It's likely that leading elements of the Pied Piper's neuronet have been in the region for the last nine months."

Royce stopped in the middle of lifting an apple slice to his mouth and frowned. "Then why hasn't he already assimilated them? Nine months, and all he got was the trapper, who the elders already cauterized?"

"Which, sir, means two things to me: Either he's assimilated more of the Tuckers than we know—"

"We'd see it in their sleeping patterns."

"—or the Tuckers have a secret network of their own set up to defend against assimilation."

Captain Carlson pursed his lips. "Their preacher. We've already arrested him for promulgating subversive elements. I'll deal with him. Anything else?"

"Nothing significant from the patrol. But... permission to speak freely, sir?"

Royce ran a hand over his growing stubble. "What is it?"

"Jarvis is... he's developed a taste for the brainshine."

"I am well aware. We need strong neurocaster networks for this line of work."

"We don't need further assimilations."

"Have *you* found the Pied Piper or his proxies yet?"

Chitman ignored the rhetorical question. "Jarvis doesn't care about the Pied Piper, except as... competition. He's going to get careless and either go rogue or get assimilated himself."

"I'll pretend you didn't just accuse a serviceman of treason without evidence."

"You know that's not what I meant—"

"I've noted your concerns. He can't go rogue and still expect my men to watch his proxies. He needs me more than I need him. And well-established networks don't get assimilated."

"The Pied Piper has already grabbed—"

"We don't know how the Pied Piper grabbed those recruits. What we *do* know is the science of how neurocasting assimilation works. Lone neurocasters are vulnerable, but even a small network distributes the subconscious among its proxies. Which means networks don't get assimilated. Which means Jarvis can't get assimilated. Period."

"All the same, sir—"

"I'll monitor Jarvis. That's why I'm selecting you for this next assignment."

"Sir?"

"That 'drifter' informant we were using—Harper and Riggs were supposed to take care of him, nice and quiet, and I'm assuming they didn't. It's been weeks now, and I've been out of contact with Colonel Armstrong too long. Take a squad and tell her I'll be departing with the Tucker neurocasters."

Roundswalks at the Grierson settlement had slowed to almost nothing—not because Captain Carlson forbade Johnny from taking such precautions, but because the Americans clearly had everything in hand.

Johnny had reached an understanding with the American captain: Let the half-and-halfs mind their business, and Johnny would look the other way. Until the Americans were gone with their Tucker draftees, he thought it best not to rub shoulders with the occupiers as much as possible.

So, when Johnny and his cousin took a stroll for fresh air away from the mine, it was, for once, precisely for leisure and not to scout for lurking enemies or unbreds. Neither of them meant to notice the crashing and rustling in the woods, but once they did, the force of long-cultivated habit compelled them to investigate.

Johnny ran through the possibilities in his mind as he picked his way through the woods. A bullhusker could stir up such all-fired consternation, but not all across a hill slope at the same time. It must be a pack of pigmen, except pigmen didn't cause such a ruckus unless they were charging, and whatever moved down in the dell seemed careless with the noise.

It was when he glimpsed movement far down in the foliage that he recognized human forms—a hundred yards out, maybe.

"Edward, get yourself along yonder, set up a firing angle," Johnny muttered.

"Greenbriers?"

Johnny shook his head. "I'd think they were nomads, but they're off the roads. Just space yourself out, in case."

Whoever was in the woods trudged on up through the trees and undergrowth, and soon, Johnny could make out the distinct shapes and military fatigues of soldiers—Americans, two score of them, easy. But they were coming from the northeast, in from the highway, not from the town direction. Newcomers, then.

While Johnny pondered this curiosity, it seemed Edward had had enough time to arrive at his own conclusion. Once the foremost elements had arrived to within rock-throwing distance, he hailed them. "Ho there! Grierson folks here. What brings so many of y'uns all the way out here?"

The Americans ducked down at first, but then, seeing they weren't being ambushed, one man—an officer of some rank Johnny didn't care to know—hiked on ahead toward Edward. "Had some trouble with some geemoes," the American explained, scanning the woods around him as he spoke. "Have you noticed any geemo activity around your settlement?"

Edward stepped out of cover to give his answer, and what had up to that point been a vague sense of wariness at the back of Johnny's mind flared to an inferno of alarm. *Wrong, wrong, wrong*—everything about this was wrong.

"Eddie, don't—" he called out to his cousin, but it was too late.

The American officer brought his rifle up and shot Edward square in the middle of the face.

Even after seeing most of his cousin's head disappear in a spray of gore, Johnny didn't call out. Not that it mattered. He'd already opened his stupid, fat mouth, and several American eyes were already looking his way.

The span between him and them wasn't far—close enough for him to hit something even firing from low ready. And through the great puff of smoke erupting from the barrel of his gun, he saw a soldier jerk and fall.

Johnny let the recoil of his rifle carry him into a pivot to hightail it out of there, and a scant few strides up the slope brought a hail of lead all around him. A piece of hot metal carried away part of his right ear, but his mind barely took note of it. Most of his focus was on putting as many trees between him and his pursuers as possible without tripping on a branch in his half-blindness. With any luck, they were still shooting at his plume of gunsmoke.

Did he have time to reload? He jumped up behind a massive oak tree and pulled out his ramrod. A bullet spat up from below and ricocheted off the tree beside him. He jumped, dropped his charge of powder, and swore. They were closer than he thought.

Johnny waved a hand so they'd mark his position, then backed up away from the tree, keeping it between him and his pursuers. Then he broke into a run, scampering from soft earth to flinty bedrock as he crossed a dried-out crick and cut his way up a game trail weaving its way around a steep precipice. Spindly trees thrust roots into the hillside like mountain-climbers clinging on for dear life. Deposits of coal-bit shale jutted out from the hillside, and his hand smeared with coal dust as he grabbed the wall for support. Beneath his feet, the mossy slope dropped away as sharp as an ax blade. In his younger days, when he had two eyes and more agile feet, he could have jumped down that slope using nothing but roots and tree trunks for footholds. Now, it was all he could do to keep his footing, and he was dead if he didn't.

Johnny didn't hear the cry of his pursuers catching sight of his fleeing backside, but he did hear the bullet they fired whizz past his head. Pieces of shale and coal from the Appalachian mountainside stung his cheek. He swung around a tree and leaped for cover on the other side of the narrow path. He ducked through the trees and slid into a crouch behind a mound of stones uphill from the path.

He ventured a peek at his quarry. The timber and undergrowth concealed them at first, but then a flash of movement down yonder gave them away. They were coming this way, still thirsty for his blood.

Johnny reloaded his gun and got himself a good firing position offset at an angle from the mountain's game trail. The Americans had made it to the narrow path now, and they were working their way across in single file, fifty yards away without a shred of cover—a whole line of sitting ducks.

He might have sent them a warning shot if they hadn't just murdered his cousin in cold blood. Instead, he lined up his sights and shot the leader high in the chest.

The American behind the leader stumbled back and fell from the path, rolling a good thirty feet down the hill before the crook of a tree broke his fall and his leg.

Johnny switched to his bow and arrow. He needed to conserve ammo, not to mention keeping his barrel clean, and this was easy shooting. One arrow through the leg was enough to turn the rest of the Americans back into the woods. He watched them go before he finished off the two screaming, crippled soldiers they'd left behind on the mountain slope. He staggered back from the stone outcropping, righting himself against an ancient oak with a quaking hand.

Footsteps stirred the loose stones behind him, but before he could even spin around to see who'd caught his flank, one of the Coles from the settlement spoke. "I heard shots, Johnny. Everything okay? Where's—"

Johnny turned to face his reinforcements—a father and his son, two of the maybe twenty able arms he could muster to defend the settlement from what was coming. His fellow half-breeds, his fellow exiles, the closest kin and clansmen a one-eyed coot could ever hope to have. They were all doomed. Edward would be the first of many to go.

"Johnny, you hurt? What's going on?"

20

He managed a few absent steps uphill, his rifle lying discarded a few thoughtless paces back, his matchet hanging half-sheathed at his side like a listing oxcart. He sank to his knees, then to all fours, shoulders shaking. A string of foul curses spewed from his spittle-frothed lips, gradually giving way to quavering senselessness.

"Those yaller ubermenschen sons-a-bitches... I can't... they shot Eddie down like a dog!"

It had been weeks since the Americans had questioned Amos and stuck him in his own bare room on the top floor of the meetinghouse. Given that he wasn't sure what would happen in the next few hours, he'd neglected to count the days and couldn't be sure how long he'd been in there past five meals he'd received daily. He knew days had indeed passed, since he had the small mercy of a window, through which spread the gradual brightening of the fall colors and the faint smell of the first fallen leaves. Other than that, he had no further means of marking the passing of time, save for the sludge-like boredom gradually accumulating around his mind. It was almost a relief when the American named Jarvis opened the door, an American regular following behind with an autorifle.

Almost.

Jarvis paced the floor in front Amos while the other American forced Amos to his knees and bound his hands behind his back. For all the American soldier's silent menace and the cold black of the polished gun barrel rubbing up against Amos' spine while he worked, it was Jarvis who unnerved him the most. The bald American paced with a predatory gleam in his eyes, a hunger only reined in by the American captain who now ran the Tucker clan like his own personal fiefdom. Amos placed little confidence in Captain Carlson's mercy, or even his ability to control this freak.

"Mmm, mmm, *mmm.*" Jarvis sounded like he was sitting down to a hearty stew after a day spent on heavy work and light vittles. "She likes you. They all do. Handsome little fella. Settle down, ladies."

Amos didn't respond. He couldn't. It took most of his concentration to keep the shock on his face from betraying his terror. He found himself grateful for already being on his knees, lest they buckle now.

"Shut up, *shut up,*" Jarvis said, swatting at the air in a spate of annoyance.

"Jesus, Jarvis." the American soldier behind Amos asked with a mixture of concern and amusement, as if he had almost, but not quite, grown used to Jarvis' antics.

"*None* of you are real," Jarvis said before shaking his head with wild vehemence and taking a deep, calming breath through his nose. "So. Little Tucker." Jarvis flashed a smile so wide it strained the muscles in his neck. It looked more like he was baring his teeth. "Royce thinks you're part of a neurocaster network."

"I—I don't know what that is," Amos answered, disarmed in a way that even torture hadn't disarmed him.

"Sure, maybe. But that's why Royce hasn't let me assimilate you yet. Could be dangerous, he said." Jarvis shrugged as if he found the concept of danger amusing. But at least he was calm now. Almost reasonable, even.

"Why don't you call him 'Captain' like all the other soldiers?"

Jarvis flashed his wolf-like grin. A raised vein in his head curved like a snake on a rock as his face contorted around his teeth. "I'm not a soldier. And you're not an adventurous young kid getting in over his head. Who's in charge in there?" He reached forward and jabbed Amos in the head with a rigid finger. "The reverend? The schoolmaster?"

Amos didn't answer.

"We're going to find out anyway."

Again, Amos said nothing.

Jarvis leaned back against the wall, his arms folded over his chest. "You don't think much of me, do you?"

"I think you've lost your mind."

Jarvis threw his head back and had himself a deep, hearty laugh. "What even is a mind?" When Amos didn't answer, he continued. "No, seriously. What do you think a mind is? How do you lose one?"

"I don't need to know the particulars to know something isn't right in your head."

"Why? Because I don't behave how people expect me to? How is that a measure of sanity? Who's to say I'm not the only sane person for a hundred fucking miles around, and it's everyone else who's crazy?"

"Your word against everyone else doesn't hold much weight."

Jarvis cocked his head to the side. "It doesn't?" He turned and left the room without another word.

Amos resisted the urge to cast a glance to the American guard behind him, and instead remained where he was in stunned silence. He'd braced himself for another beating, but just like that, the questioning was over without anyone laying a finger on him, and barely any real questions having been asked of him—certainly no reasonable ones.

Yet the soldier guarding him said nothing and made no move to throw him back with Sam.

Footsteps approached in the hall outside, and the basement door creaked open to again reveal Jarvis, this time with an escort. He stepped inside and waved someone in from the hallway. "Okay, bring him in."

Two soldiers dragged a bound and hooded prisoner between them. They forced the prisoner to his knees facing Amos before they pulled the hood off to reveal Elvin McDaniel, hollow-cheeked and dead-eyed.

"Look at your big, scary watchman." Jarvis sneered.

Amos looked around, confused.

Jarvis seized Elvin by the ear and forced his head around to look him in the eye. "Hey, watchman. Did you know I was the last to see your boy

23

alive? The kid had some equipment upstairs that you don't. Must have got it from his mother, 'cause I'm not sure you've got much of anything between your ears. Are you sure he was really your son?"

Elvin jerked his head away, his ear threatening to come loose in Jarvis's hand. His face twisted in pain and silent rage, but when his eyes met Amos's, they glistened.

"This kid and I are having a little discussion. We're not sure which one of us is crazy. Maybe you could help us out. You call the shots around here, right?"

Elvin turned back to Jarvis, but instead of answering, he spat in Jarvis's face.

Jarvis didn't bother to wipe away the spittle. "That's what I thought. So..." He turned to Amos. "Your watchman, the guy who's supposed to keep law and order in your clan, can't do anything to me. If he can't, who can?" He pointed to Elvin and proclaimed with mock seriousness, "This here is a dangerous criminal, an evil devil. And I, as the sole arbiter of truth and justice, will carry out holy judgment against this evildoer." He took an automatic rifle from one of the attendant American guards and checked the chamber.

Amos started to struggle to his feet, but the guard behind him forced him back to his knees. "Calling a dog a cat doesn't make it so," Amos growled.

Again, Jarvis cocked his head to the side. "It doesn't?"

He raised the rifle to Elvin's temple and pulled the trigger. The room rang like a bell.

When Amos opened his eyes, Elvin McDaniel lay sprawled on the floor, partly decapitated. A gory mess painted the wall, floor, and one of the nearby American guards, who was busy berating Jarvis with words Amos couldn't hear. All Amos could do was stare at the splintered edges of Elvin's skull peeking out of his face like a broken eggshell.

Amos surged to his feet in a rage and grabbed at Jarvis. "I'll kill you for this. I'll kill you!"

Jarvis drove the butt of his rifle into Amos's stomach, doubling him over. "Sure you will, Tucker. Sure."

Another pair of hands seized him from behind and threw him to the floor. A heavy boot planted in the middle of his back kept him there.

"I just checked upstairs," a voice said. "The schoolteacher's been awake this whole time. I made sure of it."

"Well, that settles that," Jarvis crossed his arms and leaned back against the cold wall. "My money was on the Reverend anyway."

Amos kicked at the American holding him down and got the breath crushed out of him for it.

"This kid's a feisty one, isn't he?" said the man with the boot on Amos's back.

"That's what makes this fun," Jarvis said, waving away the blood-stained guard's curses with one hand and grabbing Amos's face with the other. "Hey, Tucker. Look at me."

Amos couldn't resist, but when he met Jarvis's smug grin, he managed to mutter, "Murderer."

"Hey, I get it," Jarvis said with a shrug. "Only natural for you to hate me. But let's be rational. Good always triumphs in the end. So I can't be a murderer." He bent down low next to Amos, so close his breath assaulted Amos' nostrils. "It's the watchman who was the murderer. Future generations will look back on my people as the heroes, while your people will rightly take their place as the savages doomed to destruction by their own weakness and ignorance. It's the natural order of things. You and your people are the villains of history. You just don't know it yet."

"You don't get to say who's bad and who's good."

"Sure I can. And so can you. So can everyone. The difference is whatever *I* say is backed up by *this*," Jarvis said, placing the still-warm barrel of his rifle up against Amos's cheek. "Look at your watchman. What color is his blood?"

"Screw you."

"I say his blood is yellow. Unless we're going to see what color your blood is, I'd suggest you agree with me."

"Sure—it's *yellow,* you tyrant rat bastard."

"That didn't sound very convincing."

"Just because you can use your power to make me say something doesn't make it true in the end."

"Ah!" Jarvis said as if Amos had finally had his first real thought. "How right you are! You say I'm a murderer; *I* say I'm not. Who's right? Captain Royce says whoever has the most power. I say, 'Who gives a shit?' None of it matters, either the one shooting or the one getting shot."

He gestured to the corpse. About a third of Elvin's head and face were gone, including his right eye, some of his nose, and a bit of his lower jaw. Jagged bits of skull jutted out from under his scalp like the edges of a shattered bottle, and much of what had been inside had spilled out onto the floor.

"The gun shows your people for what you really are. Crazy, sane, stupid, smart, good, bad—underneath the façade, it's all a mess waiting for the maggots. What was inside his head is now outside. Big deal. The processes that make the body 'alive,' as your kind put it, have stopped. And there's an active weather system somewhere over the Amazon. Who the fuck cares? This is all it adds up to." Jarvis kicked Elvin's corpse over so that the jagged wound faced the ceiling. He stared down into the hollow where Elvin's brains used to be.

"And that's why it's natural to hate me. Not because I did anything wrong, but because I showed you that nothing is wrong in the first place. You used the antibiotics from the junkers to kill bacteria making your people sick. And suddenly *I'm* a murderer because I kill something with more biomass? Is *that* what gives something a right to live? How many pounds it weighs? And you call *me* crazy. You... hang on, I've gotta piss." Jarvis grabbed his crotch. With a crooked smile, he opened his pants and turned toward Elvin's corpse.

"No." Amos gasped as he squirmed to get free. The boot on his back ground down so hard he struggled to breathe.

"Here's as good a place as any, don't you think, Tucker?" Jarvis said before he urinated into the watchman's hollow skull.

A low, sickened moan escaped Amos's throat.

"There we go," Jarvis said, finishing up and clapping his hands. "Why waste time lecturing when a simple demonstration gets things across so much quicker? All this bullshit about honoring the dead, like *that* cares." He waved a dismissive hand at the corpse. "Why not honor the dirt we piss on, or our own piss?"

Jarvis motioned to the soldier pinning Amos to the floor, and rough hands hauled him up by the armpits, pulling and pushing him toward the door. They hadn't even bothered to get any information from him. "Why?" Amos squeaked pathetically as the door swung open to receive him.

Jarvis shrugged. "Why not?"

As two soldiers pulled Amos away, Jarvis turned the corpse over and stomped on the good part of Elvin's face, cracking and bowing the remaining skull beneath his heel. The last Amos saw of Elvin McDaniel was his face being flattened against a concrete floor. An unpersoned thing, perhaps a thing never personed at all.

They threw Amos back into his cell, empty for now, and left him alone with his thoughts and afterimages in the darkness. They left him alone with time and silence to eat into his brain—time enough for things to wriggle around in there.

# Chapter 3: In Which Amos Understands What Is Necessary

Lieutenant Chitman would not have been surprised to see any number of things on the road back to New Ashburn: nomads, marauders, unbreds—whether wild or under the influence of a neuronet—even a drifter or two. He did not expect to see an entire platoon marching under the brilliant golden canopy of yellow birch trees encroaching on the road. Before Chitman could ask what the platoon was doing, the platoon leader asked the same of him.

"Re-establishing contact with New Ashburn," Chitman gestured to his men, armed to take the teeth of every geemo in the county. The most valuable weapon, however, two of his men carried between them on a stretcher: Chitman's neurocasting proxy. "What are you all doing?"

"We're here to provide support in putting down the Tucker uprising."

Chitman cocked his head to the side. "What uprising? The Tuckers are well in hand. The watchman caused some trouble, but he's been locked up."

"Second platoon has already made contact with a settlement south south-east of the highway. We took several casualties and had to pull back to more defensive positions."

"That's just a small settlement, there's not—there's already been shooting?" Chitman could not keep the incredulity out of his voice.

"Following orders. Second platoon is to completely neutralize the halfbreed settlement and secure a corridor between New Ashburn and the neurocasting clan. I was supposed to push through, reinforce Captain Carlson, and help him put down the rebellion."

"There is no rebellion."

"Carlson sent a message to Colonel Armstrong saying the Tuckers were in revolt and that he needed fifty percent more men than he had."

Lieutenant Chitman waved for his men to set down the stretcher carrying his proxy. He paced. "Who delivered the message?" He said, stopping mid-stride.

"A Tucker defector. Works with the powdermaker." The other lieutenant's eyes widened as he caught Chitman's meaningful gaze. "But the letter was unopened, and Carlson signed it. I saw the letter myself."

Chitman pinched the bridge of his nose as he began to pace again. "Why the hell would Carlson... no. Something's up. This wasn't simple miscommunication. Someone's trying to get you away from New Ashburn."

"Who? Why?"

"I don't know. Did you leave a sufficient garrison behind to defend New Ashburn?"

"Sure. Unless there's a large force of Sylvanians heading toward us from up north, and our scouts haven't detected anything."

"The neurocasters are well protected?"

29

"They haven't even left the citadel. There's another group coming from the Baltimore enclave, but—"

"Another group of neurocasters?" Chitman spun on the other lieutenant.

"Yeah. Where you came from. But it's a relatively easy road to New Ashburn, and we've assessed that the Pied Piper is well west of the junker clan."

"That assessment may be wrong. I searched for him. *I can't find him.*"

The lieutenant's confidence cracked. "But all of the neurocasters have their own secure neuronet—"

"That message wasn't meant to get *you* ambushed. It was to keep us from reinforcing the neurocasters from Baltimore when *they're* ambushed. You're going the complete opposite direction from where you're needed."

Just then, a distant pop went off in the woods to the south, across a narrow stream which ran alongside the road. A soldier from the reinforcing platoon jerked and collapsed with a hole in his side.

"Get off the road!" Chitman ordered.

The Americans darted for cover, looking for the puff of smoke which would give away the shooter. Chitman found an ancient oak for himself, sat down safely behind it, and went still, his eyes closing.

Back on the road, two bodies lay on the cracked pavement: one leaking blood from a ragged wound, the other unharmed, on a stretcher. The unharmed body sat up, seized the autorifle from the fallen soldier, and dashed over to find the leader of the American platoon hunched behind a crook in the stream. Intermittent returning fire perforated the yellow and red undergrowth of the forest floor as the Americans searched for the shooter. The loud ricochet of another musketball told them they hadn't hit him yet.

Chitman's proxy swore. "If the Tuckers weren't in rebellion before, they are now. I can't make it to Armstrong with snipers up and down the highway."

"Conserve ammo! Spread out and push in!" the lieutenant ordered his men before turning to Chitman's proxy. "What do we do, then?"

"Change our plans. But I need to get to New Ashburn. *Fast.* And when I do," the proxy growled, "I'm going to figure out *exactly* what that Tucker messenger knew about all this."

Amos sat across the mostly bare room from Sam Chambers. The Americans had moved Amos in with the clan schoolteacher and Jarvis' pet shadower, likely to clean up the god-awful mess Jarvis had made of the watchman in Amos' previous cell. For hours, neither said anything, neither meeting each other's gaze.

"I didn't know," Sam Chambers said, responding to some unspoken accusation running circles in his mind. His voice carried a plaintive tone, but his eyes stared out into space. "I only ever wanted what was best for the clan. I had to make some sacrifices in the name of progress, but it all would have been worth it if the Americans... I wouldn't have gone along with it if I had known. The reverend kept me in the dark. Never told me what the Federation planned to do."

"How'd you find out?" Amos asked. His hand was still sore from the questioning he'd suffered at the hands of the Federation soldiers.

The battered schoolteacher nodded over to the shadower chained up across the room. "That thing has been pestering me. Not physically. Not chained up like that. But it makes me... feel things. Go ahead. Talk to it. It wants to communicate, for some reason."

The shadower kneeled with its head bent downward as if in prayer. It was like the thing was waiting for Amos.

Amos studied Sam and squinted in concentration. *Does the shadower talk to you like this?*

Sam blinked in surprise. "Yes. How..." *How did you know?*

Amos didn't bother answering, but stepped up to the shadower, almost to within striking range. The shadower made no move other than to lift its head and stare at him through slitted vertical pupils.

Amos closed his eyes and stretched out with his mind in the same way he'd heard Jarvis, the wild American. He felt something out there and grasped it with the edges of his consciousness. It was slippery. He felt it come closer, but he could not get hold of it. He concentrated and pulled it in, but he still could not get a good grasp on its mind.

Instead, the mind came to him. He scrambled for control as it approached, and he found the semblance of a mind faintly recognizable. Once he recognized it, he drew his own focus to a pinpoint and pricked the unbred consciousness.

The twisted mess of a brain inside was an alien monstrosity conceived in nightmares and born in hell. And yet there was something so familiar about it, it could have passed for a brother. Amos felt its emotions: furious, cold, miserable, gleeful—a kaleidoscope of feelings as rich as those any human felt. But the disordered emotions bubbled and mixed and spilled over each other like boiling stew. It knew, somehow, that it wasn't what it was supposed to be, and it hated being, yet it only wanted to go on living. It was like when his older sister was a kid, when she'd thought it was hilarious to go around to everyone saying, "I don't speak a word of English." Like trying to go to the moon by digging a hole.

"Whew... whoa, now."

The shadower did not move. Amos closed his eyes again, and instead of merely looking in on the unbred's mind, he opened it up and stepped inside. The weltering emotions and instincts and subconscious drives vanished in an instant, evaporating like water tossed on red-hot steel.

Amos blinked. He checked to see if the shadower was still alive.

He delved deeper and found a new mess of thoughts, not quite conscious, not quite unconscious. They were bits and pieces of—not thought, but senses—smells and sounds and sights: feasting on the rotting carcass of a deer, slurping down worms and beetles, using a stick to stir a pool of water and blur out a ghastly reflection. These were memories.

Amos saw the image of two children playing in a tree and felt the shadower's urge to tear them to pieces, felt its fear as it sensed danger nearby. He saw a cold winter day and felt the unbred's surge of recognition as another shadower emerged from the frost. Amos felt the two shadower's minds connect in the memory and felt his own mind telescope like finding infinite versions of himself caught between two mirrors.

The memories blurred, not for lack of clarity, but for lack of time. They buzzed, popped, and flashed, but only for a fraction of a moment. Somewhere in the midst of the whirl of memories, he caught the sound of voices. He saw things he couldn't understand, things that weren't possible: walls flashing with light, moving pictures, a gleaming city, people dressed in spotless old-time clothing. Amos saw memories from long ago, before this shadower was even conceived, memories that somehow were no more the shadower's than they were his.

The memories were incomplete, sketchy—fragments of old truths that broke apart and recombined in scarcely comprehensible ways, but Amos could comprehend some of what he heard and saw.

*Triumph of science... gene-modding technology has finally reinvented the Information Age... who cares what a bunch of crunchies and religious fundamentalists think? Same old tune of sacred boundaries as when scientists first started cutting up dead bodies... we've cured everything from colorblindness to Down's syndrome, but they have a problem with a little creative CRISPR application? Stop thinking of military applications, John; they aren't made for that...*

*We've already scaled-up production, and you could be looking at thousands of these young "neurocasters" serving in various industries in just the next fifteen years. They'll interact with our earlier prototypes—the servers, yes—to facilitate several information-based tasks that digital engineers have struggled with for decades. We're encouraging governments to open up the bionet to private business interests. It will speed up development... internet that can interact with you, Alan. An internet that has a physical brain, or actually millions of physical brains. And ordinary users can interact with the servers using old digital BCI inputs, but when our genetically enhanced neurocasters get old enough to take over on their own... the digital age will be obsolete in another couple decades.*

*I understand your concerns, Alan, but the neurocasters are really no different from any other enhanced human. No, they can't read your minds. They can interact with specific breeds of defense chimeras, particularly the servers. No, we don't do that, either. They'll go to school just like every other kid. They'll have special training and therapy on weekends and over the summer, but that's it. And we'll have to monitor their breeding, of course. That just comes with the territory.*

*The project director doesn't understand the potential locked up here, but you can bet your ass less-scrupulous government-funded genetic research teams will. He wants to reinvent the internet and make a trillion dollars. I'm talking about the biggest evolutionary leap since the rise of multicellular life. This is not something we want to fall behind on. Now that the development's public, we have to exploit this potential before they do.*

When Amos pulled himself out, heaving himself up from the depths of the shadower's memory, he found himself staring, face to face, into its ghoulish eyes. Amos shrieked and jumped back. The shadower never moved. It was safe, docile—but not wholly controlled.

It wasn't a random memory Amos had stumbled upon. The shadower had shown him something secret. Perhaps the same thing it had shown Sam.

"Show me more," Amos said. But the mind remained closed, the memories banished to the ether. No amount of probing could bring them back. The shadower returned to its prayerful pose, passive now.

Amos looked back at the schoolteacher, who returned the stare with an expression he couldn't read. "The reverend," Sam said, "treated knowledge as a curse. I'm beginning to understand him. We're not just—ubermenschen—we're descendants of the worst of the bunch."

Amos didn't have time to listen to Sam's woes. The young man paced the floor. There likely wasn't much time. That American, Jarvis, was planning on doing something to him, something he'd tried to do already before Captain Carlson had stopped him, and it sounded like there wasn't anything he could do about it.

What had Jarvis said when they'd first captured him? *Once there's more than one in a network, it's just a numbers game, and everyone in this fucking clan is an isolated morsel, waiting to be gobbled up.*

Amos needed a network to keep from being "gobbled up." *A network of what?*

Amos stopped pacing and examined Sam Chambers for a long time. Sam finally looked up and met his stare. "What? What is it?"

Amos didn't answer. He took a step forward.

"What is it?"

Amos stepped close to Sam and reached out with his mind. He found Sam's mind, which was just as slippery as the shadower's, if not more so. He tried to grasp Sam's mind, to envelop the thoughts simmering within with his own, but to no avail. The schoolteacher remained out of reach except for the solitary emotion that slipped through: fear.

"What are you doing?" Sam gasped, recoiling from Amos and shrinking into a corner of the room.

"Stop. Don't struggle." Amos stepped closer and reached out to Sam's head with his hands.

"No, stop. Get off me. You're—you're hurting my head, Amos!" Sam cried, his voice rising in panic. He tried to push Amos away, but Amos was a strong young man, and the physical effort of moving seemed to leave Sam's mind open to Amos's probing.

*What are you doing to me?* Sam begged silently.

*I'm sorry, Sam. It's the only way.*

Amos wrestled Sam's mind to his own and forced it open. Somewhere in the back of his head, he perceived a moan, and he clamped a hand over Sam's mouth to stifle it. But most of his mental effort went toward flinging the doors off the locked vault of Sam's thoughts, and once inside, a strange, primal instinct not unlike hunger kicked in. He could feel the horror rising up from Sam, but he found he could crush such emotions as he drilled into the schoolteacher's mind.

The next moments were messy, but, for Amos, satisfying.

When it was done, Sam's body lay limp on the floor, now more an unused appendage than a person. Amos could feel something like a mind still active there, but that mind now belonged to him—to Amos.

He sat down next to the limp body, closed his eyes, and instead of forcing open the door to Sam's mind, walked right in through the wide-open portal. Or, rather, he turned to see a new space stitched onto his own mind. He walked his mind over like he might walk from his own bedroom to the kitchen.

When he opened his eyes, his body felt different. He turned his head to see—himself, or at least his body, slumped-over and empty, waiting for his mind to return to it. He looked down at the middle-aged body he occupied. It was heavier and creakier—Sam's body.

But it wasn't Sam's body anymore. Amos lifted the hand and stroked the unfamiliar whiskers. He felt the contours of a nose broken by Elvin in a fit of rage. This was Amos's hand now, Amos's whiskers, Amos' nose. This was a spare body to walk into and out of at his pleasure.

Where, then, was Sam?

The answer was simple and obvious: inside Amos's mind, being digested.

Remorse and revulsion welled up inside him until he feared he would puke, but on its heels came a new, overwhelming, gooseflesh-raising sense of power, and the teeth-baring rage to use it.

He straightened up to see the shadower looking at him with its head cocked to the side.

"Look what you made me do," Amos said, not sure if he meant it for the shadower or the Americans or God—maybe all of them. In his anger, he returned to his body and turned back to the shadower. He came well within striking distance, as if daring the shadower to attack.

Instead, the shadower bowed prostrate, like a worshipper before the statue of a god.

Amos reached out with his mind and seized the shadower's mind in a grip now bolstered with the combined strength of two neurocasters. This time, the shadower's defenses yielded easily, and he detected a coherent thought from the creature itself: *I belong to the Pied Piper.*

Not Jarvis? "Where is he? Where is the Pied Piper?" Amos growled.

*Take care of these American neurocasters. Then we'll talk.*

The shadower went limp as if exhausted from even so brief an exchange. *Take care of the American neurocasters?* He could do that. He could do more than that. He'd make them all regret the day they'd crossed the Tucker clan. They'd wish they'd never laid eyes on Amos Taylor.

Hate was a bitter draft, but a powerful liquor. Amos would soon learn to like the taste of this new whiskey.

# Chapter 4: Predator and Pray

W hen the soldiers came for Becky Brody at the first bloom of dawn, she had as much say in it as a tree gets before the ax. They gathered her, along with her father and any of her brothers and sisters older than ten, and marched her down Market Street towards the clan main. They didn't even have to touch her; they simply advanced, raw killing power in hand, and she moved away like a magnet repelled by a familiar force. She had no real way to resist. The Americans had sealed all firearms in the clan meetinghouse weeks ago, and Becky wasn't going to face down an autopistol with a kitchen knife.

None of the other Tuckers seemed apt to raise a ruckus either—not since the Americans had dragged the watchman to jail for assaulting the schoolmaster. Neither the watchman nor the schoolmaster had been seen outside the meetinghouse since—not to rally the folkward, as Elvin might have done, nor to calm anxious nerves, as Sam would have. And Amos Taylor was not there to pull off some miraculous stunt like she somehow expected he would. No one even mentioned his absence, not even his own family.

No, the Tuckers could no longer stay firm against the most minor American orders. The soldiers no longer patrolled the outer walls. They no longer even faced outward away from the Tuckers; the soldiers' attention was all pointed inward, an ever-tightening, unbreakable grasp. The early tricky admixture of awe and admiration that had first enthralled the Tuckers had since rendered down to something more pure: raw, britches-wetting fear.

Under the barrels of a dozen sleek autorifles, the hundred-odd conscripted Tuckers went out, as meek as mice, to the open clan main. Separate from the Tucker conscripts stood the rest of the Tucker clan, no less timid and terrified for being more numerous. A half-dozen soldiers patrolled between the two segregated masses to keep them apart. The shim-sham of a cause the Americans gave for the forced meeting—news of missing Ralph McDaniel—brooked no comment, though Becky wasn't about to believe anything coming out of Captain Royce's mouth.

She scarcely believed her own eyes any better on seeing what waited in the center of the open space where Market met Main east of the meetinghouse: a noose hung from a long-disused streetlight, and below the noose, a wooden chair. Standing sandwiched between the two, his hands tied behind his back, was Reverend Brody.

Murmurs trickled through the assembled Tuckers, but most were either too shocked or too frightened to do anything but stare.

Captain Royce Carlson sauntered out from the double front doors of the clan meetinghouse, cocksure in his swagger. He strode silently to the chair where the reverend stood and placed one foot upon it as if about to kick it over. Instead, he crossed his forearms on one knee and addressed his wide-eyed audience with what he must have thought was an easy air.

"Your 'reverend,'" Captain Carlson began, sniffing at the very idea the Tuckers could revere such a man, "is guilty of conspiracy against the armed forces of the American Federation, as well as aiding and abetting the murder of Ralph McDaniel, a loyal supporter of the Federation. Since this is a Federation matter, Reverend Oliver Brody has been tried, convicted, and sentenced in military court. You all have been brought to witness the carrying-out of the sentence because there are still members of the conspiracy among you. If—"

"The Americans lie! Everything I've done, even before the Americans, I've done for love of this clan. For all the wrongs I've done, I apologize. The Americans will not be as repentant. Do not trust, do not believe, do not follow this—"

Royce kicked the chair over.

New Ashburn

Ella fought back the despair and clung to hope, even if only out of sheer stubbornness. "Do not be afraid of those that can kill the body but not the soul," the Scriptures reminded her. "Are not two sparrows sold for a chip of tooth? Yet not one of them will fall to the ground outside your Father's care. So don't be afraid; you're worth more than sparrows."

"I call on the Lord in my distress, and he answers me. I call on the Lord in my distress, and he answers me."

It was a routine that marked her confinement, though sometimes, the verses she called up into her head changed. Sometimes, the verses were comforting; sometimes, all she could think of was swords and flogging and stoning and being sawn in two. "They went about in sheepskins and goatskins, destitute, persecuted and mistreated—the world was not worthy of them."

Ella pushed the greasy scraggles of hair from her eyes and tested the silence with a timid, quavering note. "Praise God, from whom all blessings flow—"

Singing to herself in the darkness of a broom closet might be a sign that her mind was finally, truly slipping on the edges, but she didn't stop. "Praise him, all creatures here below—"

She was picking up steam now, though she didn't dare raise her voice much beyond a whisper. Mice could hum louder than her. "Praise him above, ye heavenly host. Praise Father, Son, and Holy Ghost..."

Tucker Territory

The wails of the terrified Tuckers and the creaking of the Reverend's swinging corpse still hung in the autumn air when one of the men from Chitman's platoon rode in through the gate with news at least three days earlier than Captain Carlson was expecting:

Lieutenant Chitman had run into an American relief force nearly a hundred men strong camped out on the highway only five miles out of town.

*A relief force? For what?* The Tucker situation was well in hand.

Chitman had expressed similar confusion to the captain of the relief force. Apparently, it was to secure the road from the Tucker half-breeds who'd taken up arms against the Americans.

This explanation made little more sense, and apparently it hadn't made sense to Chitman, either, at least until the reinforcing captain had explained where he'd received his information: the drifter collaborator.

"So, Mr. Walking is still alive," Captain Carlson said to himself when the puzzle came together. His instincts had been right. Not only had his two runners not accomplished their task, but his suspicion of the drifter as an unreliable collaborator had been well-founded. You couldn't trust anyone out here in the sticks. And, as a parting shot, Walking had played the messenger and tricked Colonel Armstrong into starting a premature hot war with the Tuckers, or at least the half-breed settlement. *How* he'd managed to do that remained an open question—Armstrong wouldn't accept any communication that wasn't signed by Carlson or one of his lieutenants. For now, the question was an irrelevant one. Chitman's runner reported half a dozen casualties already.

*Oh, well.* It had to happen sooner or later, and the town and its immediate inhabitants were all effectively neutralized.

Captain Carlson turned to Chitman's runner. "I assume Chitman's waiting for orders?"

The messenger nodded.

"What's the status on the half-breed settlement?"

"Slow progress. The woods along the length of the highway offer too many firing positions to the enemy, and the relief force can only guarantee security for about a mile stretch of road. They still haven't located the enemy's base of operations."

"So, you're telling me my relief force needs relief?"

"That's the situation, sir. Even our platoon received sporadic sniper fire."

"Okay. Tell Lieutenant Chitman to press on to New Ashburn and give Armstrong an *accurate* sitrep. I'll assume command of the relief force, and with our combined strength, we'll assault the settlement itself. Once we've neutralized the settlement, we'll push the Tucker neurocasters through to New Ashburn according to the original plan. Go."

Still the Tuckers on the clan main groaned in collective consternation. A few of the gathered throng shouted curses at the Americans. Before, Royce would have noted the potential malcontents and isolated them from the rest of the harvest. But he had more pressing matters to worry about now. He sent his orderly to fetch Jarvis.

"Jarvis," Captain Carlson said when the neurocaster arrived, "the drifter tried to play us, and now I have to exterminate a bunch of half-breeds. We'll be relatively short on manpower in town until I get back, and the Tucker population still conceals subversive elements. It's time to torch the chaff. Conserve ammo."

"Ask nicely."

"Torch the chaff, *please.*"

"I'd be happy to." Jarvis cocked his head. "What about the neurocasters? Who's going to guard them?"

A full-throated laugh escaped Royce. "Not you," he said. "I'm leaving a sufficient garrison in place to keep the neurocasters safe and separate from the remaining population. And the garrison will be under orders not to let you anywhere near. Take enough men to deal with the leftovers, then keep tabs on local geemo activity. If you behave, I'll see if I can grab a spare for you."

The two Americans regarded each other with a mutual amusement born of casual familiarity with death.

The door creaked open to reveal the American neurocaster, Jarvis. Amos scrambled away first from the light, then the shadow Jarvis cast over the room.

"Well, the reverend's dead," Jarvis said. "And here you are. The reverend had some compunctions about assimilation after all. None of the conscripted neurocasters croaked when the preacher swung. Just as well; more for the adepts coming out here. But the captain just left town, and no one's here to watch you. Which means you'll be for me."

He fell upon Amos.

New Ashburn

Ella didn't notice the rumble of approaching footsteps until her cell door was already creaking open. She shrank away from the sudden light in surprise. A tall male figure stood in the doorway. She blinked once, then again when the man didn't move, and she thought she recognized his outline. "Omar?"

His hips were cocked to the side, and one arm rested against the doorframe. As her eyes adjusted to the new light, she saw that the man wore army fatigues. Self-satisfied malice radiated off him like a stench. It was a man with a mind as foul as his breath and his yellow teeth—a man who took bets on how long it took a woman to strangle.

"Remember me, bitch?"

Ella gasped and scrambled to the far end of the narrow cell. "No, no, please!"

The man stepped inside the broom closet. "Don't pretend you don't want to."

"No! *Please!*"

The door clanged shut behind him, clanged shut on Ella and her screams.

## Tucker Territory

Sophie Fillmore struggled to keep her footing amid the crush of what seemed like the whole clan crowded together, even though she knew the conscripts had been taken off to the other side of the meetinghouse, across the stream towards the opposite side of town. The twins were bundled up around her, one baby strapped to her front, the other to her back. This left her hands mercifully free.

It wasn't as if the surrounding folks were *trying* to knock her down. But the heaped snarl of clansfolk trying their best not to fall down themselves while also avoiding the pointy sticks and rifle butts herding them along westward amounted to the same thing: a near-stampede of wide-eyed, huffing, stamping humans, driven to near-panic after seeing the Reverend hung like a common murderer. Sophie begged for folks around her to please, *please* be careful of her babies, but the babies were complaining with far more gut-gripping than she could muster. Even *their* cries were drowned out by everyone else's caterwauling and the harsh, tangled warbling of a Federation soldier bellowing orders into a tin bullhorn.

She couldn't see much, being on the shorter side and stuck in the middle of everything, but from the din, she guessed there must be three to four hundred Tuckers marching to... where, exactly? The empty hayloft of the butcher's stockade loomed above the crowd, but that *couldn't* be right. A hundred Tuckers couldn't fit in there, let alone most of the townfolk. Not far off, the water tower served as a guard tower, and the Federation sentry on the railing inspected them from above, waving them all right along toward the butcher's little barn.

A few stumbling strides later, she beheld the yawning double doors standing open to receive her and those around her. The movement of the other Tuckers urged her forward. If she dug in her heels, the current of the crowd might have even lifted her off her feet. The shouts and protests of the Tuckers grew louder, but the mass of people only picked up speed the closer they came to the barn.

As she passed inside, the cacophony took on a sharper, more panicked tone—a screeching, droning, plaintive, angry, despairing sound; a twisted, strained, bleeding noise, like hot water squeezed out of over-tangled washing. It echoed off the shiplap planks on the walls and the worn wooden catwalk running between the stalls. People stumbled over pitchforks and shovels as the continuing steam of folks coming in pushed them further into the tiny building. Tuckers piled up onto the raised concrete slab where Arnold Brody led animals over to the slaughterhouse, only to find that door sealed. They stumbled into the back rooms, barking their shins on discarded boxes and hoarded tools. They pried at the recently boarded-up windows. They climbed up on top of the stall dividers, slender spears of noon autumn sunlight dappling their arms and faces as they strove to escape the suffocating throng below.

All around her, crushing her and her two little ones, were her friends, neighbors, relatives—the Hadleys and Newells, the McDaniels and her own Puckett cousins, the Finches and Garmens and Buntons and Evanses. All of them lost their distinctiveness in the dim guts of the barn. Now, they were all so much noise and flesh and fear-stench.

Here and there, Sophie caught snatches of words she understood: The Americans had done something with the reverend. They'd executed all of the elders. All this was just a scare to get the Tuckers to cry uncle. The Americans were going to kill them all and settle the town with their own folks. There was some innocent reason for all of this. They were all going to die.

Then, from the double doors, came a man's cry, almost a scream. "Kerosene!"

Several hundred pairs of arms raised in the air to bang on windows and doors or to offer desperate prayers to God. Little Justin, tied to her front, reached up with his own tiny hands and grabbed at Sophie's face and hair. He was not even a year old, but even he knew something was very, very wrong.

# Chapter 5: In Which Things Heat Up

An American soldier pounded up the stairs two at a time, huffing and puffing toward the top floor of the clan meetinghouse. A scream had pulled him from the gymnasium, where he'd been packing his gear to prepare for shipping off with the Tucker neurocasters at noon. On the top floor, he nearly ran into Jarvis coming out of the last room down the hall where they kept the surviving Tucker prisoners.

"Jarvis!" The soldier stopped up short, stuttering. "What are you doing here? I thought I heard you screaming. You sounded nasty."

"Oh, that? Pffft." Jarvis waved the idea away with his left hand, but his right hand remained behind his back. "That wasn't me." His voice had an unsettling, hollow quality to it.

The soldier retreated one half-step, but not quickly enough. Jarvis brought forward a chain and manacle in a wild swing that cut the American right above the eye and sent him stumbling to the side. A second rapid strike knocked the gun out of his hand before he could bring it up, and a third backhanded strike to the cheek spun him into the wall.

"I mean, I guess it *was* me," Jarvis mused as he straddled the stumbling soldier and wrapped the chain around his throat. "But Jarvis is gone now."

The air inside the barn became unbearably stifling, but it did little to quiet the frantic Tuckers. They pounded at the door, the windows, but nothing gave. Sophie found herself near the door, whether by her own effort or because of the eddies and currents running through the simmering cauldron of humans.

"Hang on!" Charlotte Brody—Becky's mother—called out to those around her. Even in the dim light, Sophie could see Mrs. Brody's brilliant red cheeks flushed with exertion or anger—probably both. "We push together, y'hear? Together!"

Mrs. Brody tried to get folks at the door to act in concert, but nobody could keep their heads. "Together, you addles! Like a wave! Like this!"

Several started pushing with her, back and forth, like a team rowing a boat. And, for a moment, the heavy doors bowed outwards. Sophie's heart leaped up at even the slightest glimmer of hope, and she stepped forward to help push on the back of the fellow in front of her. Maybe if they could get everyone pushing—

A three-round rifle burst punched a scatterplot of holes through the barn door and upwards into the ceiling. Everyone at the door screamed and ducked. For a skipped heartbeat, everyone in the barn went quiet in momentary shock.

Over the sudden quiet, a sort of strangled, gurgling noise came in from outside on the other side of the doors. And then, a voice commanded, "Stand back from the door."

She recognized the voice. *Amos Taylor! How...*

The doors quivered as whatever was wedging them together fell away, and the doors themselves flew open to reveal her rescuer: Amos Taylor, returned to the Tuckers as if from the grave, a spray of blood drenching one side of his rage-twisted face. On the ground next to him, an American lay writhing on the ground, hands grasping at the slippery gush of scarlet pouring from his neck. Other camo-clad bodies lay motionless here and there.

Some distance behind Amos, a huddle of white-faced young women—good-looking ladies who'd been snagged from the pack for some purpose Sophie shuddered to think about—stared around with the same questions in their eyes as likely lurked in Sophie's own: Could the Americans really be killed? How had Amos been able to rescue them? And *what* end had he rescued them from?

The Tuckers poured from their prison like water from a waterskin. They broke around Amos and formed a ring around him, drawn to him by his iron will to command, but also held back in awe.

When the crowd had settled in silence around him, Amos bent down, picked up a fallen American assault rifle, and checked the rounds in the mag. "The reverend is dead. As is the watchman. Our schoolmaster"—he paused and shook his head—"is beyond our reach. A hundred twenty-seven of our clansmen are under guard across the river, on the other side of town. Arnold Brody, who would be watchman in Elvin's stead, is among them. That leaves me, the watchman's apprentice, to take his place. Does anyone have a problem with that?"

None did.

Amos reinserted the magazine into the rifle and checked the firing chamber. "The only reason soldiers haven't come running at the sound of gunshots is because they think all of you"—he swept his pointing finger in a broad arc all around him—"right now, are being executed. The Americans never meant to fight a war with us, any more than the ubermenschen meant to fight a war with the natural-bred. They meant to exterminate. They came to suck the marrow from our bones and leave the scraps to bleach in the sun." Amos chambered a round with a loud *clack*. "And those sons of bitches still have a hundred of our own under watch on the other side of town. And I know where to get the guns to free them."

The rattle of gunfire across town, so soon on the heels of the reverend's hanging and Captain Carlson's leaving, settled things for Becky Brody. One: the Americans really were lower than a snake's belly. Two: Amos, the sharp young man who'd tried to get the jump on whatever the Americans were planning, was dead. Three: the Tuckers whom the Americans had herded off to the other side of town, Sophie among them, were already being killed, and four: she and the rest of the so-called "conscripts" were soon to follow.

"Into the school!" the American sergeant shouted, pointing to the meetinghouse. "You will all remain in the auditorium until our departure! You will be fed soon! Move!"

And with no say-so either way, the Tucker conscripts found themselves pushed back out of the clan main toward the open doors of the meetinghouse, into the opening to the auditorium where they'd defended themselves last winter against a pigman onslaught. It seemed like so long ago to Becky—a strangely simpler time.

But before she plunged in with the rest of her kin, a rough hand jerked her from the mob. A leering, grizzled face lurked at the other end of the arm that held her, and Becky's fiercer instincts took hold. She wrestled her arm free with more strength than the Federation soldier was expecting, but a blow to the side of her head stunned her long enough for a second soldier to grab her other arm. Together, the two dragged her off to a smaller side door to the meetinghouse.

"The shiny ones are supposed to be kept unspoiled. If Captain Carlson hears about this, it'll be your ass."

"He's not going to hear about this, is he? And Jarvis is busy 'borting the riff-raff."

Becky came back to herself as the dark stairs into the basement slowly unspooled themselves under the soldiers' feet. One of them grabbed her by the feet, and they held her horizontally between them as he kicked the basement door open behind him. The loose pants she wore were already threatening to come loose from her hips.

Then, without warning, the American holding Becky by the armpits dropped her like a sack of potatoes as he stared, dumbfounded, into the basement and muttered, "What the—"

The other soldier dropped Becky's feet and turned to follow his partner's gaze, as did Becky. Across a narrow hall at the bottom of the basement stairs, two Tuckers were working to pry open a board placed over a broken sidelight window while a third, Cephas Finch, stood guard in front of the locked door with an American autopistol.

The Tuckers stared for a second in frozen terror, while the two American intruders stared back in stunned stupidity.

Cephas, the quickest to recover, pointed the autopistol at the foremost American and pulled the trigger. Nothing happened. "Shit," Cephas said as he fiddled with the safety.

The two Americans, woken from their stupor, raised their own weapons. The foremost got his rifle up first and pulled the trigger. Nothing happened. "*Shit,*" the soldier echoed, lowering his rifle and thumbing the safety.

Becky saw her chance and jumped up. With two hands, she seized the rifle at the pistol grip and forward rail, pulling herself up against the soldier's weight. With her foot, she drove a mule-kick right up between his legs and nearly broke her foot against the crux of his pelvis. The soldier lost his grip on the stock as he sank to his knees, even as he kept one hand clutched around the barrel.

Becky looked up. The second soldier behind the first raised his gun, trying to get a clear shot. She dropped backward, using the first soldier's grip on the rifle barrel as a hinge to swing herself down to the floor. He should have let go of the barrel; the gun, held in tension between the two, aimed itself, and he and his partner found themselves on the business end.

Becky throttled the trigger.

He somehow didn't let go of the rifle barrel until his chest, neck, and face resembled ground meat from her father's butcher shop. His partner crawled up the basement stairs, wounded and begging for help.

Becky stood up, followed him up the stairs, and pinned him face-down to the bloody concrete steps with one foot. The ringing in her ears couldn't block out the sound of his begging.

"No, no, no," the soldier pleaded.

The edge of the steps served as a handy anvil, the rifle butt a hammer, and the American's head was a piece of work that needed shaping. Two or three crunching strikes were more than enough.

Becky turned back to the three Tuckers.

"Gawdamn. Well, we're hot now," Cephas grunted and turned back to the sealed weapons cache. "No use trying to get it open quiet-like. Stand back." He pointed the gun at the lock, but before he could blast it loose, another burst of gunfire sounded elsewhere in the building.

Becky picked up the other American's fallen rifle and made doubly sure the safety was off. "Where's the rest of the clan? Anybody else armed?" she asked as she posted up on the basement stairway.

An answer came to her—not from the three Tucker men, but seemingly from her own head. *The rest of the clan is free, but the folkward is unarmed. I'm coming down.*

Becky blinked in confusion. "What—" she said aloud.

A pistol shot and the clink of shattered metal on the concrete floor spun her around, and footsteps clapping down the basement stairs over the dead bodies spun her back again. Amos Taylor almost ran right into her. He surveyed the rifle in her hands and the bloody corpses on the stairs next to him. "I see you're taking care of yourself, as usual." He spoke with approval, almost joking, as if she'd swatted away an insult with a witty comeback rather than brutally killing two men.

In the moment it took her to blink back her surprise at seeing him alive, she almost said the same thing to him, but more pressing matters asserted themselves. "They're keeping the conscripts in the meeting-hall."

"I know. But we don't have enough arms to spring them loose. I've got Shane Bunton holding them off upstairs, and ten volunteers to run this stuff out." Amos gestured into the dim basement room which, now open, held an army's worth of arms and ammo. Next to them, a tangle of female bodies lay on the bare floor. "Who—" Becky stuttered. "Who are those?"

"Don't worry about that right now. We can still rescue the conscripts if we can get these guns out to the folkward."

"What about the—the folks the Americans already took away? The kids and old folks and—" *Sophie*, she thought to herself.

"This is how we help them. They're okay for now, and the plan is to head for the hills and meet up at Job Brody's farm. But they haven't made it outside the walls yet, and I need more guns outside to cover the retreat."

Becky nodded, still sorting all the news in her head. She stooped and tapped the side of what she judged was a powder keg and lifted it up. She pointed up the basement stairs with the muzzle of the American chatter gun. "These stairs are the only way out."

"The only *easy* way out. We won't stay too long. Let's go." Amos ordered the Tuckers moving weapons, powder, and shot from the storeroom through the dank recesses of the basement to a set of open windows high along the wall. They lifted the supplies up to the dust-speckled windows, and hands reached in from outside to receive them like a bucket brigade. A muffled gunshot reverberated from upstairs across the myriad hard surfaces in the meetinghouse's underbelly. "It's gonna be tight," Finch said.

"The west side of the meetinghouse is clear," Amos explained, leading Becky back to the main stairs up from the basement. "If we can get enough guns and set up firing positions, we can out-shoot them."

They reached the hallway intersection where the storeroom sat across from the first floor stairs. He shouldered the American rifle he carried and stepped up the stairs, past the mangled bodies of Becky's erstwhile captors. She followed him up to the first floor hallway, where Shane Bunton lay prone in a classroom door, another captured American rifle trained down towards the meeting-room.

"What's the word?" Amos asked.

"Keepin' their heads down for now, but I don't want a stray shot going into the meetin'-room, and they know it. I keep having to fall back." Shane grunted, shifting the bulk of his body further into the disused classroom, out of the line of fire.

"I'll get another firing angle."

"What firing angle?" Becky said. "There's only one hallway down the whole length of this here wing." She rolled into the spinning and weaving room across the hall from Shane.

"What the hell are you doing?" Amos ducked down and followed after her.

"We need to get us a sightline east of—" a salvo of bullets tore through the window and cut her off. She dove to the floor as glass rained on her back and rounds peppered the opposite wall. The long automatic burst raked the length of the meeting hall.

"We don't win this way, Becky! We have to retreat and get them when we're ready!"

Becky rolled onto her back to catch a glance at Amos, crouched low in the doorway. A shroud of fear flickered across his face—not for himself, she realized, but for her.

"They'll get away. We can't just—" Becky flinched as another round buried itself in the wall across from the window.

"Can't save them if you're dead. We have to—"

A shadow cast from the window appeared across the floor. Becky jerked around as an American soldier swept into the window to clear the room.

A deafening gun blast set Becky's ears to ringing again, and when her eyes opened from her momentary blink, the American was gone. Amos was still in the doorway behind her, an autorifle she hadn't seen him raise smoking from the barrel. Another three-round burst peppered the wall above her.

He was right; they had to get out of there. She crawled across the rubble-strewn floor to Amos and back to the central hallway. He held her close in the scant cover they could find. The east side of the meetinghouse offered the Americans one firing angle, and those at the door of the auditorium were trying to get another one. If they broke free of their position, they could shoot straight down the hallway clear to the other end of the meetinghouse.

"Get going, Becky. The west side is safe. That way, you hear?" Amos pointed toward the outward-facing doors in case she couldn't hear. Indeed, she couldn't hear much. "We want to keep the garrison pinned in here until we get the others out of the basement. Get outside and cover our retreat." Several thunderous gunshots echoed off the tiled floor and plaster walls behind them, but Amos didn't flinch. "The moment you're clear, get out of here and find cover across the street, west-side," he ordered.

"And Becky?" Their eyes met for a moment. "I'm glad we got you out, even if no one else."

Becky nodded and closed her eyes to focus. When she opened them again, Amos was gone.

Shane Bunton fired his gun again, sending a single brass shell casing spinning across the tile floor. Becky took her chance and bolted across the open hallway after the spent shell. She plowed through the two sets of exterior doors opening to the outside, barely taking in the stack of dead Americans piled up in an out-of-the-way corner like cordwood.

Once outside, though, she had the good sense to scan the open air for living Americans on the chance this side of the meetinghouse wasn't as clear as Amos had said. The streets outside stretched out empty except for the scattering of Tuckers running north from the meetinghouse windows with arms full of combat materiel. Whatever American soldiers there were remaining outside must still be on the east side, their view blocked by the immensity of the meetinghouse.

Becky took off after her clansmen, her own mother up ahead, watching over the withdrawal from behind a horse trough, an American firearm in her hands.

"Ma, what do we do? The Americans are onto us! There's a gunfight going on inside the meetin'-house!"

"They still got your daddy in there. We're gonna get 'im out." It was all Charlotte Brody said in return, never taking her eyes from the gun's iron sights.

A flicker of dark movement on the limestone parapet of the meetinghouse rooftop flitted for a second, settled, and opened up with ear-splitting automatic fire on the Tuckers retreating through the open. One of the Tuckers jerked as if in surprise as dust and debris jumped up around him like water flicked into hot oil. He fell and went still, the small canister of shot he carried rolling on a couple more feet.

Becky's mother held her breath and squeezed off a single shot at the shooter. The bullet tore a chunk of stone loose close to the shooter's head, driving him into cover.

Lower down, on the third story, a window went up. Becky didn't bother waiting to return fire. The rifle bucked twice in her hands, and then the mother and her daughter were the ones taking fire, likely from some window closer to ground level. Becky couldn't see where from; it was all she could do to keep her head below the lip of the embankment and run further north to a new firing position.

"Folkward!" Becky's mother called out. "Load your guns and give 'em hell!"

From the upper story of the Evanses' home, a musket belched smoke towards the meetinghouse, and Becky's heart buoyed with hope. *The clan's armed.*

She popped her head up long enough to line up a shot on an American changing cover outside the meetinghouse, but ducked again when high-velocity rounds snapped over her head. Her mother ran up about ten paces to her left and squeezed off three rounds at the meetinghouse.

In a battle of equal numbers against muzzle-loaders, it would have been enough to warn off the enemy. A neat three-round burst spoke pretty elegantly. *We've got automatics and aren't afraid to burn an entire jaw's worth of money to kill you.*

But the Americans also had automatics, and more of them. And they seemed willing to burn fifty charges just to keep Becky and her mother pinned.

There were too many soldiers, and Becky didn't have any more bullets than what she had in the magazine. As she had when facing off against the Greenbriers, she knew there was only one thing left to do.

She gritted her teeth and peeked over the brim of the embankment. She willed her mind to ignore the bullets whizzing overhead and kicking up dust around her—if they didn't hit her, they didn't matter—and instead focus on the important details, like the American breaking from cover to catch her and her mother's flank. A single well-placed shot spun the soldier like a top.

Another musket boomed with a nitrogel round, followed by a crackle of musket fire as Tuckers brought their arms to bear. Becky changed places again, moving steadily north, keeping her head below the level of the stream bisecting the town.

The Tucker guns went quiet, and the dadgum belt-fed bullet-eater on the roof of the meetinghouse opened up again. A scream of pain from behind her signaled a Tucker had been hit. She spun to see Cephas Finch and a couple other Tuckers dart into an alleyway, retreating from the never-ending American gunfire, leaving one of their fallen comrades behind.

Becky's heart crashed into her stomach. "Give us some cover, you yaller-bellies!"

"Retreat!" someone called out. *Amos.* "Get out of there! We're outgunned! Regroup at the Brody farm!"

Another fusillade answered the American assault, but it wasn't enough to turn back the onslaught. Deek Evans, set up north closer to the wall, dropped his gun and bucked backward with a ragged crimson wound on his arm. Becky and her mother ran in a crouch under the edge of a shallow drainage ditch until the carpenter's place stood between them and sight of the meetinghouse. There, they pulled back from the ditch into a nearby stable, where Cynthia Hicks was tearing open a charge of powder for her musket. An American round punched right through the wooden wall of the stable, killing her where she stood. Becky stared, horrified, into Cynthia's glassy eyes and regretted ever thinking ill of her.

And still the machine gun stuttered its deathly drumbeat.

Charlotte Brody went to take Cynthia's place and fired back at the Americans.

"Ma, we got to go!"

Her mother flattened herself to the ground and crawled over to Becky. "They'll take them away. We'll never see them again if we don't beat the Americans here."

"We'll get 'em, Ma. But we gotta live long enough to do it."

Her mother's face set in that grim way of hers, like when she wrung a chicken's neck, and she nodded.

They made quick time weaving their way through the narrow streets, but the American guards chasing the fleeing Tuckers had a straighter shot up the main road. Becky skidded to a halt at the sight of three soldiers already at the gate. If the soldiers hadn't been looking forest-wise, they would have capped her right there.

Becky rolled back into the cover of the adjacent alleyway in time to stop her mother from charging out into the open, but not in time to escape the soldiers' notice.

"We're cut off!"

Worse, they were stuck. If they retreated to the east, even assuming that side of town was empty, they'd have to ford the stream and cross a wide stretch of open street.

A stone's throw away, a section of the northern palisade jutted out towards the woods in a redan, breaking sightline of the gate interior. It could serve as a quick escape if Becky and her mother had enough time to climb up to the catwalk before the soldiers closed on them.

Becky's mother must have had the same thought, because she pointed towards the redan and shouted, "Wait for my shot!"

Charlotte Brody dropped to a crouch at the corner of the house, leaned out of cover, and unleashed a steady tap of semi-automatic fire. Becky steeled herself again and sprinted across the gap between the town buildings and the palisade. Even with her mother's covering fire, an American bullet tore a chip of wood from the palisade interior as she passed into the wedge-like redan and scrambled up the ladder.

She reached the top, turned, and shouted for her mother to follow. Mrs. Brody gathered her skirts and hustled to the ladder, her empty gun discarded behind her. "Becky, you get on over the wall. You're right the heck out in the open, girl!" her mother hollered as pulled herself up the ladder after Becky.

Becky ignored her mother. If the soldiers gave chase along the wall—she glimpsed the movement of an over-zealous soldier and sent him ducking back to cover with a shot that barely missed his head. The bolt clicked on an empty chamber, and she hoped she'd bought the two of them enough time.

Becky vaulted over the wall and fell into a rolling landing on the forest side. She turned and extended a hand upward. "C'mon, Ma! Jump!"

Her mother's face appeared at the top of the wall, looking down on Becky as if to gauge the distance, then twisted in pain and shock as a lance of gunfire perforated the palisade breastworks where she stood.

"Mama!" Becky cried in horror.

Charlotte Brody nearly collapsed backwards, out of sight. At the last moment, she caught herself long enough to look down at her daughter. She gave the gentlest smile Becky had ever seen, waved her on, then slumped below the line of the parapet.

# Chapter 6: Bodies and Brains

In what amounted to a closet in the meetinghouse basement, five soldiers' cooling bodies lay stacked on top of each other behind the remnants of a boiler that had been stripped for parts decades ago. Leaned up against the back wall was the body of the bald man who had lured the soldiers from their posts—Jarvis.

When his eyes fluttered open, it was Amos who looked out of them. The knowledge and skills Jarvis possessed were still inside—a much more useful and illuminating set than Sam's—but the person known as Jarvis only existed now as an incoherent, silent howl; an unthinking thought, an unfeeling pain.

His hand went to the pistol and bloody knife at his side. They were still there. He reached out and brushed the cold basement wall with his hand, then the barrel of his assault rifle lying next to it. They were still there. He scanned the dark room and found the surrounding space just as he'd left it.

He seized the automatic rifle from behind the boiler and checked the mag, safety, and firing chamber with a practiced familiarity Amos had never had with old-time weapons.

He rose, stepped to the t-hallway as delicately as his combat boots would allow, and approached the stairs and the emptied supply room. Smoke clouded the already dim air, and within the storage room, he could make out the glow of flames. Actually, the storeroom wasn't totally empty. The people Jarvis had consumed remained where they'd been kept, less useful to the Americans than the guns and ammo. Six proxies waited for him, all laid out in orderly rows on the bare floor like felled tree logs. They were all young women or girls.

*Of course*, Amos thought to himself.

He charged in, his foot brushing that of Jarvis' proxies—now his proxies—and stamped the flames to mere embers. Good enough for now.

He moved out of the supply room and looked up the basement stairs. The two Americans Becky had killed had already been moved aside to clear the way for the plundering of the storage rooms. He held his nose against the sharp tang of smoke and melting laminate as he followed the sound of harsh cries coming from upstairs in the direction of the main foyer.

"That's enough!" said a voice that the Jarvis part of him recognized as belonging to a soldier named Crawford. "Hitch up the wagons and torch the rest. We've got to move before those assholes come back."

"What about Jarvis's proxies? They were supposed to—"

"Forget about that freak! If he's still alive, they're his problem now."

"Where's Stein?"

"Let's gooooooo!"

Jarvis's body ascended the last few stairs and stepped outside into the main hallway. Smoke from the basement and from rooms along the first floor hallway pooled against the ceiling. Two soldiers fled the building, one with a stuffed rucksack slung over his shoulder. Neither gave Jarvis so much as a passing glance. Boxes, barrels, and shattered jars lay scattered across the floor. The American neurocaster darted to an open window across the hall, careful not to slip in the briny vinegar coating the weathered laminate tiles, and peered through the wire mesh grate at the clan main outside.

The spacious street intersection east of the meetinghouse was already emptying, with a knot of tightly packed Tuckers moving toward the eastern half of town. A score of Federation soldiers forced them along with sharp words, gestures, and occasionally the butts of rifles. He could hear the screams and wails of his terrified kin, the sporadic thumps of rifle reports, and the bellowing and bleating of the various cows, hogs, and goats dying at the hands of the soldiers. Any livestock the Americans thought they could get away with followed the train of captives. Several horses and oxen hauled trailers loaded with stolen booty. He spotted Tucker weapons on one of the wagons.

The Tuckers' brainshine called out to him. It had always been there, and he'd always been dimly aware of it, but he'd never had a name for that glow he felt from some clansmen and not from others. No one spoke of it, and he hadn't spoken of it to anyone else. He'd long ago dismissed the feeling as naught, and there it had atrophied to unconsciousness. With Sam, Jarvis, and Jarvis' network under his sway, however, the instinct came roaring back far stronger than it had ever been, and with it came a hunger for more. He could sense his clansmen's brainshine now with the acuity of a starving dog smelling seared meat.

He bolted away from the window, back to the hall, and out the east-facing double doors to the outside. He slowed to a brisk walk as he exited the great double doors, the last American to leave the conflagration. He resisted the urge to run for cover; he was wearing Jarvis's face, and none of the other soldiers had any cause to suspect Jarvis yet. No one was looking back his direction, anyway. The stream of people and animals had made their way across to the far side of town, and in the distance, the eastern gates trembled open to release the first trickle of the American exodus.

He raised the rifle towards the trailing soldiers running to catch up to the convoy. All were out in the open, lined up not more than a hundred paces away. He lowered the rifle again. *Not this way.* The Americans thought he was still one of theirs. He could run up, take charge, stop the caravan. He could make up an excuse, some subterfuge, and then—

A cache of powder the Americans must have left behind went off, blowing flame, smoke and debris from all the lower windows on the south side of the building and sending him diving for cover. He looked back at the meetinghouse. Smoke billowed from nearly every window, not just from the basement. His body—Amos's body—was safe, hidden away in a corner of Arnold Brody's butcher shop. But Sam's body, and the ones Jarvis had brought with him—they were still in the burning building. Resources he could not afford to lose.

Jarvis's eyes swept back to look one more time at the retreating caravan. Amos already knew what he had to do. He cursed with Jarvis's mouth and turned Jarvis's body back to the meetinghouse, casting his rifle aside.

He jumped back down the basement steps two at a time, past the two American corpses.

As he stood deciding which one to start with, he recalled their names: Pamela. Audrey. That was Jarvis's first one—Audrey—all the way from back in the D.C. neuroclave. The one next to her had been a Sylvanian refugee, fleeing the neurocaster purges. He shook off the irrelevant details and the gnawing unease that came with them. He had a lot of heavy lifting to do.

He started to heave one of the bodies onto his shoulder, bracing himself for a trek back up the stairs and out of the building, before he stopped in thought. *Idiot,* he thought.

He bolted back up the stairs.

He dashed up past the first floor, up the flights of quarried stone stairs to the top floor, where Amos had been locked up with Sam and the shadower. On his way up, he passed that blasted printing press. The piles of American paper, which would have been worth a fortune only six months ago, were now a roaring inferno. The same paper they'd used to mesmerize the Tuckers now served as the clan's pyre. All that wealth and power, mere kindling.

Many of the old-world building materials were slow to catch fire, but the soldiers had done their work with pitch and strategically placed piles of crackling coals. The flames and smoke would spread. He had little time.

He reached the top floor and found the hallway door still locked. The locked door yielded to his pistol, and the successive side door beyond yielded to his booted foot. Sam's body lay just as he'd left it, as well as the chained shadower. *There. All bodies accounted for.* He unholstered his pistol and laid it on the floor.

Jarvis's body sprinted back downstairs, through the ever-thickening smoke, back outside until he was well clear of the building. He closed his eyes, reached out with his mind, felt the nearby glow of a consciousness he knew belonged to him, and seized it.

And then he was no longer in Jarvis's body, but in a female in the basement, smoke wafting of her—over his—head. Her body straightened up, but a bit too quickly. This body was smaller than Jarvis's, weaker, having had almost no exercise of any kind since her assimilation. She was a tool, in Jarvis's mind, not someone in need of anything more than basic maintenance.

Amos remembered the assimilation, both through Jarvis's eyes and the girl's. He remembered her terror, the profound heart-sinking feeling as her mind washed away.

The granite-etched flashback dogged him as he threw the unfamiliar dimensions of her body up the basement stairs to safety. He remembered her name, her family, her loved ones circling the drain of Jarvis's will, warped and erased for his perverse amusement. The usefulness of her brain was secondary. Jarvis had liked to see them squirm before they went down. Parts of her were still squirming even now inside Amos—just like Jarvis now squirmed.

*I'll keep you squirming, you son of a bitch.*

Her body was outside now, and Amos left her next to Jarvis'. He occupied the next female and brought her out, and so he continued, one by one, as the flames crept up the stairwell and the basement became almost black with smoke. Each of their final moments warbled in his mind, but he grew better at quieting them as he worked. They were nothing but hollow brainpans. They were no different from a pisspot except for their usefulness to him, the soot in their lungs and the cough in their throats only a fact to weigh along with the weather and the time of day.

Sam's body was the last to receive Amos. As the schoolteacher's middle-aged knees cracked on the way to the door, the chained shadower reached out to him. *I can serve you.*

Sam's eyes gazed into the shadower's slitted pupils. *I thought you belonged to the Pied Piper.*

*The Pied Piper has gone away to feed on the eastern ones.*

Sam's hand lifted the pistol with Jarvis's swiftness and turned to face the shadower with Amos's intensity. He raised the pistol to the glassy surface of the shadower's head, but it did not flinch. He angled the barrel downward and pulled the trigger. One of the rusty chain links shattered, and the shadower stood upright, almost like a man, its long-fingered arms dangling nearly past its knees.

He didn't even look to see if the shadower would follow. It was another empty vessel for his will, another dark corner needing that hale light burning hot inside him.

# Chapter 7: Next Steps

Amos walked the empty streets of the clan. An unnatural quiet gripped the town deeper than a midwinter witching hour. The horses were all gone, along with the goats and hogs. Even the chickens had been lifted with the plundering of the town. The carcasses of various livestock littered the clan main. They could salvage the meat, though it would have been easier if the clan's butcher hadn't been among the conscripts taken from town. The meetinghouse still stood, but only as a smoking husk, its stone and brick walls blackened with soot. A breeze carried bright leaves like fallen plumage in front of him in a rustling whisper. Clouds hung dark and gray overhead, threatening rain.

The wide-open area around the meetinghouse ensured the blaze hadn't spread to the other homes and shops in town, but the Americans had seen fit to put the light to the eastern gate as they left. The clan stores of food and supplies inside the meetinghouse had either been pillaged or burned, and it was doubtful most of the families had squirreled away enough victuals in their own homes and cellars to last them through the coming winter. At least, with the hundred twenty-seven conscripts gone, it left fewer mouths to feed.

He'd already scoured Sam Chamber's home for an item he already knew would be there: a sealed envelope. Elvin had given Sam a letter for Ralph, in the event the boy was found alive. It was a long shot, but Elvin might have known something to give Amos an edge, something he'd written for Ralph in that letter. But Amos had already broken the seal and gotten nothing. Dead ends at every turn. The combined knowledge of Sam Chambers and Jarvis, as well as his newfound power drawn from his neurocaster network, left him stronger than ever before. But all too late.

By now, the convoy of guards had surely caught up with Royce Carlson's detachment, and Amos did not expect Johnny Grierson's ragtag bunch of half-breeds to be anything more than a hiccup in the face of far superior numbers and firepower. And that was even assuming Johnny would actually put up any resistance beyond saving his own settlement in the first place. Knowing now what Jarvis knew about the Griersons, Amos didn't trust Johnny any more than the Americans, which meant the Tucker neurocasters were gone—gone beyond his ability to feel their brainshine. He was alone. Utterly alone.

Then why did he still grip the American rifle so tightly?

A neurocaster was skulking around—and not one of his own. He examined the eight neurocasters he held in his thrall, all lined up in a neat row on the cold ground, their bodies open to receive his mind. A different glow, slippery and hard, resisted his grasp.

Amos wandered toward the eastern gate. He rounded a corner in the wending road to see a hunched figure standing in the gate's charred ruins.

Amos leveled the autorifle at the figure, the neurocaster who was the source of the alien brainshine. It was an old crone, withered and frail, scarcely alive. He didn't recognize her. Yet she couldn't be an American; nothing so fragile could have survived a journey out here. He struggled to understand, and then put it together the moment the old woman spoke.

"Amos Taylor," she said to him, her voice thin and reedy. "We don't have much time. Come with me. Come with me and understand."

She beckoned him to follow and hobbled off the main road to the north end of town. She moved slowly, painfully. He offered her support, more out of impatience than concern. The woman accepted his help, more out of necessity than gratitude.

The old woman had a strong smell about her that went beyond unwashed bodies. She smelled earthy, musty, like the long-abandoned cellars in the old town, overgrown with moss and blanketed with gently rotting leaves.

With Amos helping, it took the two of them only five minutes to reach the open door of Old Man Brody's home. They went inside without any words or thoughts exchanged between them. She led him into the bedroom, and he followed, both accepting and dreading what he already knew he would find inside.

In the old man's empty room, then in the connecting closet, a trap door stood propped open, revealing a crude ladder disappearing into the yawning black darkness below.

"Took me ten minutes to get out. This body hasn't had this much exercise in years," the old crone said, gesturing to her own nearly skeletal frame. "You could hop down in one jump. It isn't far. But I'll understand if you want to take a lantern with you."

Amos took the bedside lantern and lit it. Walking up to the closet, he raised the lantern to see where the trap door led. A sturdy deadbolt attached to the underside of the trap door sealed out intruders rather than sealed anyone inside. The ladder ended on a bare concrete floor only six feet down—shallow enough that when he had climbed down, he still had to duck in the narrow passage below the house.

The short passage ended in a cellar. An ancient toilet sat in the corner, but the pipes running into the ceiling likely still carried water in from the water tower, and the sewage pipe likely ran into the same septic tank everyone knew lay attached to Old Man Brody's house. A pantry with a few bland morsels lay open on one end, as well as a washbasin with a likely functioning tap. A small vent near the ceiling opened to the outside to circulate air, but there were no windows, no ornaments, no decorations or comforts of any sort.

Several metal bunk beds lining the walls took up most of the meager space the room could offer. This room was a cellar, not a bedroom, and cellars were meant for storing things. This cellar stored several people, laid out sleeping on bare mattresses, all of them old, withered, and naked, and all of them apparently not far from death.

"You've figured out enough to start your own network," the old woman said as Amos stared at the bodies. "How much do you know?"

"Mostly what Jarvis knew, which wasn't much. He liked consuming people, but he didn't know how—or why—all this started."

The old woman sighed. "Where do you want to begin?"

"What do I need to do to win?"

"Know what you're up against. I don't have much time. I'm with the convoy now, you know. These proxies have been part of my network so long, their brainshine is as familiar to me as my own. But even still, it's weak."

"Is someone carrying you in the convoy?"

"Last time I checked, it was my sons, Arnie and Job. They assumed it was because I was too old to keep up the march, and the Americans will probably swallow that for the time being. Everyone in the convoy is scared and confused, but healthy. I counted twenty-five soldiers. We haven't made it more than two miles yet. You're too late to stop them from rejoining the other Federation detachment, but not too late to keep them from getting to New Ashburn."

Amos paced. "Jarvis knew of reinforcements coming from out east. That puts the number of soldiers at well over a hundred. With the weapons we've freed up, I could arm maybe twenty clansmen."

"The soldiers aren't your biggest problem," Old Man Brody said through the woman. "It's this drifting neurocaster."

"The Pied Piper. The Americans were hunting him. Jarvis knew about him but didn't think he was anything special."

"It looks like the New American Federation's restarted the research that drove people like me to the hills fifty years ago. They're chasing the golden goose again. This Pied Piper character is almost surely what came of it."

"What's the golden goose? Are they trying to get control over all the unbreds?"

She chuckled without humor. "That's what they thought we could do with neurocaster networks sometime between the first and second generation of neurocasters. Back when the bioengineers realized assimilation was possible in the first place. But stronger control over the unbreds only scratches the surface of what neurocaster networks can do."

"Then what is it?" Amos asked.

The old woman didn't answer. She tilted forward as if about to faint, and Amos stepped up to catch her. She came back to herself at the last moment and sat on the bunk that was apparently hers. "The golden goose," she went on, "was what I was supposed to... be a part of. I was supposed to be sacrificed to a network, but I ended up subsuming her root instead." The crone gestured to her own body. "A stunt like that wasn't supposed to be possible, but that's how I got out."

"Same here. How did you do it?"

The old woman shrugged. "It was so long ago. Neurocasting assimilators are conditioned to go for the jugular, you might say, but I knew I was over-matched. Had to bleed the network slow. It was like—eating a man alive, from the feet on up. I had to do it to survive, but... the more time passes, the more I feel like I lost a part of me that day, instead of—"

"I don't have time for your boo-hoo shit, old man," Amos said. "Why did you go to the trouble of hiding your own little network under the house if you weren't going to use it?"

"I did use it. But our clan's breeding is a blessing and a curse. I can ward off wild unbreds, and have done so since the founding of the clan. But pigman armies answer to a network. To a cabal of shadowers, say. And the shadowers answer to any neurocaster powerful enough to master an unbred legion and hungry enough to go after a community of free neurocasters. Four withered old proxies aren't enough to ward off that kind of pressure."

The woman started to slump over, but again caught herself before she hit the bunk.

"There used to be more," she said of the other bodies. "Most of them were free neurocasters I picked up over the Scavenging Years. Not likely to get much more mileage out of them. I lost three over the past ten years. Cut up the bodies myself. Carried them out at night and buried the pieces in the garden."

"What was your plan after the rest of these go?" Amos pointed to the sleeping proxies.

"Didn't really have one. I tried to pass this along to my son, but he refused. He was about your age when he found out. It was all he could do then not to disown me on the spot and have me banished. But even he couldn't deny my usefulness. So, he took up his place as the clan Reverend and preached a holy condemnation of our unbred heritage, all the while secretly nurturing my proxies, caring for me when I was sick, ensuring my survival through famine and war. I taught him the rudiments of unbred shepherding. But he himself refused to partake in the fruit of fellow neurocasters, even those from outside the clan, and I don't blame him for that."

"If he wouldn't do it, why didn't you go out, then? Why wait for some other son of a bullhusker to get an edge on you?"

"Increased risk with small chance of reward. In the early days, I thought about breeding some in secret with the proxies I already had and assimilating the young neurocasters around the age of five or six. But the logistics of caring for an infant and young child in secret proved too difficult to manage on my own. Even aside from the practical difficulties—I couldn't go through with it. Not to a child. That's the real reason the butcher looks nothing like me. I told my second wife he was my bastard child by a nomad prostitute, and she helped me raise him without a complaint. She knew, I think, what he really was. A little tomcatting seemed like such a nice lie in comparison. And knowing I wouldn't do to him what I'd originally intended kept her sleeping by my side, even to the end. She was scared of me," the old crone said, staring off at a memory too distant and painful to warrant frequent revisitation. The woman spoke as if realizing something obvious for the first time. "She was scared of me, but because of Arnie, she trusted I'd go only as far as I had to, and no further. No further. She went to her grave too young—all of us do—but at least she went with her mind still her own."

Amos was about to snap at Old Man Brody's proxy again for his pathetic self-justification, but the proxy fell to the side on the bunk.

Amos swore and shook the woman by the shoulders. "Come back to me. Hey. Come back to me, old man; I need to know what to do about the Pied Piper."

The woman's eyes opened, but she did not get up this time. "The convoy's close to the top of a hill. If we go over, I'll lose contact."

"Then tell me. What. Is. The golden. Goose. Jarvis didn't know anything about a 'golden goose.'"

She didn't answer right away. "It's hard to explain," she said. "What do you know about the brain?"

"Enough. I learned about it in school." Amos hadn't actually paid much attention to what he'd thought of at the time as irrelevant information, but Sam Chambers had known quite a lot. And whatever Sam had known, Amos now knew.

"How does the brain do the thinking?"

"Brain's made out of little cells called neurons, and they think using electricity."

"*How*, though? What does electricity have to do with it?"

Amos shrugged. "This isn't important. What does—"

"Communication. Your neurons are talking to each other all the time. Sometimes all over, sometimes quietly, in small areas. But they're always talking. Individually, they're stupid, insignificant, and totally expendable, but through communication, they come together to make a whole."

"Okay, so?"

"Take a step out. What are we doing right now?"

"Talking."

"Which makes us neurons. Stupid, insignificant, and expendable, unless we're talking to each other. Then we become something more."

"The golden goose?"

"Not with normal, person-to-person communication, though even that has allowed humanity to do as a whole what a single person could not: Planes. Refrigeration. Plastics. Spaceships. A primitive mind. A long way from achieving true consciousness. But our neurons had to start somewhere, too. Think about the distant ancestors of the neurons in your brain."

"You mean ancient humans?"

"No, much further back. Billions of years ago, when the only life was single cells. For ages, that's all there was. Single microscopic cells fighting for their own lives, or at most, small colonies barely working together for mutual survival. Then one day—" the old woman tried to snap her fingers, but her trembling arm was now too weak. She stared straight up to the bunk above her, not even able to meet Amos' eyes. "The cells came together in a way that made them part of something bigger. A multicellular organism. And suddenly, the individual cells didn't matter anymore. A single cell could die, but the organism lived on. Compared to an amoeba, a human life would seem like immortality."

"Now *we* are the single-celled organisms."

The woman nodded, her eyes closing. "A neurocaster network is just a colony, still under the direct control of the root. You assimilate enough neurocasters, however, and the intelligence becomes distributed throughout the network. The network gains sentience, and there's no longer any distinction between root and proxy. The individual bodies cease to matter, as long as the whole... lives on."

Amos remembered speaking with the shadower, which had since disappeared into the wilderness. He remembered the memories passed down through the lives of whatever creature lived long enough to receive them, there for any neurocaster strong enough to bring it all together. Someone like the Pied Piper. Or someone like Amos Taylor.

"Beyond that veil," she said, "you have continuous, unbroken consciousness for as long as you've got fresh bodies to throw into the network. *That's* the golden goose."

"Immortality. Godhood."

"That's what the Pied Piper wants, if he hasn't become that already. You'll know if he can occupy all his proxies at once."

"And you never wanted to follow that path?" Amos asked.

The old woman paused. "Yeah, well—the individual cells... always mattered to me." her eyes fluttered open, shining now with tears, before they closed again.

"How can I stop him?" Amos asked.

She didn't answer.

"Is he strong enough to take the convoy before I can catch up with you?"

No answer. He shook her again, but Old Man Brody was gone for good now. Amos cursed again and paced the little cellar. He had to keep the Pied Piper from getting any more neurocasters in his network. Amos would have to kill any proxies that didn't belong to him. He looked at

Old Man Brody's sleeping proxies. If the Pied Piper got to Old Man Brody...

"Sorry Gramps," Amos said, unsheathing his matchet, "these were about out of juice, anyway."

As blood ran into the drain in the middle of the floor, Amos considered his next steps. He'd need help with the proxies in his network. Not just whatever unbreds he could get control of. Human neurocasters to stand watch while he was hopping bodies. The Americans had taken nearly everybody. Becky Brody had escaped, but other than that... wait. He knew where another one might be.

A harvest moon hung over the crowd of Tuckers sheltering in the reinforced corral out in front of the big barn. But they hadn't come to hold a threshing bee or hoedown. The moon and stars were the only light; none dared stoke coals for a fire, even for warmth against the autumn chill. Job Brody's wife, who alone among her kin had avoided conscription, quietly distributed all the crackers and pickled goods from her larder, but the repast didn't go far to satisfy several hundred ravenous stomachs. No one complained, though. The bereaved and worried wept silent tears. Even the children spoke only in whispers.

The few Tuckers bearing arms stood watch in the night against the encroachment of unbreds or pursuing soldiers. Becky still grasped the automatic rifle she'd taken from town, having scavenged six bullets for its magazine. Her eyes remained dry, unblinking, fixed on the dark tree line to the south.

Someone stepped up beside her—Sophie, with one of her twins cradled in her arms. "My father-in-law's watching Justin," she explained softly. Her children were safe, at least. For now. "Do you think it's safe, spending the night this close to town?"

"Not sure where else we could go. Nobody's got a plan past getting to this place. If you're worried about the Americans chasing us, I don't think they'll want to spare any extra hands pulled away from guarding their big prize." She meant, of course, the hundred-odd Tucker conscripts left behind, Becky's father among them.

Without preamble, a voice called out from the dark treeline, loud and clear in the still night air. "Don't shoot! I'm alone, and I'm coming out."

Sophie gasped. "Is that—"

It was Sam Chambers. His form coalesced around his voice as he approached the revetment behind the dual-purpose irrigation ditch and moat surrounding the farmstead.

"How did you escape? I thought Amos said you were dead," Sophie said.

"I didn't... Amos was mistaken. But it is true that I'm unwell. I'll need to rest soon, once I've relayed our next course of action to the survivors. How many have we lost?"

"Where's Amos?" Becky demanded. "He never came back with the other volunteers. Did you see him when you escaped?"

Sam raised his hands to calm Becky's rapid-fire interrogation. "Amos is alive. He wanted to be here in person, but he has other plans that require his direct attention. He's sent me here to act in his place.

"Are these plans going to get him killed?"

"No need to panic, Miss Brody," Sam said, now close enough he could meet her gaze directly in the moonlight. *Remember, Becky: We got you out, even if no one else. That's worth it to me.*

Becky stutter-stepped back in shock at the thought—the memory, or the voice—intruding into her mind. That wasn't her thought. That was... "Amos?"

Sophie gave Becky a quizzical look. "Huh?"

Sam ignored Becky's spoken bewilderment as one might ignore a social gaffe. "I need to know where things stand. What are our casualties so far?"

When Becky said nothing, Sophie spoke up. "Shane's counted eight of the volunteers dead for sure. Charlotte Brody..." She looked sideways at Becky. "Becky's mother among them."

"How many weapons did we get out?"

"Job's bolt-action. A couple Armalites with enough .223 ammo for some smart action, this gun here, and eleven muzzle-loaders. A bit of black powder, and a couple shots' worth of nitrogel. It's not enough to take on even the town garrison, let alone all the soldiers who left town earlier to do who-knows-what."

"They're headed to kill everyone at the Grierson settlement," Sam Chambers said, examining the barrel and rubbing his thumb over the threads cut onto the outside. "And these weapons *will* be enough." He let out a satisfied sigh. "We'll be safe here tonight, but I need to rest. You probably won't be able to wake me in the morning. If that's the case, make a stretcher for me and carry me along with the rest."

Becky shook her head, still confused. "Carry you where?"

"The Grierson settlement, of course." Sam walked into the temporary camp and faded into the tangle of Tuckers huddled together for warmth.

"It sounds like there's some kind of plan. That's good, right?" Sophie said.

"I don't know." Becky's voice teeter-tottered between overwhelmed bewilderment and overwhelmed despair.

"Hey." Sophie reached out to comfort Becky, but they'd been friends long enough for her to know Becky hated being touched. She withdrew her arm. "Don't you give up now. We've lost too many people to give up on the ones we've left behind."

Becky gave no answer but for a slight shake of her head.

"You don't have any hope for them?"

"Don't make me say what I'm thinking, Sophie."

Sophie stared at her friend. "You already said it."

"I'm sorry. I wish things were different. I'll make it back to you, if I can."

"You may still save your pa. You've got to hold on to hope. What else have you got besides hope?"

It wasn't a question meant for an answer, but Becky answered it anyway. "Hate. That's what I got. I don't know if I can save my pa. I don't know if Amos can. But I know he can hurt the Americans. I know I can. And I aim to."

Sophie stared into the darkness for a long time. "Would Ella have stood for that notion?"

"Ella ain't here."

"What difference does that make?"

"She's gone with the Americans to New Ashburn. Along with *your* pa. What do you think the Americans have done to them, huh?"

# Chapter 8: In Which Sparks and Dry Forests Make for Lively Companions

N ew Ashburn

"I want to talk to Colonel Armstrong," Bill said to the guards through lips pursed around a cigar on one side of his mouth, a reddening mark blooming on the other side. "The workers are striking. They've holed themselves up amongst the kilns, and I barely kept my head on my shoulders long enough to run to you. They want shorter hours, extra rations—"

"Armstrong won't care what they want," Lieutenant Harlow said, striding up with other guards in tow. He wore his American-issued uniform and assault rifle, and all the authority that came with them, as if he'd been born with them. "Tell them they have five minutes, by my count, to get back to work at their assigned stations, before I take the most infirm from the group and start breaking kneecaps."

"Ain't no way I'm going back in there on my own."

"If I have to go in there, I'm going to hurt people."

"Better them than me," Bill said. "I'll come along with you. You'll need more men, though. They got the numbers in there."

"We have the guns," Lieutenant Harlow answered, but he waved to one of the attendant guards anyway and waited for reinforcements to arrive.

With twenty guards in a tangle of unwashed junker hooligans and slightly more washed American regulars, they made their way to the brickworks. The massive double doors, usually open to provide better ventilation, remained closed.

"They didn't even barricade the doors?" Harlow asked.

"Not from this side, anyway."

"Go open them, then."

Bill turned to look at the guards beside and behind him. "Why me? They're not armed with anything worse than bricks."

"Your factory, your workers. Go." Harlow waved him on with his assault rifle.

The guards fanned out to get better firing lines on the brickworks interior.

Bill took a few tentative steps and stopped with a frustrated puff on his American-made cigar. He turned to face the half-ring of guards. "Could you lower them weapons at least until I get the doors open? I don't wanna get shot."

The American lieutenant shrugged and waved the guns down.

But Bill didn't turn back toward the doors. He stood like a man facing a firing squad, feet planted square with his shoulders, one arm crossed over his chest to tuck under the other. He took a long, sumptuous drag from his cigar. The smoke he exhaled masked the slight upward curl of his lips. The smile may have looked like one of grim resignation to those who hadn't known him. Those who did would have seen an ornery streak he'd never grown out of. "I coulda got used to these smokes," he sighed, taking a wistful look at the glowing end of his cigar. He raised his head to meet his bodyguard's eyes, long enough for his smile to freeze the lieutenant in confusion, then alarm.

Bill casually flicked the cigar at Harlow, and the entire detachment of guards disappeared in a blinding white flash.

The sound—a powerful *whump* not quite the thunderclap of an explosion—smote Bill in the face, making him recoil as much from the noise and whoosh of hot air as the brilliant light and flash of heat.

On the heels of the fulgurating blaze came the cries of the guards, at once shocked, outraged, and humiliated. They were all stark naked.

Twenty young men stood in a ring, their skin reddening from the flash of heat that had vanished their clothing as a wizard's wand might have done. They'd dropped their weapons to pat their bare, tender skin, to tamp out the flicker of flames that might have caught on their hair, but mainly to cover their denuded butts and genitals.

A couple had the presence of mind to reach down to grab their discarded weapons, but it was already too late.

"Don't even think about it," came a voice from behind the guards: Omar Walking. He held one of the discarded rifles at hip level, which he used to wave them all to the side. "Over there. Snappy now. This thing ain't loaded with goose feathers."

Bill called out, and the double doors behind him opened to let forth a swarm of workers, who raced to gather the fallen weapons as Omar herded the guards next to the shed's outside wall.

Bill stepped forward to examine his captives. "Huh. Will you look at that?" Bill said in mock surprise to Omar. "Take away their fancy uniforms, and they ain't any different than the rest of us. Y'all know what happens when you treat cellulose material—say, cotton—with nitric acid? You get what y'all were wearing until about a minute ago: gun-cotton. *Now* y'all ain't got nothin' on but boots and singed waistbands. I ain't sure y'all ever had much more'n that. Just a bunch of boys too big for their britches, I say."

The workers guffawed with the glee of the oppressed finally getting their long-overdue payback. They laughed and jeered with the kind of hard-edged mirth that only stopped at a superior's orders or a victim's death. It wasn't yet clear which would come first.

One of the Ashburnite guards, one of the low-down Rockhurst boys, shivered from terror, cold, or both. "What are you a-gonna do to us, mister?"

"I'm gonna march you smack dab in front of me and all these fine folks here," Bill gestured to the armed workers, "right into town and up to Armstrong's castle. We're going to have us a... re-negotiation."

A patter of rapidly approaching footsteps whirled Omar to face the Ashburnite apprentices who'd come running to investigate the ruckus. They stopped cold in their tracks, though whether at the sight of a bunch of unclothed guards or their guns in the hands of the workers couldn't be certain.

"What's going on?" exclaimed Jody, the naturally colored part of her face going a lighter shade of white.

"It's a mutiny," Bill explained with barely a glance her direction. "And wouldn't you know, I'm the one leading it. These here are my hostages. If you don't want to be a hostage yourself, you'd best stand aside.

The Rockhurst kid shook his head in a near panic. "The Americans don't care about hostages. They'll gun us down along with you."

"They're welcome to try. They ain't the only ones with guns now, but they *are* the only ones with matchsticks for clothes. If they feel like going naked to a gunfight, I guess that's up to them." Bill walked over to Lieutenant Harlow, who seemed to be trying to keep his composure more than the rest of the guards. "Like it or not, *sir*," Bill said, "I'm calling the shots now."

"You're going to pay for this."

Bill snorted. "We'll see about that. You two," Bill ordered two workers, "Put his bare butt all the way up to the front of the line. I want *everybody* to get a good look at this big guy. Okay, you rascals, let's get moving."

The Rockhurst boy still wasn't convinced. "You can't beat Armstrong. She runs this whole area. What are you gonna do to her?"

Bill stepped up close enough to let the kid smell the cigar smoke still on his breath. "I'm going to teach her never to get into a pissing contest with a chemist who knows what to do with ammonia."

Tucker Territory

Johnny Grierson passed off his watch to the Coles and warned them to keep their outlines low. The overnight downturn in the temperatures did not put his mind at ease. The cat-and-mouse skirmishes his sharpshooters had been playing with the Federation soldiers had only become more dangerous. Reinforcements had come from town, and the soldiers were acting more boldly, chasing his fighters back away from the road and keeping up a presence in the forest. The Americans still lurked out there in the woods, likely defiling his kin's half-bred corpse. Their stench wafted to him every time the wind shifted from the north, carried on the breeze to any halfway sensitive nose: several days worth of unwashed travel, and an untold number of warm bodies. The invaders had broken out of the pen Johnny had made for them, and now it was only a matter of time before they found their way to his settlement and penned him in. They were waiting out there, outnumbering and outgunning him. Damn the ubermenschen.

For now, the Coles manned a handy killzone about a quarter-mile downhill from the settlement, and the American soldiers hadn't been dumb or unlucky enough to walk into it. He hoped he could cull enough of their numbers there to forestall the inevitable siege, but if they were any kind of smart, the Americans would creep the long way around, scouting in force to outflank his fighters and locate the settlement. Johnny could only spare ten woodsmen to screen what amounted to three square miles of wilderness. And signs of more pigman doings topped this dung heap he'd found himself waist-deep in. He'd have to recall everyone to the settlement palisade by the next watch, or else risk the loss of critical manpower.

The promise of a warm bed and a scant breakfast after a twelve-hour watch offered little rest to Johnny's buzzing mind. Rest would come later. He still had business to attend to. The business in question waited for him at the settlement gate with folded arms and a crooked nose.

"Sam Chambers," Johnny Grierson growled. "You got news from town?"

Sam carried a rifle with what looked like an ugly metal plug stuck onto the end of the barrel. "There's been shooting. The Americans burned the meeting-house and eastern gate, along with clan stores of gunpowder and most foodstuffs they didn't steal. I have three hundred sixty-one clansmen hiding out at the Brody farm. A hundred twenty-seven more are held captive. Right now, you're the only thing keeping them bottled up on the highway."

"Any good news?"

"Amos Taylor is in charge now."

"The blacksmith's kid? What the hell's he gonna do?"

"Everything. He's going to do everything, as long as you keep the Americans from breaking through on the highway and getting away with the captives."

"You're too late, then. They done pushed my people back from the highway. They can waltz east any time they want."

"They haven't. Not yet. Royce Carlson wants to neutralize your settlement before he breaks for New Ashburn."

"How you know that, schoolteacher?"

"I have sources."

"Then I gotta shore up the bull-works around here," Johnny gestured to the settlement palisade. "I can't keep fighting the Americans in open country without more hands."

Sam Chambers regarded Johnny with a naked scorn he'd scarcely seen from any Tuckers, let alone the schoolmaster. "This isn't a request. You're going to take every able gun-hand and get control over that highway."

"Then who's going to ward up the settlement? You bring any armed town Tuckers out here?"

"We'll send reinforcements."

"I want to see the reinforcements before I stick my neck out."

Sam shook his head, his glare twisting into a grin. "Oh, Johnny." Sam clucked his tongue. "You don't know how far out your neck already is. This isn't a haggle, and I'm not done giving orders."

"Where do you think you are, Sam?" Johnny blustered, incredulous. "You want me to pull *your* town clansmen out of their own smoker, you better give me a good reason."

Sam stared blankly back at Johnny for a full five seconds before punching him square in the face. Johnny stumbled back, holding his nose. Sam seized his collar and battered him around his good eye with vicious, evenly spaced hammer-blows.

"Are you listening, Johnny?" Sam said, his voice level but tense with anger.

"Kiss my half-bred ass, Tucker," Johnny wheezed.

Another blow to his nose, this one breaking it. Johnny hadn't reckoned the schoolteacher could hit that hard.

"I *saaaid*, 'Are you lisssstening, Johnny?'" Sam said through clenched teeth.

"What do you want?" Johnny's voice cracked.

"Those hundred clansmen are in the smoker because of you. I know you sold us out to the Americans, you useless half-and-half crapsack. What did you do with Ralph McDaniel? Royce Carlson let you have him. Did you kill him to keep your little secret?"

"What—how do you know—"

"*I have my sources.*"

"I never did you any worse than you've done to me. I already lost my cousin fighting the Americans."

"If I didn't have a use for you, I'd kill you right here."

A gun cocked from atop the palisade. "Back away from Johnny." One of the half-breed Craines, who'd left town after marrying up with the Coles, pointed a musket at Sam.

"You want to fight the town Tuckers and the Americans both?" Sam said. "Shoot me if you want. But Amos Taylor is in charge of the clan now, and if he decides to pay you back properly, you'll *wish* for an American bullet before it's all done."

The guard lowered his gun, his bluff evaporating in the face of Sam's cold stare.

Sam turned back to the one-eyed Grierson. "So what's it gonna be, Johnny?"

Grierson wiped at the blood pouring from his nose. The grip on his collar loosened, and he fell back to the ground, utterly spent. A coughing sigh escaped him as he struggled to his feet. "Open the goddamn gate," Johnny said to the guard with a nasally growl.

The gate open, Johnny led Sam past the settlement's few ramshackle homes, past the temporary piles of mine tailings kept well separate of the rest of the settlement interior, up to the dark maw of the mine entrance. Johnny laid hand to an available lantern hanging on the post outside the mine entrance, lit the coal-oil wick, and motioned for Sam to follow before he plunged into the darkness.

The two passed a series of rough-cut wood-paneled walls with padlocked or barred barn doors every few feet. Some were emergency stalls for livestock, others storerooms and cellars belonging to the individual families of the settlement. All of it lay within reach of daylight, before the slope of the mine dove sharply down into the mountain, but they still kept a bird in a cage in this section of the mine whenever the stalls held anything living.

One such birdcage hung outside the last stall in the tunnel. Johnny unlatched the door and pulled it open. Inside, a prisoner blinked in the lantern light.

"So you didn't kill him," Sam said, looking in at Ralph McDaniel.

"We done him the best turn we could, under our set of stances. The Americans wanted him dead, and I swayed 'em to let me deal with him. Said I could make it look like an accident, and keep the rest of the Tuckers from raising a fuss over it. You can ask him yourself. We kept him fed and—"

"Enough." Sam stopped Johnny with a wave of his hand and took the lantern. "Leave the two of us. When I decide to go, he's walking out of here with me. Take your fighters—every single one—and stop the Americans from passing through the gap. I'll get you your reinforcements. But Johnny," Sam said as Johnny turned away with a sigh, "Remember who your real enemies are and pray the Tuckers never become one of them."

Johnny sighed again and did as he was told.

"What's going on, Mr. Chambers?" Ralph asked.

Sam Chambers did not answer, but instead stared at Ralph. Gauging.

"Mr. Chambers?"

Sam raised the lantern higher and stepped forward into the stall.

Ralph shrank back to the bare rock wall. "Mr. Chambers? Are you okay? What's going on? What happened to your nose?"

Finally, Sam answered. "My nose is the least of our worries. A lot has happened. We're at war with the Americans, and Amos Taylor has something he wants you to help with. But I'll have to teach you how to do it. Come outside with me."

Sam turned to lead Ralph from his confinement, but stopped in the stall doorway. "Your—your father is dead." Sam said, reaching into his inner coat pocket. "He wanted you—to have this." Sam turned and handed Ralph an opened envelope containing fine American paper. "I'm... I'm sorry. I thought he had something... useful to tell you."

New Ashburn

The procession of naked hostages and their bedraggled captors marched unopposed through the asphalt streets of New Ashburn, right up past the super-mart to the palisade at the base of the hill behind it. Whispers, glances, and occasionally even citizens followed the march, adding to the size and weight of the crowd. No Federation guards, or even their Ashburnite lapdogs, came to stop them.

Bill, walking at the head of his impromptu army of half-starved slaves, kept steeling himself for the inevitable brawl he was sure lay in store. The leaders among the slaves—those few who seemed to have actual military experience—rallied the workers and kept the hostages in line. Their harsh orders to "follow the powderman!" were perhaps meant to bolster Bill's confidence, but they instead reminded him how badly things would go if they indeed went bad. It wasn't the chest-thumping that kept him walking. Ella was cooped up in that citadel. Whatever Armstrong or the Federation or whoever said about it, there wasn't any call for such nonsense. None at all.

It wasn't Armstrong who met him at the palisade gate, or any American at all. It was Mr. Salazar.

"I don't reckon on you joinin' me," Bill said. "But you'd best stand aside."

"I need to know what you intend."

"I intend to air my terms in as peaceful a way as I'm allowed."

Mr. Salazar bent his head toward Bill without moving from the gate. "Go ahead, then. You can air them here."

"I want Ella Holland back. Right now. I want full rations, proper housing, and three teeth's daily wages to every worker at my factory."

"You know I can't grant you that."

"Then stop wasting my time and let me talk to the one who can."

"You know I can't do that, either."

"Oh you can't?" Bill crossed his arms.

"You think I had a choice in this?" Mr. Salazar's voice rose, either in anger or desperation.

"You can't hide behind that. I licked Federation boots same as you. You want to be Armstrong's mouthpiece, that's on you."

"You want me to throw in with your lot, just like that?"

"Just like that."

"It's not that simple!"

"Sure it is."

"For you. Not for us. All *you* ever had to worry about was your nitrogel factory. Us Ashburnites have only ever had two choices when it came to the Americans!" Salazar jabbed two fingers skyward as much in defiance of Bill's needling as to emphasize his point. "Submit or die. We were nothing more than a bump in the road to the first wave of Americans who came through here, chasing some super-caster. You think folks out east think any better of us junkers than hillfolk do 'round here? Around anywhere? Armstrong wanted to kick us out, ship us all off to work at their dockyards or their paper mills. To live in their slums. It took every bit of convincing and groveling I could do to keep my kin here."

"If you don't think it's a fair deal, why stick with it when a better one comes along?"

"*What better deal?* To pay your workers with money we already gave up to the Federation, house your workers in the barracks we built for Federation soldiers, and feed your workers with provisions we had to send away two months ago? Workers, I might add, who are prisoners of war? A war that makes them my clan's mortal enemies?" Mayce Salazar shook his head, eyes shut against the ridiculousness of Bill's demands. "Pretend the Federation soldiers at the gate didn't have two light machine guns aimed at us right now. Even then, do you think your workers, with their new guns, wouldn't put my kin under their boots? It's the same deal, Mr. Puckett. Just a different administrator."

Jody Perkins spoke up from near the back of the procession, now mixed in the with the workers. "Bill Puckett ain't our enemy, Mr. Salazar! Nor the workers, neither! We're all just prisoners of different sorts!"

"What does it matter what we are?" Mr. Salazar screamed. "If this rabble ain't my enemy, then the folks at the top of the hill are! And where does that leave New Ashburn? A turncoat ally for the Federation to swat like a horsefly?"

"I got no dog in this fight other than my own people. I don't see why your people are any different," Bill said.

"You're an idiot, Mr. Puckett. You're up to your neck in this war, whether you asked for it or not. You were in this war the moment your nitrogel sold on the open market. Armstrong was going to have you and your nitrogel, one way or another. You're with her or against her. Submit or die."

Bill put his hands on his hips. "Didn't have to be this way."

"But this is the way it is."

Bill turned away, then turned back to face Mr. Salazar again. "Okay. Then your clan's in the middle of a war no matter what you do, same as mine." He stepped forward, pointing to the ground between them. "If you were picking sides again, who'd you rather have? The one who saw you as a trash-picker, or the one who saw you as an equal?"

Mayce Salazar stared back. He didn't answer, nor blink, nor even breathe, it seemed.

The soldier atop the gate had finally seen enough. He racked the charging handle on his machine gun and shouted, "That's it, *everyone* on the ground, face-down, hands behind your head! You have to the count of three!"

Mayce Salazar was the first to his knees, before the soldier had even counted "one." But his eyes locked with Bill's, and those eyes showed not resignation, but acceptance. Mr. Salazar stooped to pick up a palm-sized rock from the worn footpath. The last thing he ever did was rise again, spinning, to chuck the stone at his Federation masters. He missed, and the gun cut him down.

The machine gun fire from atop the palisade ceased the moment it began as the soldiers' clothes burst into flame. They rose from their cover out of instinct, presenting themselves as shaking pink targets. Close-range gunfire removed their brains from their skulls, and the whole exchange ended in less than a second with the dual *thud* of two corpses hitting the ground on the other side of the palisade.

Bill ducked down and ran to Mr. Salazar's prone form. The junker's eyes had already glassed over, and Bill closed them.

"It didn't have to be this a-way," Bill said again, looking up to the citadel atop the hill. But this was the way it was, and now with Mayce Salazar dead, the American Federation wasn't just looking at a prisoner revolt.

All of New Ashburn had turned against the Americans.

# Chapter 9: Sending a Message

Becky's shock at seeing Ralph McDaniel alive lasted about as long as it took to make sure it really was him and not an American lost in the woods. She had no more room for surprise, even a good one. The sudden appearance of a presumed dead neurocaster merited little more than a "Good morning. Welcome to the team."

Becky still wasn't sure what the team was, though. Sam Chambers had returned from the Grierson settlement with Ralph McDaniel in tow, only to climb onto the wagon with Amos Taylor and six other sleeping people—all neurocasters—and go to sleep himself. Then Amos had gotten up and walked off without a word.

"What's going on?" Ralph asked, staring with barely contained terror at the American soldier sleeping right next to Sam Chambers. "Why is *he* here?" he asked, pointing to the man Becky knew as Jarvis.

"I don't know much. Amos said they're all working for us. Even this jackass." Becky slapped Jarvis's knee.

Ralph shook his head. "No way. That feller said he'd eat me before one of the Griersons nabbed me. Ain't no way he agreed to join up with us."

Becky mused, "I think he's a hostage. Amos said they're all harmless and told me to keep them safe. He hasn't moved since we left town. Look." She jabbed the American in the shin and got no response. "Cold as a stunned fish."

"Sam said we're both neurocasters, and only neurocasters would understand Amos's plan."

Becky nodded. "That's what Amos said, too. But he ain't told me more than that. He's playing it pretty close to—"

A rustle in the grass sent them both whirling around as Amos returned from a pocket of dense undergrowth.

*I told you both not to speak out loud.* Amos's tone of rebuke intruded on Becky's mind, and apparently on Ralph's as well.

Ralph's eyes squinted in concentration. *I smell unbreds, Amos. Were you followed?*

Amos smiled. *Of course.*

A shadower emerged not far behind Amos, and then an entire host of pigmen. Both Becky and Ralph recoiled at the sight, though Becky had the presence of mind to toss Ralph a spear before she raised her gun.

*Easy,* Amos cautioned them both. *They're with me.*

The foremost pigman came to a stop, lifted one clawed hand, and gave Becky and Ralph a casual two-fingered salute—the same gesture Amos might have given to a fellow roundswalker on a night patrol.

"What in blue blazes—" Becky said aloud.

*No spoken words,* Amos reiterated. *We sit here and wait.*

*For what?* Becky asked.

The distant rumble of gunfire reached them. Becky peered out to the southeast and spotted, far beyond the crest of the hilly horizon, a plume of thickening smoke.

*That'll be the Grierson settlement. That's our signal. Let's go.*

95

A dozen pigmen transferred the eight sleeping people to the slapped-together stretchers while half a dozen others heaved the satchels and travel-packs Amos had brought with them on the wagon. Becky watched with unmasked awe and confusion tinged with a hint of distaste. *You figured out how to use unbreds as packhorses?*

*How'd you think we were going to get all this stuff over hill and dale? We can't take the highway, but thanks to the Griersons' little distraction, the way north of the highway should be clear.*

"But I thought—" Ralph McDaniel began before speaking with his mind. *I thought we were sending reinforcements to help the Griersons.*

*I thought it would be nice to see Johnny Grierson stabbed in the back for a change. Don't you agree?*

Neither Becky nor Ralph answered. For her part, Becky was too busy grasping the latest in a long line of shocks. Maybe she wasn't too full up on surprises after all.

She cast one last glance over her shoulder in the direction of the far-off rumble before she followed Amos's strange procession of unbreds and sleeping neurocasters.

New Ashburn

Lieutenant William Chitman and his small scout team had ridden hard to make it to New Ashburn and warn Colonel Armstrong of the deception the drifter collaborator had played against them. Their horses were nearly spent, and the small cart carrying his proxy wobbled and rattled on its single axle in an effort to shake apart. When they crested the last hill and descended into the winding river valley that marked the last stretch to New Ashburn, he breathed a sigh of relief. Chitman would get answers soon.

The settlement came into view around a bend in the river, then the westernmost gates as they entered the clear zone. The dark form of a sentry sat atop the parapet, watching his squad approach.

He raised his arm to hail the sentry as they neared earshot, but he stopped before his throat could open. Alarm sparked in his mind. He squinted out towards the gate. Was that sentry in uniform?

The light machine gun at the parapet flickered at them, and Chitman didn't have time to pull up on the reins before the clarion crackle of gunfire cut through his squad. His focus drew to a knife-point, blocking out his squad mates reeling under the fusillade and instead centering on his horse and wheeling it around. His mount nearly bucked him off as a bullet nicked it, and by the time he'd seized the packhorse hauling his proxy by the bridle, the three men he had left in his squad were already ahead of him in their mad retreat for the safety of the treeline.

As he got the packhorse turned around, the buzz of a round passed his ear. He abandoned his proxy with a curse and kicked his mount ahead in a full-tilt gallop back up the road where he'd come. He took little notice of the two bodies on the road, certainly not enough to tell whether they were alive or dead.

He was right at the edge of the gate's sightline when his horse stumbled. He threw himself from his mount before the horse's fall could pin him underneath. He dropped into a rolling fall that bruised his ribs before scrambling the last few feet and taking cover behind a thick oak tree. He looked back to scan the killing field. One of his team limped toward him, only to take a bullet through the side and collapse well short of safety.

Chitman retreated further into the woods, tripping over deadfall and the stony talus washed into the valley by eons of rainfall. It wasn't until he had broken contact by a quarter mile and the gunfire had long since ceased that he dared approach the road or inspect himself for wounds. Something had torn a ragged hole through the shoulder of his uniform, but he didn't appear to be bleeding. He checked his gun, lay down, and abandoned his body for the faint brainshine of his proxy still breathing in the killzone.

He opened his proxy's eyes to find it laying splayed out on the ground next to the overturned cart. He risked a glance up at the gate where the sentry still stood behind the machine gun, watching but not firing. It was too far to tell whether the guard wore an American uniform, but he didn't need to see to know Armstrong no longer controlled New Ashburn.

One of his men lay nearby, his moans masked by the fallen horses' agonized whinnies. Without rising, Chitman turned his proxy's head and gauged the distance to the safety of the woods. About two hundred feet, not too far at a dead sprint. A fallen travel pack lay discarded along the way, which he'd need if he got away from this current debacle.

With the precision and rapidity of a machine, the proxy jumped up and dashed for cover, scooping up one shoulder strap of the travel pack as it ran. A dozen bounding strides later, the machine gun opened up again, and the proxy altered its trajectory to a diagonal. It found the same tree its root had used for cover as the sound of a loud ricochet zipped deep through the forest.

The proxy moved to catch up to its root while Chitman's mind whirled inside the braincase. Maybe the Sylvanians had sent some expeditionary force to storm the settlement. Whatever it was, he was sure that drifter was behind this, somehow. Now it was up to him to get back to Royce and warn him that New Ashburn was no longer a safe haven.

Bill Puckett paced behind the newly assembled breastworks erected at the base of the hill. Every now and then, he checked the citadel for some sign of movement. "It oughtn't take this long," he said.

Melissa Daly leaned up against the wall as he paced. "For what? To hear what those shots were about, or hear back from Armstrong?"

"Both, but since we ain't heard any more shootin' from the western gate, I'm guessing that's handled. What I don't get is Armstrong. My terms were simple and generous. Armstrong would be a fool not to jump at my offer."

The Ashburnite chemist, Cora Compton, who had taken Mr. Salazar's place as speaker for New Ashburn's interests, only frowned at the ground. Melissa Daly, however, had no problem airing her thoughts. "Armstrong doesn't trust us."

"Why the heck not? I ain't the one been double-dealing."

"Armstrong's problem is she thinks, deep down, everyone's like her," Daly said, her arms folded. "And your problem is, deep down, you think everyone's like you."

Bill turned towards Melissa. "What's that supposed to mean?"

Melissa regarded Bill with a mixture of exasperation and admiration. "You're the kind of feller who'll kick and scream and finally do what's decent and honorable. Armstrong ain't got a decent bone in her body."

Bill grunted. "It's that Holland girl they got locked up there. Her pa warned me she'd make me soft."

He wasn't looking when Melissa cracked a small smile at him as he paced, but he did hold up when her voice rose behind him. "Here comes the messenger," she said.

The messenger was Ricky Brody, and he returned to them just as he'd left them: naked. Bill instinctively recoiled at Ricky's blank-faced shamelessness as the kid hailed them from the last stretch of open no-man's land between the gate at the base of the hill and the citadel.

"No deal," Ricky said, deadpan.

Bill looked in dismay at his compatriots. Mrs. Compton had returned her gaze to the ground in embarrassment, but Melissa stared back at Ricky, her eyebrows arched like the back of a cornered cat. "Something's not right with him," she said.

Bill shook his head at Ricky with disgust and disappointment. "You were such a promising kid." Bill shook his head, staring at Ricky's implacable young face. "I know I mighta been a tough bird sometimes, but I ain't treated you any worse than the others. You remember them, right? Ella? Omar? Melissa?"

"You should worry more about yourself. If you run now, you might give yourself a few days' head-start."

Bill crossed his arms. "What do you mean?"

"I mean Colonel Armstrong has a zero-tolerance policy for traitors and insurgents. When this rabble is disarmed, she'll be the judge of who qualifies as an insurgent. And right now, she's not feeling magnanimous."

"What's she going to do? We've surrounded this whole hill. We've got half her men under lock and key."

Ricky turned, waving off Bill's protests with a dismissive flick of the wrist over his shoulder. "We're done here. The only negotiations available now involve you on your knees, begging Armstrong for your life."

"You've lost!" Bill shouted at Ricky's retreating backside. "The only reason any of you Americans are still alive is because I don't want to get a bunch of folks kill't!"

Ricky slowed enough to turn and taunt Bill. "And that's why you'll never win."

Bill's jaw hung agape, his head wagging from side to side in disbelief as Ricky returned to his American masters. "I don't get it," he said. "They can't have more than a couple dozen soldiers left in there. Not enough to take us in a fight."

"We cut off the pumps supplying the citadel with water," Cora said. "And even if it rains every day for a month, they can't have enough food to last them more than a couple weeks."

A new voice came up from behind them—Omar Walking. "The sentry at the gate spotted an American squad coming in from out west. Just walked straight up the road. The machine gun got most of 'em, but likely a couple got away."

Bill ran a hand through his thinning hair. "I can't tell if that muddies the water or clears it."

"You think Armstrong's got something up her sleeve?" Omar asked.

Bill shook his head. "If it was just one squad walking out in the open at a chattergun, that ain't what I'd call an ace. She's bluffing. We'll let her sweat in there another day, and then she'll want to bargain."

"I don't reckon she needs to bluff anymore."

"What are you gettin' at?"

"If you got an advantage over your enemy, you don't give 'em a chance to sneak in a knife jab." Omar jerked a thumb over to a couple of the Sylvanian workers up on the wall, watching over the citadel with their newly acquired weapons. "If the Americans got some free scouts running out for reinforcements, we can't afford to wait around for Armstrong to make up her mind. You got the numbers and the weapons to charge up that hill now."

"You outta your head, Omar? The Americans still have the guns and bullets to kill half of them before they get to the top."

"What about Ella? She's still cooped up in there with them. Didn't we do this whole thing to get her out in the first place?"

"Them's ain't my tools." Bill pointed at his Sylvanian militia. "Them's my people, and I told you, I'm done having my people do my dirty work for me."

"Then I reckon you've got to choose which of your people's more dear to you. If it were up to me—"

"It *ain't* up to you." Bill shook a warning finger at Omar. "You think you were any different than these half-starved slaves when you came crawling into my shop last year? But I still took you in, didn't I? And stood up for you when the clan turned against you, too."

Omar didn't turn to meet Bill's stare, nor did he answer except with a long, slow sigh.

"Fine," Cora Compton said. "We're not going to try an attack just yet. But we need to catch what's left of that American patrol."

Omar turned on his heel and walked back toward the apprentice quarters without a word. "Where you going?" Bill hollered.

"Going to do what I do best," Omar answered without looking back. "I'm gonna go after those American scouts. I'll see if I can be back by morning."

The porcelain chip, not much bigger than a piece of hardtack, caught the last light of the sunset on the horizon. Omar could see quite a distance in every direction from halfway up the cell tower, from the trees and broken antennas of New Ashburn's citadel, all the way to the highway running in between two mountains to the west some ten miles away. The distant hills sparked with shades of red and yellow trees among the shortleaf pines still holding their green.

It was a useless instinct with so much sweeping territory around him, but he nevertheless scanned the woods and brush and trees all around him for any sudden movement or out-of-the-ordinary shape or gleam. It wasn't only the fear of falling that kept folks from climbing these old perches.

His first warning was the complete cessation of the autumn wildlife—no bugs, no birds. When new movement stirred in the woods below, he returned the white chip to his pocket. With both hands free, he unslung the American assault rifle he sported now and steadied it on one of the tower's metal crossbraces.

A lone pigman emerged from the woods and looked directly up at him. Unbred and human stared at each other across the darkening space between them. "Clint. I want to talk to Clint," Omar said.

The pigman went back the way it came, and Omar waited as the orange disk of the setting sun became a waning glow under the curve of the hills.

Then a bald human came forth. "Hello, Omar," the man called.

"I might need a hand."

"With what?"

"We've—the workers revolted at New Ashburn. They got the Americans pinned up in their citadel, but it's turning into a siege neither side can get an edge on. And it looks like Americans outside of town found out about our little hell-raising. I reckon Armstrong's expecting help."

"She is. The Americans have gone back to their original plan: consolidate their forces and any free neurocasters back at New Ashburn. Thanks to your little misdirection, they've spread their forces out over fifty miles of roads, rivers, and hills. But they've emptied the Tucker town, and it will only be a day or two at most before the convoys they sent to clear out the Tuckers return. The thing I don't understand is why you care."

"I've got unfinished business, and I can't finish it with American reinforcements riding in from everywhere. Can you—deal with them?"

"Sure." The bald man smiled, his lips peeling back from his teeth. "Anything for a fellow Greenbrier."

Amos waited, watching the moonlight scatter on a bubbling brook some fifty feet below. He felt its brainshine before he heard or saw it: the glow of a foreign unbred carrying tidings for him. When it finally came, Amos' own unbreds parted for it like court attendants parting for the emissary of a distant land's king.

Instead of passing any sealed scroll, however, the shadower simply kneeled and opened up its mind to Amos.

Amos spoke first. "Jarvis knew there would be trained American neurocasters coming out here from D.C. to harvest the Tuckers. And since I've eliminated Jarvis, I've put you in a place to take the Americans more easily. What you do with them is of no concern to me. But the Tuckers are under my protection."

*You cannot dictate terms to me. For the continued safety of your clan, I require sacrifice. Do not interfere with the Tucker neurocasters captive to the Americans. They belong to me.*

"Or else what?"

*A god is omnipresent. I can harrow the defenseless clansmen you left behind just as easily as I can harvest the minds of the neurocasters many miles from here. Would you trade four hundred souls for one hundred? If you try to stop me, all of them will be mine, both those you pursue and the ones you abandoned.*

Its message delivered, the shadower left Amos alone with his rage.

The night teemed with the far-off eyeshine of pigmen watching Becky and Ralph. "It looks like Amos has got these unbreds standing watch for us," Becky said. "No need to stay up. We should get some rest while we can. I don't suppose we're too far ahead of the Americans."

Ralph sat on the rusty remains of a metal fence stretched between the hulking vegetation of a tree belt. He stared down at the brown, overgrown pasture below. "Go ahead," he said without breaking off his absent gaze. "I ain't tired yet."

Becky shrugged and left him to his pondering.

When she was gone, Ralph unclutched his fist, and the crumpled letter from his father fell to the withered grass at his feet.

Everything felt heavy—the paper he'd avoided reading, the musket he'd laid against the fence, the worn-out rags on his back. He'd lied, of course. He was tired. However many days or weeks he'd languished in the Griersons' mine hadn't rested him any. A chill wind worked its way up under Ralph's collar, but he didn't bother to pull his jacket closer against the harbinger of coming winter. Amos had said he had a use for Ralph, but all Ralph had done was walk limply behind Amos's train of tamed unbreds until they'd stopped early to camp. Putting one foot in front of the other was all he could do, and all he'd likely ever be able to do.

He felt useless.

He closed his eyes and saw the look on a man's face as he stabbed him. His pulse quickened. He saw Jarvis's hungry eyes, then Johnny's unreadable face disappearing behind the padlocked door after bringing the daily rations of a lowly prisoner. His ears rang, but through it all, he still heard his father and felt his scorn. It was barely a passable showing—not good enough for the son of a watchman. Elvin McDaniel would have killed ten men without pause—the great Paul McDaniel would have killed twenty men. Paul McDaniel would have overpowered a man like Jarvis, licked the Americans, and cowed the Griersons. There was no room for pity or fear. *Worthless little shit*—

"Shut up, you old warmonger. I tried," Ralph said to the empty air.

It did nothing to quiet the ringing in his ears. He was fighting with a ghost. The harsh voice in his head was his own, even if it had his father's timbre.

The same lot that had fallen to his father would fall to him: the mantle of failure and humiliation waiting behind every tree, the danger of being exposed as a coward. Ralph had to have gotten it from somewhere. It was odd that he'd never consciously thought it until now, but he knew it to be true. He'd seen the furtive glances, the shifting uncertainty, the doglike retreating and raised hackles whenever the clansmen weren't looking. Ralph had never called his father out for it, because he was afraid, too. He and the cowhide had met far too many times for him to cross his father. But he'd gotten it from somewhere.

Ralph stared between his knees at the unopened letter on the ground. Sam had said there wasn't anything useful in it. No need to read it. The last sight he'd had of his pa had been through tear-blurred eyes. He had punched his own father, then run away with his tail between his legs rather than face up to it.

His pa would have the last word, one way or another. The letter was one last insult from beyond the grave. *Traitor, coward, troublemaker, disrespectful, lazy, stupid—maybe all the above.*

*And not even man enough to face a dead man's letter?*

He sighed and picked it up. Best to get it over with, have it all out, and move on with life.

*Dear Ralph,*

*I'm sorry. I want you to do whatever you can with your life. Become whatever kind of a man you want to. Only promise you won't become a man like me.*

*I'm awful proud of you, son. More than I could ever say.*

*Pa*

As the letter trembled in Ralph's hand, a nearly forgotten memory bubbled up. Over the drone of his father's incessant, sharp rebukes, an old, barely remembered murmur rose to the surface—the voice of a younger watchman dandling a small boy on his lap, a sing-song thrum bouncing in time to the father's knee. *Who's Papa's boy? You are. Who's Papa's boy? You are.*

Ralph held his face in his hands as his shoulders shook.

# Chapter 10: In Which Ralph McDaniel Settles a Score

The gunfire in the dell gave way to screams of terror and rage, and then those screams gave way to screams of agony—the gut-wrenching, quavering wails of someone reduced to a tiny world of mortal pain. Soon after, even those screams went silent.

Yet when Ralph looked over to Amos Taylor, he was still concentrating, still giving orders and receiving feedback from his inhuman servants. "Huh," Amos said finally. "That's interesting."

"What's interesting?" Becky asked.

"Someone's still alive down there. Let's check it out." Amos picked up his rifle and stutter-stepped down the leaf-littered slope.

Becky and Ralph passed a look between them—something that had become common practice lately—and followed.

The site of the massacre lay only a couple hundred paces downhill, around the bend of a great rocky outcropping. Fresh scarlet blood smeared the yellow-and-gold leaves on the forest floor amid entrails and skin and torn clothing hanging from the underbrush like some sick mockery of a tanner's shop. Enough remained undefiled of the scattered bodies for Ralph to count thirteen dead, and judging by what remained of their uniforms, all of them were Federation soldiers.

A score of dead or dying pigmen lay jumbled about the vegetation and on the rocks under the cliffside to add to the carnage, but at least two-score more unbreds continued undeterred about their work, hauling the bodies off to feed the rest of Amos's army and throwing salvageable booty like ration packs, guns, and ammo into separate piles. A shadower watched them like an overseer, directing them not with gestures, but with delicate ripples of almost warm, almost visible glow emanating from its body, a glow Ralph was growing ever more aware of. Becky had a similar glow. Amos' was much stronger, so much so as to be something different altogether.

Leaning back against the stone cliff underneath the rocky outcropping, Johnny Grierson half-stood with a still-smoking gun at his side and a bloody spear grasped with both hands to keep the unbreds away—as if such a paltry weapon could do anything when so outnumbered. He seemed to favor one leg. A bloody hole oozed a steady stream of gore a few inches above his knee.

The pigmen keeping Johnny hemmed in scattered as Amos approached. Becky and Ralph followed behind. "So, that's why the Americans peeled a squad off the caravan. They caught your scent," Amos said, amused. "I got more use out of you than I expected. How many of your folks survived Carlson's attack?"

Johnny glared with his one good eye at Amos. "I did like you wanted. You said you'd send help."

"You know how it is, Grierson. Got too busy. Looks like I won't have to worry about your little settlement anymore, though, and I'm guessing you took some of the Americans with you. If it makes you feel any better, the rest of them will end up like this when I'm done." Amos swept a hand over the blood-spattered rocks and foliage.

"You used me for kindling."

"Sucks, doesn't it?" Amos slapped his knees, kneeling down close to Johnny. "Tell you what, Grierson: You've done your fair share to fight the Americans. I'll give you a running head start." He chambered a round in his rifle. "I'll give you to the count of ten."

"You're shittin' me."

Amos's forced smile faded. "One."

"Goddamn you."

"Two."

Johnny Grierson struggled to stand. Using the spear as a support, he limped up the hill, cursing with each step.

"Three."

"Amos, no." Ralph reached out and laid a hand on the gun. "I want to do it. Let me finish him."

Amos locked eyes with Ralph, then nodded and passed off the rifle.

Ralph ran up behind Johnny and kicked him in the back of his wounded leg. Johnny fell with a cry, rolling down the far side of the hill, where he came to rest crookedly against an old hickory tree. "That was for selling us out!" he shouted, spittle flying from his lips. He turned to see Becky and Amos watching him from below, and his cheeks flushed in spite of himself. "Go on." He waved the two of them away. "I'll catch up. I—I need to deal with this myself."

Amos shrugged and went on his way, his unbreds coming with him. Becky followed, but not immediately. She lowered her head, grim-faced, before turning her back on Ralph, leaving unsaid whatever she was going to say.

When Ralph turned back to look at Johnny Grierson, he was still lying askew between the hill slope and the old tree, his spear out of reach. "Listen, Ralph, I never—"

"*Shut up!*" Ralph screamed, his voice cracking with the strain.

He raised the rifle and pulled the trigger. The shot went wide—stupidly wide, way off downhill, well clear of his point-blank target still lying against the hickory tree.

Ralph dropped the gun. He met Johnny's good eye before approaching slowly.

"You gotta bind that leg up 'fore you bleed to death," he muttered. He grabbed a fistful of fabric at Johnny's shirtsleeve and ripped the stitches free. He pulled out his knife and opened a small tear at one end of the sleeve before pulling it into two long strips. Then he did the same with Johnny's other sleeve.

"Why—"

"You think Amos was going to let you live just 'cause I asked him to? Had to give him a show." Ralph examined the entrance and exit wounds on Johnny's leg.

"But why'd you—"

"I think you're a low-down, ornery cuss. But you never stopped being a clansman, not even when you locked me inside your mine. I know the difference between an enemy and someone just looking to get out of the crossfire. It don't mean I like you any, but I'm not about to shoot a wounded man while he's down. My pa didn't raise me that a-way."

Ralph balled up two strips of cloth, ramming one into the entrance wound and the other into the exit wound. Johnny merely grunted against the pain. Ralph wrapped a strip around the leg to keep the cloth in place and bound it good and tight, just like his father had taught him. "There. We'll see if that stops the bleeding." He sighed and rested back on his haunches. "So, what happened at your settlement?"

"What do you think? Weren't enough folks left to defend the wall. The Americans killed my rear guards and torched the whole place. Stove in the mine. We lost a quarter of our people. Whoever was left broke for the town—see if they can scrape a living as a farmhand, or else sign up with the next nomad clan."

"Except you."

"No going back for me, and I ain't about to sell myself to two-timing nomads. I figgered I'd have one last go at the Americans."

Ralph scratched the back of his neck. "I gotta go. Here's my canteen. Keep yourself watered. If you nab some of the Americans' food packs yonder, you'd have enough supplies to keep you fed for a few days. You'd better clean that wound when you get the chance, and fresh-boiled—"

"I know." Johnny sounded annoyed.

"If you want to eat your gun, that's up to you. But if you want to survive, and maybe even start over somewhere new, well, I reckon that's your choice, too. My hands are clean of it either way."

Becky and Ralph looked down on Amos as he exchanged some sort of information with a glassy-skulled shadower. Ralph thought he saw the shadower present a white pebble or small trinket to Amos before it left, but he had no idea what the purpose behind it could be.

Becky Brody stared intently at Ralph. *I ain't used to these tamed unbreds running around us. I keep jumping at every rustle in the bush, but these pigmen and shadowers and screevlers keep doing Amos's little two-fingered howdy at me, so I guess they're still our unbreds.*

"You know, Amos can hear your brainshine when you do that," Ralph whispered.

*I know. Just figured I could use the practice, is all.*

Amos, having finished his business with the shadower, came back up the hill to their temporary shelter, where his sundry thralls lay sleeping in a neat line right across the fire pit from Ralph and Becky. "The Americans are playing it cagey since that last platoon never came back. They're nervous, and hauling so many Tucker neurocasters along isn't making it easier. Captain Carlson is holding them together. We take him down, the rest could be easy pickings."

"I don't suppose you could just bum-rush the guards with a couple bullhuskers or something," Becky mused.

"With their numbers and guns, I'm not sure I've got enough unbreds under my control to pull it off. Certainly not to still have enough left over to take New Ashburn. Anyway, that's not—"

"Wait, New Ashburn?"

"You want to get Sophie's daddy back, don't you? And Ella?"

"Yeah, but... I didn't think—"

"I'm getting all of our people out. Whatever it takes."

"And if we're too late?" Becky asked.

"Then we'll still have to deal with that American colonel before she sends out for even more reinforcements. These Federation assholes are persistent, and if all we do is whip them once, they'll come back angrier." Amos picked up his canteen and took a swig. "It'll take a lot more dead bodies before they go from angry to scared. And I mean to go well beyond scared. But we can't be planning for that part before we're done with this first part. I can't free the Tuckers while the American soldiers are holding their formation, and I can't break up their formation with unbreds, because they've got a neurocaster trained to keep off unbreds. If I push the unbreds toward the caravan, the American neurocaster will push them back. Which means we need to take care of the neurocaster first."

"You got a plan for that?"

Amos pointed to one of his sleeping thralls: Jarvis. "The Americans will still think he's one of theirs."

"Are you sure he's one of ours?" Becky didn't sound sure.

Amos smiled. "He's one of *mine.* I'm going to lay down and take a rest. Jarvis here will go to get things ready tonight. In a few minutes, some more unbreds will come and haul me and all these"—again, he gestured to the sleeping people—"up to the top of this mountain. In the morning, I'll have to leave. You guard the bodies until I get back. Don't go running off for any reason *until* I get back; I wouldn't want you two to get hurt, yeah?"

"What about the folks back home?" Becky asked. "The Americans cooked the meetinghouse, burned the gate and half our powder, and rode off with anything that weren't tied down."

"They're not the ones in greatest danger. We've got to get to the convoy first."

"I know, I know."

Amos lay down and was instantly unconscious. The next instant, Jarvis sat up and retrieved Amos's automatic rifle. He smoothed out the wrinkles in his uniform and shook loose the leaves clinging to his back. "Remember," he said, "wherever these bodies go, you go, and nowhere else." He gave the two Tuckers a casual two-fingered salute and took off into the woods with just his gun and a small travel pack.

Becky and Ralph sat until the rustling of Jarvis's boots in the forest undergrowth had receded to total silence. The dry rattle of dead leaves covered over the quiet he left in his wake.

"What. The heck. Is going on." Ralph said.

Becky shook her head. "I don't know. But I'm glad he's on our side."

"Who? Who's on our side? The American?"

"Amos."

"And what about the American? What about those women lying there? What about Mr. Chambers?" Ralph stabbed a finger at Sam's still body.

"Sure, they're helping us, too."

"*How* are they helping us, Becky?"

Becky stammered. "I—I don't know. They're all neurocasters. They must be helping Amos control the unbreds."

"And how come none of us ever knew a doggone thing about this neurocasting stuff until the Americans showed up?"

"I don't—what are you getting at?"

"When Amos told us to stay put, was that a warning or a threat?"

"He's on our side, Ralph."

"Sure, he's on *your* side, maybe. Who's to say what he's gonna do to me once I ain't useful to him? Is he gonna do to me like he done to Johnny?"

"Johnny betrayed us. You didn't."

Ralph's musket, now with an ungainly silencer screwed onto the barrel, was too long to have slung over his shoulder without catching on nearby branches. He leaned it against a tree and started pacing. "He hasn't once told us what all the sleeping folks here are for, and ain't a one of 'em right in the head. I don't know what happened to Mr. Chambers."

"They're helping us. Maybe they have to—dream, or something. To help control the unbreds."

"Have you *talked* to Mr. Chambers? I'm tellin' you, he ain't himself even when he's awake. He's—not right."

"Okay, fine. He seemed a little weird when he pulled me from the Brody farm. Maybe the Americans knocked a screw loose. It don't mean Amos is mixed up with it."

"Oh my *word*." Ralph groaned as if he were dealing with the town imbecile. "He's *totally* mixed up with it. You can't see it because you're smitten with the feller."

"Beg pardon?" Becky rose to her feet now, her face glowing with either embarrassment or anger—probably both. "What are you, twelve? Have your balls even dropped yet?"

"I'm *sixteen*."

"You've still enough freckles to spackle a pheasant. Unless that's mud on you."

"I'm old enough to know there ain't a girl in the clan who ain't swooned over Amos at least once."

Becky raised an exaggerated hand to her ear. "Is that jealousy I hear?"

"What you hear is somebody who's still thinkin' with his head."

"Well, then, think about this, as long as you're thinkin': These Americans could kill every Tucker in the clan, and they pert' near did. How do you plan on rescuing the prisoners—my pa amongst 'em—without Amos's help?"

Ralph said nothing.

"Huh. 'Cause *Amos* seems like he can do it all without putting any extra Tuckers in danger. You got a plan for what to do when the Americans come back, looking for revenge? 'Cause *Amos* thought enough ahead to have a plan for that, too. If you don't have a better idea, leave it for the real men to take care of."

"Fine. But there's something ugly going on. When it's all done and we're counting up the ledgers, don't say you didn't know if the costs come up higher than you were wanting."

# Chapter 11: Showdown at the Abandoned Barn

I t was a cold, misty morning when Jarvis hailed the night watch and nearly caught a bullet for his trouble. Having applauded the watch for its restraint, he requested an audience with Captain Carlson before the convoy got on its way.

The guard led him past the host of Tucker neurocasters huddled on the ground in groups for warmth. Few were still sleeping, and all of them looked haggard. Jarvis kicked the foot of one of their men. "Hey, Tucker," he said to the man. "What's your name?"

The man squinted up at Jarvis before rising stiffly to one elbow. He favored his side with a wince. "Phil Holland. Sir."

"Say, Phil, don't you Tuckers know when to give up?"

The servility in his face gave way to confusion. "Huh?"

"I said, 'Don't you know when to give up?' Your clan's been chasing the convoy ever since you left town."

The Tucker had the good sense to look down and shrug in answer to the morsel of hope tossed to him like a stale breadcrumb. Jarvis shrugged in his turn and continued to where the proper camp was set up.

William Chitman's proxy chewed a hunk of dry bread as he examined a topographic map spread out over a wide, flat rock. Chitman's body lay stretched out on a bedroll not far beyond. Jarvis exchanged glances with Chitman's proxy before coming to a halt outside one of the few canvas tents.

Royce emerged from the nearby tent, wearing breeches and an undershirt. At the sight of Jarvis, he stopped and examined the American neurocaster closely. "Where have you been?" he said after a silence most people would have found uncomfortable.

"You left without me. I didn't have anyone to help me carry my proxies."

"So you brought them with you?"

"I've got them stashed nearby. I'll explain later. What's he doing here?" Jarvis pointed at Chitman's comatose body.

"We've lost control of New Ashburn," Chitman's proxy said. "Whoever's occupying it now fired on my men. I was the only one who got out."

"With your proxy, I see."

"You got yours out as well, apparently."

Jarvis and the proxy stared at each other for a moment before Jarvis broke the silence. "We've got some urgent things to deal with."

"No shit," Captain Carlson said. "How'd you avoid the Tucker war party that's been picking off my guys the last couple days?"

Jarvis shook his head. "I've been using unbreds as a screen. And they're not Tuckers."

"Marauders?"

"It's all unbreds. The Pied Piper's onto you."

"It can't be." William Chitman's proxy broke in. "He pushed southeast weeks ago. Every indicator supports my assessment."

"And you've been tied to the Tucker neurocasters for the past week," Jarvis rejoined, pointing to the mass of huddled wretches camped out in the open air. "That's plenty of time for the Pied Piper to make a move on the convoy. You think the Tuckers could have staged an uprising like that on their own?"

"I assumed you fucked up," Royce said, staring at Jarvis.

"On the contrary." Jarvis folded his arms. "I saved all your asses."

"How many of your men made it out, besides you? Stein? Gustavson?"

"I thought you didn't care about casualties."

"I do if I don't get anything out of it."

"You get intel out of it. The Pied Piper's attack was too well-timed to have been an accident. He waited until our forces were split before he attacked."

Royce stepped toward Jarvis. "He had eyes in town?"

"Or he's the one who pulled you out of town in the first place."

"What do you mean?"

"Who asked for reinforcements to help deal with the Grierson settlement off the highway? Who said it isn't safe to go to New Ashburn?"

Royce shot a glance at Chitman's proxy.

"Captain, don't tell me you believe him!" the proxy cried.

"No, I don't." Royce turned back towards Jarvis. "To pull that off, the Pied Piper would have to assimilate Chitman's neuronet. Neurocaster networks don't get assimilated."

Jarvis shrugged. "Then it could be one of the Tucker neurocasters you have in the convoy. The good news is, the Pied Piper showed his hand. He's north of the highway, personally directing the unbreds from his root. May I?" He moved over to the topo map, found their camp, and drew a line with his finger northwest over the snarl of contour lines that marked the surrounding territory. "He's somewhere boxed into this ravine, a little more than two miles out. If you and Chitman could come with a few guys..."

"Yeah, maybe," Royce said, still thinking. He pointed at the map and pushed his own finger south of the ravine to a penciled-in landmark. "There's an old abandoned farm maybe three clicks from here. I'll meet you there and use it as a staging area. Sound good?"

Jarvis nodded. Royce dismissed the neurocaster, who left the camp the way he'd come.

Forty-five minutes later, Royce led a squad of six soldiers across the grass-overgrown remnants of an old paved road snaking along a stream at the bottom of a vale. The trees broke on the gentle uphill slope to reveal a wrecked homestead beyond. A dilapidated but mostly intact red barn stood out against the dry, reedy grass and young trees around it, and a single-story house not far beyond. Jarvis's outline stood in the open barn doorway, hailing them. They'd made the short trek without any hostile contact, but Royce only tightened the grip on his rifle.

The forest was quiet, but not peaceful—like it was waiting. A breeze stirred the branches overhead, and colorful leaves drifted to the forest floor like falling snow.

Royce led his men up to the barn, where they fanned out to form a perimeter. "Okay, Jarvis, let's go inside. I want a word."

Jarvis nodded and led Royce inside the barn. A narrow corridor extended into darkness between the feed troughs on the left and the wooden cribs built for horses on the right. The air was old and musty. "Where's Chitman? We'll need both of our networks to take down the Pied Piper."

"He's bringing up the rear." Royce reached inside his camo jacket. "Hey, Jarvis. Hang on a second," he said as the door banged shut behind them.

Jarvis turned to face the captain. Royce grabbed him by the back of the neck with one hand as if bringing him in for a hug, and with the other hand, plunged a combat knife into his gut with three sawing stabs. Royce's calm never wavered as he pulled the knife free and shoved Jarvis away.

Jarvis stumbled back, his hands clutching his perforated belly, his face contorted in surprise. Then, in the dim light of the barn, his grimace stretched into his unnatural smile. "How'd you know?" Jarvis asked, his voice weak but free of pain.

"You rogue neurocasters all think you're so good at pretending. It's not hard to tell when something's off. You called the geemoes 'unbreds,' which was weird. But then you tried to convince me Chitman had been assimilated. Come on. *Chitman?*" Royce said as if disappointed. "Never mind Jarvis was even more convinced than I was that networks never get assimilated. Even assuming Jarvis changed his mind, there's a hand-picked team watching Chitman's every move. If it's possible for a network to be assimilated, which I'm guessing now it is, it would be Mr. 'Fly-with-his-own-ass-cheeks' Jarvis, not Chitman. Not a professional. And you tried to get me to walk into that ravine, which, frankly, couldn't have been a more obvious trap."

"I guess Chitman's not meeting us there."

"No. I sent him with his squad to hunt down your root. Which brings me to my question," Royce said, returning his knife to its sheath with a satisfied grunt. "Whose neuronet am I talking to now? The Pied Piper, I presume?"

Jarvis laughed, his head lolling languidly back against the wooden timbers at the opposite end of the corridor. At almost the same instant, a scream and a gunshot coincided outside.

Royce whirled from Jarvis to the door behind him. One of his soldiers appeared in the door, already breathless. "Geemoes! They got Chantelle!"

Royce assessed the situation and determined Chantelle was not, in fact, dead yet. He lay writhing in the grass, a pigman in its own death throes next to him, and several more closing fast. "Inside. Quick," Royce ordered, shouldering his rifle and popping off the two foremost pigmen with carefully placed shots. Rather than scattering, the remaining pigmen sprinted through the brush to catch the retreating soldiers.

"It's a small wave! Post up and 'bort 'em!" Royce shouted. A succession of eye-watering rifle blasts felled the charging pigmen. The last geemo collapsed only a few paces from the soldiers outside the barn door.

Royce waved his remaining men inside the barn and ordered them to find positions on various windows. He turned back to Jarvis, who by now had sagged to the floor.

"If you're wielding geemoes, your root must be closer than I thought," Royce said. "I was planning to talk to your proxy, but I guess I'll talk to you in person."

"You idiots still don't know who you're dealing with."

As Captain Carlson approached, Jarvis stared back at him with unseeing eyes. Dead. Who, then, had just spoken with Jarvis' voice?

"What happened to Jarvis?" one of his men asked in the silence that followed.

"Sssshh!" Carlson chopped a hand through the murky air. "The Pied Piper is close," he whispered, gesturing to emphasize his orders. "Harden up. I want a sightline on the house, then the woods. Somebody clear these stalls." Royce hammered a fist against the boards paneling the barn cribs.

"Wait—what was that?" a soldier gasped in the dark.

Everyone froze, muscles tensed in the still air. Nothing moved outside. The minute disturbance in the air came from inside, with them.

The weight of some living body shifted on the creaking oak floor-boards above their heads. Three rifles jumped up and turned the hay loft floor into a strainer. A screevler screeched in pain over the din of the guns, skittering over the floorboards above their heads with frantic, jumbled claws.

The head-splitting gunfire ceased at a raised fist from Royce. A splintered plank tumbled down amid the shower of dust and the smell of freshly disturbed dry rot. They waited for any other sign of movement and sensed none.

"You two." Royce pointed at the two nearest soldiers, then at the crude boards forming rungs on the wall behind Jarvis's corpse. "Into the loft. Now."

The two soldiers crept down the narrow corridor between the stalls and feed troughs while the others crouched low, their rifles still pointed upwards—the wrong direction, as it turned out.

*Thunk!* The wooden door of the crib next to the point man exploded open behind him, knocking the soldier off-balance. A young human stepped out and swung upwards with a short sword in a single fluid motion.

The second soldier reeled to the side from the uppercut of the young man's blade, a trail of blood following the arc of the sword upward through the air like paint flicked from a brush. The downstroke caught the point man in the neck before he could recover, before Royce could even bring his own rifle to bear.

A blocky shape in the young man's other hand spewed a wild shower of fire.

Royce rolled out of the narrow hallway into the adjacent cattle stall to his left, snapping up his M4 as his last two men crumpled in the hall.

It was a kid armed with a submachine gun. He might have wasted the full mag.

Royce darted forward again, trying to sneak a shot from cover. He peeked into the passageway and jerked back as a gun spat bullets at him, one of them nicking his ear. The offending gun—an assault rifle this time—continued its hammering rhythm, punching holes in the walls of the stall, kicking up dust inside, and keeping Royce's head down as he scrambled for the back corner.

Royce righted himself and unloaded every round left in his magazine through the wall, fanning back and forth with suppressing hip-fire. The bolt finally clicked on an empty chamber. Silence gradually resolved into a guttural moan as his ears recovered from the thunderous point-blank exchange. Was it the kid moaning out in the hallway, or one of his own men?

"I remember you," the kid said somewhere farther out in the barn. "You're the guy who smashed my hand. 'The strong do what they can. The weak do what they must.' Something like that."

"And I remember you, kid," Royce said, ejecting his spent magazine and pulling out a fresh one. "You're that little punk who tried to steal Federation property. Had to make an example of your reverend for that. You understand how it goes. Nothing personal." He inserted the magazine, chambered a round, and shifted positions. The hay loft above him had a few floorboards missing. If he was careful about it, he might just climb up without being seen...

"I understand. I've got to make an example of you, too. Nothing personal," the kid answered from between the intervening planks in the worn-out walls. Royce searched for some flicker of movement between the gaps in the boards, but no target presented itself. He climbed up onto the barn's stone foundation footing to get within arm's reach of the hole in the ceiling. "So, did you get the kid first, or Jarvis?"

"You still think you're talking to the Pied Piper?" the kid's voice called from somewhere across the corridor.

"You expect me to think there are *two* independent neurocaster networks able to assimilate other networks?" Royce scoffed. He slung the rifle over his shoulder and jumped up as silently as he could.

"That would be a scary thing for you to accept, wouldn't it? You're right—it's much easier to assume all of this is the work of the Pied Piper. Or maybe the neurocasters are evolving. Not all breeding gets done in a scientist's lab, you know. You probably think all of us hillbillies are hopeless, inbred animals, but the law of nature demands that, when it all shakes out, the strong will eat the weak. Jarvis sure found that out in a way he didn't expect. You should have heard his screams. And you know the really crazy thing? There's some morsel of Jarvis still kicking around in my neuronet, in some wordless, thoughtless way, still existing. Still screaming." The voice was coming from the other side of the barn, out under the overhang where a tractor would have been parked decades ago. The kid had retreated to one of the barn's exits.

Now in the hay loft, Royce crept along the attic floor, avoiding weak spots, taking note of the smeared bloodstain where they'd shot the screevler. An open trapdoor lay a few meters in front of him, leading down into another empty crib. Royce dropped through the trapdoor without a word and scarcely a sound while the kid kept talking.

"I can see why you wanted to kill that rogue neurocaster. So he calls himself the Pied Piper now. Are you afraid he'll run off with all your children? Guy like him could put an end to your whole empire. I wonder if it was guys like him who finished off the world fifty years ago. It would make sense. The people who planned the Pandemic must have known that killing ninety percent of the world would destroy any long-term military power they could hope to muster. But you don't need a factory or international shipping to raise an army of pigmen. You just need a male and a female, maybe a shadower, and some time. But I guess the planners didn't plan on their neurocasters deciding to do their own thing.

"You thought you could do better than the old breedcrafters and figure out how to set neurocasters loose while still keeping them safe. Thing is, you can't plant new crops without burning the old ones. They didn't understand that back then, and it looks like you don't understand that now. But I don't suppose it matters whether you understand. You've helped restore things to their natural order. I'll finish the work our forefathers started."

Beams of light cut down through the barn, illuminating patches in the darkness. Royce stepped over the bodies of his fallen men, noted one of the automatic rifles was absent, and made his slow, careful way to the origin of the kid's voice, weaving through the oak support beams of the old corral lean-to and around the withered remains of a long-forgotten farm implement. Still no sight of the kid, but he homed in on the sound of the kid's voice as surely as a wolf stalking its prey.

Still, the kid kept talking. "We're the new breed of ubermenschen, and your kind are now nothing but grist for our mill. In the next hundreds and thousands of years, *I* will set forth right and wrong, for I will be God."

Close. Royce rounded the corner, bringing his rifle stock up to his cheek, finger tightening on the trigger. A bleeding, six-armed monstrosity lay where the kid should have been, mouth forming English words with the kid's voice. The young man himself was nowhere to be seen.

Shit.

A murderous, stabbing punch in his back carried Royce forward, then everything below his waist went numb. He couldn't recall hearing a gunshot. He careened off the rusting farm implement and collapsed onto his back, watching holes in the barn roof twinkling with daylight until a silhouette blotted them out.

"Well, lookee here," the kid said. "Looks like the hotshot army guy got outsmarted by some goat-humping redneck. I could have popped you in the head easy, but then it's over, and you don't get to think about what's ahead of you and really look into the blackness. I wanted to let you know what I'm going to do after all your men are dead."

The kid grabbed a fistful of Royce's hair and forced him to look into his cold, unsmiling eyes. "I'm going to find where you came from and kill everyone you ever knew. Everyone will know the sound a human makes when they're eaten alive. I'm going to starve your dogs until their ribs show, then lock them up with your children. I'm going to rape your women. I'm going to burn your homes with your old ones inside and spit on their graves. And if anyone's still alive in the end, they'll look on my deeds and worship me for them. Bye, now. Have fun bleeding out."

The kid left, though Royce still found the strength to curse the empty air.

Arnold Brody watched from where he crouched with the other Tucker conscripts—prisoners, hostages, he wasn't sure what they were—while his American captors kept up their perimeter watch with twitchy glances and itchy trigger fingers. The party on the road had caught the sound of gunfire a long ways distant, but the day had gone long in the tooth with no sign of Captain Carlson and his fireteam. The Americans' stark unease gradually crawled under Arnold's own skin, leaving gooseflesh in its wake. The caw of a couple nearby crows in the bloodshot forest canopy heralded their coming doom.

A hiss and a dull thunk sent one of the American soldiers falling backward like a sawn tree. The others darted for cover on either side of the road amid curses and frantic questions. The Tuckers stayed put, frozen as much in fear of the Americans as whatever lay out there.

Another hiss and thunk marked the loss of another guard, this one reaching haplessly with contorted arms to the ragged hole in his back before pitching off the side of the road and down the steep downhill slope beyond.

"The shooter's uphill! Eyes up, eyes up!"

Two more shots—they must have been shots—followed in quick succession, one tearing out a good chunk of a man's face, the other a good chunk of a man's shoulder. Neither shot proved deadly, and no rifle reports carried over the sounds of their screams.

"Did anyone see it? Anyone?"

"Shit, Sarge, I didn't fucking hear it!"

The officer in charge wiped the cold sweat from his forehead. "We've got to get in there and clear them out! Reed, Whitehead, Carter, Case, Mikey, and Dickface! On me!"

"I'm not going in there!" One soldier complained before a faint crack in the woods sparked and sent him reeling backwards with his collarbone caved in at the base of his throat.

"There! Chisolm, take his place and let's go! Move up or get shot!"

The soldiers bolted into the woods, and their forms faded against the backdrop of yellow and red leaves clinging to the hillside slope and scant undergrowth. The remaining soldiers watched with Arnold, giving no care to either the Tucker prisoners or their own writhing wounded.

Then came the horror: a quick pop-pop-pop of automatic gunfire, followed by a great chorus of pigmen squeals, followed by human screams.

When the shrieks finally went quiet, one of the few remaining soldiers looked at his partner. "Maybe they got the shooters, too."

A hiss and snap put the lie to that hope with grim finality. Arnold counted the American guards still whole and hale: seven left. American guns lay scattered here and there, only a few paces away.

"Fuck this shit, man. I'm outta here." Another soldier got up, sprinted across the open roadway, swore again as a bullet zipped out of nowhere and chipped the ancient pavement, and plunged down the hillside opposite, away from the unbreds and shooters and the whole mess. Six left.

One of the six also broke from cover, found himself the nearest Tucker woman, and pulled her up off the ground. Several Tuckers rose up as if to stop him, but pulled back when he waved his gun at them.

The other five Americans got the idea and took their own hostages, one of them being Arnold himself.

"Easy, easy now," Arnold said, raising his hands as the American pulled him forward and kicked him back down onto his knees.

"Shut the *fuck* up," the American said, panting.

The American who'd first pulled the woman out from the prisoners called out to the uphill forest. "Whoever you are out there, I've got a hundred people you probably don't want dead and more than enough ammo to make them dead! You get me? I swear to God, if there's one more shot, I'll blow her fucking brains out!"

The wounded soldiers moaned, swore if they were able, even pled for help, for all the good it did them. The soldier with his lower jaw missing could only gurgle. The Tuckers for the most part kept from audibly weeping in terror. A cold gun barrel stabbed at the base of Arnold's skull, a reminder of what would happen if he made one wrong move. He realized he was holding his breath.

Then the soldier guarding him shifted behind him. "Hey!"

Arnold tilted his head to the left, glancing down the road behind the procession to see a figure striding down the center of the highway, arms outstretched as if it were Sam Chambers greeting a nomad clan.

Wait a second, it *was* Sam Chambers, wearing the same patched and worn topcoat he always wore when the weather turned chilly.

"That's far enough!" Arnold's guard shouted. "Not one step further!"

"Sure, whatever." Sam shrugged.

The woods came alive again with the sounds of pigmen, turning Arnold's attention back to the woods. Scores of the creatures swarmed down the slope. He crushed his hands over his ears as the American guards mag-dumped into the unbred throng.

From the corner of his eye, he saw Sam flash into motion. There was a pistol in his hand, a sudden look of savagery on his face as he brought the gun into a two-hand stance. The pistol bucked in Sam's hands once, twice, three times, spitting brass casings out to the side. A fourth shot, a fifth, and then Sam's shoulder jerked backwards, and he spun around from the force of an autorifle burst. He fell to one knee, listing to the side like one of the countless blown-out trucks they'd passed on their journey, the pistol flying out of his hand.

Arnold called out something he didn't fully understand as he watched the man he'd known since they were both boys get up and stagger forward with baleful hate. The American behind Arnold shot Sam again, then again. He didn't stop. A bullet punched clean through the center of Sam's chest, and still he didn't stop. He unsheathed a matchet hidden under his topcoat.

"Die, you motherf—"

Sam cut him off. He slashed the American soldier's right forearm to the bone. Rather than finish him right there, though, Sam dropped his matchet and leaned in, knocking the assault rifle to the side. For a moment, it seemed to Arnold's addled brain like Sam might kiss the screaming American.

Instead, he tore the American's throat out with his bare teeth.

Sam kept the American's arms pinned to his sides as the dying man sank slowly to his knees before him. It was only after the American collapsed that Sam raised his gore-smeared face and gazed one last time upon his clansmen. He crumpled like an old scarecrow knocked down in the wind.

Trembling, Arnold rose to his feet and found the other American guards already dead or dying: felled by Sam's pistol or dragged off by the sudden unbred attack. Arnold came to himself and seized the American's fallen autorifle to fight off the pigmen, but they were already retreating. And so, while the road, and the ditch, and the woods beyond were all strewn with the bodies of American soldiers and the unlucky unbreds who'd attacked them, the knot of Tucker prisoners remained, abandoned and unharmed.

The Tuckers were alone when three voices called to them from the hill above the stream: Becky Brody, Ralph McDaniel, and Amos

Taylor, all carrying rifles with Phil Holland's newfangled silencers. For Becky and Ralph, their joy was as palpable as Arnold's. He grabbed his daughter in a tight embrace when she burst from the woods.

"Sam Chambers..." Arnold Brody tried to explain to Amos over Becky's shoulder, his face still white from the ordeal, "He saved me. He saved us."

Amos looked over to the schoolteacher's corpse. "We all make sacrifices for the clan," he said. His gaze drifted to the crowd—to his mother, it looked like. "But I was the one who saved you all. The unbreds were mine. And so was this rescue."

The crowd of freed Tucker neurocasters cheered and scrambled for the supply carts, but Mrs. Taylor remained motionless before her son. "Do you think," his mother said, "that this will bring my Dale back to me? Do you think this will make up for what you've done?"

"Mother, you misunderstand me. I don't intend to bring Dale back. I'm going to send the rest of the world to meet him. And this"—Amos placed his heel on a dead American—"was because I wanted to thank you. You helped make me what I am."

# Chapter 12: Domino Effect

Nighttime descended upon the forest. Taking with them the convoy of plunder the Americans had pillaged from town, the Tuckers moved off the road and lit feeble fires for warmth and some semblance of security. Sam, Amos, Becky, and Ralph had saved them, sure. The Americans were dead, and the Tuckers now had their fancy guns, even if ammo was short. And yet the Tuckers were adrift, caught out in the wilderness, unbreds acting strangely all about, and their new leader a maelstrom of magnetism; sometimes attracting them, sometimes repelling them, and the force behind it beyond the periphery of their senses.

Tuckers here and there prepared for a restless night of sleep. Amos produced a couple deer carcasses bearing the claw and fang marks of pigmen. Arnold Brody reckoned they'd make a passable breakfast if they let them hang until morning. He did not ask how Amos had got the deer from the unbreds in the first place.

Ralph McDaniel returned to camp after a brief scout in the woods. He enlisted an elder's help dragging Sam Chambers' body to a section of slope strewn with rocks. He didn't have any tools for digging a proper grave, but he had plenty of stones at hand. He cleared a man-sized area of earth and leveled it as best he could before rolling his mentor's corpse into the shallow depression. He gathered stones from all around and placed them on the body with heavy slowness, first forming a ring around it before stacking the rocks on top.

It was difficult work for Ralph.

"There's no point to this, Ralph."

Ralph didn't turn to acknowledge Amos. He placed another rock over his teacher and wiped the sweat from his face. "You gonna help me?"

"You'd do better to save your energy."

Ralph kept working.

"I'm not saying I don't understand your sentiment. I'm saying its stupid. Why bury the dead? To keep disease away, or starve the unbreds, maybe?"

"I'm doing it to keep myself human," Ralph spat. "To show that I'm not an animal, like..." He shook his head and stood to gather more rocks.

"So, to keep up the lie, in other words."

"To honor those I cared for."

"There is no honor, Ralph. Only winning. Only surviving. It's the only way any of this, any of *you* will ever matter. If you want his death, or your little life to mean *anything,* you do it by carving your name into the hearts of your enemies and your friends. This," Amos pointed at the mound of rocks, "is a waste of time. Nothing but playing pretend."

Ralph stopped working. He rested on his knees, his head down and his shoulders sagging. "'I am...'" he began, "'Ozymandias, King of Kings. Look upon my works ye mighty, and despair.' Mr. Chambers taught me that poem."

"Percy Shelley," Amos nodded. "Now you're getting the idea."

"No. The rest of the poem: 'Nothing beside remains. Around the decay of that colossal wreck... boundless and bare...'" Ralph got to his feet and locked eyes with Amos. "'The lone and level sands stretch on away.' Are you getting *my* idea?" He stormed off before Amos could answer.

Amos shrugged and rested a foot upon the stone heap, surveying the downhill slope shrouded in nighttime stillness. Words bubbled up out of him, a deep croaking at first, then up above the level of hearing. "...don't talk to me that way. I was right, and he couldn't handle it. I just... stop. You're not even supposed to be here any more. You're not real."

"Amos?"

Amos spun, his hand darting to the matchet at his side. He relaxed at the sight of Becky coming down from the camp.

"Who were you talking to?"

Amos shook his head. "No one."

"Do you, uh... want to be alone for a while?"

"No, it's fine. Come on over. I was just... thinking about Mr. Chambers."

Amos moved away from the grave and tested a fallen tree before sitting down. Becky followed suit, setting her silenced rifle aside and leaning onto her knees as she sat. She rubbed her hands together.

"You think there was something going on with me and Mr. Chambers," Amos said.

"I... don't think Mr. Chambers was acting himself these last few days."

"I've kept you and Ralph in the dark for your own good. So you could focus on rescuing your kin instead of this." Amos indicated Sam's grave. "But you deserve to know the truth. Neurocasters don't just talk with their minds. They can also consume each other. Feed off the minds of other neurocasters and grow fat off their brainshine. That's what the Americans wanted you and the rest of the 'conscripts' for. That American, Jarvis, he tortured me and Mr. Chambers both. I watched him..." Amos closed his eyes and pulled a deep breath through his nose.

"I watched him consume Mr. Chambers right in front of me. But when he came for me, I won. I consumed him. And then, like it or not, I got everyone Jarvis had ever consumed, too."

"Oh my word, Amos." Becky's breathless exclamation spanned both horror and pity.

"*That's* how I could control the unbreds. It's how I know things. Everything Jarvis knew, I know."

"What a thing to know."

"It's a lot."

"Did they do it to... did they consume Ella?"

Amos turned his head to look at her. "Ella was how the Americans found out our clan was full of neurocasters."

Becky rested her head in one hand. "Not Ella. Not her. Not—"

"I don't know if they've assimilated her or Ricky yet. Those were the only two neurocasters who went to New Ashburn. I intend to find out what happened."

"Then I'm coming with you."

"Of course you are. Everybody is."

"You're not sending the convoy back?"

"Can't."

"Why not?"

Amos sighed. "The Americans, Jarvis in particular, were looking for a nasty piece of work. A few years ago, some free neurocaster sought shelter with them out in Baltimore. They trained him, and he distinguished himself in repelling a massive unbred attack. A real special talent. But he was an out-of-towner, so they sacrificed him to their established neuronets. They fed him to one of their choice neurocasters. Or they tried to. Instead, he assimilated the whole neuronet, along with a whole school's worth of their young neurocaster trainees, and took off for the hills. He calls himself the Pied Piper, and he's been trailing us for at least a day."

Becky turned as if expecting to see glowing eyes watching them from the brush. "How do you know?"

"I spoke with him. Tried to negotiate. It's no use. He's after this convoy, and if I try to stop him, he'll turn around and take it out on the town Tuckers we left behind. He's not far behind us. I can feel flashes of some brainshine at the edges of my neuronet. Peeps and prods from the shadowers out there I control. I'm pulling as many unbreds as I can close to me, but not fast enough. I keep feeling a pack of pigmen or a screevler fall out of my neuronet. My guess is it's the Pied Piper absorbing them."

"If he's so close to us, he can't be close to town. It would take him days to get to 'em, wouldn't it?"

Amos shook his head. "I don't know how he'd manage it, but he's not bluffing."

"It couldn't be... some other neurocaster? Maybe someone working with him?"

"There was supposed to be a big group of American neurocasters coming out our direction to harvest the Tuckers, but their brainshine wouldn't be coming out of the woods like this. And they sure as hell wouldn't be teaming up with him."

"Maybe..." Becky paused. "Maybe you could teach me to... consume neurocasters. Maybe if *we* team up—"

"*NO!*" Amos leaped up, his whole body tensed like a tomcat with its hackles raised. "They're *mine!*" He raised a hand to the side of his head and took a deep breath through his nose. "I mean..."

"I'm—I'm sorry, Amos."

"No, you don't understand. I didn't mean to scare you. I just don't want you to... it takes a toll."

"What do we do, then?"

Amos wandered to where a bone-white branch forked from the main trunk of their slapdash bench. He waited as if building up to some de-cisive proclamation, but then reached out and snapped a twig between his clenched fists. "I don't know. You're right, he shouldn't be able to reach us and the town at the same time. I don't understand how he's able to do it. It's miles and miles between town and where the caravan is, with hills and trees and mountains in between to boot. The shine can't reach that far. My best plan is to keep him interested in us. Draw him further and further away from town."

"I think I know how he does it," Ralph said from behind them.

Becky and Amos whirled to see Ralph carrying an armful of stones for Sam's grave. "I thought you were done with me," Amos said.

Ralph stared long and hard at Amos, the muscles in his jaw flexing and relaxing. "Do you want to deal with the Pied Piper or not?"

Amos shrugged. "Go ahead."

"I know how he does it. And I think I know how you can do it, too, as long as you've got these... shadowers under your control."

Both Amos and Becky looked in Ralph's direction. "How?" They asked in unison.

"Have either of you ever... played with dominos?"

Tucker Territory

Shane Bunton drove the last two pack animals left in town to haul a felled log from the woods, his eldest son tending the log sledge three paces behind. The animals were old and not well suited to timberwork, but Shane had come near to blows with the Garmens for even these. Shane had tried to assert his authority as a clan elder and marshal the survivors to repair the town defenses, but the clan's hunger asserted itself more. The past few days, most folks had done nothing but strike out into the wilderness to forage for victuals. With so many bare larders, everyone worried about what they would eat come January.

Without the eastern gate repaired and a regular watch on the walls, however, they were liable not to make it to January. Not that any of these boneheads listened to him. So Shane had rallied his family, down to his six- and seven-year-old daughters, to take on the repairs. If they worked before sunrise to an hour or two after sundown, they might get something passable set up by the end of the week.

The draft animals jerked in their traces as the log sledge tilted and slid to the side. Shane spun and yelled at his son, "Dad-burn it, Nigel, keep the sled steady over the ruts!"

But his son wasn't minding the sledge, nor even Shane's rebuke. Rather, he stood mute, his eyes turned upward to the break in the scrub brush to the north. Shane followed his son's gaze to glimpse the stock-still form of a shadower.

Shane dove for the musket sheathed alongside his mule, but his son's lips loosened. "It's Amos Taylor, Pa."

"What?" Shane looked to see the shadower raise one hand and give them a two-fingered salute. "What in blue blazes?"

"I don't know how, but that's... that's Amos."

The unbred creature pointed out to the east and crossed its forearms in front of its face. It repeated the gesture three times while Shane puzzled over it. "Don't go east, or some problem that-a-way."

"Danger? Danger from out east?" Nigel suggested. "Or does Amos need help out east?"

"I don't think a big 'X' means 'come this way,' Nigel," Shane grunted.

The shadower pointed west, then placed its long-fingered hands one on top of the other and ground them together in a circular motion.

"The old mill out west," Nigel said a split second before Shane could.

The shadower repeated the motion, but Shane had gotten the message. "There's something coming our way. We need to get everyone together and hide out in the old mill."

"Why there, Pa?"

Shane frowned in thought, then spat. "'Cause it's on the crick. If we wade upstream a-ways, whatever's coming won't be able to sniff out our trail."

Dawn broke with a thin layer of frost overlaying the fallen leaves, stubbly grass, and stones with glittering silver. The Tuckers finished the meal of tough venison and ash-baked sweet potatoes they'd prepared in the lightening fog of a dim morning twilight. Amos paced the outskirts of the mist-shrouded camp, silent agitation etched in his face. How much had he slept, and how well?

Amos' instructions to the clansmen were clear and simple: the convoy was to push on to New Ashburn, where they would kill the American garrison and liberate the Tuckers there. Only Job Brody seemed to have any doubts about this plan. He raised a hand to put his question to Amos: "What makes you think we'll be able to storm New Ashburn with a dozen chatterguns?"

"I don't expect..." Amos began, but faltered. His eyes closed. Then they were open again, his self-assuredness back as if it had never left him. "I don't expect to fire a single shot. All you have to worry about is getting there."

The Tuckers raised no further questions. The convoy assembled itself, together with all its livestock, its carts and wagons, its little ones and old codgers, while the sun yet hugged the eastern horizon. They began their march with the vitality brought about not by ample rest, but by a purpose they held as their own.

Amos took up the rear, and most of the convoy carried on without commenting on Amos' brief lapse. Except for his two lieutenants, Ralph and Becky.

"What's going on? Is it the Pied Piper?" Becky asked.

Amos nodded.

"Did it work?" Ralph asked. "Did you get a warning through to the town?"

"I couldn't exactly walk a shadower through the eastern gate. But," he said, raising a hand to his temple and furrowing his brow, "I spelled it out for them so that they couldn't miss it. If it's as hard for the Pied Piper to do anything fancy that far out as it is for me, we should be all right. I guess I'll know if it worked when he has to choose between going after us or the town Tuckers."

Which meant there was nothing to do but press forward and see what happened. The thick fog never abated, not even as they started uphill. Drab branches and bristly heath reached out at them through the gloom like knobby hands.

"We have to pick up the pace," Amos said.

Becky turned and placed a hand under Amos' elbow, but he remained steady, silent, eyes fixed forward with single-minded resolve.

Folks squinted into the cloying mist, searching in vain for signs of stalkers they knew must lurk out there somewhere. The Tuckers could feel it without Amos telling them the exact nature of what hunted them. The animals could feel it. Things moved deep in the woods beyond their sight. Susurrations shot through the convoy like shivers, but none dared voice anything louder than a whisper. Most needed little urging to season their tread, but there were children and older folks who drifted further and further toward the back of the procession as the convoy moved.

"Will it come to a fight?" Becky asked.

"We'll see."

"Will we make it to New Ashburn before the Pied Piper catches up with us?"

Amos didn't answer for a long time. "No."

As the morning ripened and the convoy climbed out of the valley to attain the ridgeline, the fog dropped away to reveal scattered calico mountaintops afloat in a sea of gray. The road carried them along the headlands a full mile, across treeless balds and flinty, thin-soiled knolls and glades. Those bearing arms took up watches along the sides and vanguard, scanning the scree slopes for danger and finding none. The Tuckers relaxed, even if their pace did not. Perhaps they would make it, after all.

All wonderings melted away to leave a needle-sharp point of certainty as the Tucker convoy trudged over the crest of a hill to see their path blocked by a single bald man astride a bullhusker.

Amos tried to pull the unbred under his sway, but he might as well have tried to climb an icicle with his bare hands.

Job Brody raised a long rifle.

"Don't shoot!" Amos ordered, shouldering his way to the front of the group.

"Don't tell me he's friendly. He's just standing there. It's an easy shot," Job said.

"He's bait. Don't waste your ammo. I've got a cheaper defense. Ralph! Becky! Hold me up!" Without waiting for his lieutenants to catch him, he reached out to all the unbreds still with him and drew them in from the brush and woods at either side of the ridge into a tight ring around the convoy. One of the Tucker women blasted a pigman with a black-powder-charged shotgun. "Cease fire!" Amos ordered. "These unbreds will not attack us. Only use muskets and hand-weapons, and even then, not until I say so! Brace yourselves!" Climbing onto a wagon next to his proxies, he turned to Becky and Ralph. "Whatever happens, protect me and all the sleeping people in this wagon."

The elders among the convoy acted as Amos's sergeants, directing the fighters. "Old folks and young 'uns in the middle!" Arnold Brody shouted even as the woods came alive with the shouts of pigmen rallying for a charge. "Circle the wagons!"

The Tuckers didn't have time to prepare proper defenses, but they didn't need to. The pigman onslaught broke before it ever reached the unbreds under Amos's sway. The two opposing lines of pigmen howled and snapped at each other, but never got into it tooth-and-claw.

"So, I guess Amos ain't the only one 'round here who can play shadower to the pigmen," Arnold Brody said with a sideways glance Amos didn't miss.

Amos ignored the wary tone in the butcher's voice. He sat up in the wagon and scanned the woods, reaching out with his mind as understanding dawned on him. "There's not—he doesn't have enough. He tried to get my unbreds, but he's not strong enough to flip them. There aren't enough in the area for him to take us head-on. Which means..." He jumped to his feet. "Fire, fire, *fire!*" A thunderstorm of musket fire sent the attacking unbreds reeling back into the forest.

The moment they'd dispersed, Amos called out his next order. "We make for New Ashburn, *now*. Drop anything you can't carry on your back and move!"

Becky spun toward Amos as if he'd told them to saw off their own legs. "But—most of our food—the livestock—"

"We have to get out of here before the Pied Piper gets enough unbreds to actually stop us. We take weapons, ammo, and rations! Now *move!*"

The Tucker convoy lurched forward, picking up the pace until everyone was puffing with exertion. They'd already loaded up the slowest onto horses and mules, but there weren't enough pack animals to go around, even piling the children on together. First, the smaller animals failed to keep up, followed by the cows and oxen. Some Tuckers slackened their tempo to shepherd their cattle, but Amos took his matchet and beheaded one goat before anyone could object. No turning back. The unbreds were coming, and there wasn't anything they could do for the animals who couldn't keep up.

They unhitched the wagons, already lightened, from the horses, and the older Tuckers who'd been riding in them had to dismount. Soon, they were starting to lag behind. The one wagon they kept held the sleeping people Amos had brought with him. The Tuckers stayed their course with the grim understanding that even if they outran the unbred swarm, they would have to storm the walls of New Ashburn to gain a modicum of safety.

Amos trotted back to the end of the column and found Old Man Brody heaving up another never-ending hill along with a bunch of tired old goats. "Let's go, Brody. You can do it. New Ashburn's not far. We can make it by nightfall."

"I won't make it. I can't."

"Take a turn on a horse."

"You have to save them for the kidlin's."

"You can make it. It's only ten miles more."

"Leave me, Amos. I've had enough. I'll—I'll slow them down."

Amos paused only a moment before giving the old man his matchet. "For the clan," he said.

"As always. For the clan," Salvador Brody wheezed.

Amos, bringing up the convoy's rear to kick the heels of any further stragglers, threw one last glance over his shoulder before they passed around a bend in the valley. Old Man Brody sat in the middle of the road, looking westward, toward home.

# Chapter 13: Diplomacy by Other Means

B ill Puckett paced the charred wooden floor of his office as the
evening sun outside gave him one last mischievous wink over the
edge of the western hills. Each passing day taunted him. He'd thought
the pressure of keeping up nitrogel production was enough; now he felt
time pinching him like a vise. Melissa Daly arrived with grits and beans.
This last week, he'd slept little and eaten less. The hard lines on his face
now appeared permanent.

"You gotta eat somethin', Bill. You ain't doin' no good half-starved."

"I can't hardly stand all this waitin'. I keep doin' my figures. Unless
Mrs. Compton's got herself a secret stash, the junkers don't hardly
have enough food to get themselves through the winter, let alone a
couple hundred workers. And we ain't gonna see any nomad clans soon,
neither. The ones friendly with the Federation won't come no more,

and any free traders will think we're still under the Federation's thumb, and we might as well be, 'cause Armstrong *still* ain't cried uncle. Who knows when the American cavalry will get here, and if we'll be able to fight 'em off when they do?"

Melissa had noticed how quickly Bill took to saying "we" whenever he talked about the junkers, just like he'd talked about the Sylvanian slaves. It was likely more than warm fellow-feeling, though; they were all under the same rain-cloud now. "Folks can start foraging," she said. "It ain't the best eating, but acorns are in season, and they'll get us through the winter all right. And my folks ate grubs before all right. We can do it again if we need to."

"Foraging's too risky if we're worried about a bunch of reinforcements coming over the hill—"

"Mr. Puckett?" Omar knocked on the door. "Lookouts spotted a whole ruck coming from out east."

Bill sighed. "They ain't started shooting yet?"

"They don't look like Americans."

Bill topped the ladder to the palisade walkway with fervent energy. "What's the word?"

The Sylvanian who'd become Bill's second-in-command crouched behind the parapet, the bipod of an M249 machine gun resting atop the wall. "They've taken up positions in the treeline. Someone out there is telling us to surrender or he'll kill us all."

"Numbers?" Bill asked.

"I'd say a hundred-fifty. Certainly no more than that."

"Whoever it is ain't taking on chatterguns with a force like that and coming out with the same number of holes he went in with. What's he about?"

The Sylvanian shrugged.

"Ho there!" Bill Puckett called. "Just who do you think you are, calling for us to throw down arms?"

The answer didn't come right away, and when it did, Bill could not have predicted it. "Bill Puckett? Is that you?"

"Amos Taylor? What the heck is going on? What are you doing all the way out here?"

"Open the gate and let us in. I'll explain once we don't have a pigman swarm nipping at our heels."

Bill turned to two Sylvanian guards on the wall. "Throw open the gate, quick-like. Them there's my folks."

Human figures surged from the treeline a hundred paces off and resolved themselves as they came closer into the shapes of men, women, and children, then into faces and figures he recognized. Brodys. Hadleys. Finches. His friend, Phil. They looked tired. Care-worn. Terrified. Road-dust clung to their clothes up to their waists, and some of their shoes were in a sorry state. A wagon laden with corpses rattled through the gate, but they bore no other baggage train.

"What it be, Arnie?" Bill asked of the butcher as he staggered into New Ashburn.

"Gotta ask Amos," came the only reply. "He's in charge, now."

Bill looked to Amos, who was already ascending the ladder to join the powdermaker on the catwalk. Before he could open his mouth, Amos cut in. "Have your men cover the forest. Once we're inside, I don't expect a direct assault yet. The Pied Piper doesn't have enough unbreds yet."

"The Pied Piper? What—"

"Doesn't matter to you. Are these guys junkers?" Amos pointed to the armed Sylvanians. What happened to the Americans?"

"No, they're, uh, Sylvanians. The Americans weren't treating us too good, so we got together and raised a little hell."

Amos nodded in approval, though the permanent scowl that seemed attached to his face never softened. "You've got New Ashburn under your control?"

"Well, not all of it. The junkers kinda came over to our side, but Armstrong, she's the commander, see—"

"I know who Armstrong is. Is she dead yet?"

"I—not yet. What's going on, Amos? You're not acting like you used to. Why are you in charge here?"

"'Cause everybody else is dead and I'm done putting up with bullshit. The Americans killed Elvin McDaniel, Sam Chambers, and the reverend."

Bill's hand lifted itself to the side of his head as the color drained from his face. "What happened?"

"The Americans are worthless bastards who tried to kill three quarters of the clan and ship this last quarter here for human experimentation."

"What about Sophie and the kids?" Bill interrupted. "I heard Victor—"

"Sophie and the kids are fine. Victor's not. Others have died. The Grierson settlement is toast, but they had it coming. I've saved most of Tuckers, though, and now I'm here to show the Americans what happens when they screw around with me. Now give me your sitrep."

"Sit-what?"

"Tell me what the hell's going on here."

"We got us about thirty American prisoners, with the rest buttoned up with Armstrong in a fort back hills-wise. We were worried you were that big American army sent out west a few weeks back. Do you know what happened to them?"

"I happened to them. Where do you think all these Tuckers got assault rifles from?" Amos nodded, unsmiling, to the passel of Tuckers huddling amongst the workshops of lower New Ashburn. Job Brody and Phil

Holland broke from the group and strode toward the palisade ladder with the same question on their lips: "Where's my kid?"

"It's, uh... complicated." Bill turned away from them, his hands on his hips. "The Americans have Ella locked up in their fort. Ricky... he's gone over to the Americans' side."

Amos's eyes narrowed. "What do you mean?"

"I've been trying to strike a deal, but the Americans won't budge. They won't even talk to me directly. They've been having Ricky do their talking for them."

Amos was already walking past Bill towards the gate to the citadel as if he knew the exact layout of New Ashburn. "I'm taking control of this operation, Bill. You can get back to your powdermaking, but leave the folkward and the negotiations to me now. I want to talk to Ricky."

"Well, uh, not that I don't think you don't got the gumption, but the Sylvanians here don't know you like they know me. Are you sure you can command them?"

Amos stopped and looked at Bill, then at a squad of nearby armed Sylvanian workers. "You," he said, pointing at them. "Do you want to see the American neurocasters suffer a fate worse than death?"

The former slaves traded glances, the guns they carried hanging limp at their sides. One of them turned to face Amos and nodded without meeting his eyes.

"Then follow me and do as I say."

The Sylvanian guards weren't the only ones to follow Amos. Bill followed, too, as well as Job Brody and Phil Holland, along with his lieutenants, Becky and Ralph, and a gaggle of curious junkers taking up the rear. He drew them all along like a magnet drawing iron filings. He held them under his sway by that powerful, invisible attraction he always had, which awed both neurocaster and brain-dark.

He picked up one more follower on his way to the base of the citadel hill: Omar Walking. Amos stopped long enough to nod his direction.

"Didn't quite expect to see you still alive, after the plan we hatched together went sour," Amos said.

"Can't say I expected to see you, either. When you didn't come back out of the meetinghouse, I thought you was dead."

"Thought I was, too. They knew I was coming."

"I'm sorry, Amos."

Amos stared at Omar. "Yeah."

Omar returned Amos' penetrating gaze. "How'd you get out?"

"They underestimated me," Amos said, turning back toward the citadel.

When Ricky Brody came forth as a distant figure from the concrete citadel, Amos Taylor sat at the gates waiting for him, flanked by several of the new Tucker arrivals. Ella's father, Phil Holland, and Ricky's father, Job Brody, peered through the gunports. A small, gawking crowd of intermixed junkers and Sylvanians gathered further back. Everyone, whether Tucker, Ashburnite, or Sylvanian, recognized the now infamous fellow known as Ricky before he was halfway down the hill.

"So, Ricky's gone over to the Americans, huh?" Amos said to Bill.

"Yeah. I can't account for it. But yeah," Bill said.

"My son would never betray the clan that a-way," Job said.

Amos didn't comment either way. "Hmm."

Ricky closed the remaining distance before hailing Bill Puckett. "In light of recent developments," he said to Bill, glancing at the Tucker reinforcements behind the wall, "Colonel Armstrong would like to renegotiate—"

"Hey, whoever you are," Amos called down from his perch on the palisade. "You had your chance to make a deal with Puckett. Now you talk to me. I don't have time for screwing around, and I don't make deals with proxies. Send out your root and we'll talk."

Ricky regarded Amos with barely concealed contempt. "Who gave you the authority to negotiate here?"

"I did."

"I'm not going to pass along terms from some kid."

Amos turned and held Job Brody in a grim stare. "Sorry, Job. Becky," he said. "I was afraid of that. You know that's not really Ricky there anymore. You'd better look away."

Ricky scowled up at Amos. "Hey, boy. What are you—"

Amos shot Ricky in the face.

"*No!*" A scream burst forth from Job Brody, followed by a weaker, deflating moan. "No..." He ended with more of a confused whimper than a cry, as if he were coming to after being knocked unconscious and couldn't make sense of his surroundings. Even Becky held her hand over her mouth, her eyes darting open in utter disbelief.

Amos put down his rifle and stared up at the citadel. "Job, at least you know your son never betrayed us. He was loyal to the end. He's no longer their puppet."

Job gave no sign of having heard him. The rest of the Tuckers stood there, frozen in shock. Finally, Amos noticed Becky climbing the ladder up next to him. "What now?" she asked, white-faced, looking down at her cousin's body.

"Now we wait for the Americans to send out someone important."

"Are you sure that wasn't—"

"It wasn't Ricky. Ricky's been gone ever since the Americans took him."

"Are you sure there's no way—"

"Trust me. Once they've been assimilated, even a bullet won't make much difference to them. He was gone, long gone."

"Like Sam Chambers was gone?"

Amos swatted the irritating question away. "I did what I had to do, Becky. For the clan. For you. They would have made you like Ricky."

"Ella's in there. Do you reckon they done the same to her?"

Amos lifted a pair of bird-watching glasses and scanned the roof of the citadel. "Probably. I'll find out."

Becky made a funny choking sound into her elbow.

"There we go," Amos said cheerfully, still staring out through the binoculars as if Ricky had been nothing more than a passing hiccup. A bald human had emerged from the building and was walking the same path down to them that Ricky had walked. "Looks like they're ready to talk."

"You sure about that?" Becky asked.

The figure—apparently a woman, despite her lack of hair—stopped halfway down the hill as if waiting.

"If they're not, they will be by the time I'm done with them." Amos handed Becky the binoculars and climbed down. "Keep watch. Don't do anything crazy."

Amos left his guns and knife behind, stripped off his coat, and walked through the gates to meet the American neurocaster.

"That's far enough," the woman called when Amos came within ten feet of her.

Amos spread out his arms and turned a full circle. "I don't have any weapons." He stepped closer to her.

For now, she stood her ground. "I have multiple soldiers covering you in case you try anything funny."

Amos continued his approach. "And I've got my own people covering you. But we both know it won't do either of us any good. It's just you and me."

The woman's brow furrowed in her first sign of uncertainty. "Why?"

Amos took a step closer. "Because at this range, neither your guys nor mine can hit one of us without hitting the other. I'm too close."

The woman took a step backward, but Amos closed the last distance.

"What do you think you're doing?" she demanded, but the command in her voice faltered.

"Hold on, sweetheart. Come here," Amos said, reaching up and around the back of her neck in an intimate gesture. "No reason to fuss. Nobody will shoot if nobody makes a scene, see?"

"They'll shoot at my signal." The woman gasped, her eyes going wide as Amos drew close to her.

"Go ahead, then." Amos gave her a nod, his eyes locked with hers. "Scream if you need to."

The woman quivered, but said nothing. She merely stood there, rigid, in his hands.

"See there? They can't tell anything's going on. We're just talking. Just talking, right?"

"I can..." The woman's voice dropped to a whisper, sweat beading on her face. "I can get Armstrong to surrender."

Amos nodded. "Oh, I know you will."

Whatever effort the woman put into pushing him away, it wasn't enough. Her hand twitched, then returned to its side. She opened her mouth as if to scream, only for it to close again without a sound. *How are you doing this?*

"I'm sure you've never felt trapped like this. Like a slave or a dog on a leash. Savor this moment. Do you want to scream? You look like you want to scream."

She said nothing. A rivulet of sweat ran down her bald head.

"The American guards up there are curious as to what's going on. All you have to do is turn around and call out to them. Come on. Try reeeeaally hard."

Only her eyes moved. *I'll do anything you want. Please.*

"That's right, you *will* do anything I want. Have you ever wanted to jab your fingers into your eye holes and pull your own mind out by the roots? To step out of that festering sore that is your brain and walk around outside yourself for a bit? But you can't. No matter how hard you try, you're trapped, because you *are* your brain. We're all sealed-off in our own little prisons. You understand that, right?"

The woman said nothing, only stared, wide-eyed, back at him.

"Oh, but of course you wouldn't understand it. You're an American, upper-story, special-bred ubermensch. You can't see it, is all." Amos leaned in towards her, nose-to-nose. "But I can make you see it."

*Please...* she pleaded, tears leaking down her face. *Don't do this. Now. See.*

A deep shudder ran through her, but it was Amos who sank to his knees and fell to the ground, unconscious.

The woman took on the slouch of a confident young man, wiping away the tears and sweat as if cleaning dirt off her face. She grabbed Amos by the collar and hauled him back down the hill. "Becky," the woman called out to the butcher's daughter, "keep watch over my body. I'll be right back."

She turned around without bothering to gauge the response from the other Tuckers; their response was irrelevant and likely a predictable set of slack jaws and limp minds. A minute later, she was back at the top of the hill.

"What the hell's going on? What happened out there?" The guard on watch demanded.

"Negotiations."

She knocked on the steel door and was given admittance. She made her way by lantern-light—the electric lights had long-since gone dark—past the rooms where the neurocasting roots had taken refuge from the worker uprising, as well as the adjacent room where their proxies slept on racks. She moved to the deepest interior of the citadel, where a certain broom closet waited.

Colonel Armstrong stopped her before she ever got there. "Well?" Armstrong asked. "What are his terms?"

"He wants the Tucker girl released first."

"No way. That Tucker girl is the only reason we're still alive. Go back out there and tell him we're walking out of here with her as insurance. Tell him we'll release her once we're clear of New Ashburn's outer walls."

"Are we actually going to release her?"

"What does it matter to you? That's what you'll tell him."

The bald woman sighed. "I know what he'll say: He'll tell us to surrender and release her immediately, or he'll take any survivors and nail them to a tree for the... geemoes."

Armstrong tensed ever so slightly, but not so slightly as to escape the woman's notice. Armstrong drew a pistol and pointed it at the bald neurocaster. "You're not Candice."

The bald woman shrugged. "It depends on what you mean, Selina. Are any of us the same people we were when we were children? Did you really even know me then?"

Armstrong's unreadable visage melted into something else for a bare instant before hardening into a glower. "Who are you? Really?"

The bald woman sighed. "I'm the one who calls the shots now, and since you insist on doing things in the most difficult way possible, I suppose I can offer you my demands directly."

"I am the highest-ranking officer of the New American Federation for a hundred miles. I will *not* be dictated to by shit-shoveling hillbillies!"

The bald woman's stare hardened to match Armstrong's in the flickering lantern-light. "I'll state my terms once, and then it's up to you. You and your soldiers, along with any New Ashburnite collaborators, will immediately lay down your arms and march down, single-file, with nothing but the clothes on your backs, and surrender yourselves to the Tucker clan. You will keep your lives. In exchange, I want every neurocaster living here. And Ella Holland, of course."

Colonel Armstrong didn't move. She stared hard at the bald woman, and the bald woman stared back. "How can I be certain you won't double-cross me the moment my people surrender?" Armstrong asked.

"I'll need someone to deliver a message back to your masters for me."

"Which is?"

"Any Federation settler, soldier, trader— *anyone* who enters these mountains is mine."

"This is Federation territory."

"Then I guess I don't need to send a message. If you want to fight this out, I'm *perfectly* happy to oblige. By the way, in case you were wondering, Candice wished you'd confided in her more, or anyone at all. So sad." The woman shook her head with a pouting lip.

"I'll kill every last one of you."

"You already tried that, long before we'd done *anything* to you. You just saw us as a resource to be exploited. Harvested. Butchered," the bald woman spat, her eyes flaring.

"Don't take your judgmental tone with me. It's clear you've done the same. Don't act as if you're any different."

"We're nothing alike," the bald woman said, her lips curling to reveal glittering teeth. She leaned forward and murmured in a gentle whisper, "I'm much, *much* worse. Last chance before you have to fight this proxy in the dark."

Armstrong's scowl didn't fade, but she lowered her gun. "Fine. I surrender."

"Good." The bald woman straightened up and held out her hand. "Give it over. Come on, now."

Armstrong shook her head in frustration, but she laid her pistol on the floor before stepping back.

"The other one, too."

Armstrong undid both holsters and slid them down the hallway toward the bald woman, then motioned for the nearby guard to lower his gun. He obeyed, unslinging the strap and setting the rifle on the floor.

"Okay, hands on your head and out the doors. You will command everyone here to lay down their arms outside the citadel and march down the hill with their hands on their heads. You first, then the soldiers.

The neurocasters stay up here. Anyone else still up here when I check the rooms dies."

Armstrong's jaw clenched as if she were chewing leather before she barked an order which passed on through the narrow corridors down the chain of command. It wasn't far back to the entrance, but by the time they'd reached the rusty steel door, American soldiers lined both sides of the hallway, most of them looking dirty and frightened in the dimness. They should be frightened. They were at Amos' mercy now.

"Cheer up, fellas," the bald woman said. "Your colonel just made a deal for your lives. You're all about to walk free, just as soon your commander leads the way."

The Americans marched down across the broad slope with their hands over their heads as Amos's proxy had instructed. By the time they reached the bottom of the hill, Amos was back in his own body and ready to greet them at the gates. He strode up past Ricky Brody's corpse, where Job Brody sat staring out at nothing.

"Becky," Amos said, "you and Ralph give me a headcount, then get all the prisoners out the eastern gate. Every American, every single collaborator Puckett captured during the uprising—all of them. Then these fresh prisoners after that." He pointed to Armstrong and the bedraggled soldiers marching down from the citadel.

Becky turned toward Amos, pain in her face. "Amos, have a heart, please. Just give me a minute."

"*Now*, Becky," Amos ordered. "You can cry about your cousin later. We got Ella, and that's all that matters."

"Can I go up and see her?"

"We've got more important things to do. There are a bunch of American prisoners who need watching and an unbred army not far outside town. Get all the Americans together at the eastern gate, and I'll tell you what to do next. Have your pa help you if you need the extra hands."

Amos turned to Omar. "Omar. These Sylvanians you got patrolling the clan. You trust them?"

Omar shrugged. "Enough to put a gun in their hands."

"Then take yourself five and form a ring around the outside of the citadel. I'm going in personally to clear the rooms."

Omar looked up at the citadel. "What about Ella?"

"I have to clear the building first. The bald people in there are dangerous to the Tuckers. That's what happened to Ricky Brody. But they can't do that to you or the Sylvanians. If any try to escape or maybe crawl up the side of the mountain, shoot them."

Omar frowned as if Amos had walked into an obvious snare. "If they're dangerous to the Tuckers, won't they be dangerous to Ella? Couldn't she be like Ricky?"

"No, but it wasn't for lack of trying. It's the funniest thing." Amos shook his head in amused bewilderment. "Ella seems like she's immune to assimilation. At least she's immune to the pathetic enclave-trained neurocasters the Americans brought in with them."

Omar didn't take his eyes off the building where Ella lay captive. "How do you know?"

"I know everything that American neurocaster knew." Amos stepped up beside Omar and pointed at the unconscious bald woman at the base of the hill. "And she saw everything the Americans did to her."

Amos found all the neurocaster roots in the same common room, some of them sitting, some of them standing, all of them frozen in mute worry. When he entered, one of them surged towards him, then backed up when Amos aimed a pistol. "Where's Candice?"

"She's with Armstrong. We've come to terms. You," Amos said to the neurocaster who'd first approached him, "come with me. The rest of you, wait here. Our clan's schoolteacher wants to interview each of you individually before you're released."

Great cauldrons of stew bubbled over grates throughout the town square. The aromas of sage and smoked pork wafted seductively to the noses of the surrounding Tuckers. Bill had ordered the food whipped up to celebrate the Americans' surrender and the safe arrival of his Tucker clansmen, but Amos had ordered Becky and Ralph to keep folks away from the food for now. He needed the full attention of all the Tuckers, and this was the easiest way to get it. The pots held enough food for both the Tuckers and the Sylvanians. As to how this would affect New Ashburn's stores going into winter—well, that was their problem, as far as Amos was concerned.

A different kind of feast waited at the top of the hill, just for Amos: the collective brainshine of a hundred-fifty bodies, ripe and fresh. But first, like a prayer before the meal, he needed to give the mass of gathered onlookers a demonstration.

He turned to the many men, women, and children, Tuckers and Sylvanians, but also the few Ashburnites hoping to sneak past the guards for a free meal.

"We've won a great victory over our enemies, but most of you don't realize how great a victory it truly was, and how much work our clan has left to do. Soon, we Tuckers will all pack up and go home, but we cannot leave this place like we found it. The world has changed for everyone, and there's no point in going back to the old ways. When you Tuckers return to your kin, whom I have saved, you will tell them the truth of what you saw here. You will help bring about the new order of things, not just for our clan, but for every clan in these mountains, friend and foe, familiar and strange."

Amos paused to sweep his penetrating gaze over the wide arc of transfixed onlookers. He was no longer merely a promising young lad or a headstrong whelp. He wasn't even merely a leader. He was a force, elemental and implacable. The hale light within him burned so hot he threatened to sear the minds of anyone who drew too close.

"Before I do this," Amos said to the people, "I want you to know I'm doing this because I care about you, and you deserve to know the truth. The problem is, when you've been brought up your whole life with a lie, you wouldn't believe the truth if I told you. So I have to show you. I have to show you what we're all capable of, and what the Americans would have done to you if I hadn't stopped them."

Amos turned to the first bald American. "You are an acceptable sacrifice," he said.

"Wait, wait, please," the neurocaster begged.

This time, Amos let him scream. The Tuckers needed to hear the screams dissipating into the autumn air like incense.

# Chapter 14: Will to Power

Ella jumped in her prison at the sound of the moans and shrieks of men and women cutting through the thick darkness. She made out protests, curses, and pathetic imprecations at first, but they all slipped into the same uniform wail of minds being shackled to glowing iron. They all sounded like Ricky in the end. It went on for ages.

When it did end, however, she heard footsteps on the concrete floor become louder. The bolt holding the door shut slipped, and her mouth watered in anticipation of the gruel she took whenever the door opened.

But instead of an American guard, it was Amos, holding a lantern in one hand and his nose with the other. "God, Ella. What did they do to you?"

"Wha..." Ella mumbled a question she didn't finish, either because she was too tired or the answer was obvious. She wasn't sure which.

"I've beaten the Americans. You're free." He reached down to help Ella up.

But Ella didn't take his hand. "Amos, what have you done?" She shrank away from him as if he were the yellow-toothed guard.

The shadows cast by the lantern hardened the glower on Amos's face. "I did what I had to do. For the good of the clan." When she still didn't take his hand, he reached down and grabbed her by the elbow as if she were an impetuous child.

She yelped and pulled away from him, and he finally gave up with a huff. "Ungrateful little—fine, stay there." He threw up one hand in frustration and left her in the dark.

She sat trying to think about what to do and coming up short every time. Perhaps she should leave. But the Americans were out there. They had to be out there, regardless of what Amos' presence meant. But if the Americans were gone, what waited for her out there? The uncertainty kept her rooted where she sat. She didn't have to sit long, however, before she heard another voice come ringing through the blackness—a voice she recognized, indignant and hurried.

"Can't believe I had to wait outside this long. Bunch of hooey, is what it is. Where is she? Where—"

"Papa?"

He held the lantern aloft and looked down into the closet at her, lines of care deep in his face.

Ella turned away, crouching into the corner. "I'm disgusting."

"Ah, sweetheart," he said, his voice melting like butter. He dropped to a squat and turned her head to meet him square in the eye. "You'll never be too dirty for me. You need a hand? Come with Papa, now."

"I..." Ella said. "I don't want them to see me like this. I don't want them to see me like this, Papa." She didn't resist, however, when her father pulled her up and looped her arm over his shoulder.

"We gotta get you outta here. Get some food in your belly. Becky Brody is here. She's been asking about you. Everybody has. Can't say my stomach's settled, but it never is these days," he joked weakly as he walked her down the empty corridors. "We've all been worried just about sick."

The door out front squeaked on its hinges, and Ella blinked in the daylight. She pulled up a shaking hand to shield her pale, drawn face and took a tentative step outside, the greasy strings of her hair clinging to her face and neck. The light of day showed her dress was filthy and torn.

Omar was there, waiting for them. At the sight of her, a tremor rocked the fault-lines on his normally impassive face, but he looked down so quickly she may have imagined it. When Ella stumbled in the harsh light of day, he caught her other side and, together with her father, walked her on down the hill.

Ella sniffed a little. "I don't... I don't want everybody to see me like this."

"Everybody quit your gawking and clear on out of here!" Phil Holland yelled at the folks on the palisade at the bottom of the hill. Then, turning to shield Ella from those downhill, he said, "Is there anyone you'd like to see to you?"

"Mrs. Daly. Becky."

"Mrs. Daly's already waiting for you," her father said. "Where's Becky?"

Omar answered. "She went with Amos. They're hunting collaborators."

The freed Sylvanian slaves had thrown in with Amos after seeing the ease with which he'd forced Armstrong's hand, but they still held to their distaste for neurocasters and recoiled at the idea of handling Amos'

proxies, which meant the task of collecting all the comatose bodies together fell to the Tuckers who were still scrambling to get their wits about them in a clan they'd never seen before. While the Sylvanians may not have wanted to touch the proxies, they had no compunctions about carrying out Amos' next task: throwing Mayce Salazar's widow and her six wailing children out on their ear so Amos could set up his headquarters in their home. The junker woman and her brood were collaborators, beneficiaries of the Americans' exploitation of slave labor, and even technically New American citizens, and therefore enemies of the Sylvanians. Amos didn't have them stop at Salazar's family. Mr. Salazar's next-door apprentice was the next collaborator on his list.

A Sylvanian hammered on the door to the Perkins home with the butt of an American rifle while Amos waited with arms crossed. A man answered, hunched and meek, lenses suspended on thin wires perched on the bridge of his nose. Her father.

"You can't have her, young man," the father said, his voice trembling and his gaze dropping to Amos' feet. The father wrung his hands together in front of him, pathetic worm of a man.

"Take him, too," was Amos' only reply.

Two Sylvanians dragged him out of the way, and two others stormed into the house to extract the young junker archivist.

"Jody Perkins, you have collaborated with the Americans and caused great harm to my people. I sentence you to banishment."

Jody Perkins blinked in surprise at the accusation, then recoiled when Amos drew a pistol to make his intentions clear. "I never served in the militia! I—I helped with the worker's uprising!"

"You worked with Salazar. You helped him with his bookkeeping. One of those records reported on how many neurocasters the Tucker clan had."

"How could you know that?"

"I know everything. Out."

Jody's mother cried out from somewhere inside the house, but Jody waved her back. "Don't get mixed up in this, Mama. I'll figure this out." She took a deep breath and brushed away the hair that covered the burns on her face. "I don't reckon I'm getting a trial?"

"Trials are for people who aren't sure of the truth. I know exactly what happened. I know you knew what you were doing. We'll see how the Americans will repay a two-tone trash picker like you, since you're getting banished right along with the rest of them."

"I did what I could with the choices I had."

Amos sneered at her. "I don't care. You're going, and anyone who tries to pull you out gets one between the eyes."

Amos and his Sylvanian bodyguard went from house to house and through the town, picking out the last stragglers of collaborators he deemed guilty enough to warrant a trip out the eastern gate, which turned out to be a tidy sum. By the time he had worked his way through town, he had twice again as many New Ashburnites driven ahead of him as he had captive Americans.

Behind Amos followed what remained of the town's population, as well as the swarm of Tuckers and Sylvanians along with them. A growing caterwaul rose from the exiled Ashburnites in front and their kin who followed behind, but the Americans' automatic weapons now lay in the hands of the Sylvanian ex-slaves who separated the condemned from their kin, and the Sylvanians answered to Amos.

Most of the Tuckers, being new to New Ashburn and therefore unacquainted with the junker exiles, had no stake in the matter and were still too stunned from watching Amos' little demonstration with the American neurocaster earlier to do anything about it if they had. Bill Puckett had not been so overawed by Amos' power that he offered no protests, weak though they may be. He broke out from the shuffling throng and matched Amos' insistent stride.

"Amos, we're all mighty happy to see y'all come through for us here, but does it have to go this far? Shouldn't we think this through a little?"

"I'm not going too far. I'm being merciful. If I thought I could afford the time, I'd take these greedy, backstabbing liars three miles out, break their legs, and leave them."

Bill turned to the Sylvanian guards who flanked Amos. "Y'uns can't go along with this. I helped get you free."

One of the pair slowed, turning his head in uncertainty. Amos made a full stop and whirled on his heel. "You want to challenge my authority here? Steal my men out from under me?"

"I didn't... they're *my* men, Amos."

"They *were* your men. People like you are the middle-men of the world. You do okay in a pinch, but once a real man comes along, you'd better step aside or get crushed underfoot. So what's it going to be?"

"Amos, I'm just saying I—"

"Quit talking and *act.* What's it going to be? Are you with me or against me?"

Bill raised his hands in surrender. "I'm a fellow Tucker, here. I didn't aim to start a fight."

"Then back off. The Ashburnites are collaborators. We are under no obligation to show any more mercy than necessary."

The eastern gate awaited them. A light machine gun sat perched atop the parapet, pointed out at the American soldiers-turned-refugees already outside the wall. The gates opened, and the two Tuckers guarding the Americans turned to see the wave of expelled Ashburnites join them. Amos heard the Perkins girl cry out from the crowd in recognition. "Ralph?!? Ralph, you're alive! Ralph!" she called.

"Miss Perkins!" Ralph's eyes widened as he turned from the American exiles he guarded to find her among the Ashburnite herd.

Amos sighed and climbed the ladder to the palisade. Teenagers.

Ralph was already out of position, his rifle down, his head up, darting for a better look as he skirted the edge of the crowd. "Miss Perkins, what's—" He looked up to see Amos atop the palisade gate. "Amos! What's going on?"

Amos didn't bother to answer. "Becky, Ralph, come on back inside. I'm going to give a last farewell."

They both obeyed, Becky with a hesitant glance over her shoulder at the mob now numbering well over a hundred, Ralph at a near sprint for the gate.

Amos began to address the exiled—the condemned—American soldiers and Ashburnite junkers alike. "You've got road, your feet, and the clothes on your backs. The next settlement east of here might be—"

"Amos!" Ralph interrupted, clambering up the ladder behind him. "You can't do this! You won, okay? You got what you needed; just let them go!"

Amos laughed mirthlessly. "That's exactly what I'm doing."

"I won't let you kick the Ashburnites out of their own clan. This isn't right!"

Before Ralph could get to the top of the ladder, Amos placed a foot on his shoulder and shoved him back down. "Take his gun and shut him up!" he snarled. Two Sylvanians pinned Ralph's arms to his side as he struggled. "Your father would be ashamed of you," Amos said.

Ralph stared back up at him with a defiance Amos had never seen from the young McDaniel. "You don't know the first thing about my f—" Someone shoved a rag in his mouth. He continued to grunt useless objections into the gag as the Sylvanians dragged him off.

"Don't take him away, yet." Amos held out his hand in command. "I want him to watch." He raised his voice so the entire crowd of Tuckers, Sylvanians, and terrified junkers inside the wall could hear him. "Let me make one thing clear before I continue. This clan doesn't belong to the trash pickers anymore. It belongs to me, and I decide what happens here."

Ralph, sitting on his knees, his arms pinned to his sides, stared out at the people beyond the open gate, his face turning yellow like the withering autumn leaves.

"Right now,"—Amos turned back to the exiles on the other side of the wall—"you all are hereby banished. On foot, I'm guessing it will take you four to six days to reach the nearest settlement past here, and maybe another three to get to what you think of as proper Federation territory. How you get there, and how to get food along the way, is up to you. Stay here, and you get to talk to a machine gun." He slapped the M249 resting on its bipod next to him. "Go." He waved a hand at them with no further ceremony.

He turned and called down to Becky. "Becky, get up here and—" One of the exiled American soldiers shouted an insult up at him. "Hang on," Amos said. He steadied the machine gun, turned one more time towards the idling mob of exiles, and kneecapped the American who'd dared annoy him. With the American on the ground, Amos took his time lining up his next shot to blow out the other knee. He didn't need any more words to set the rest of the exiled prisoners and collaborators on their way.

Over the receding din, Amos called down to Becky again. "Get up here and make sure I'm not interrupted. I need to focus."

Becky was already halfway up the ladder, her mouth slack and her eyes unfocused. She mumbled the beginning of a question. "Focus on wha—"

Amos shushed her with a gesture as he sat cross-legged on the catwalk and closed his eyes as if to meditate. Presently, his eyes opened again, but the irises had rolled back into his skull, leaving only pale orbs staring out at nothing.

The forest beyond the clear zone came alive with the calls of hundreds of waiting pigmen. An entire shadower army's worth of unbreds hooted and screeched in the brush, and the renewed screams of humans burst forth to answer them. Dimly, Amos heard the gasps, moans, and low screams of the onlookers still inside the walls as his true intentions became clear.

He relished the moment of clarity he bestowed upon his flock as he worked. They needed to know there was no quarter for Amos's foes, to know his instruments were not guns, but the very unbred legions of the apocalypse.

The calls of the hunters and the cries of the hunted steadily converged. Amos willed his army on.

*Click.*

"Call them off."

Amos turned his head to stare down the barrel of Becky's rifle. But Becky stood back several paces, unarmed and befuddled. The one holding the gun to Amos's head was Ella Holland.

Amos sighed. "I thought I told you to keep everyone away, Becky."

"But," Becky pleaded helplessly, "it's Ella." As if that explained a single goddamned thing.

"You leave those people alone, y'hear?" Ella ordered, her jaw clenched so tight it twisted the words coming out of her mouth.

"Or what?" Amos scoffed.

"I'll pull this trigger."

"I don't think you've got it in you."

"One." Ella said, tears of anger or anguish leaving trails in the dirt on her face.

"You want to save those sons-of-bitches? After everything they've done to you? I know better than anyone else. The man who raped you is out there. I'll feed him to my unbreds, piece by—"

"*Two.*"

"If you kill me, the unbreds will go wild. Those people will be just as dead, and then you'll have to—"

"Thr—" Ella's finger tightened on the trigger, even as her whole body trembled.

"Okay, okay." Amos held up his hands in surrender and closed his eyes, and the unbred battle-cries in the forest went silent. Soon after, the terrified shrieks of the humans quieted as well.

Ella kept the gun on Amos until he opened his eyes again. He glowered at her with cold anger. "It's done. Your pets are safe."

The multitude, north of three hundred strong by now, stirred as if awoken from a spell. Many stared up at Amos and Ella, but they also looked at each other like they were just now noticing all the other folks swept along in Amos' abortive blood-frenzy. Most of the junkers simply collapsed or hugged each other in relief.

Ella called out to the crowd, her voice already quivering. "I need some folks to go with me and fetch back the Ashburnites! Mrs. Compton, you out there?"

A hand waved from further on back. "I'm here! Yes, I'll go with you. We have horses stabled back yonder; I can get them ready."

Ralph shook himself free of his stunned captors, tore the gag from his mouth, and shouted, "I'll go with you, too!"

Ella sensed movement at her side and turned as Amos rose to his feet. "*Stupid* girl," he spat. "You think you can order me around 'cause you put a gun to my head? Becky, take your gun back."

Ella looked Becky's direction and saw she hadn't moved. Instead, Becky's eyes darted from Ella to Amos, then back to Ella again.

"Becky, I want you to *deal with her.*"

"Amos, I..." Becky faltered.

"Listen to me. *I* was the one who saved the Tuckers. *I* was the one who rescued the Tucker neurocasters. *I* was the one who beat the Americans. The neurocaster who chased us here—I can beat him now. You want me to finish off the Greenbriers? I can do that, too. But I need you to hang with me. We've got a good thing going. I know how you

169

really feel about me, and I feel that way about you, too. Just trust me a little longer."

Though Ella made no effort to threaten Becky—the gun was still aimed skyward—Becky still didn't move. *They killed my mom, Ella. If I don't pay them back, what else am I going to do?*

*I'm sorry, Becky. I'm sorry about your Ma. I'm sorry about everything.*

Amos pressed on. "Becky, we can't let them go free. You get a bleeding heart, those trash-picking collaborators will stick a knife right into it. And if the Americans go free, you can bet they'll be back. Except they'll send a five-thousand-man army against us next time. I know you like strong men. I'm the *only* man strong enough to stop the Americans. They fear me. You think they're scared of a wispy little goodie-goodie like Ella? She's not made to survive in a world like ours."

Ella locked eyes with Becky but said nothing.

Becky's jaw set and her nostrils flared like her mother's always used to when she dug in her heels. "No, Amos," she said. "I thought—I thought I'd foller you to the end of the world. But I done follered you too far already."

"She's right, Amos," Bill Puckett hollered from the crowd. "This has to stop."

"What about you, Sylvanians?" Amos shouted to the workers. "You want mercy for those American slavedrivers?"

The Sylvanians looked at each other, confused and uncertain. Except for one. "I'm with the boss," said a man who'd previously helped Amos drag Ashburnites from their homes. He nudged the stock of his rifle in Bill's direction. "He's the one who got us free of Armstrong, and he didn't need to leave a trail of bodies to do it. I liked the powdermaking better than the soldiering anyway."

Another Sylvanian joined him. "The government kicked out neuro-casters in the first place, and this is why! I can't believe we were all about to follow some psycho-caster who had the stones to eat someone's mind right in front of us!"

Still another Sylvanian spoke up. "The girl's the one who had our back from the very beginning. The Americans locked her up on our account. If she wants to spare the Americans, I say she's got the right to it."

Amos measured them all with a contemptuous stare. "To hell with all of you," he said. He slid down the ladder and shoved his way through the crowd, disappearing through the doors of the main clan building.

Now, Ella commanded the attention of the diverse assembly. She wasn't sure what to do with it, though the groans of the injured American outside the gate suggested they'd need to do something about him soon.

"Ella?" Becky prodded, her confidence coming back to her by degrees. "I reckon we oughta to haul the whole lot back here, don't you think? We could sort things out in a more reasonable manner then."

"Well..." Ella swallowed. "If it were up to me, I'd give the junkers a pass, but I reckon it oughta be up to the New Ashburnites what to do. Maybe a trial will fare well enough. I don't think the Americans would want to stay if they couldn't be in charge, but I think it would be decent to give them at least a day's rations and some charred spears before we send them packing. We'll need to get the doctor to look after that feller Amos shot, get some tourniquets on them there legs and such. I ain't one for herding chickens, but I think we'll get everything sorted out if we all get organized and everyone has their say."

Bill stepped in, barking orders and taking to the chicken-herding without stopping for breath. The Sylvanians and New Ashburnites jumped into action. When Cora Compton came thundering back to the gates with a couple horses, Bill was quick to direct her outward.

"Hurry on out and tell them the news," he said. "They'll need to hear it from an Ashburnite if they're gonna believe a word of it. Ella, any put-ins you'd like to make?"

"I... I think I'm too wore out to make it any longer." Ella's shoulders sagged as if someone had slung an invisible weight over her back. She held Becky's gun out for her to take back. By the time she'd plopped onto her seat with her legs dangling over the edge of the catwalk, her arms were shaking as if from a powerful chill.

Now, Melissa Daly fought her way through the crowd. "You've done enough, Miss Holland. You aren't going to lift a finger more until you're good and ready. First things first. What'll it be? Food, or a warm bath?"

"Bath," Ella said, shoulders sagging still further. "I want a bath."

Ralph found them about a mile out from town. The exiles had reached a disused watchtower, and Armstrong and some of the senior officers had climbed on top, likely to leave the rest as a buffer for whatever unbred attack they were expecting next.

Ralph wasn't concerned about the people at the top of the watchtower; he had eyes only for the folks at the bottom.

At the sound of galloping hooves and the rattling of dry weeds, the exiles turned as one to face their rescuers. "You're safe!" Cora Compton called out. "Mr. Puckett's convinced the Tucker boss to abide by his original terms! Come on back to the clan so we can sort it all out." It wasn't the truth, but it was close enough. They could work out the details once they all got back to town.

Again, Ralph didn't pay it much heed. He needed to make sure everyone was safe, that all the Ashburnites were okay—that one specific Ashburnite was okay. She shouldn't have been hard to pick out from a crowd. He scanned the junkers without finding her. He felt his heart drop—

"Ralph!"

His heart came springing back and overshot to his throat. There she was, away from the rest of the group, already cast out as a sacrificial lamb for the unbreds. She clambered up from the ditch where she'd been hiding.

Ralph didn't say a word. He jumped down from his horse as Jody Perkins ran up to him. He took three bold steps to meet her halfway, caught her in his arms, and dogged if he didn't kiss her right smack on the mouth.

He'd never kissed a girl before. It wasn't like what he'd read about in books. He hadn't bathed or brushed properly for days. She'd narrowly escaped being eaten alive, and he could still smell her fear.

But dogged if she didn't throw her arms around his neck and kiss him right back.

It wasn't anything like the books. It was a fair sight better.

# Chapter 15:
# In Which Amos
# Realizes the
# Importance of
# Geometry

The rest of the day passed like a long, drawn-out sigh of relief. The Ashburnites, Bill Puckett, Melissa Daly, Ella Holland, the rest of the newly-arrived Tucker neurocasters, even the Americans; all took in the strange new aroma of a place free of cutthroat power grabs and callous retribution.

With a crisis averted, folks tended to other concerns: Ella to a hot bath, Bill Puckett to his workers, Cora Compton to the Ashburnite exiles pulled back from the brink at the last minute. The Brodys, who'd come out of every corner of town back home, gathered together to prepare Ricky for burial. Once Ella was taken care of, Melissa Daly helped distribute rations to the Americans before they departed once again. They had the good sense not to hurl insults this time—the American who'd tried was now a cripple for life—but they regarded her with disgust for her half-bred bloodline as they left.

It was only that evening, when the available Tucker elders and their New Ashburnite equivalents met together with the few folks the Sylvanians had chosen to represent them that anyone noticed a critical missing person.

Amos was gone, along with several wagons, draft animals, and all the proxies.

Ella lay stretched out on a sleeping mat on the super-mart roof, staring at the stars.

"I brought you some soup."

Ella looked over to see Melissa Daly bearing a steaming bowl with mittens. Becky Brody followed behind.

Ella straightened up. "How'd you get that up the ladder without scalding every inch of you?"

"Carefully. Eat up. This'll do the body good." Melissa sat the bowl in front of Ella and backed away, crossing her arms in front of her chest.

"You okay, Ella?" Becky asked.

"Yeah," Ella said in a way that wouldn't have convinced a nomad's patsy. She picked up the bowl and tested a small spoonful of broth.

Becky kneeled down beside Ella and put a hand on her shoulder.

Ella stopped blowing on the spoon and went rigid.

"What's the matter?"

Ella dropped the spoon back into the bowl and touched her brow. "It's nothing, I just—"

"You know what?" Melissa broke in, lifting Becky's hand. "How's about we give Ella some breathing room."

"You sure you don't want some company, Ella?"

"I appreciate you. Really, I do. I... could you go see if Omar's around?"

Becky nodded, concern etched on her face. "Sure, Ella. Whatever you say."

Becky left her with Melissa, who stood several paces off with her arms crossed. Ella nursed a few sips of soup and caught the taste of fresh sage. Her mouth watered, but the soup was still too hot. She set it down and pulled her knees up to her chin, never meeting Melissa's eyes.

"We don't have to talk about it if you don't want to," Melissa said.

Ella didn't answer.

"Mind if I tell you my... side of things?"

Ella shook her head. "I don't mind."

"My first time was when I was ten. My pa. It went on for five years, until a screevler got him. Bert picked me up pretty quick after that. Out of the frying pan and into the fire, they say."

"I'm sorry."

"Was this your first time?"

Ella gave a gentle nod.

"Not what you hoped it would be, huh? First times are dressed-up dolls anyhow. I don't expect you'd've had a much better time either way."

"I didn't... I didn't fight, really. Overstandingly not after the first time. Felt like fighting wouldn't get me anywhere, so I just... let it happen."

"You know what's real bad? By the time I was twelve, I'd convinced myself I really kinda liked it. So who can blame my pa if I went along with it so easy?"

"You were a child."

"Then don't you go blaming yourself either. I spent more than half my life thinking it was all my fault, that I was just a dirty whore whose only use was what was between her legs. If that's how you feel, well, then that's how you feel." Melissa tapped her head. "But you gotta know up here it ain't true, and you don't need to take eighteen years to learn that."

"How'd you learn it?"

"You taught me."

Ella tried another taste of soup and slurped it down. "I'll have to tell Omar."

Melissa pursed her lips. "Maybe you should wait on that."

Ella nodded. "Should I wait until I'm over it?"

"Sure. Until you're over it."

"How long will it take?"

"Dunno. How long ago did your brother die? Your ma? You over that yet?"

Ella sighed. "It doesn't get better?"

Melissa's voice softened with a sigh of her own. "Listen, I don't know much. I barely learned my letters and sums. I know you'll have good days and bad 'uns. And I know for every good day, I'll have a hug just for you. And for every bad day, I'll make sure you get what you need. Company, alone time, vittles, anything. And I know I'll keep that up 'til you don't need me no more. I know you treated me like a clansman when no one else would, and I know I won't let nothin' bad come to you so long's as I can help it."

Omar paced outside the gate to the citadel pathway, the shrinking cinnabar sunset on the jagged western horizon rapidly giving way to a chilly autumn darkness. A rifle protruded from over his shoulder as he walked his patrol.

Becky Brody neared, an autorifle slung over her own shoulder. "Ella wants you," she said, jerking a thumb over her shoulder. "She's up on the roof of the super-mart."

"What's she doin' up there?"

"She's been cooped up weeks. I reckon she wanted to be outdoors, away from folks."

"Then what's she want with me?"

"I don't know, you go ask her," Becky asked, cracking a grin that vanished almost as soon as it showed. A shadow passed over her face where the smile had been. "Any sign of Amos?" she asked.

Omar shook his head.

"Any telling what he's up to?"

Omar shook his head again. "I would have said he'd gone after the Americans on his own, but that seems pretty boneheaded with that other unbred shepherd still on the prowl out there."

"The Pied Piper? You think the Pied Piper might go after the Americans instead?"

Omar shrugged. "Sounds like he was after neurocasters. The only neurocasters left are tucked in here, safe and sound."

"Maybe Amos went to take him out?"

"Maybe."

"You were friends with him, weren't you? Back before the Tuckers kicked you out?"

"As much as I could be friends with anyone, I reckon."

"What is it about him that..." Becky shook her head, trying to find the words.

"He follows his own path, no matter what you or me or anyone tells him."

"That's it. I saw it in him from so long ago, and it..." Becky looked away.

"If it puts you at ease, he probably knows what he's doing." Omar gave Becky a reassuring slap on the shoulder as he walked past her to leave.

Omar was out of earshot before Becky said to herself, "That's what worries me."

Melissa left Ella, bundled against the night chill, on the roof. She brought out soup for herself and Earnest and fed her son at bottom of the closed door leading to the ladder access to the roof. She blew wisps of steam from each spoonful she held up to the bandaged child's lips, murmuring encouragements and promises as he ate up.

Approaching footsteps turned her toward a figure emerging from the dimming twilight. "Hey, Bill!" she called, a smile spreading on her face. "You came to see me?"

"Actually, I... thought I'd see how Ella was doing."

Melissa's smile faded. "I think Ella wants left alone."

Bill put his hands on his hips and looked up the ladder at the roof. His eyes glistened in the moonlight. He looked down again, this time at little Earnest. "How's this big boy doing?" He lowered himself into a squat and patted her son on the back.

"Healing up, slow but sure."

Bill kept on rubbing Earnest's back. "I wanted to say... it was my fault all this happened. With Earnest and Ella and Ricky."

"You already told me that."

"I ain't told Ella."

"You don't have to. Not yet. And... it weren't your fault. Not really."

"Now I don't believe that for a minute. I been trying to tell myself that ever since I came here with that dad-blasted nitrogel. And because of it, Ricky's dead. Ella and Earnest liketa died, too. All for the same hullaballoo that took my Martha."

"But I don't blame you for it. And Ella don't either."

"But I still don't know what to do. I got a mind for the cookery, for the mixin's, for the figures and pipes and glassware. Not for... what matters."

"You were the one who saved the slaves."

"So what'll I do now that I freed my own blasted workforce?" Bill asked, turning toward her, the light of the moon glinting through the thinning hair on his scalp.

"I reckon you'll need to start up the fact'ry again somehow, right? I don't have the head for figures like you do, but I'm sure you'll squeeze teeth out of the operation again soon."

Bill turned away from her, a hand reaching up to massage his creased forehead. "I don't know. I been doing me a lot of thinkin' lately."

When he didn't elaborate, Melissa asked, "What about?"

"About what kind of folks were they who created the unbreds. The oldsters said they was some wicked 'ole jaspers, but I think they was just some folks too clever for their own good, trying to keep ahead of the rest, be the next big thing, show what they could do. Be remembered. Like me." Bill rose from his squat next to Earnest and spat to the side. "Do I want to be remembered for giving armies the tools to kill everybody? Or for propping up a tyrant like Armstrong?"

"You don't have to be remembered for any of that."

"But what would it cost me?"

"More than most folks would be willing to pay," Melissa admitted. "But... Bill, I think the world of you just for asking the question."

"There's a million things I could do with my mix-craft. Good things. I don't have to make nitrogel. I could make fertilizer just as easy. I'll clean this soot off my soul."

"Don't have to use the nitrogel for killing. Could be mighty useful in Johnny Grierson's mine. Could help against the unbreds."

"Maybe." Bill sighed.

"But if you're askin' me, and it seems like you is, I think you really oughta watch out for the real danger: power."

"I ain't ever gonna let someone like Armstrong take over on my watch ever again."

"I'm talking about you."

"Me? Why me?"

"'Cause, Bill," Melissa explained as if stating something that should have been perfectly obvious, "you're going to be a rich man, whatever you do. You'll be rich and powerful and probably famous. And before you know it, you'll have to choose between giving up some power and letting some other rotten feller take it for ornery ends, or get the jump on him and do the nasty business yourself. Armstrongs don't come from nowhere, Bill."

"If you were in my place, what would you do, then?"

"Hell if I know. Have someone close to me I can trust to shoot me straight."

Bill turned a long, penetrating gaze toward Melissa, but not the kind of leering, slimy look she was used to getting. "Yeah," Bill said, his mouth hanging open. "You might be right. Want me to take Earnest in? Get those bandages changed?"

"Go ahead."

Melissa watched him go, carrying her son against his shoulder as if the child were his own. She paced in the night, guarding the white-painted ladder leading up to the rooftop as if she were on patrol. She waited for the one she knew was coming. And in a few minutes' time, here he came, just like clockwork. Just like a man. So predictable.

"Where do you think you're going?" Melissa asked.

Omar nodded up to the rust-bitten metal door behind her. "Thought Ella asked for me."

"She needs some peace and quiet, and you aren't going to help her with either."

"After what she's been through, I figure she has the right—"

Melissa gazed at Omar with disdain weathered by a weariness beyond her years. "You don't got *any* idea what she's been through."

His gaze dropped. "She asked for me, I tell you."

"Ah, bless it. She cares about you for some reason. But you don't care about her. To you, she's just a—a match for you to light up and throw away."

Omar folded his arms. "Where's your ankle-biter?"

"Bill's tending his burns for the night."

Omar stared at her. "Bill, huh?"

Melissa stiffened at his tone. "He offered. Don't you be gettin' ideas."

Omar sniffed. "You ain't foolin' me, and I guess I ain't foolin' you, either. Everybody's twistin' to get somethin' they want." He turned to leave.

Melissa's eyes narrowed. "All I ever wanted was a gentle hand and a kind word. What are you after? Least I can say I ain't gonna hurt no one."

"And you think I am?"

"All I'm sayin' is you better not." She peered after him as Omar left without a word. "You better not, y'hear?"

In the dimness of twilight, a form shifted almost imperceptibly in the brush. Not an unbred, or if it was, not one of his own. Amos reached out consciously—something he rarely troubled with anymore since his army now acted as a mere extension of his will—and checked his unbred thralls acting as his bodyguards. It was like flexing fingers and toes to keep them from going numb. All were compliant, even eager. In fact, Amos often had to quell and ignore the insistent inputs from the hundreds of unbreds acting as his eyes and ears. Before he'd scouted out this area, he rode on a cart pulled by a team of pigmen with his eyes firmly shut. It took all of his concentration, pulling from all his collected proxies, to attend directly to each sight, sound, and smell reaching the fingertips of his vast neuronet.

What moved in the darkness wasn't part of his neuronet, but the fingertip of a different one. A shadower not his own emerged from the undergrowth, but out of deference to the neurocaster Amos was here to parlay with, he didn't try to pull it under his influence. Amos had sensed the Pied Piper's nearby neuronet long before the first tendrils showed their ugly faces. A proxy followed not far behind the shadower; no surprise there. Amos' own proxy rose from its hiding place and greeted it.

Amos spilled his thoughts into the silence between them, the first spark across the synapse. *I thought it was time we had a meeting of the minds.*

*Quite. Why did you send a proxy?*

*Probably for the same reason you sent yours.*

*You've gobbled yourself up quite a network. The proxy you're using is one of the ones I particularly wanted.*

*I didn't know you had claim to this one. You won't get any more out here, I'm sorry to say.*

The Pied Piper's proxy glowed with amused bafflement. *You came to give me an ultimatum?*

*That, or an offer of cooperation.*

*Indeed? Go on.*

*First, what you won't likely want to hear: the neurocasters in this area are under my protection. I shouldn't have to tell you how much power I've accrued since you first tried to subsume me, or even since you tried to catch us all out on the road.*

The Pied Piper's proxy raised its hands diplomatically. *No need at all.*

*The way I see it, we could battle it out between us, my neuronet against yours. And you know at this point you can't win. Or I can help you find greener pastures.*

183

*Such as?*

*When you first escaped the American neurocaster enclaves, the combined might of the Federation military was too much for you to manage. I'm willing to bet that's no longer the case. And who knows how many neurocaster enclaves they still have set up?*

The proxy laughed. Both of them knew how many enclaves there were, or at least, the American neurocasters they'd both subsumed had known. *You want to send me away to plague the Americans?*

*I wouldn't be sending you as much as going with you. I have unfinished business with them. And again, I think you do, too. I know you wanted the Tucker neurocasters as much as the Americans did, but I understand why. I'm willing to put that all behind me. The enemy of my enemy, and all that.*

The proxy laughed audibly. *I knew you could handle yourself, Tucker. Still, I'll admit. I underestimated you.*

The Pied Piper's proxy went limp, the hum of consciousness falling from a bright clarion to a dim whisper. Amos cast about, trying to find where the mind had gone. Back to the root? Or another proxy? Why? Had something happp—

*Sorry about that, Tucker.*

*What happened?*

*Just taking care of some stuff. I look forward to the day when I don't have to keep up this whole hopping between bodies drudgery and LIVE. With every assimilation, I can feel myself coming closer to it. Funny how that is. There's a threshold, for sure. The researchers theorized about it, and I came up with my own theories. But in the end it comes down to a feeling, like—*

The proxy went limp again, cut off mid-thought. Amos concentrated. The Pied Piper's root had to be close, no more than half a mile away, likely less than a quarter. Amos caught the murky signatures of sundry overswayed unbreds scurrying about under the loose influence of the Pied Piper's mind. Something wasn't right. The subterranean sea of assimilated minds boiled up in a frothing tide of noise and disjointed alarm. He detected the aftertaste of Jarvis and Sam Chambers among the wraith-like simulacra. Amos crushed the swell of wails and reached out to see if he could wrest control of the unbreds away, without success. Not that it mattered. He had his own army, and if the Pied Piper tried anything, Amos' own root was well hidden—

*I'm back. As I was saying—*

*What about my proposal?* Amos cut in. He didn't have time for this neurocaster's rambling thoughts, and something made him nervous. *I'm willing to offer you every neurocaster east of New Ashburn.*

*That's a right generous offer, I'd reckon.*

I'd reckon? Amos paced within his proxy's skull. He dropped out of his proxy and opened his own eyes on the first stars winking on in a deep purple sky. He sat up and peered through the thick foliage that covered him and saw nothing amiss. Some two hundred yards down the hill, well beyond his visible sight, he could feel his proxy's faint hum, waiting for his mind to return. The Pied Piper's proxy was still dark, which meant that his mind was occupied with something else as well, somewhere nearby. He could feel the Pied Piper's hum, but without testing the strength of the hum at several distances, he couldn't get an idea of the source.

Wait.

Amos left his body and returned to the proxy at almost the same time as the Pied Piper returned to his.

*What are you doing, Tucker?*

*Trying to figure out what you're doing. Why do you keep dropping out?*

*I'm feeling things out. It's called trilateration. It's a little like bee hunting. It's some math I could do with chalk and slate, but like everything else a neurocaster does, the mind does it more by feeling than thinking about every single little piece. Like how you catch something thrown to you. Your eyes see it, and your hand just knows what to do. Except with what I'm doing, I can only have one eye open at a time, so to speak. But now...*

Amos could *feel* the Pied Piper's laughter, even as it dawned on him what was happening.

*I've found your beehive.*

Amos dropped out of his proxy and jumped back into his own body—to stare into the black eyes of a screevler. He tried to reach for his sword, but his arms were already pinned at his side. He squeezed his eyes shut and waited for the mandibles to clamp around his neck, but the screevler just held him there. Waiting for its master. Amos reached out with his mind and felt the ever-strengthening hum of the Pied Piper, coming in from his left.

He struggled against the grip, but it was useless. He might as well have tried to buck a bullhusker. Pigmen ringed the nest he'd built for himself, cutting off any chance of escape, awaiting his sacrifice. He reached out with his mind for his own army of unbreds and found them stubbornly passive. They had all bowed to the will of a stronger neurocaster.

*Slippery little devil, ain't ya?*

If Amos wasn't about to die, he'd have found the Pied Piper's manner curious. *How are you doing this? I assimilated the entire American convoy!*

*You think that was the only convoy of neurocasters Armstrong sent for?*

Amos struggled again. *You still need me, Piper. You still need me!*

*Just the opposite, really. I can't afford to keep you alive. Should've known a talented neurocaster like you would be too hard to control. Just about made the same mistake the Americans made with me. But here you are: as delicious a will to power as I've had since I busted loose of Armstrong's little science project in Annapolis. And even aside from all that... I've got my own business with you Tuckers.*

Amos could not yet see the Pied Piper, but he could feel him. He couldn't move an inch. Trapped like a rat. Hold on...

Two hundred yards away at their original meeting place, Amos' proxy snapped up and scrambled to its feet. It picked up a nearby rock and kneeled beside the Pied Piper's abandoned proxy. Panting and grunting with fury and fear, Amos bashed in the female's skull with two quick strikes before he sent his own proxy running up the hill as fast as its feet could manage.

How long did he have? The hum in his mind spiked into coherent thought as he came closer.

*I think it'll be fun when the Tuckers return home only to knife all their families in the middle of the night. The Tuckers won't know what hit 'em. Maybe I can leave a couple of them with hale minds, so as no one can tell who's been assimilated and who hasn't. Wonder how long it would take for them to start knifing each other on their own. There you are, little Tucker.*

Amos saw the form of a man hunched over Amos' root just twenty yards further. The man reached out with his hands and placed them upon Amos' resting head. A knife of white-hot pain shot through his mind—whether it was in his own head or that of his proxy's, he couldn't tell; the difference had become increasingly meaningless. He pulled on the strength of his neuronet, but it was too weak. The Pied Piper's network wasn't simply bigger; it was used more skillfully than any neurocaster's brainshine Amos had ever seen. He couldn't resist, let alone try to assimilate the Pied Piper.

He reared back with his proxy and hurled the stone in its hand in one desperate throw, and through the blinding pain and the flashes of the Pied Piper's memory bleeding over his own, he glimpsed the rock sailing past the pigmen, right over the screevler, to its target.

*Word from the nomads about a big-time government operation out east, he'd heard with his own ears. Roundabouts D.C. area, or what used to be D.C. Offering teeth for all manner of information and service, looking for recruits from the mountain clans. None of his kin or clans-*

*men were interested in that kind of rainbow-chasing nonsense, but he had the wanderlust bad, and it didn't sound like folks out east had the same worries about neurocasting his clanfolk did. They'd change their tune if they found a government ally in this part of the mountains. He'd put the Greenbriers on the map, all right.*

The rock connected with the back of the Pied Piper's head. A glancing blow, but enough to knock him over and send a shock wave rippling through the surrounding unbreds. In another moment, Amos was looking down at his own body.

The Pied Piper's root staggered to the side, an arm flailing blindly in an arc around him, his unbred thralls stunned and confused. It was a moment that wouldn't last. Leaving his proxy behind, Amos scrambled to his feet and fled.

Something vicious and sinewy tackled him from behind before he'd made it ten paces. He stared up into the Pied Piper's hollow eye sockets as a pair of hands seized his head. Amos reached up with his own hands to return the twisted embrace and screamed.

In the end, pain was just another kind of talking, all of it merely neurons, all of it of no real consequence.

# Chapter 16: The Siege of New Ashburn

They brought lanterns for the meeting into the space the Ashburnites used for church services, weddings, and funerals. There was no electricity for lights; ever since the Americans had shipped off their methane-powered generator, electricity was only for heating and refrigeration.

Cora Compton and a handful of other prominent Ashburnites sat at the table in the middle of the room. At the other end sat Frank Cooper, the elected leader of the Sylvanians and one of the few who may actually have been a prisoner of war and not an enslaved farmer. Splitting the difference between the junkers and Sylvanians, several Tucker elders settled into their chairs, careful not to scuff up the remnant clumps of polyester carpet still clinging to the floor.

Two folks remained standing: Ella Holland, who kept to the periphery of the lantern-light, and Bill Puckett, who paced as he tried to untangle the threads brought by so many different interests. "Whether or not my factory stays open will depend on how many of you Sylvanians elect to stay," he said. "With the Americans gone, I can warrant better housing. I can almost warrant better pay once we find us new buyers. What I can't warrant, and what worries me the most, is food."

Arnold Brody spoke up. "Bill, it hurts me to say it, but I think we might need to shutter your operation at least until spring. We need to get all the Tuckers back to town, and I think we'll need to send the Sylvanians home as well."

Bill opened his mouth to speak, but the Sylvanian leader beat him to it. "Just as winter comes?" Frank Cooper said. "It's two hundred miles to Sylvania. How are we supposed to make it?"

"You won't," Ella said. "We can't send them out without enough supplies to make safe the journey."

"Short supplies are the reason we'd send them home in the first place. I just don't know how we're gonna keep everybody fed." Arnold shook his head. He looked tired—more than the long trip from home could account for. "We left tons, and I mean actual tons, of food back on the highway when we started running from the unbreds, and the livestock the clan has left is gonna be close to zero. We can go back and see what the unbreds didn't plunder, but I can't imagine there's much. We've lost..." He rubbed his eyes at the enormity of the loss. "So much food. We're gettin' along together now, but after two months of wild turnips, we're liable to go after each other. I know you ain't keen on that, Ella, but them's facts. This'll be the second tough winter in a row for us Tuckers. We can get back to co-operating come spring."

"When I do come back, I'm bringing Sophie with me. I ain't leaving my daughter a widow back there," Bill said.

"I want to get back to the problem at hand," Frank said. "We've lost two dozen of our number due to hunger, overwork, and abuse, not to mention outright execution."

"From the Americans," Cora Compton clarified.

"Because we were slaves. This no longer being the case," Frank leaned back, crossing his arms, "the Sylvanians will not tolerate second-class status, especially not to neurocasters."

"Hey, now," Job Brody said, grief adding an edge to the irritation in his voice. "I just got wind of this neuro-whatchamacallit stuff, and it's looking like that's what done in my oldest son. So don't you be lookin' at *me* like—"

"What Job's saying," Arnold said, interrupting his brother, "is that we can't help being what we are, and we don't want treated like half-and-halfs or junkers."

Cora gave the butcher the kind of dangerous glance Arnold recognized from his late wife—a sort of *I-can't-believe-you-just-said-that* look. "Pardon me?" she asked.

"Oh, you..." Arnold swallowed. "You know what I mean... not talking about y'all... I mean..."

"Again," Frank cut in, "the Sylvanians here are through being slaves or footstools or workhorses. If we want to stay, we stay as partners. If we want to leave, we leave whenever we want. And in either case, we leave with the same provisions you would send with your own people. Is that clear?"

Cora met his piercing gaze. "We don't even have enough food for our own clan. Nomads working with the Americans went off with most of our clan's reserve foodstores. It wasn't too big a problem at the time; we had a trade deal worked out with the Federation, and the supplies came in every seven days without a miss. That's done for now. We here in New Ashburn gave up our only standworthy lifeline to throw in with you."

Frank rose to his feet. "Are you blaming us?"

"No. I want to be sure you're not blaming *us.*"

"My people are not going to go hungry, one way or another."

"Do you know what's sad?" Ella said, staring at the floor as if musing on something for the first time, though she had a hard set to her jaw as she spoke. "There weren't no good reason we couldn't work everything out with the Americans just fine."

"There's no making deals with a bunch of enslavers and imperialists," the Sylvanian leader objected.

"But that's the thing. If the Americans had been willing to work with us instead of treating us like herd animals, they wouldn't be marching back home now with their tails between their legs. We'd all be sitting in clover right now."

"What's that got to do with us?"

Ella shrugged. "Seems to me the best way to end up with nothing is to try and grab everything."

"Okay." The Sylvanian crossed his arms. "That's fair. But someone has to make the first move. Why should we be the ones to sacrifice first?"

"Then us Tuckers will tighten our belts first."

"Hold on, now," Arnold said before Ella could commit the clan to anything too radical. "Let's think our way to some fit and handy workarounds. It's clear to me we gotta get ahold of free nomad clans or another clan who's keen to do business. We got plenty to offer, between the nitrogel and the penicillin—"

"And baking soda," Bill said.

"And baking—baking soda, really? And the Americans' paper and guns they done left behind. Let's figure out what's closest and send us out a scout force."

A knock on the door interrupted the proceedings, and the cacophony of frantic hurrying announced the message before the actual messenger did. "There's trouble outside."

They piled outside to hear a commotion in the factory district—no, farther beyond that, at the wall. A couple muzzle flashes burst in the night, with the pop of their reports soon following.

"An attack?" Cora asked.

"Unbreds," the messenger confirmed.

"Must be the neuro-castrater who followed us up the highway," Job said.

"Neuro-what?" Cora spun, blinking.

"What about Amos?" Arnold said. "Couldn't he—do you think he..." He trailed off. Amos either wouldn't or couldn't save them, and everyone knew it. For all they knew, he was the *cause* of the unbred attack.

"Can the defenders hold?" Cora asked.

More gunshots sparked in the darkness. "Not for long," the messenger said.

"Sound the alarms. Get everyone inside the super-mart. Everyone!"

And so, the guards at the walls carried out their fighting retreat as the last few people outside the super-mart got inside and the Ashburnite folkward battened down their hatches.

Omar fought against the steady current of Ashburnites, Sylvanians, and Tuckers streaming through the wide doors of the super-mart. Ella had gone out with the elders, but she hadn't come back in with them when the attack had started. He called for her, but his voice was lost in the foment.

In the end, he found her as the one unmoving stone in the stream of terrified people. She faced outward, toward the west, staring at nothing.

"Ella," Omar shouted when he got within shouting distance.

She gave him no sign she had heard him.

"Ella, we've got to get inside. They'll scale the walls soon if they ain't done it already."

"I can't go back in there. I can't," Ella said, her gaze still out at the open sky.

"What are you talking about? You were just in there. Come on," he said, grabbing her hand.

She pulled back against him. "No. Don't make me go in there."

Omar turned her to face him. "Listen to me. If you don't get out of your head and move, you'll get chewed to bits, y'hear?"

Ella's neck strained as she looked away from him, trying to turn her whole body away, to run for the hills. But she did hear him. He saw it as the wild went out of her eyes, as they screwed together in focus and anguish.

"We're just going inside for a little bit," Omar lied. "We'll come right back out. Whenever you want."

"Whenever I want," Ella repeated. She took a deep breath and turned toward the super-mart. "I can walk myself in."

And so, as early night turned into late night, Ella and Omar followed the last of the souls into the super-mart and, packed in much too tight for comfort, they sealed themselves inside like a giant tomb. Together they waited until the first dawn of the siege of New Ashburn, Omar sleeping in fits and starts, Ella in a corner next to a bright lantern, her knees pulled up to her chest, eyes wide, unblinking.

A gnarled yellow hedge tree twisted its way out of a dry streambed, and the thorny branches on the leeward side hung down in a thicket that masked someone sleeping underneath. As the sun rose to drive away the clinging mists, the figure shifted and untied the barrier of thorny branches he'd made for himself.

It was William Chitman, the last surviving member of his platoon, and indeed the entire battalion sent west of New Ashburn.

He'd survived multiple shit assignments meant as much to keep him out of the way as to accomplish anything of value. Armstrong had sent him after the Pied Piper on deep recon missions more than once, sent him as a glorified postman back to Annapolis, then again out to the Tucker clan, then back to New Ashburn, then back west with only himself and his proxy still breathing. He'd been shot at, stalked by unbreds, and toyed with by an impish rogue neurocaster. And after all that, where did he end up? Under Captain Royce Carlson's thumb.

Ever true to form, Carlson's assessment of the tactical situation had proven as confident as it had been wrong. When Jarvis had miraculously—Chitman thought suspiciously—returned, the plan was for Carlson to distract the Pied Piper while Chitman took a squad out to strike at the root. This plan was, of course, all dependent on there being only one hostile neuronet out there to contend with. That had not been the case.

So instead of completing his mission, his squad foundered as he detected coherent brainshine coming from multiple directions. Some of it had to be the Pied Piper; some of it belonged to something else.

Geemo activity in the area had spiked, then surged. The pigmen that had swarmed them were remarkably well-coordinated, and they'd all found themselves on their last mags within minutes.

What had started out as a pitched battle became a rout, with his men disappearing one by one. He hadn't even tried to make it back to the convoy. He'd lost most of his men, his proxy, his *second* horse, and a costly portion of his supplies. The nature of the mission had become clear: they had lost, and now the best they could do was survive.

For the last several days, he and his few surviving soldiers had made their desperate way east, skirting around far north of New Ashburn, trying to reach the highway and from there return to civilized lands. He and his last man had attained the eastbound road yesterday, only to find they weren't the first to flee this direction: amongst the pile of bones, scraps of viscera, and a mostly stripped skull, they could perceive a shredded, bloody uniform. The American garrison at New Ashburn had fled ahead of them, with no more success than Chitman's platoon.

And now, he was alone again, his last soldier dead yesterday to a bullhusker. There were so many goddamn geemoes out here, and not nearly enough bullets.

Chitman found a more or less straight branch on the hedge tree he'd slept under, and with great effort, he hacked a six-foot length piece free with his machete. They told you to char the points of any wood spears you made, but hedge trees had such a dense grain, they didn't need charring. If you couldn't or didn't want to make a fire, hedge would make a hard point on its own as long as you could work the wood.

He'd learned that from the hill folk out here. There was a lot to learn from them if one paid attention. He had his orders and understood the Federation's wariness toward such wild savages, but he also respected the way people did things in these parts.

Colonel Armstrong certainly did not see things his way. None of the officers did, which was why he'd been on permanent recon and escort duty, and, as a bitter, ironic twist, was why he'd likely outlived many of them. He was the problem child, the one to be ignored and put away, lest he see and report back to D.C. what was going on.

But now that everything had gone to shit, he *would* go back, and he *would* have a report. He wasn't sure who would survive the journey home—the colonel, Captain Carlson, Jarvis, whoever—but he would make sure he *would* survive, and he would have choice words for every single one of them.

But first, he had to survive.

He slung his automatic rifle over his shoulder—he could only use it now in an emergency—and used his hedge-wood spear as a walking stick as he returned to the highway and continued east. The morning wore on, and every now and then, he spotted the gory splats that marked the final moments of those who'd gone on before him. His jaw set a little tighter for each one he passed, but he marched on, ignoring the evil forest watching him from both sides.

As Chitman passed a massive truck half-blocking the road, he heard something move in the forward cab. A quick investigation behind the safety of an extended spearpoint revealed a resting American soldier, still alive. His gun was gone, his travel pack flopped over the gearshift like a gutted carcass, his empty canteen on the dash. No spear. No tarp or blanket. Chitman could smell the stench of a wound even from the other end of his spear.

"Hey," Chitman said, prodding the man's foot with the tip of his spear.

The soldier stirred and stared with a pale face and half-lidded eyes at Chitman. "Water," the soldier murmured, his gawping mouth barely getting the word past his yellow teeth.

Chitman took his own canteen and, not wanting to touch it to the soldier's lips, measured some out into the empty canteen. Once the soldier had taken a few sips, Chitman asked, "Can you walk?"

The yellow-toothed soldier returned the question with a gormless stare, his canteen held in a limp grip. His jacket and pants were shredded and stained crimson-brown.

Chitman looked away, then turned back. "I can't stop, and you wouldn't make it even if I did. You know that. I can... I can make it quick. Just nod if you want me to."

It was a minute before Chitman got his answer. The soldier's eyes flared wild, and he growled, "*You did this.*" He leaped from the truck cab, brandishing a knife with a final burst of strength.

Chitman ducked backwards in time, darting away as the soldier struck out with impotent slashes far astray of the mark. The soldier finally sank to his knees, utterly spent—a picture of hopeless defiance.

Chitman shook his head and moved on, leaving the wretch to his fate.

The carnage along the road continued—apparently Chitman wasn't the only one to have left that soldier for dead—and the unease returned, stronger this time. He couldn't understand why the soldier had accused *him* of this calamity, as if Chitman was the true enemy, as if his offer to help had merely been that of a predator toying with his prey. Had they even known each other?

*You did this.*

He finally understood when he sensed the familiar glow of a nearby brainshine. It was harder to pick it up without his proxy; whatever it was had to be close. When he came to the disemboweled corpse of a soldier tossed up into a tree, its arms and flayed skin crucified on bare branches like a scarecrow, Chitman's shoulders sagged. This wasn't pigman work. No more sense running.

He sighed and turned to face the pigmen he knew were there, following him. There were more than he'd expected.

With one fluid motion, he dropped his spear and unslung his rifle as the pigmen charged. He placed each round carefully—one shot, two, three. The fourth missed; the bugger hopped to the side. The bolt clicked on an empty chamber, and Chitman ejected his mag while pulling free his emergency black powder mag. The black powder mags were for last-ditch situations, and not just because they lacked the power of the old ammunition.

The space between Chitman and the geemoes turned smoky as he fired off a spray of bullets, backpedaling away from them. The fouling and inefficient burn rate would wreck the barrel's service life, but that was the least of his worries. More immediate was the jam that stopped him halfway through the mag.

He tried a manual cycle, but that caught, too. With the foremost pigman within twenty feet and closing fast, he went back for his spear. That slowed them down, but it didn't stop them, and he couldn't backpedal fast enough. He drove the spearpoint home through a pigman's torso, but it only made the geemo angry. While still skewered, it grasped the shaft with its gnarled opposable thumbs and wrested the spear from Chitman's grip.

Chitman reached for his machete, too late. They surrounded him, divided his attention, and caught his flank. A pigman got inside his arm reach and tore at him with its claws. The claws, curved like talons, hooked on his clothes and opened up deep gashes in his flesh, though he could barely feel the cuts. Maybe this wasn't the worst way to go.

But the pigmen didn't finish him off. They merely kept his arms and legs pinned, with the extras scurrying aside to make way for their master. *The* master. He ambled up to Chitman, grinning and eyeless.

"Oh, my God," William Chitman said, raising his hands in supplication.

The Sylvanians, the Ashburnites, and the Tuckers together found new common ground in the same place that had threatened to divide them: their suffering. Chill morning brought the changing of the guard—one man slapping the relieved watch in a wordless, plodding gesture of solidarity. Regardless of rank, origin, or manner of speech, everyone ate from the same stew the clan cooked in its giant kettles every day. They huddled together for warmth without respect for past allegiances or animosities. Neurocaster, ubermensch, and half-breed alike all united against the horror that lurked beyond the walls.

It was days before the collective garrison of New Ashburn—now pushing well past a thousand souls—could venture outside the super-mart. Ella Holland spent those days alternating between silent staring and frantic pacing, and neither Omar, nor Becky, nor her own father could shake her from her state. The only one who could calm her nerves was Melissa, who watched over her like some mix of older sister and guard-dog.

When sharpshooters and pikemen had given the unbreds enough of a bloody nose to convince the horde that the treeline outside the walls made for a better staging ground than inside, Ella was one of the first to break free of the cramped quarters of the super-mart.

A further week stretched on with no break in the siege, and Ella spent her days up on the super-mart roof, watching the comings and goings of the guards and the workers tending to essential tasks. She carried no weapon with her, but folks still felt her stern eyes as they might have felt the watchman's. Ella even slept up on the roof when the weather was warm enough. The weather did not cooperate for long. Soon the nighttime temperatures fell, and the super-mart interior took on the faint but pervasive stench of stale air and the multitude of bodies living in perpetual proximity.

In the vacuum left by the Americans' departure and Amos' disappearance, new lines of power coalesced around what were now the de facto leaders of each population. These bonds strained with the passing days, but nevertheless mutual need and Ella's unspoken vigilance held them fast. A grim but steady resolve settled upon the people, a resolve that promised to hold, provided no surprise right hook caught them in the ear.

The surprise right hook came a week later.

Clouds hung heavy in the bleak sky as a woman strode up to the eastern gate from the direction of the old hydroplant. An escort of pigmen accompanied her. She asked to talk to the leader of New Ashburn, but the leaders of all three groups assembled to hear her message. Even Ella came down from her perch to listen in. They all gathered while the visitor stood outside the eastern gate, under the guns of two white-knuckled Sylvanian guards atop the parapet.

The weather promised a chill turn. The proxy regarded the guns pointed at her and the biting wind tugging at her thin frock with the same detachment. When she judged the leaders sufficiently settled, she spoke, anticipating the leaders' question before they'd asked it. "Are you ready to hear my terms?" the strange woman asked.

Mrs. Compton looked left and right, opened her mouth to speak, and, in the end, nodded her assent.

"I don't care about New Ashburn. I'm after the Tucker neurocasters."

Mrs. Compton sighed. "Why am I not surprised?"

"Whoever you are," Bill Puckett cut in, "you can't have 'em!"

"I've already got one. Good luck finding which one." She waved a dismissive hand at the settlement they guarded. With a simple utterance, she'd proclaimed the neurocasters a greater threat than all the unbreds outside.

"I'll get them all," the proxy said. "The only question is how many Ashburnites and Sylvanians die before I eat."

# Chapter 17: Cold Comfort

Ella paced a well-trodden path along the super-mart rooftop, stopping at intervals to survey the somber horizon or pull up the collar on the padded coveralls Melissa Daly had scrounged up for her. The heavy *clunk* of footsteps on expansion steel grating turned her toward the roof access door.

It opened to reveal a dour Job Brody. "Mind if I join you?" he asked.

Ella patted the chest-high rooftop ledge. "Go ahead."

Job walked over and leaned next to her. "Pardon my language, Miss, but this is a head-first dunk in the shit-house."

Ella didn't answer.

"I can't even... I can't even grieve my son. Or my brother. Or my father."

"I understand." Ella waited for Job to say why he really came. The leaders had come up more than once since the siege began, looking for advice, or more often to ease a guilty conscience. She was willing to offer the former, but had less and less patience for the latter.

"That woman... she didn't say much, but it was enough to get near everybody at each others' throats."

"You don't think that's what she wanted?"

"She wants us. The Tuckers. The neuro-whatsits."

"That's what she said she wants, but that isn't really it. She—the Pied Piper—wants us lesser humans to scatter and set against each other. Because the very idea of us holding together threatens the whole point of the Pied Piper existing."

Job shook his head. "I don't go out of my way to wish these folks harm, but ain't none of this is lookin' good. It's lookin' like last winter's siege, with more mouths to feed, less food to feed 'em with, and a bigger army surrounding us. I don't want to say it, but this axle won't hold true. The only question is, who's gonna jump the cart first, and why shouldn't it be us?" Job Brody said.

"That's wicked talk."

"Come on, Ella. It's real talk. If we're going to be fighting each other for scraps, best do it earlier, when there's still food to be had. You know the Sylvanians are already having this very talk. We're a bunch of Jonahs to them. Toss us out to save their own hides; that's what they're thinkin'."

"If I had my druthers, I'd have every Tucker hanging from the palisade before I murdered an entire town's worth of people," Ella said, her voice as cold and unyielding as a headstone.

"That's not what I'm saying, I—"

"Then what are you saying?"

"All I'm saying is, haven't we suffered enough? Ain't it about time we quit having everything taken from us and take something back for once?"

"You think them Sylvanians ain't had everything taken from them? You think *I* ain't suffered?" Ella's voice rose, the hard bite of anger sharpening her words.

"Ella, I'm sorry, we all care about you. We just—"

"I suffered plenty already. I'm about fed up with the suffering. But you know what I'm fed up with more? I'm fed up with *Tuckers*. I'm fed up with *clan*. I'm fed up with y'all being so tough when you're fighting a battle, only to show less backbone than a soggy worm whenever an outsider needs a pinch of decency." Ella turned away from Job to pound a fist into the ledge. "Everybody thinks they're fine folk, but when they have to choose between the right thing and their own life—or even their own *comfort*—they'll choose their own good-for-nothing hind end every single time. And then they'll go on and say they ain't never had a choice, to hide the truth that they're all cowards and pushovers. We call ourselves warriors. Ain't a warrior among us what'll fight any battle what matters."

Job faced off with her, anger and pain and grief vying to gain purchase on his face. "So we just lie down and take it?"

Ella squeezed her eyes shut and balled her fists against the rooftop ledge. Her head stooped, but the tension coursed through her body. "*Yes*. That's what I'm saying." Ella righted herself stormed off. "If anybody's hungry, they can have my rations. I done lost my appetite."

When Omar didn't find Ella on the roof, he found her in the next likely place: curled up in the corner on the floor of the room she'd had when she first came to New Ashburn, her back up against the unpainted OSB plywood walls.

"Don't blame you for coming inside. The air out there's taking a turn for the chilly."

"I'd like to be alone for a little while, Omar."

"What happened?"

Ella didn't look at him, only stared in front of her and gave him a slight shake of her head. "Don't take it personal. Just not up for talking."

"That's good, 'cause I ain't here for talking." Omar reached back out into the hall and produced his banjo. "What'll it be? 'Daisy May, Maisy Day' makes for a tune."

Ella shrugged. "Just noodle around a bit. That'll do fine."

Omar obliged.

Ella sat and stared at nothing while Omar plucked away at the banjo, stopping now and then to adjust a tuning knob. He tried a few different licks before ambling his way through some bump ditty variations on a melody he'd once practiced with his kin. It was a tune that had always reminded him of home.

"Are you here because of the neurocaster?" she asked.

Omar finished a phrase on his banjo before he stopped to consider his answer. "I came... because I figured you could use a little something to salve the mind. The only time I ain't seen the whites of your eyes these last days is when you look like you're making a caterpillar outta your eyebrows."

Ella cracked a smile and looked over at him for the first time since he'd entered. "That's sweet of you. Just got a lot on my mind, is all." Her smile sagged. She rested her chin on her knees.

"Music goes a long way to help."

"I'm glad you're thinking of me. I really am," Ella said. "But I'm afraid you can't fix what's wrong with me."

Omar hit a dissonant note and tried again. "I'm sorry to hear that."

"It's not your fault."

Omar nodded, this time not meeting her gaze. "Who's fault is it?"

Ella didn't answer.

"I won't tell anyone if you won't."

Ella exhaled deeply. "Nobody's. Everybody's. Sometimes there's nothing to do. The way of the world, I guess."

"It is what it is."

"Yeah. It is what it is."

Omar clawhammered a couple strings. "The elders are meeting soon to see about the neurocaster. I don't expect what she said to do much for the fellow-feeling."

Ella shrugged. "The elders can do whatever they want."

"They'd let you have a say."

"I've said my piece. If I opened my mouth right now, nothing too nice would come out."

"Not feeling too charitable, huh?"

"I shouldn't feel this way, I—"

"At this point, I'd say you can feel whatever way you damn well please."

"Okay, fine. I feel like God ain't finished punishing us ubermenschen for what we done, and there ain't a single soul in this place who deserves to make it out of here alive, but everybody will still have the crust to think they're being dealt sore. I feel like I could say what I think until I'm blue in the face and it won't make no difference, 'cause folks only listen to you when you have power and mean to use it. I feel like I ain't hardly ever spoke up before because I knew, deep down, nobody would care to hear me."

"I care to hear you."

Ella's eyes shot up. "Did you care to hear me when I asked to be alone?"

Omar pursed his lips and scratched at his jaw. He nodded and stood without meeting her eyes. "You got me."

"I'm sorry, Omar, I didn't meant it like—"

"Don't have to explain. I asked for it. Take care, Ella." He picked up his banjo and left her in her corner.

"Everyone simmer down now!" Job Brody shouted to calm the horde of people jabbering and jawing and nigh-on panicking outside in front of the super-mart. He wasn't the only elder shouting for calm, and he'd been shouting for some time now. Finally, he loaded a charge of powder without a ball and blasted it skyward. That did the trick. "Now, all of you, listen up," he yelled, his voice carrying over the cowed audience, the pungent fog of gunsmoke heavy in the air.

Mrs. Compton raised her voice. "The woman claims to be the proxy of a neurocaster called the Pied Piper. He says—or she says—she'll let us all go free... if we give up all the Tuckers."

"Over my dead body!" a Tucker man shouted, threatening to send the crowd back into pandemonium.

"*Shut up!*" Job Brody hollered. "Now, we ain't settled on any plan just yet, and we got ourselves a lot of things to decide on before it comes to something like that."

"But we're running low on food as it is, and can't no one go outside the walls with bullhuskers watching the gates!" an Ashburnite woman with a baby at her breast wailed.

"This is why us Sylvanians got rid of neurocasters in the first place!" someone else shouted.

The tenuous hold the elders had over the mob failed, and once again, the crowd fell into an arguing, shouting, jumbling mess. Some folks came close to blows.

Amidst the confusion, Omar Walking broke free from the group, heading north.

Omar stopped long enough to retrieve an American autorifle and a pistol he'd hidden away near the wall before he slipped outside the postern door on the north wall. With the chattergun slung across his chest, his matchet and pistol at his side, and a bow and quiver strapped to his backpack, he shifted his muzzle-loader to his left hand and followed the path out east across a bend in the river, toward the landfill, before turning north once again.

.

# Chapter 18:
# In Which
# One Hare-Brained
# Scheme Runs
# Contrawise to
# Another

I n a secluded tangle of bracken, Omar worked the action on his American automatic back and forth, feeling for grit or wear that might cause a jam. It was flawless. He fed a single round into the firing chamber and racked the charging handle to eject the round. A smooth, satisfying *click* sent it spinning free. Omar snatched it out of the air and admired the steel and composite feat of deadly engineering he held in his arms. He would save this as a close-range, last-ditch weapon, and not just because the ammo came dear. He figured the gun could hit targets well beyond that of his musket, but he didn't trust himself with an unfamiliar weapon. He'd seen and even held a couple guns like this before, but folks would not waste ammo to train him on it. Same with the autopistol holstered under his brown duck overcoat.

He took a deep breath, inhaling the scent of fallen leaves touched with the first blight of decay. He reached into his pocket and rolled the white porcelain chip between his fingers.

A distant rustle in the dry scrub to the south had him whirling in an instant. He dropped into concealment as he scanned the calcareous scree he'd descended minutes earlier in this trek beyond the walls of New Ashburn. Was something following him? The valley channeled the winds cross-wise to the hill, so he couldn't get a whiff of whatever it was.

He waited, stone-like. He'd kept the pan on his musket primed for smart action. He would need less movement to ready his rifle, and so was less likely to tip off his stalker, but his bow would be quieter, and so less likely to alert every blasted creature within half a mile. He pinpointed a scuttling several stone's throws uphill, judged his quarry to be alone, and elected to use the bow. Still prone and careful to keep his eyes on the moving figure, he bent the yellow Osage Orange bow against his outstretched foot to string it.

He fitted an arrow and waited. He stirred one numbing leg to restore feeling while the figure resolved itself to the form of a person. His brow furrowed. The human figure by degrees showed to be a woman. A woman with light loamy hair, wide eyes, and a graceful oval face.

Omar cursed under his breath. Ella was dressed in padded workman's coveralls and carried a stuffed backpack, but no weapons that he could see.

He stood once she'd wandered within earshot. "What the hell do you think you're doing?"

Ella's head snapped toward him. "Omar!"

"Sssh! Tamp your pipe."

"Watch your language." Ella altered her course and picked her way down to him, keeping her arms out for balance.

"What do you think you're doing?" Omar asked again in a cautious voice once Ella had reached him.

"Helping you hunt the Pied Piper. Saw you trying to sneak away while I was out on the rooftop. Don't know how you thought you'd find him without a neurocaster."

Omar felt the chip in his pocket and thought better of telling her what he was thinking. "I've got a plan, and it didn't allow for dragging a stuck plow behind me."

"Does it allow for getting 'et by unbreds? 'Cause you ain't gonna make it far with just your good looks. You need yourself a neurocaster to keep the unbreds away."

"Then why don't you go ahead and break the siege, if you can control the unbreds so good?"

"I can't really *control* them, just push them away. And even then, I reckon it's only thems what's close enough for me to see."

"You ain't steadying my nerves."

"Unless you want me going all the way back by myself, your nerves will have to put up with me. I'm coming to help."

Omar shook his head and muttered about how his better judgement was leaving him, but he handed her his chattergun—he figured, as a gunsmith's daughter, she'd be more familiar with it than he—his hunting knife, and his autopistol. He kept for himself his musket, matchet, and bow.

"Here's what we do," Omar said, his voice still low. "We move up that hill over yonder. Get a lay of the land. Move to the next hilltop, and so on. You don't speak unless there's an unbred about to skin you alive. You stay right on my tail, eyes up. And neither of us pees or takes a dump outta sight of the other'n, y'hear?"

Ella made a face, but she shrugged and nodded. The pair set out combing through the denuded brush and snarled deadfall. Upon finding a narrow hollow carved into the mountain by the steady hand of trickling ages, they moved upwards, shielded beyond fifty yards on either side by the edges of the hollow.

Twice they stopped at pigman calls close enough to make their hoots and growls almost sound like some form of speech, speech humans had never fathomed but which nevertheless carried some meaning. Ella and Omar ducked low both times, Omar's buckskin and weathered brown coat and Ella's drab coveralls blending in with the winter thickets. Once, while hugging the ground, Omar glimpsed a detachment of pigmen through the timber skirting the edge of the hollow. Their going was slow, incremental. The whole time Ella remained silent behind him, at times only her fogging breath reminding him she was there at all.

They stopped at noon to munch on a brief repast of hard biscuits washed down with water from a plastic jug Ella had packed. He hadn't planned on taking this long, but then again, he hadn't planned on tending to Ella, either. From their vantage point, he could see a fair stretch down one side of the hill under an even canopy of low-growing pitch pines. The far side of the hill across the hollow lay half-obscured from him, a final dome that rose away from them in a slight grade before cresting on a forlorn glade with stones poking through thin soil like bones through the hide of a rotting carcass. Around them, they still had plenty of cover.

Omar took a swig of water and whispered to Ella. "Need to pee?"

Ella nodded. "You first or me?"

"You first." He pointed at a more-or-less private spot, then the gun she carried with her. "Keep low."

She sighed. "You don't need to tell me." She made her way over to the densest bushes, setting the autorifle up next to a great elm tree. Omar turned away and scanned the downhill slope.

He cradled his musket in the crook of one arm and touched the porcelain chip with the other hand as he surveyed the woods. What had before been an uncertain plan was now an all-fired mess. That girl was just as likely to attract unbreds as drive them away. He weighed the worthiness of slipping away now, with her pants literally around her ankles.

His hand went from his pocket to the stock of his rifle. Down through the twisting, narrow trunks of the pitch pines, something moved. A hunched, ape-like form, but with a familiar bipedal gait and those cursed grasping, clawing hands. Had it seen him? It loped in an unhurried gait over fallen logs, its blunt nose turned downward toward the ground, for now. Omar restrung his bow.

It came closer, uphill, heading straight toward him, still apparently unaware of him. Maybe something beyond sight drew it his direction, something to do with the girl. The memory of his discovery by a pigman swarm a year ago trespassed his mind as he nocked an arrow. Just as now, it had started with a lone pigman and ended with him nearly becoming unbred dung.

It was still beyond his ability to hit with any surety. If it turned back now—

The pigman stopped, looked up, and locked eyes with Omar. It was still too far away for Omar to see the whites of its eyes, but he thought he could still see an eagerness there. It was a smaller one, just a young shoat. He reached into his coat pocket, withdrew the chip, and held it aloft, a white flag of truce. Human and pigman regarded each other in frozen silence. Ella rustled in the bushes behind him, now finished and coming to take his place.

Omar returned the chip to his pocket. "Stay down," he said without breaking eye contact with the unbred. The rustling behind him ceased.

The unbred started up the hill again at the same unhurried pace, this time cutting across the slope to sidestep Ella and Omar. They watched it, themselves rooted in place, as it attained the crest to the north-east of them and disappeared over the curve of the bald.

Omar motioned for Ella to follow, and she nodded. The short trek was no more taxing than usual, but his heart was hammering in his throat by the time they'd trailed the pigman over the patchwork of lichen-covered bedrock and hardy grasses at the top of the hill. Once they'd reached the military crest on the other side, he beheld a winding valley dropping down beneath them with the steepness of an ax-head.

A couple hundred yards below, a network of abandoned brick industrial buildings hugged the far hillside across a bottomland of cracked asphalt and tall grass. Ella tapped Omar on the shoulder and swept a hand in an arc over the knot of structures. She didn't have to say anything. He was no neurocaster, but with her, he knew: the Pied Piper was somewhere down there. She could sense it. Omar gave her a thumbs-up and scanned the nearby woods for the pigman they had tracked.

It was hard to pick out its hunched form, not because it was too distant or because the cover screened it from his sight, but because the hillside below them *squirmed* with its kind. Were they all attending to the Pied Piper, or—

The swarm charged up the hill at them as one. The scout had merely led them into an ambush. Clever little bastards.

He expected Ella to cry out, but she stepped forward next to him and closed her eyes, one hand on his shoulder for support. The touch was light, even tender, in the face of coming death. Her eyes and mouth pinched together. A vein stood out on her temple as she brought her strange shine to bear.

The wave of pigmen, already struggling up the steep incline, faltered. It crossed Omar's mind that having a neurocaster on hand might have been worth the while after all. But the pigmen rallied and continued up after them, if at a slower pace.

Ella gasped, her eyes darting open. "I can't—he's too strong. The brainshine's so bright."

Omar glanced to their right along the slope. The grade steepened even more sharply, and a stony rock outcropping jutted outwards from the defile like a craggy bastion. "This way," Omar said.

"They're after *me*, Omar," she said. "You don't have to—"

"The hell I don't. Follow me." Omar seized her by the elbow and dragged her along. She got the idea.

The two of them tore through the undergrowth, using their advantage in elevation to stay ahead of the pigmen. Their pursuers made no war cries, no barks or hoots or shrieks, only the rasp and rattle of a hundred pigmen clawing their way after them in an inexorable wave. Neither of them had the fast-twitch genes which allowed a body to outrun a horse for short sprints. Ella panted next to him, taking large strides to avoid fallen branches and buried vines, holding the chattergun she carried slung close to her side with one arm, the other arm pumping in wild swings in her headlong flight. The outcropping loomed closer. Maybe thirty yards. Twenty yards. Ten.

Now he heard grunts and unhuman panting ahead of him, and a pigman appeared on the stone precipice overhead. It stood above them a moment, toned muscles bulging under the coarse hair of its arms, rough claws clenched into fists.

It leaped from its perch before Omar could bring up his musket.

# Chapter 19: Stuck Between a Rock and a Hard Place

There was no time to think, only react, as the pigman dove through the air from the boulder overhead. The creature slammed into Ella, who'd had the presence of mind to sling her gun forward to ward off the full force of the strike. The pigman's pounce sent her reeling backward, tumbling down the scabrous slope toward the approaching swarm. Omar dropped his musket as he unsheathed his matchet and, grabbing Ella's booted foot in one hand, slashed the pigman through the side with the other. The unbred fell, howling, down toward its brethren clambering up to meet him.

Ella scrambled to her feet as she unslung the autorifle and thumbed the safety.

"No time to lose," Omar panted, picking up his musket, "up over the rocks."

The two of them resumed their ascent, sweat now pouring down their faces despite the winter chill. As they crested the lip of the flintrock outcropping, another pigman appeared over the edge to meet them.

Its head shattered in a pink mist at the thunder of Ella's gun, fired from the hip at point-blank range. Omar bounded up the last few steps to see one final pigman scurrying off the flat, barren prominence, leaving them the masters of this natural stronghold, for now. He turned and gave Ella a hand up.

"Cover me. Make your shots count," he said. He dumped his entire quiver of arrows onto the ground around him and nocked an arrow.

The autorifle boomed again, and the pigman at the head of the approaching swarm toppled like a house made of straw. Ella swept the barrel to the next target, her face set in grim purpose. She fired three more rounds—*boom boom boom*—and the surviving pigmen at the vanguard balked at the fearsome firepower. They retreated backwards, but not down the slope.

Omar drew sixty pounds and nailed a pigman on the run. He took a moment to watch the horde navigate around the boulders scattered around the sides of the outcropping, making their way to the earthen rampart connecting the hillside to the precipice on which Ella and Omar made their stand. He drew another arrow and drilled a pigman clean through, though it only made this one angry.

He reached for his musket, drew a bead, and dropped the wounded pigman to make sure the rest got the message: back off. So rather than assaulting straight down onto the outcropping, the pigmen scattered among the trees on the hillside above Omar and Ella, taking cover behind the sturdy trunks.

"Reloading," Omar said, pulling a paper cartridge from his pack and tearing it open with his teeth. He dumped the powder into the muzzle and stopped. He heard a claw scratch against stone.

"Behind you! The cliff!" Ella shouted, spinning with her gun.

"Watch the woods! I'll watch the cliff." Omar snatched up his matchet and peered over the brink to see a dozen pigmen scaling the scarp like ants, the foremost unbred within a couple feet of the top. Omar kneeled and cleaved the pigman's skull in two with his heavy blade. Another darted up alongside its fallen comrade, and Omar sliced its arm open to the bone. The others stopped, neither climbing back down nor advancing, but waiting beyond the reach of his steel.

His ringing ears quivered again at the report of Ella's rifle. He turned to see a pigman, foolish enough to have left cover, squealing on the ground about thirty paces distant. He spun in a circle to observe their surroundings. No unbreds negotiating the stones and boulders falling away from the sides of the natural fastness on which he stood. He finished his reload and slipped the ramrod into its groove. About half a minute, all told. With a breech-loader, he could have cranked out at least three shots for every one these simple muzzle-loaders could fire. Not that it mattered much. There were far more unbreds than either Ella or Omar had bullets, and he didn't trust his matchet-work.

"How much did you shoot?" Omar asked.

"Four, maybe five rounds, I think?" Ella answered, her gun held steady on the uphill trees hiding a gathering number of pigmen. The creatures flitted from cover to cover, working their way forward, keeping their profiles low.

Omar pulled the chattergun's ammo pouch from his back and plopped it next to her. "Top off your mag. I'll cover."

Quick as a flash, Ella ejected the magazine and pulled a handful of bullets from the pouch. It was only once she'd started feeding them into the magazine that he noticed her hands trembling. He watched the woods, daring the first unbred to make a move and take a ball between the eyes. At this range, it was easy shooting, and they only had one straight lane of attack.

He heard the skittering sound of claws on rock behind him. They were trying to sneak up on them again, but he'd been waiting for it.

Without even making a full turn, he lunged backward and drove the stock of his musket into a pigman's ribcage like a battering ram. He felt bone crunch. The unbred sailed backwards over the ledge two full yards before plunging down into the forest below. A second pigman climbed up to his left on the heels of the first. Omar pivoted on one foot and two-handed his musket barrel as he brought his gun around in a savage tree-chopping swing. The gun stock connected with its head with a loud *crack.*

Ella tapped the magazine on the hard ground and clicked it into the receiver. She gave it a wiggle to make sure she'd seated it aright, then resumed her shooting stance. The girl knew how to get steel-eyed when the times called for it, he had to admit to himself.

He turned back to the cliff and saw three more pigmen retreat down the rocks away from him. They were waiting for him to turn his attention elsewhere. He had no spear, fool that he was. He picked up his bow and one of his arrows scattered on the ground and sent the shaft straight down into a pigman's throat. The rest backed all the way down and took cover beyond his sight line.

"Good on your end?" Ella asked.

"For now. You?"

"They ain't moving. I think we got 'em corralled."

"But they're the ones who can out-wait us. Sure you can't push them back with your weird mind tricks?"

"I could try, but I don't think it'll do much good, as close as we are to the Pied Piper."

Omar looked down at the decrepit huddle of brick buildings peeking through the canopy of bare branches between the cliff-side and the valley below. "We did get close. So close."

"Looks like there are more pigmen coming. Got ourselves quite a—" Ella broke off as a heavy footfall almost below their range of hearing thumped up on the bald overhead. Then came the crack and crash of a hulking body charging through the brush.

Omar seized his rifle and pulled the hammer back to full-cocked. "Looks like they ain't out-waiting us after all."

Ella backed up along the precipice until she was shoulder-to-shoulder with Omar. She raised her gun and sighted down the barrel.

The bullhusker broke from the treeline at a full sprint, and Omar fired his musket at the same time that Ella held down the trigger on her chattergun for a full auto salvo. Even if they'd killed it right there, though, its sheer weight and speed would crush them as it careened across the outcropping.

"Over the edge!" Omar shouted, tugging at Ella's left arm.

The two of them hopped down the sharpest ledge, slinging their guns over their heads in as fluid a motion as they could manage while diving for their lives. No sooner had they dodged down the cliff face than the wounded bullhusker rocketed over their heads and plummeted down to the waiting hillside below.

But the bullhusker was merely the tip of the spear. The pigmen sheltering below scampered up after them, and the host in the forest broke for the rampart leading out from the hill. They were attacking from front and back. Omar reached over and, still clutching the rocky outcropping for purchase, heaved Ella back up. She wasn't fully on her feet when the first pigmen reached her. She fired into them from the hip, kneeling, unbalanced, in full auto. Omar couldn't believe she didn't pitch backward off the cliff. But the old-world ammunition did its grisly work, punching through the unbreds two or three at a time, mincing their charge to a gory mess. The bodies piled up, and their fellows clambered over the fallen to get at her, slowed, but not yet stopped.

Omar reached to pull himself up, but a pigman grabbed his ankle from below, pulling him downward. He tried to shake it loose. No good.

"Little help here!" he shouted.

Ella righted herself and turned to see the pigman dragging Omar back down away from her. She lined up a careful shot and blasted the unbred wide open. Omar forced his way to level ground as Ella spun to face the charging unbreds again, but her bolt clicked on an empty chamber. She'd fired the last round to save Omar. Their spare bullets lay scattered over the rocks and among the stubbly grass from the bullhusker's charge.

In a single fluid motion, Omar stood full upright in a stride that put himself between her and the unbreds, unsheathing his matchet and opening a pouncing pigman from belly to jaw. He cinched the wrist-strap of his matchet on down and lowered the blade, daring the next pigman to try something.

And try they did.

Omar's first swing passed clean through the first's throat, his return stroke lopping off an extended arm at the elbow. His third went lower, tearing open an unbred's stomach. He was careful to avoid ribs, vertebrae, hips—anything that might get his blade stuck, even for a moment. If he couldn't kill, he wounded, and if he couldn't wound, he swiped the empty air close by to remind them what lay inside the reach of his arm. He cut his assailants to ribbons with rapid slashes, nothing fancy. Blood arced through the air with each swipe of his blade. An arterial spray hissed in the winter breeze. His nose caught a metallic scent. His arms ached. A pigman made a bold move, and Omar two-handed his weapon and unstitched the creature's head from its shoulders.

The wave of pigmen piled up on the precipice, forming a tightening crescent around Ella and Omar. He heard Ella scream and whipped his head around to see still another pigman dragging her back toward the edge of the prominence. Her gun lay on the ground, the ejected magazine half loaded. He stepped to help her, but it was ground he couldn't afford to give. A pigman grasped him around the middle and pulled him away from her.

Omar glimpsed flashing steel, and the pigman wrestling with Ella fell away with the hunting knife buried in its shoulder. Omar rammed his matchet into the guts of his own adversary and shoved it off his blade. But the distraction had afforded the horde the window they needed, and they closed in on him faster than he could bring his sword to bear. A chitinous, segmented arm pinioned his own, and he found himself staring into a screevler's sunken eyes. He fell to the ground.

The screevler's skull-like mandibles opened, but instead of biting, it spoke: "I'll let you go if you let me have the girl. I'll have her anyw—"

Omar grabbed one of the fallen arrows with his free hand and gouged the creature through one of its beetle-like eyes. His sword arm got free as the shrieking screevler threw itself back. He tried to get to his feet, knowing pigman claws awaited him, but Ella hollered behind him, "Stay down!"

Another ear-shattering rattle of gunfire tore through the unbreds. This time, their ranks broke. The surviving pigmen beat a hasty retreat to the cover of sturdy boulders and tree trunks, where they could wait for more reinforcements and begin their attack anew. The sudden peace tingled. Quiet and still, but only from the shock of the last wave and the taut threat of another yet to come.

"How many in the mag?" Omar said, gasping for air and getting to his feet.

Ella popped the magazine free of the magwell and checked the top before reinserting it. "A few." Wisps of smoke rose from the sizzling barrel, and he could smell the tang of scorching metal.

Omar gathered his scattered supplies and reloaded his musket. He raised the touch hole to his mouth and blew soot from the barrel. Tore open the cartridge. Dumped the powder down the barrel. Placed the paper and ball over the muzzle. Forced them down together with the ramrod. Sprinkled primer in the pan. Closed the frizzen over the primer. God, his arms ached.

But the attack had stalled, held off, for now. He scanned the ground for more ammunition for Ella's gun. Five rounds. Maybe there were more in the pouch—he picked it up—no, it was empty. He had a good thirty cartridges for his smooth-bore musket, but he couldn't keep up a fire rate to keep off another attack without the chattergun covering him.

"Ella."

"Yeah?"

"You got eight rounds in the autopistol. If you have to use it, don't shoot more'n six."

"Why?" she asked, but when she turned to meet his gaze, understanding flashed across her face. One bullet for him, one for her.

Omar collected his remaining arrows and counted eight. He nocked an arrow and rested on his knees. "Now we wait."

"Think we could make a break for those buildings down yonder?" Ella asked.

"I reckon there's a couple hundred unbreds between us and the Pied Piper, if that's what you're thinking. He won't let us get to him unless he wants us to."

"He'd let me get to him."

"Not before he had you stretched out between a rut of hefty pigman boars, nice and helpless."

They shared a silence between them while they watched the surrounding unbreds spying on them from behind trees and the heap of corpses forming a gruesome barricade. Omar stood and walked to the ledge. No pigmen or screevlers showed themselves on the face of the cliff, and the bullhusker lay groaning some thirty feet downslope.

"Omar, if... if this is it..."

"This ain't it. I'll think of something. Top off your mag; I can cover."

The unbreds made no move, and some of them even withdrew. But they maintained a watch to ensure Omar and Ella could not escape. And so the afternoon wore on, the early winter sun skimming the southwest horizon as the shortened day drew to a close, the temperature dipping with it. The wounded bullhusker's bellows rose and fell in intensity, becoming weaker as the hours passed. If he'd had plentiful ammunition,

Omar would have put it out of its misery, but this was not the place for him to be wasting ammo.

They took turns with the water Ella had brought with her, and Omar took the liberty of relieving himself off the side of the precipice. Ella claimed not to need a break, and he didn't question it.

"Why you think they haven't rushed us again?" Ella asked as the first stars winked on in the darkening sky.

"Don't know," he answered, scratching his chin. He had himself an idea, though.

"Figure it's a good sign or a bad 'un? I reckon it can't be too bad, seein' how we're still breathin'."

The waning daylight gave way to moonlight, and still the pigmen only watched, their eyeshine glinting in the gloom. Omar and Ella took turns again urinating, and this time Ella had the misfortune of having nothing better than a pair of largish rocks to serve for her latrine and Omar's turned back for privacy. The hours went by in a sludge, and still the unbreds waited, unmoving. Several of the pigmen piled on top of each other and slept, using their body warmth to stay comfortable. At the base of the cliff, another rut of unbreds nuzzled under the exposed belly of the bullhusker's corpse. Even dead, the brown fat on a bullhusker could activate with the right physical stimulation and keep the body warm for many hours. As the cold began to bite, Omar wished the hulking creature could have had the decency to die up on the cliff with them. Omar and Ella's breath fogged the frigid air. Ella lay prone, her gun propped up against her backpack for support.

He paced to keep himself alert and circulating. His mind was getting fuzzy. "You keeping warm?" Omar asked.

She didn't move as she spoke. "Warm enough. I'm just so doggone *tired.*"

Omar looked down at her, then kneeled, shifting his gun to his other hand. He slipped a bare hand down the back of Ella's coveralls.

Her reaction was immediate and visceral. "What in blue blazes you *doin?!?*" she shouted, spinning around on the ground and bringing the gun dangerously close to pointing Omar's way.

"Sorry, sorry." Omar backed away. "Checking for hypothermy, is all."

"Well, you could've warned me. Your hands are like ice." Ella repositioned herself. "Maybe I oughta be checking *you* for hypothermy."

"I'm sorry. You had me worried."

"Ain't a gal allowed to be tired without hands all over her?"

"You're allowed."

"Well, I'm awake now. Sheesh."

The quiet returned, and it stretched with an insistence on its unending duration.

Omar cleared his throat. "You know I would never, uh..."

When he hadn't finished his thought for a full minute, Ella asked, "Never what?"

"Never... you know... do you that a-way."

Ella laughed without her normal gentle cheerfulness. "On these rocks, with a dozen unbreds watching? I wouldn't think so."

"I know, but you came off strong when—"

"Your hand was just cold. That's all."

Omar nodded and went back to his pacing while Ella rested her cheek against the polymer stock of the chattergun. He heard her sniffing in the raw air. She wiped her nose on her sleeve and sniffed again.

"It's just..." Ella said, and her voice was thick with tears.

"What? What's the matter?"

"I just... why didn't you come?"

"I tried," Omar said, though his words came hollow. "I saw them take you away. I didn't know what would happen to you. It... hurt me... every day you were in there." It was all limp excuses, and he knew it.

"I thought no one would ever come. I kept hoping for someone to come, anyone but him, and end it. And I *saved* him, Omar."

"You done more than I ever would have. But you saved a bunch of Ashburnites 'cause of it."

"But I didn't do it for them. I did it for him."

"Why?"

"Because I felt like I had to. I thought I could forgive him. But I can't." There was a venom in Ella's voice he'd never heard before. "I hope he rots in hell." And like a dam breaking, she burst into tears.

Omar reached down with an uncertain hand and patted her on the back, and though she didn't flinch this time, her hackles went up like a frightened cat. He withdrew his hand, then tried again, then backed off for good. Ella went on weeping, her shoulders heaving while Omar looked on, useless as tits on a boar. Her sobs gave way to hiccups, and then those stilled as well, just as a dim pink band shone on the eastern horizon.

Ella's shoulders were rising and falling now with the regular breathing of exhausted sleep. Her forehead burrowed into her backpack now, her chattergun lolling to the side.

Omar stood up and stretched his aching limbs. He shook off the fatigue clinging to him like a cloak, stepped forward, and raised his porcelain chip a final time.

A pigman stepped out of cover as if intrigued.

"I want to talk to the Pied Piper, dammit," he said, growling like two grinding millstones.

The pigman motioned for Omar to follow, and he did, leaving Ella alone on the precipice.

# Chapter 20: He Who Digs a Pit

Omar followed the pigman in the dim twilight of dawn down the hill past the scattered corpses of the attackers he'd knocked off the rocky escarpment. Other pigmen watched him along the way, but they remained resting on their haunches, somewhat like sitting dogs, yet somewhat like squatting humans, their sinewy arms rested upon their knees. Omar and his unhuman guide walked in silence into the complex of disused industrial buildings, long since stripped for parts. A concrete-lined drainage canal ran along the path, the two joining where a retaining wall had collapsed and the earth spilled out into the channel. A two-story brick building lay not far beyond, its shattered windows staring back at Omar like empty eye sockets.

The valley turned gray with coming morning light. A small footbridge mottled with rust traversed the drainage ditch further down, past a mass of brambles clogging the path and canal. The pigman leading him climbed down and crossed up the other side without looking back to see if Omar would follow.

Omar jumped five feet down and found a spot where a stout tree root threaded its way down into the fissured cement wall of the canal. He seized hold of it and hoisted himself up. He looked either way to see if aught were amiss, and, at an unsteady ease, swung one leg up, followed by the other.

He stepped around the rusted chassis of an old truck and crossed a wide open space to the brick building, bypassing junk so thick with weeds it had nearly returned to nature. The area lay still and quiet, but the air was thick with the scent of pigmen and other unbreds. Omar walked along the wall of the brick building, sidled up to one of the yawning portals, and risked a gander. The dust on the floor had been scuffed, either by footprints or paw prints or both. His pigman guide was gone, nowhere to be seen.

"Clint?" Omar said in a low voice, nearly a whisper. "Clint, you there? It's Omar."

A metal door lay askew on one remaining rusty hinge. He checked from the window to see if there were any nasty surprises rigged to the doorway inside, but he could see none. The empty complex around him was quiet as a graveyard, so that his own heaving breaths sounded like cursed-loud gasps.

"Clint?" Omar asked again. No answer.

By the time he'd rounded the corner and stepped through a gap between the door and the frame, his labored breathing grew choppier, hitching and halting with each step. Despite the early winter chill, sweat beaded on his face and neck. He stood just inside the door a few moments, the musket in his hands trembling.

"Clint?" Still no answer.

He risked a single step forward. Nothing happened. Gun gripped in both hands now, he continued on into the murky interior. Rubble and broken glass crumbled underfoot like dry crackers.

"Dammit, Clint. It's me, Omar."

Something shifted on the floor above him, the sound of it conveyed down the stairs more leisurely than a creak should. Omar tested the steps, found them firm, and crept up.

He had neared the top when someone spoke out of the shadowy silence and made him jump. "Omar Walking. It's been a while." The smile was a thin mask, the friendliness in his voice even thinner.

Omar reached the top of the stairs enough to see through the shattered railing. The form of a man sat cross-legged on the floor, hands delicately perched on its knees in some sort of obscene zen. Through the shrouded gloom, Omar could see the man staring back at him through black holes where the eyes should have been.

"Decided to get out while the getting was good, Omar?"

"What the hell, Clint? Your unbreds liketa chewed me to bits out there."

"You had something I wanted."

"Yeah, I want to talk to you about that."

"Don't worry. My unbreds won't eat her. I want her brain working long enough for me to absorb her shine."

"Listen. I need her and some of the Tuckers alive. The formula—"

"Ah, Omar." The Pied Piper shook its head in amused resignation. "Your cops and robbers act is cute, but your job is obsolete. You *know* this battle's over, and I've won. You wouldn't have tried to escape otherwise. If I want the formula, I'll rip it right out of her mind. Just like that Tucker neurocaster and his neuronet I snacked on. Coming here to help you out proved to be worth my time. For that you have my thanks. Now you just need to get out of the way."

"So Amos really is gone, then." Omar fingered a chink in the buttstock of his gun.

The Pied Piper cocked its head. "You seem nervous, Omar. You never seemed like the nervous type to me."

"You, uh, talk... different. And if you don't mind me sayin', you don't look—"

The Pied Piper struck out with a foot at a skittering black speck on the floor, killing it instantly. The Piper snatched up the still-wriggling cockroach and munched on it while it spoke. "I'd hook this meatbag up to feeding tubes if I could." He gestured to himself. "All of them, really. Eating stopped being interesting to me over a year ago."

"You don't seem like Clint no more."

"I understand your uneasiness. In a very real sense I no longer am Clint, the same way you are no longer the little squid-like creature that grew in your mother's womb. Put yourself at ease. You don't have the brainshine. You're inedible."

Omar coughed. "Do you still think of yourself as—"

"I can see right through you to the other side. I know why you're here. You, the Tuckers, the Americans, the Greenbriers, everyone. When I finally convinced the clan elders it was really me, they wanted to use me as a radio. A *radio*. It's like watching worms figure out what to do with an oxcart. All of you are like little spiders spinning webs on a burning pyre, oblivious to the growing fire underneath. No understanding, no foresight, no vision."

"Then why'd you talk to me in the first place?"

"It's amusing."

"I reckon your new... understanding... hasn't given you a high regard for your fellow man?"

"That would be hard, given that you need a healthy contempt for humanity to become what I am at all. All the men, women, and children whose minds I consumed, all the insights into their memories and personalities before I absorbed them or scrubbed them all away—profoundly uninteresting. The mind is such a weak, paltry thing, only useful for—"

Omar blew the top off the Pied Piper's head with a well-placed shot from his musket.

A moment of ringing silence curled in on itself like a wisp of swirling gunsmoke before Omar let out a sigh.

"Sorry, Clint," Omar said to the sprawled corpse, "I'll be seein' to things my way. No hard feelings." He turned to leave.

"No hard feelings at all, Omar."

The voice behind him jerked Omar around again. An old man hobbled in from the adjacent room, ignored and forgotten until now. It was the body of Old Man Brody, but something alien had scrubbed away and replaced the essence of the old man. Something sneered at Omar from behind those eyes.

Omar tripped over the lopsided door as he fled. The rifle slung across his back wedged in the crook of the doorway, keeping him from struggling to his feet, and he cast it off with a curse. He ran back the way he'd come, angling toward the drainage channel with no other thought in his mind than putting as much space as possible between him and the thing he'd spoken with.

His mad flight kept him from noticing the charging bullhusker until it had nearly taken him in the flank. Only the barest twitch saved him as he ducked under a long tusk and sidestepped the great moving mass in a crouched, whirling pivot, his right toe sweeping a broad arc in the dust. The bullhusker's attack roar swept over and through him, so much so he could feel the thrum coming off its body like sweaty heat. Omar changed course as he came out of his spin and sprinted back the way he came before the bullhusker could turn its knotted head and ravenous maw to strike at him again.

Outrunning a bullhusker was a fool's task, and outmaneuvering it only bought time. Omar streaked past the entrance to the building and plunged into the dense jungle of a towering canebrake that had taken over the parking lot beyond the dilapidated industrial building. If he could only break line of sight long enough, he might get away.

The bullhusker hit the copse of cane behind him a few skinny seconds after he did and charged into the thick of it in a straight line. Omar dove to his right quick enough to dodge the bullhusker's charge a second time, but not quick enough to escape the bullhusker's notice. The bullhusker wheeled around, tearing the grasping, rope-like weeds straight from the earth in flurries of uprooted soil and rubble while Omar zig-zagged through the brush. The remains of another chain-link fence stopped Omar in his tracks in the middle of the head-high grass, but the fence proved to be his salvation. Omar was already pushing to his right again, heading out of the weed thicket, when the gigantic unbred wrapped itself up in the same mess of twisted wire and steel poles. Omar pulled out his matchet and scythed his way out into the open again, where the concrete still more or less held the vegetation at bay.

He sprinted for the concrete drainage ditch again, the sounds of the bullhusker's furious scuffle with its rusty net propelling him forward with renewed vigor. Omar stutter-stepped at the edge to find a spot where he could drop down without twisting an ankle and thanked his stars he hadn't leaped blind. Just under his feet, a swath of thorny bushes had taken over this side of the canal.

He looked up at a flutter of movement among the ruins beyond the canal. A child in a ragged shift climbed past the remains of a cinder-block wall. An adult with a drawn face followed the child, then another kid after that. Omar spun to scan the area around him. Faces and figures of people emerged from the buildings at all sides, laughing at him, mocking his pathetic efforts to escape.

A horde of neurocasters, hollowed out like a gourd and filled with the Pied Piper's noxious soul, closed in on him with the mechanical steadiness of a ratchet crank.

A couple proxies blocked his path to where the canal ran clear of brush. He looked to the opposite side of the concrete ditch. It was a long jump, but he could make it with a running start.

He hesitated for one second, but a second was enough for the pigman to get him. From behind, the unbred appeared as if from nowhere and sent him flying headlong into the drainage channel and the waiting brambles below. Omar's sword left his grip as a thicket of thorns rushed up to meet him. He never touched the ground; a thousand tiny points broke his fall, suspending him like a living scarecrow. He reflexively jolted back off the bed of thorns with a curse. His feet broke through and hit more or less firm ground, but whip-like tendrils peeled his britches and coat sleeves up over his calves and forearms as if they wanted to skin him alive. The wooden shards and splinters of snapped twigs submerged him up to his neck. The air that finally found its way into Omar's lungs spent itself on a howl.

The pigman snarled and looked for a way down the sheer retaining wall. The unbred found a collapsed section a hundred feet back and skittered down the earth that spilled through. Now it only had to find a way through the thorns to get at its prey. As small as it was, it would find a way in much faster than Omar would find a way out.

Where was his sword? He saw a glint a mere ten feet beyond his reach, nestled in its own bed of needles.

Omar looked back at the eagerly grunting pigman and gritted his teeth. He put one hand over his eyes—those would not heal as easily—and charged forward with something between a scream and a growl gurgling up in his throat. A thousand wooden claws and talons grabbed his feet and arms, raked his face and neck, slowly stripping the exposed flesh from his bones as he fought through the brambles for dear life. His right foot tangled in a fibrous web of thorns and was not there when he needed it. Omar pitched forward again onto one foot. Omar ripped his leg forward in fury and agony, only to have his arm caught by the sleeve on another thorny branch. The sweat from his forehead stung the cuts around his eyes.

Something that was not a branch grabbed his foot, and he felt claws that were not wooden. Omar summoned the strength of a bullhusker and leaped for the sword. He pulled against the hungry pigman and reached out with his hand through the bramble, into the tightest nest of thistles, and laid a hand on the hilt of his sword. Finally! Take this you—a thorny whip seized his wrist mid-swing. He jerked it free, shredding his hand still further. The pigman crawled its way up Omar's body, heading for the throat.

"Not like this. *Not like this*," Omar snarled as he kicked the unbred back in vain.

Omar rolled onto his back as best he could and kept the creature down with one hand while he tried to get his sword into a stabbing angle with the other. If he could only—get—free—

A gunshot cracked, and the pigman jerked off of Omar, dead in an instant. Omar rolled away from the twitching body and heaved a breath of relief and agony. At the prodding of his living razor-wire cage, he began to pick his way out of the thorns.

"You okay?" Ella asked, the barrel of a rifle she carried still smoking.

"Just help me get out of this, for God's sake," Omar gasped as he pulled vines off him with trembling hands and arms.

When he was out, he picked broken thorns out of his hands, arms and legs with sputtering curses. "I think I done crawled through every inch of stickers there is."

"You look terrible."

"Good. That's how I feel."

"Here, let me see your hand. Can you walk?" Ella asked as she tried to help him to his feet.

"Everything hurts," Omar said, wincing as he took a tentative step. "What are you doing here?"

"When I woke up, you were gone. Wasn't hard to figure out where you'd gone, and the pigmen didn't stop me once I headed your way."

"Shoulda stayed put."

"Last time I did that, I lost someone I cared about very much."

Omar winced again with the next step. "I—I messed up."

"It's okay, Omar. It's okay."

He held his arms out from his sides, every movement painful. "I don't know what to do. That thing is just taking its time. It's cat-and-mousing us."

"It's okay," Ella said again, brushing debris from Omar's shoulders and dabbing at his dirty, bloody hands with her sleeve. "You tried, and that's the important thing."

"I... Gimme the pistol. I can slow them down for you if—"

"I'm not leaving you behind."

"Amos would."

"I won't."

The two of them hobbled under the arch of an overpassing railway bridge. "Thanks," Omar said.

Footsteps approached, and from either side of the canal, the Pied Piper's proxies arose to watch the two limp along. They were men, women, and children. Some well-fed, some skin and bones. Some of them were bald American neurocasters, others, strangers from who-knows-where.

Ella paused and looked up at the many eyes of the Pied Piper. "Which one of you wants to speak to me?"

"Any one of me will do," one of the male proxies began. "It's all the same to me," finished a female proxy from the other side of the canal.

Ella looked behind her and spotted Old Man Brody's body on the railway bridge they'd left behind.

"You got Mr. Brody?" Ella said mournfully, then sighed. "I guess I'll talk to him. Let's get this over with." She let Omar down easy, propping him up against the concrete wall of the ditch and placing his pistol and the chattergun with him. "You'll need these more than I will."

Omar grabbed Ella by the wrist as she tried to leave. Their eyes met. "I'm not gonna let him do it to you," he said.

"Omar, trust me."

He let go of her; he couldn't have resisted much in his state anyway.

She climbed up onto the bridge and stopped just short of the halfway point in front of Old Man Brody's body.

*You wanted to speak with me?*

"I'd prefer to do this with spoken words, Mr. Piper."

"No need to be formal with me, Ella Holland. I've known you all your life. Watched you grow from a little slip of a girl."

"You're not Mr. Brody."

"I've kept of him what was useful to me. Just as I will keep of you what is useful to me. Which, I must admit, is not much. A silly bargain, trying to save the lives of loved ones by offering your own, as if you held anything of worth to me."

"And yet, here you are."

"Your boldness intrigued me, nothing more. Holding off my cabal of shadowers without any training was impressive, for a neophyte. And I'm curious about how you managed to resist assimilation by the Americans. But everything else about you is so conventional," the old man let out an affected sigh of exasperation. "Your obsession with slave morality, your stubborn altruism, your rambling thoughts of love, love, love—it's a sticky sweetness." He smacked his lips in obnoxious exaggeration. "Quick to draw grime and filth. In the end, you are naught but a tiresome thing. Boring, childish, and blind."

"Perhaps, from a certain point of view."

"From every point of view except your own, it seems," the Pied Piper said. "Oblivious to the fact that your very weakness, your very personality, everything in your worldview was handed down to you by your DNA, by those traits selected by scientists to conform to a bygone ideal of a saint. There's nothing you have that's really yours."

"I can agree with you on that. Every good thing I have has been given to me."

"And even what you have will be taken away."

When the conversation stopped, Omar raised the pistol to shoot. But Old Man Brody hadn't laid a finger on Ella yet. The two stood there, staring at each other, their bodies rigid. Omar expected a scream, or an utterance, or at least some kind of tremble from Ella, but she remained motionless.

Rather, it was Old Man Brody who trembled. A spasm shook him, and without any sound or further fuss, plunged headfirst into the concrete ditch. At the same time, Omar heard the thud and thump of a dozen bodies hitting the ground. A couple of the proxies spilled over into the ditch around Omar, one of them right next to him. He didn't need to check the pulse to know what had happened, but out of shock and disbelief he did so anyway.

Dead. The proxies were all dead.

The Pied Piper was dead.

And Ella stood in the morning light above the corpses as if she hadn't even broken a sweat.

# Chapter 21: A Thorny Subject

By the time Ella had returned to Omar, he'd understood. "This was your plan all along. You weren't going as sacrifice; you were going as bait. Amos was right, what he said about you. You can't be assimilated, and you knew the Pied Piper couldn't force it."

Ella shrugged. "It ain't magic."

"And just like that, you killed him?"

"I don't know if I would go that far. He brought it on himself. All I did was give him a little nudge. I hate to see it happen, but it was all over for him but the shouting. These neurocasters"—Ella said the word as if she weren't one herself—"know the whole is stronger than the parts, but they think the only way to get the whole is to crush the parts. I don't understand how folks so smart can't see what lies at the end of that road." She heaved a breath heavy with pity. "I hope Mr. Brody's found some peace."

"Why didn't you tell me your plan?" Omar asked.

"Well, I didn't know *for sure* it would work. And you wouldn't have believed me if I'd told you, would you?"

Omar closed his eyes and shook his head gently against the solid wall at his back. "Probably not. 'Cause I'm an idiot." He worked loose a fragment of a broken-off splinter from between his knuckles.

"Tell you what," Ella said, sitting down next to him and leaning her head against his shoulder with a sigh of deep—but contented—exhaustion. "You work on listening to me more often, and I'll work on making sure I'm heard. Deal?"

"Deal."

The two sat in silent companionship for a while. Ella made no effort to remove her head from Omar's shoulder, and he made no effort to shift out from under her. The hard concrete and dry weeds and cold gray weather made for poor resting, but the morning's toil had drained both of them.

"I never told you about the neurocasters. About what they could do." Omar said.

"I don't blame you. I don't reckon you were too keen to cross Reverend Brody."

"I could've warned you once we were out here. Just didn't think the Americans... would ever go that far. My old clan, we kept a close watch over those with the brainshine. You grow up in that, you never think one feller would up and cross that line, let alone a whole empire."

"I had warnings a-plenty. You grow up in a clan like mine, it gets hard to accept that you're an ubermensch, let alone a neurocaster."

Omar nodded. Easy moments passed them by like a lazy stream.

"You worried about the unbreds?" he asked.

"Without the Pied Piper? Not right now. They're confused and scared. It'll take a day or so before any shadowers around carve up the army for themselves."

"Never thought of an unbred as a thing to get scared."

"Someday we'll have to deal with the fact that these critters carry some sliver of God's image. But I'm too tired to think about it now."

"Then go ahead and rest."

The silence returned long enough for their mutual body heat to bleed through their clothes and warm the other.

"This is nice," Ella said, as if there weren't a dead body lying not fifteen feet away and Omar weren't still oozing blood from many shallow cuts.

"We should get back," Omar said, though he made no effort to get up. He did make some effort to pick at another sliver of wood in the back of his hand.

"Do we have to? Back to the arguing and fretting and fussing?"

"I do like the quiet," Omar admitted, then hissed as he got the sliver free.

"About last night..."

"We don't have to talk about it if you don't want to."

"I do."

Omar pressed his hand against a cut on his temple that hadn't stopped bleeding. "I'm sorry about last night. Wasn't thinking."

"Omar, for once in your life I wish you'd do a little less thinking and a little more feeling." Her rebuke came gentle and jocular.

"I don't have much experience with this sort of thing."

Ella snorted. "I can tell."

"I'm sorry."

"I'm sorry, too. Shouldn't have snapped at you."

"The situation was a mite tense."

"It was, wasn't it?"

They both chuckled and returned to their quiet contemplation.

"The other night, after I'd been freed," Ella spoke into the calm between them, "I was up on the roof to look at the stars. Why didn't you come, Omar?"

"Figured you wanted to be alone," he lied.

"See, that's what I'm talking about. Always assuming no one wants you around. I wanted this," Ella said, patting Omar on the hand. "I was sad and wanted a shoulder."

"Mine in particular?"

"I reckon so. Really, why didn't you come?"

"I want... I wanted to. So I could tell you I was sorry. For what happened. I can't imagine... what it was like in there..." Omar's body grew stiffer as he spoke. "'Sorry' won't cut it, but it's all I could think to say."

"'Sorry' would have been enough."

A cardinal sang off in the distance, but the bugs this time of year were quiet. The morning air was heavy in its stillness. "It ain't enough," Omar said. "You tell me so 'cause you're a sweetheart, but it ain't enough."

"On its own, I guess. But just you sittin' here, keepin' me company, does me more good than a heap of sorrys."

Omar nodded, and there the two sat, but the quiet had taken on a feverish hum. His back stayed rigid. "If everything were on the level, I'd be glad to comfort you. And go on sittin' here with you to watch the sunrise, and stay here all day until the stars came out again. Be a right honor, even. But I ain't so sure I should be the one."

Ella finally turned to look at him, though he didn't meet her gaze. "Why, Omar?"

He pressed his lips together. "I'm a coward," he said as dispassionately as if he were judging the wind.

"You just went out on your own to try and face down a wicked neurocaster by yourself."

"That wasn't brave. I thought I knew what the neurocaster wanted and figured I could pull a fast one on it. Every brave thing I done, I done with my back to the wall. I fought the unbreds alongside your clan 'cause I had nowhere else to run. I went after the shadower with Amos 'cause I had to or get my neck stretched. I ain't never done nothin' without a thought to how it would get me ahead, or at least keep me quick. I've always told myself it was what needed to be done, that I was being smart, that I had to pick my battles. It's how I coped. But you knew, right when I made a deal with that one-eyed half-and-half to spy on Mr. Puckett back when. Gotta do whatever it takes to save my own hide."

"You saved my life."

"No, I didn't. Amos did, when he came running in with his army of neurocaster slaves. I mighta helped with the uprising against the Americans, but that was because they'd got their use outta me and wanted to get rid of... witnesses. Really, I'm more of a collaborator than any of the Ashburnites were, and saving you was just a... side thing."

"I ain't talking about none of that. You saved me long before all of that. When that pigman jumped me last year. Back when you'd scarcely known me more than an hour."

Omar's gaze fell.

"A coward's just somebody who's got nobody more important to look out for than himself. And for a drifter, that's just the way life is. But you ain't a drifter, not anymore."

"I ain't left my drifterly ways behind."

"You don't want to?"

"Don't know how."

"It ain't obvious? A coward don't care about anyone more than himself. Care about someone more than yourself, and you ain't a coward anymore. It's just love, is all."

"Ain't that simple."

"Ain't it?" Ella said, leaning closer to him. "Last June, the Greenbriers raided the Hadley farm. I got caught in the wrong place, and my horse threw me way out in the open. A couple Greenbriers rode up to finish me off. Somebody came up over the hill and drove them away, and I'll be darned if I didn't think it was you."

The tendons in Omar's neck stood out. "I was banished and long gone by then. You know that."

"And only a fool would've hung around to make sure the clan what banished him was safe. What could've made you do such a thing?"

Omar shook his head. "It wasn't me. One of your own clansmen."

"Nobody took credit for it, and there was plenty of cause to."

Omar made to jump up, but winced at the cuts and lacerations on his hands, arms, neck and face. The pain only gave his protest more heat. "Then it was marauders, or a guardian angel, or whatever! Whatever it was, it wasn't me, and you oughtn't make more out of me than what I am."

"What are you, Omar?"

"I'm a coward and a collaborator and a treacheratin' little weasel. I'm a waste of your time. I ain't gonna do nothin' but break your heart. I didn't want to make you feel better that night up on the roof because I knew... *this* would happen. What the Americans did to you, you didn't deserve any of it, and the last thing you need is to heap more hurt on yourself by running to a turncoat like me for comfort, y'hear?"

Ella stood as Omar looked away. "Cowards don't fess up to being cowards, and weasels don't fess up to being weasels, neither. And I already knew all of that anyhow. I *know* you've been lying to me, Omar."

Omar stayed firmly facing the other direction to hide his face, lest he betray something he didn't want to.

Ella continued. "I know Melissa thinks you're up to ornery business. Even got me to make a copy of Bill's notes in my own journal in case you ran off with 'em. I expect you were working with the Americans so you could steal Bill's formula, maybe to sell it, maybe 'cause they put the screws to you. Melissa would likely say you only saved me to get at the notes I hid."

"What are you gettin' at?"

"There comes a time when folks have to settle on how much they trust each other. You were just honest with me, as honest as I've ever seen you. Now, it's my turn. I wrapped Bill's notes in oilskin together with my own copy and hid it behind a loose stone back at the railroad bridge, where you and I once talked about how clever and stupid humans were. You can fetch it for Bill if you want. I'm a smidge too tired to go after it myself, and I've set on trusting you."

Ralph McDaniel picked up a yellowed, friable copy of *Nature* magazine from the littered floor of New Ashburn's sprawling library and returned it to a shelf where he assumed it belonged. The unbreds had worked over most of New Ashburn outside of the citadel and the supermart, feasting on what they could and making a general mess of what they couldn't. Amid the siege, the cleanup of the library had been low on the to-do list. Now came the breathing space to allow for the task, a task his father would have deemed a waste of time. Or perhaps not. He picked up a stained hardback and examined the spine.

"Did you hear the unbreds are retreating?" A young female voice came from behind him.

He turned to face Jody Perkins and nodded. "Becky Brody told me. She weren't exactly sure how it happened, but she seemed a bit upset."

"Folks are saying Omar and Ella killed the neurocaster, but your friend, Amos Taylor, he had to sacrifice himself so they could do it."

Ralph turned away from her. "Yeah, that's a good enough story for the Tuckers. It'll help them heal. We'll memorialize him when the exiles get on home again. He can join the rest of the nice little lies we've kept."

"It's not true?"

Ralph turned back to her. "At the end, do you think Amos Taylor would have sacrificed himself for anything?"

Jody didn't answer.

"Becky's lost a lot of kin. No need to make it worse by giving her sweetheart an untidy ending."

"Well, not every ending has to be untidy." She drew up next to Ralph and slipped her arm around his. A frisson of exhilaration ran up his arm and down his spine. "If you're feelin' pondersome, I can go," she said.

"No, your company's good for the melancholy."

"Will you be leaving with the other Tuckers, then?"

"I ain't sure what's gonna happen with me. I guess I'll have to decide what I'm a-gonna do. Not really used to making my own choices."

"Do you know what we're going to do now?"

"You mean with the library, or everybody here at New Ashburn, or... you and me?"

Jody shrugged. "Whatever you want."

Ralph sighed. "I ain't got the faintest idea any which way."

"Not even about us?"

"Well, no, I guess, but..."

"But what?"

"There's something I figure I oughta tell you, now that things are on the near side of serious. I... there ain't many folks know this about me... my pa never knew this, or he woulda killed me."

"What is it?" Jody's face turned grave.

Ralph ran his thumb along a book's pages. "There's this game, see. Not like soccer or wicketball. It's uh, something I play with a few fellers back home. A... this sounds dumb as a box of rocks, but a pretend game, where we act like characters in the old times, with cars and tv's and such, and—"

Jody's grip tightened on his arm as she gasped. "Are you talking about... *Pillars of Modernity?*"

"You... you know about that?"

"We got a copy of the game here in New Ashburn, but no one ever wanted to play with me!" Jody let go of his armed and jumped—*jumped*—in delight. "Will you teach me how to play?"

Ralph took a beat to recover from the shock, but once he had, he couldn't contain an ear-to-ear smile. "Miss, it would be my pleasure."

Omar trudged up the path to the outer gates of New Ashburn to find someone waiting for him, a small, bandaged child riding on one hip.

"What are you skulking around for?" Melissa Daly asked.

"Running an errand for Ella." Omar crossed through the gate and brushed past the wary widow.

"What kind of errand?"

"You know, if you take a step back from the diggin'-hole, you're less liable to get a shovel-full of dirt in your face."

"You're a-fixin' to run off with Bill's formula, ain't you?"

"Oh, 'cause I'm headed straight for the hills, is that right?"

"If your arrow flies so true, then how about you go ahead and just give it to me, seein' how I'm so close to him and all."

Omar locked silent eyes with Melissa before he slipped his ruck-sack from his shoulder and thrust a hand inside, withdrawing an oil-skin-bound sheaf of papers. "Sure. Seeing as how you're so close to Bill."

Melissa snatched the papers away, opened them up, and leafed through them. She threw searching glances up at him as she scanned the pages. "What are you at?"

Omar shrugged. "My job, maybe?"

"You think this is going to make me trust you?"

"You're never going to trust me, and I don't really give a damn. Ella wanted me to get this for Bill, so I did."

"Simple as that?"

"Simple as that. Or maybe you cinched the reins down on me so tight I never got the chance to do whatever you thought I would," he said, the mockery in his voice cold and low.

"What really happened out there with the Pied Piper?"

"Ella killed him and saved us all."

"But what were *you* doing? How'd your face get all cut up?"

Omar smiled without humor, the scratches around his mouth stretching and threatening to crack. "Got the notion to chase a rabbit through a briar."

Omar took his leave before the Daly widow could hassle him any more, and the formula he'd given her seemed to satisfy her, at least for now.

Under the cold blanket of clouds scudding across the sky, Omar made his way towards the supermart before angling to the right with a discreet glance behind him. He bypassed the main entrance and let himself in through a side door. He wove his way through the housing units, passing the apartment he used to share with Ricky Brody and which now housed ten Tucker men. He strode up to the room which Melissa Daly had insisted go to Ella and rapped his knuckles at the recycled pressboard door. No answer.

He eased the door open and stepped inside the dim room. Empty. He reached inside his rucksack and withdrew Ella's copy of the formula, contained in a patent leather-bound journal. He stared at her cot, weighing the journal in his hand. He flipped open the small book and pinched the pages between his thumb and forefinger. A ripple of tension traced his scarred jaw as he rubbed the sheets between his fingers.

He snapped the journal shut. With one hand clenched into a trembling fist, he took a bold stride forward, lifted the pillow on Ella's bed, and hid the formula under it. He turned and left the small dormitory without looking back, Ella's journal still unread.

The news of the lifted siege and the miraculous death of the Pied Piper removed the last specter of strife from the coalition. For now, with the confirmed scattering of the unbred hordes, all that remained was the food problem, and problems, as Bill Puckett put it, were things you could solve.

The solution in this instance was to send out a well-protected, well-provisioned convoy to strike a new trade deal. This trade deal, however, would involve the Sylvanian people far to the north. New Ashburn reckoned on a month or so of modest rations for everyone, which should give enough time for the envoys to work out a deal. This would allow the New Ashburnites to repatriate the women and children and any other Sylvanian ex-slaves who did not wish to remain in Bill's employment, to ensure guides for the Tucker and Ashburnite emissaries, and to increase the chance of getting a favorable arrangement, seeing as how the Sylvanians and the Tuckers and Ashburnites now shared a mortal enemy.

Still, Ralph McDaniel pointed out some aims that had to be ironclad in any negotiations going forward: no armed Sylvanian soldiers would be allowed within the Tuckers' or New Ashburn's walls. Bill would accept and compensate Sylvanian workers on a contract basis, but his nitrogel formula—now returned and kept firmly on Bill's person—and the various industrial processes he used to produce the nitrogel, would remain a strict trade secret. The same would apply to New Ashburn's antibiotics. The Tuckers and the Ashburnites would not, under any circumstances, agree to support any Sylvanian military endeavors as part their trade deal. Any attempt at price gouging, whether to leverage the Ashburnite need for food or the Sylvanian need for nitrogel and antibiotics, would be seen as bad-faith negotiation and would result in the delegation finding business elsewhere.

The Ashburnites had no difficulty picking their emissary. Cora Compton had the experience and expertise necessary for the job, not to mention knowing the particulars of their antibiotics. Jody Perkins would travel as her assistant, which in turn meant that Ralph McDaniel would come as well to assist whoever the Tuckers picked for their emissary.

But the Tuckers had no obvious pick. Sam Chambers was dead, and Bill Puckett insisted on returning to Tucker territory and visiting his widowed daughter. The butcher, Arnold Brody, would have been the next pick, but he wanted to return with his daughter and say goodbye to his own late wife, brother, and father. Most of the Tuckers, homesick to the point of actual sickness, desperately wanted to return to their kin and to see who had survived in their absence and what had been salvaged from the destruction of the clan meeting-hall. Job Brody offered to go, since there wasn't much for him to do during winter back on his farm, but he didn't think he could keep everything straight in his head *and* work out a deal with folks he'd never met before.

What they really needed was someone with the smarts for diplomacy and the combat experience of a watchman.

So, even though he hadn't volunteered for the job, one person soon became the obvious choice for the Tucker emissary: Ralph McDaniel himself.

And so young Ralph, still three months shy of seventeen, found himself sitting atop a horse at the northern gate of New Ashburn, one Tucker elder, two Ashburnite women, and eighty-two Sylvanians lined up behind him, ready to start a long journey.

Arnold Brody, the butcher, was there at the gate to watch him go. He noticed the blemished Ashburnite girl staring at Ralph from behind, chin propped up in her hands, but he ignored her twitterpated gaze. "Most of the Tuckers won't be here in New Ashburn by the time you get back. *If* you get back. We'll all be heading back home not long after you leave. This is a mighty big responsibility for a raw upstart like you," he warned. "Job's gonna be with you to make sure those Sylvanians don't look down on a kid, but you'll be the one calling the shots, understand? This is a longer trip than any clansman's made in over thirty years, and there's cause for that."

Ralph gave a weighty nod, but without fear. "I understand."

Arnold glanced back at the Ashburnite girl. "You don't think you might be getting your feet before your head, now?"

Ralph tapped the sheathed musket on his horse's saddle. "Come on, now, Mr. Brody. I'm Elvin McDaniel's son."

Later, after Ralph and his entourage had left, Arnold's daughter Becky kept asking him what was so gosh-darned funny. He never answered—only shook his head, wiped his eyes, and laughed again.

# Chapter 22: No Rest for the Wicked

After weeks of scant vittles and no news, Nigel Bunton and an Ashburnite came in through the eastern gate with a message from Shane Bunton, the current elder in rotation as a diplomat to New Ashburn. Shane had detailed the news on leftover American paper in his clunky chalk-and-slate handwriting, and the news was good: the Slylvanians had agreed to the terms Ralph McDaniel had set forth nearly as soon as he'd had the chance to state them. He'd encountered a sizeable Sylvanian settlement up north on Highway 76, which, Ralph McDaniel felt compelled to pass along, was a *proper* highway. The joint delegation had since returned, along with *wagonloads* of supplies for the Ashburn-Tucker alliance, some of which Nigel and his posse escorted behind them as a midwinter treat for the Tuckers—if extra calories beyond mere subsistence could be considered a treat.

The money side of the negotiations had been a tricky bargain, but a reasonable one, considering recent history. The Sylvanians demanded high wages and regular inspections of housing and workplace conditions by their own people, and Bill's operation had to bear the cost. It was a necessary compromise, and one that Ralph had been expecting to make. In the meantime, Bill's nitrogel operation would remain shuttered until he returned to New Ashburn, and it would operate with a skeleton crew until the first big Sylvanian crews came out in spring.

It was good news indeed for a clan that desperately needed it. The price for their freedom from the Americans and the Pied Piper had been paid in blood. More than two dozen were dead, four of them clan elders—three dozen, if one included the Grierson settlement. And this brutal ledger didn't include those who'd already died fighting in the pigman siege last winter, or the Greenbriers last summer.

The Tucker neurocasters had returned home to find the great clan meetinghouse a charred, blackened ruin. The stone foundation remained, but the great four-story walls had collapsed, and it was all the clan could do to clean up the mess, let alone rebuild anything approaching the wonder of the old building. The Americans had torched workshops, homes, and sections of the eastern wall on their way out as well. The defenses were vulnerable, and another pigman army the size of last winter's, however unlikely, would spell their doom.

The butcher, Arnold Brody, had taken on Elvin's role as watchman for the time being and directed the restoration of the outer defenses, but everyone could see his heart wasn't in it. His wife would have made a better watchman, and she'd died fighting the Americans. He drooped. His daughter Becky held him up and encouraged him, but he drooped nonetheless.

Most people drooped. There was joy and relief, to be sure, but now, in the dregs of winter, with so much loss behind them and so much work ahead of them, the Tuckers found themselves in the place they'd been so many times before: persisting and striving, not through hope or ambition, but through grit and plain stubbornness. Folks went out to forage pine nuts, honey locust pods, and wild onions. The Fillmores—what was left of them—brought in yearling coons to cook slow in boiling water before baking to render the gamey flesh edible. Clansmen hunted for turkey tail mushrooms and wild rosehips to ward off scurvy. Much of the eating was bland, and no one cared. As long as they got their calories, they had other things to dwell on as the gray winter plodded by.

Most of the glum, even the raw, choking grief, ebbed and flowed under the balm of restored kinsmen. Sophie Fillmore found comfort in friends and family gone from her for many months. Ella, Becky, Sophie's father, and even the widow Melissa Daly cared for her and her twins while her third child grew within her. Little Earnest somehow got it into his head that he was to be the big brother to Sophie's kids and took on such imagined responsibilities accordingly.

What restored fortunes couldn't help were the gnawing questions left in the wake of such upheaval. Victor was dead, doomed by his own breeding. And though Sophie was no neurocaster, her twins were, and presumably, the infant inside her would be as well.

The clan was full of a kind of people most hadn't known existed a year ago. And with that knowledge came the obvious, awful conclusion: the purity of the Tucker's breeding was all a tremendous lie, and the ones to answer for it were dead. What would happen next? What Amos had done, could they all do? Could what had been done to Victor and Ricky be done to them?

Most folks in the clan worried about it, but no one spoke of it, neither to fellow neurocasters nor to their non-neurocasting clansmen. Maybe if they ignored it, it would fade away, like the bite of loss at missing a kinsman at the breakfast table.

The day came, most of the way through January, when Shane returned home. The Tuckers needed their carpenter, and New Ashburn needed a powdermaker. Bill Puckett made no objection to going back to New Ashburn as the Tuckers' next envoy; he could no longer stand being "useless," by which he meant working night and day repairing the eastern gate. Even without a factory going full tilt, he had a mountain of tasks that needed done if he had any hope of cooking more than "a mouse fart's worth of nitrogel" come spring.

The problem was Sophie. Bill wanted his widowed daughter to come with him, but the idea of a pregnant woman making such a wintry journey, let alone with two babies only just a year old, was empty-headed. But he wouldn't leave her back home alone and uncared-for again, which meant leaving behind help he'd grown used to having: Ella.

"We ain't got any contract written up this time, so you don't have to go if you don't want to," Bill explained to his apprentices as he packed his things. "I understand if you've got a mind to finish out the winter here, or even find a new job, if you get the itchin'. Ralph McDaniel's still out there; I can likely get him to pick up the slack, and if I can get him, I reckon I can get that Ashburnite book-girl, too." He rolled his eyes.

Ella nodded. "Sophie needs somebody."

Bill agreed. He had expected nothing less.

"I just need to know you'll keep safe out there, Bill."

"The Americans are gone. The Pied Piper's gone. What's there to be afraid of, other than my own blasted self? I'm more worried about you home folks. The Americans ain't coming back. The Greenbriers... they always come back."

"I'm staying, too," Omar said.

"You is? You itchin' to fight the Greenies?"

Omar stroked one of the many softening scars on his face. "Mr. Holland's lost his apprentice, and I could... pick up the slack. I ain't keen on going back to New Ashburn just yet."

Bill's final surprise had yet to come.

"I'll come with you, though," Mrs. Daly said.

"You want to come all the way back out there, 'Lissa?" Bill asked. "With little Earnest?"

"I done it once. I can do it again."

"You're sure, Melissa?" Ella asked.

"I know what I'm doing. I can take care of myself now."

Bill caught a glance passing between Melissa and Omar but couldn't grasp its meaning. When Melissa turned her full attention back to him, he forgot whatever interaction had gone on between them in the first place.

"But, Bill," she said, "I got one firm standing: I want you to put more teeth toward that baking soda idea of your'n. And I want you to teach me how you do it, with all the steps. And when spring comes," she said with a rare twinkle in her eye, "I want you to give me the reins."

Arnold Brody stumped his slow way along the haphazard southern patrol route the previous watchman had done twice a week. How Elvin had managed to keep up a good pace and a wary eye out for danger at the same time was beyond him. By midday, he couldn't even do one of the two.

His mind wandered in spite of itself. If the journey had gone well, Bill and Melissa and their Ashburnite escort would be in New Ashburn by now, and well settled. In other times, the two running off together might have stirred up scandalous gossip among the town's busybodies. Now, the scuttlebutt ran more along the lines of "Huh. He always was a do-things-his-own-way kind of feller. I wonder if they'll elect to marry back here, or if we'll just get a news-letter about it."

When he came upon a broken twig upon a game trail, he paused more to rest than to investigate. Even a cursory glance showed the exposed green quick of the scrub oak. A fresh break. Probably nothing. Deer, or at worst a roving pigman.

His heart sank at the sight of a thread of snagged fabric dangling from a sumac grove beyond. Arnold closed his eyes and rested his head against the cobblestone bark of an ancient persimmon tree. The air hung sharp and still as a blade pressed to his throat. He refused to believe it. Some other explanation, anything but the obvious. Anything to keep him from riding back to town to rally for war again. To beat the war drums for so small a thing as a single thread. But one loose thread was enough to unravel a blanket.

Arnold's frayed thoughts kept him from hearing his own daughter come up behind him, hissing from the brush, "Hey, Pa."

He exhaled slowly. That was it. The thread was from Becky's padded shirt. He still had the good sense not to answer until he'd removed himself from the narrow footpath and hunkered into the concealing undergrowth, but he allowed his old heart a gasp of hope. "What's the word?"

"Two humans, a couple good rifle shots southwest of here, heading north."

Dread clutched his chest again. He tried and failed to quell the tremor in his voice before he spoke. "That'd put them on track for the Newells, roughly speaking. You're sure you saw them?"

"I've got eyes, Pa," Becky snapped, clutching her bow. "They were moving real slow, careful-like. I had to sneak out myself to keep from gettin' spotted. Saw 'em maybe half an hour ago."

Arnold rubbed a hand over his face. He trusted her—he had to—but trust didn't ease the weight pressing on his chest. "Let's go check it out, then," he managed with a sigh. "You roust the Newells and meet me up the mount southwest of the Newells' field." The prospect of danger didn't reinvigorate his weary legs and back, though his heart beat faster than his legs ever could.

He nevertheless forced himself to make good time to the rally point, keeping the crest of any elevation between himself and where he imagined the mystery humans might be. Is that how Elvin would have done it? Could he be sure he hadn't been seen, heard, or smelled? He wiped the damp sweat that clung to his brow despite the chill.

Some minutes later, he heard steps behind him and turned to see his daughter and four of the Newell kids running up to reinforce him. "What's the orders, watchman?" the eldest Newell asked.

Wishing he were doing something more pleasant, such as slitting a hog's throat, Arnold directed the young folks to spread out over the crest and watch for any movement, with orders to shoot only if shot at and to move only to keep out of danger.

As midday moved into midafternoon, Arnold saw something. He waited for and recognized the pattern of a cautious interloper: starting from cover, moving to the next good cover, and getting the lay of the land: Stop, look, run. Stop, look, run. They were too far out for a shot any better than pure luck.

So far, none of his own had moved to go from looking to shooting. He couldn't brook the foolhardiness of youth at a time like this. He had enough folks to bury already.

He tracked the flickers of movement through the timber and the occasional rustle of dead leaves. The shadows darted between trees like ghosts, and Arnold's grip on his musket turned his knuckles white as they came close enough to resolve themselves into separate figures. "Two," he whispered to himself. The two strangers kept up their stutter-step advance, and when Arnold was sure they weren't getting any closer and also sure there were only two of them, he risked calling out. "Halt! Who goes there?" he hollered.

The two distant figures bolted between the trees and into cover. Had they seen him? He hadn't moved. They likely couldn't spot his low profile among the brown leaves and brown branches of the vast wintertime woods, right? He couldn't see them, but... he knew where they had to be. Unless they snuck around to catch a flank somehow, or maybe he'd counted wrong. Maybe there were others. Even if they didn't see him, they knew what direction he'd shouted from. They could be drawing a bead on him right now.

Arnold swallowed the thick lump in his throat, fighting the urge to flee and wishing for the thousandth time that Elvin were here to call the shots. He couldn't let this turn into a day-long staring contest. He gathered his nerve and called out again. "Come on out with your hands up and tell us who you—"

They took a potshot at him before running for the hills.

The panic splintered the barred door of his heart, threatening to overwhelm him. It was only once the shooters had passed beyond rifle range that he mastered himself and replaced the panic with grim certainty. "I guess that answers my question," he muttered as he arose from prone. He may have been tired before, but a musketball shot his direction had a way of making a body forget.

It was time to rally the folkward, send out scouts, and set up runners on horses to keep everybody linked up. This wasn't over. Not by a country mile.

The Greenbriers had returned.

# Chapter 23: The Unkindest Cut

"**D**oggone it, couldn't them Greenies keep well enough alone?" Phil Holland complained as he measured out powder for cartridges on a slapdash assembly line put together in the gunsmithy. Neither Ella nor Omar said anything.

Nigel Bunton hollered in through the open street-facing door without dismounting his horse. "Watchman wants volunteers to scout south of the farms."

Omar didn't hesitate. "I'll go. Let me go get my gear." He darted off toward his quarters in Bill's nearly empty home.

"Omar, let me go with you!" She reached out as if to physically pull him back from the door.

"Sit back down, girl, and tie off them cartridges. He can snag a buddy from the menfolk. I'm through with you stickin' your neck out and worryin' me sick." Phil muttered something unintelligible, likely about how his eldest surviving child would drive him to an early grave.

"Trust me, Ella," Omar said before he walked out, meeting her eyes. "I'll be okay."

By the time Ella had delivered the ammunition to the canvas tent that served as the clan's meeting area and returned to the gunsmithy, Omar was gone.

The rusting bulk of the old cell tower hadn't changed in Omar's absence, but it looked older now, more bedraggled among the reedy stalks of overgrown grass and the sagging brown branches of trees denuded of leaves.

Omar paused to scan the area, gave the roadway a cursory glance, and darted over to the downward-sloping embankment on the southern side. He checked the culvert under the road for any occupants. It, like everything else in the area, seemed empty and dead.

But only seemingly so.

Omar stiffened at a new smell on the wind, then relaxed. It was a familiar scent. A rustling not far off brought his attention to the camouflaged Greenbrier waiting for him. In the Pied Piper's absence, they must have decided to start manning this outpost again, which was what Omar had been banking on.

"Omar," the Greenbrier said.

"Jacks," Omar answered. "I have news: Clint is dead. Probably served the bastard right, but now, the Tuckers are wise to your movement. They're pushing south, and they've got manpower from other clans behind them."

Jacks didn't answer. It didn't seem as if he'd heard at all.

"Listen, we need to rethink the plan. I know you likely thought I'd have the formula by now, but... a lot's gone on since the summer. The

Americans hurt them worse than we ever could, and I think we oughta let the dead bury the dead. They ain't gonna attack us, Jacks. Ain't a one of the elders still alive who wants to come after us, and with me on the inside, I can tip you off if ever they do."

Again, Jacks gave no response. Something stirred up the hill behind him, which he also didn't acknowledge.

Omar peered up through the naked trees at the human silhouettes arising from their coverings of leaves. "What's that?" he asked, suddenly wary.

"Don't worry about them; they're with me," Jacks said.

"Are you okay?"

"He's fine. He just hasn't felt like himself lately," said a familiar voice behind Omar—the voice of someone who, a year ago, had helped him bag a shadower.

Omar closed his eyes to the voice behind him. "Not Jacks. Not him."

"Did I hear you right, Omar?" the voice behind him said. "Were you thinking of burying the hatchet? After everything the Tuckers did? That doesn't sound like you."

Omar shook his head, almost whispering to himself. "Not Jacks. Not... not him."

"Oh, I know. Oh dear. He was a friend of yours, wasn't he?" Amos clucked his tongue in mock pity.

Omar turned to face Amos, who'd arisen from his own hiding place dug into the road embankment and covered with dry grass.

Amos didn't return his stare. He couldn't. He had no eyes. "If your folks only knew how much time you spent fishing with Jacks when the two of you should have been tending the sugar maples. He never told you this, but when you first disappeared and everyone thought the pigmen had got you, Jacks didn't eat for days."

"How many?" Omar asked.

"Thought the Pied Piper got me, didn't you? But the Pied Piper—Clint, right?—made the same mistake you and everyone else did: I'm Amos *fucking* Taylor," Amos said. "Didn't expect you to blow Clint's head off during our tete-a-tete, but it was a fun little game we had going there until Ella stepped in. She's too toxic for my proxies to handle, so I had to prune that part of my network." A brief pall of unease swept over Amos's face as if remembering a bout of nausea, but it passed as soon as it came. "No matter; there's plenty more for me to harvest."

"How many of them did you take?" Omar repeated.

"Not nearly enough."

"What did you do, you son of a bitch?" Omar asked, his voice holding level.

"You'll have to be more specific. Hunting down the Americans, or consuming your friend here while he was manning this outpost?" Amos said, pointing to Proxy Jacks. "Or sending him back to convince your clan to mount a suicidal attack?"

"They wouldn't be that dumb."

"They don't know Clint's gone. They'll be camped in an old quarry with only one easy way in or out to bait the Tuckers in. They think they're getting unbred reinforcements. But there's not going to be a battle. I've already got a swarm of unbreds headed there. By the time the Tuckers get there, there will only be meat. Because that's all you are: so much meat. The neurocasters, I'll drag off for special treatment. And after that?" Amos shrugged. "I'll have my way with what's left of your pathetic brood."

Omar turned again to see nearly a score of Amos's proxies emerge from the forest, their faces deadpan, their strides even and calm. Around and in between, pigmen and shadowers escorted them.

"I'm sorry you won't be around to see all of it. You'll have to make do with seeing your childhood friend cut out your beating heart."

Omar's eyebrows pinched into a glare as his jaw clenched in cold, wordless fury, the scars on his face standing out on his winter-chilled cheeks. Amos answered with his casual two-fingered salute, a mockery of their companionship and shared suffering.

Omar pulled the American autopistol from his holster, but instead of pointing it at Amos, or his proxies, or the unbreds, he lifted the barrel up under his chin. Still staring at Amos with defiant eyes, he flicked off the safety and moved his finger to the trigger.

Amos stretched out a hand as if to cast a spell and caught the matchet tossed by Proxy Jacks. "Okay, fine. Are you going to take the coward's way out, or are you going to defend yourself?"

Omar held his trigger finger still, but his pistol stayed under his chin. "You afraid to fight a blind kid?"

"You've got eyes a-plenty." Omar surveyed the ring of shadowers and proxies forming an arena around the two of them.

Amos shrugged. "Your choice."

Omar stared back in a lengthy silence before he finally said, "Screw you," and aimed the pistol.

Amos made no effort to avoid the bullet; he couldn't see. The shot missed the mark anyway. A flash of movement hit Omar from the side, knocking the pistol clean out of his hand. He tripped and saw his assailant: a shadower, breaking ranks to assist its master. His long rifle, too, was out of reach.

With Omar stretched out on the ground, the shadower had a chance to press the attack, but hesitated. He got his matchet free, but the shadower backed away, kicking away the pistol and rifle.

Amos clucked his tongue. "That always was your problem, Omar. You never were very sporting. And at the end of all things, sporting is all you have left." He stepped closer, his guard down, his left hand extended out as if inviting Omar to take the first swipe.

He did, lunging desperately to catch an opening. Though eyeless, Amos swatted the thrust aside as if not even trying.

Omar pulled the matchet back into a high guard to close the opening he'd left from his failed thrust, but Amos stood lackadaisically to the side, his sword in the same place it had started: hanging limply at his side.

Omar feinted and struck again, and again made no connection. He backed off and waited for Amos to make a move this time.

"What's the matter, Omar?" Amos taunted. "Out of fencing practice?" He disengaged their blades, but only to spook Omar.

Omar jumped back, inching towards the edge of the ring. Rather than try to fight Amos's preternatural quickness, he took a swipe at one of his proxies, but of course, the proxy had the same quickness. It ducked under the swing, then pivoted behind Omar and reached under his armpits to get him pinned in a headlock.

"Still trying to fight dirty, huh, Omar?" Amos said, approaching. "Were you going to kill all my proxies before going after me? Think that was going to work?"

With Omar held in place, Amos pulled his sword arm back to thrust the blade into Omar's guts. Omar got his foot on the other side of the proxy's and, with the advantage in leverage, swung the body in between him and Amos to act as a shield. He rolled out of the lock and brought his matchet up to block the first real attack Amos launched.

The two were at it then with rapid strokes and counterstrokes. Omar swiped at Amos's feet, and Amos deftly hopped over the swing. The grin never left his face, and with no eyes, it was impossible to read his next move.

The next move was a thrust that turned into a low-guard blade lock as Amos stepped closer, his hollow eye sockets coming within inches of Omar's face. Amos twisted his matchet with a lightning-quick motion, and Omar's sword twirled harmlessly to the side. Omar scarcely had time to realize what had happened before Amos's foot hooked behind his knees and a fist to the chest propelled him backwards next to a fallen log.

When Omar's eyes opened again, Amos's blade was hovering over his prone body. Omar raised a hand to shield himself.

"To think I once called you a friend." Amos's smug grin was gone now, replaced with a lip-curled sneer. "You lowdown worm of a thing."

Omar lowered his hand. *"Do it."*

Amos obliged. He lifted the matchet up high and brought it down two-handed, like an ax—except he missed, burying the blade into the rotten log next to Omar. His eyeless face twisted in disgust or agony, but it was impossible to tell which.

The proxies and shadowers watched passively as Amos pulled the matchet free, raised it again, and again chopped down into the log. He attacked the dead thing with a growing, animalistic fury. Chips of damp black wood and scraggly moss flew. Omar scrambled to the side, and still Amos chopped at the log. When he was panting with the effort, Amos finally threw the matchet aside as if he'd finished butchering Omar.

But the butchery had not sated him. He fell to his knees, clawing spongy bits and detritus free from the tree with his bare hands and stuffed his maw.

"Meat," Amos snarled to himself as he feasted. "Meat. *Meat,*" he repeated with growing hunger. His hands trembled from his ravenous appetite. The bark stuck to his teeth, worming under his chipped fingernails, and still the word worked its way up his throat past the rot. *"Meat."*

And still, the proxies watched, echoing like dutiful parishioners: "Meat." The shadowers had come a step closer, closing the ring. Amos seemed to give no thought to anything but his rapacious hunger. He leaned down and gnawed on the wood like a pigman on a fresh kill. *"Meat,"* he said between mouthfuls.

The shadowers closed the loop in perfect lockstep. They stepped past Omar, ignoring him as one already dead.

Amos chewed and gnawed. He spoke one word again and again, but he no longer sounded human. He was a hunched thing, wretched and blind, choking down the grit of his awesome vengeance, a god and a goblin. The shadowers closed around him as if part of a heathen ritual. But they had not come to worship.

Shadowers had little occasion to use their claws, but this was one such occasion. They rent the flesh of his back and arms, dragging him back away from his feast.

"*Meat!*" Amos shrieked. "*We're meeaaat!*"

The proxies did not intervene. They watched with detached blandness as the shadowers tore Amos to shreds. Perhaps they were waiting their own turn.

It was all Amos, after all: root, proxies, and shadowers.

Omar pulled himself to his feet. Leaving his guns, his sword, and his travel pack behind, he ran from that cursed outpost, Amos's screams nipping at his heels. *Let the shadowers take it all!*

# Chapter 24: The Tipping Point

Omar returned to find the clan buzzing like a young rascal had been casting stones at it. He walked up through the old town in a daze as if a rascal had missed his throw and dinged him in the head. It didn't take long for someone to mark his unusual bearing. Job Brody called down at him from up on the south gate. "You're lucky I didn't take a shot at you, traipsin' through no-go zones like that! Where's your kit? Ain't even got a spear or a matchet with you?"

Omar didn't answer or even acknowledge Job's presence. He merely pulled the gate open far enough to gain entry to the town and stumbled inside.

"Hey! Omar!" Job called. "What's going on? Did you see anything on your route?"

"I'll give tale to the watchman," Omar called without looking back.

"He's at the big tent, then. He's readyin' the folkward. You sure…" Job began, but he turned away as Omar walked on in the vague direction of where the meetinghouse used to be.

Omar shuffled through the clan, jaw clenched and eyes staring. He saw Mr. and Mrs. Taylor across the clan main, now bereft of two sons, and their remaining sons folded up into the folkward. Omar probably looked the same as them. It was a common enough look that none likely questioned it. It was a withering-from-the-inside-out look, a brooding, stewing look. The only question was what loss in particular had set him such a-way.

If they only knew.

Arnold Brody was briefing the gathered fighters when Omar wandered up. "Scouts have picked up Greenbrier doings south of the Hadley and Newell homesteads, but not within striking range yet. Speaking of which, do you have anything to add, Omar?"

Several dozen heads turned to look at him. "Nothing. Didn't see nothing," he croaked.

Arnold shrugged and pointed to the charred topo map they'd salvaged from the meetinghouse basement. "Best I can figure it, they were looking for a place to hit us, and our patrols got the heads-up on 'em. They ain't tried to fight it out with us any, likely 'cause they know we got the range on 'em. So, they keep sneaking in this way and that, then running as soon as they come across our scouts or defenses. Thing is, them's all falling back the same direction. You can't see it 'cause of the burned spot, but 'ere's a box canyon here, and I'd be willing to bet teeth they've staked out their little base yonder, hoping we won't find them."

"Then why ain't we gone up 'ere and killed them sons of bullhuskers already?" one of the Finches asked.

"'Cause our scouts just picked up a bunch of unbred doings, as well."

"An army?"

"No. Best I can tell, it's an army that just scattered. Pigman groups going out every direction. I've back-called the patrols to the outer farmsteads until the hills settle a little."

Omar perked up, leaning forward now to get a good look at the topo map. "Think any of the unbreds mighta caught the Greenbriers out?" he asked.

Arnold shook his head. "Scouts ain't heard shots. Woulda made things simpler, but we don't get that lucky. We'll head out in a little, once I reckon we got us a clear path out to the holler. We get the folkward into that opening and watch our flanks, there won't be a thing the Greenbriers can do about it. So, here's what we're going to do—"

"What about the unbreds?" Omar broke in.

"I already said they're clearing out."

"But they could come back."

"And we could all die of a plague," Job Brody growled, a flinty bite to his voice. "We get a shot to kill Greenbriers on our own turf, we take it. We don't, then you bet your sorry behind *they'll* come back. What would Elvin say, huh?"

"Hear, hear!" came a voice from the gathered folkward.

Omar didn't hear the rest. He broke away from the group with brisk strides, heading toward the gunsmithy.

"Omar, where are you going?" The carpenter's son stopped him on his way, but Omar brushed him off. "Omar, I'm not kidding. We're about to head out—" Nigel Bunton stretched out a hand to slow him down.

Omar slapped Nigel away, whirling as he did. "Get your filthy hands off me, Tucker." The gashes from the thorns stood out, garish, on his face.

Nigel stepped back. "Okay, okay. What's gotten into you, man?"

"Beat it."

No one else tried to stop him as he stepped into the narrow alleyway separating Bill's shop from Phil Holland's. Bill Puckett was gone, and with him the formula—his copy, at least. But Ella's copy had remained with Ella, returning with her to the town. Omar had seen it, bound in black patent leather, small flakes of material peeling away with age. She had taken it back with her from New Ashburn, and she likely kept it where anyone would.

He stepped around the back way of the Hollands' home and peeked in through the back window at the Hollands' kitchen. Occupied. Mrs. Holland was distracting Clive and Margaret from the mustering folk-ward.

*Now or never.*

Omar looked up to the second-story window and got a running wall-kick off Mr. Puckett's wall to grab onto the first-story eaves of the Holland home. He pulled himself up and crept along the wood-shake to Ella's bedroom window.

He was about to lift the window open when he froze at the sound of Ella's voice calling for him from the street out front. "Omar! Has anyone seen Omar? I need to tell him something!"

He waited until her voice faded, then slipped into her room. He didn't even have to look for it. There was her notebook, right there on her desk. He flipped through the first few pages. Where was the formula? Where was it? He stopped at the sight of his name and flipped back a page or two.

His mouth went slack, but his hands went so rigid around the little book that his knuckles turned as white as his face.

"Omar!" Phil Holland shouted at Bill's place from the floor below, snapping him out of his trance. "It's time to go! Pack your crap already, and let's get the heck out of here!"

Omar stuffed the diary into his breast pocket and left the way he came, his hands shaking as he lowered the window behind him. He was already down and back inside Bill's house when Mr. Holland came over from next door to physically roust him. "Where've you been, Omar?"

"I..." Omar gestured impotently toward his effects, but Phil was in too big of a hurry to notice or care that his face had gone completely pale.

"Arnold Brody's out front. Seems you and the carpenter's boy had a spat. Fall in and take your drubbing. The folkward's moving out."

Ella couldn't find him. She'd checked the meeting-tent and had been told he'd been there not long ago. She'd heard he'd had a run-in with Nigel Bunton, but no one could tell her where he'd gone from there.

He wasn't at Bill's, or anywhere around her house, and then Dr. Bernhard conscripted her to prep bandages. She paced as she worked, her mind barely on the task at hand, not heeding Sophie's questions, nor even Sophie's presence.

Finally, something she said came through. "If you're worried about Omar, I'm sure he'll be okay. Before the folkward moved out, Becky told me they've got the numbers, range, and even the terrain on their side against the Greenbriers."

"Was he with the folkward?"

"Of course. He'd already come back from his scouting run, and we're getting all able fighters behind this push. You don't think he'd try to bolt, do you?"

Ella stared into space for a minute. "I'll be right back," she said before running off toward her own home, her own room, her own writing desk, where she'd left her own diary.

Tracking down the folkward over difficult terrain was a chore even in a calm state of mind; now, it was a nightmare. Of course, she didn't know where the quarry was, other than somewhere to the southwest of the Newell farm. In the end, she found herself wandering further and further into the wilderness, her heart in her throat most of the time, going from a walk to a run and back to a walk again in a frantic gait, and only the first distant gunshot told her she was headed the right direction.

A lone girl in the woods made a prime target for roving unbreds, but she didn't care, at least until she looked up a nearby hillock and spotted a shadower sitting astride a bullhusker like the pale rider from hell. Ella kept going, and the unbreds followed at a leisurely pace, neither stalking nor pursuing—more like closing the loop of a noose.

It wasn't just Ella's neck on the line. She had to pick up the pace.

*Dear diary,*

*I haven't written in you since Jim was killed. Yesterday, I saw the man who killed him. The other Tuckers were saying he was a drifter, that he had saved Amos and Dale Taylor from a bunch of pigmen. He called himself Omar Walking. Whether or not that's his real name doesn't matter; I know who he really is. I've seen him before. Two years is not enough time for me to forget the face of the man who murdered my brother.*

Ella broke into a run when she picked up a definite trail again. Now, she had to worry about finding Omar amidst the chaos of a battle. She hoped that first gunshot hadn't been meant for him. Another rifle report echoed through the naked trees, and she surged ahead, stopping only to catch her breath.

*December 7th,*

*He was right there in front of me, and all I had to do was unmask him and watch the clan hang him from a tree.*

*I couldn't bring myself to do it. And then the pigmen came, and he saved my life. What am I supposed to do? He's a Greenbrier, and he knows we're all Tuckers. I expected him to cut my throat just as soon as save me. Am I to return an act of kindness, even an unthinking one, with betrayal? Dear God, what am I supposed to do?*

*December 10th,*
*I heard a sermon today that said love never fails. I think that's what God has told me to do. I'm supposed to forgive this Greenbrier.*

The sound of gunfire grew closer and more frequent, but it hadn't yet taken on the cadence of a pitched battle. There was still time. She had a lost friend to find.

Omar wasn't with the main group of fighters chasing the heels of the lead scouts who'd started skirmishing with the Greenbrier sentries. He was away from the battle entirely, like a coward or a turncoat or both. Ella saw his gun first, lying discarded along with a rusty matchet and a charred spear.

Omar himself was slumped down against a tree like a man already dead or dying, her diary open in his lap.

"Omar! Are you okay? Are you hurt?"

Omar didn't quite seem to hear her, but he blinked at the sound of her voice. What visions flashed before his eyes, Ella couldn't tell. When he saw her approaching with her face flushed and her skirts hiked up for running, he looked dazed. "Miss Holland? You knew? Why...?"

"I'm sorry. I meant to tell you earlier, but I wasn't sure... I couldn't find the gumption, or... I don't know, but it doesn't matter. We've got to stop this, and we've got to hurry! There's unbreds on the way!" Ella blurted between breaths.

"I—I tried... I didn't mean for it to go this far."

"Omar, I *know*. I know who you are and what you did to my brother. I know you were after the formula. I know that's why you came back. I know you played the spy, and I know you worked for the Americans."

Omar still looked like he'd been struck with a heavy club. "I've told so many lies... I don't know what's true anymore. I can't believe it. It ain't possible. Some kind of trap."

"I *never* wanted to trap you, Omar. I forgave you. For all of it. Every day, I forgave you all over again. And together, we can stop the killing. You and me."

Another gunshot barked, and this one came with an answer shortly after it. "I tried to warn my kin, to get them out. Wasn't fast enough. I'm too late. The unbreds coming..." Omar shook his head. "They were Amos's. Might as well get all of us, for what we deserve."

"We can stop them, both of us."

"There's no way. They hate each other too much."

Ella kneeled down in front of Omar and took his face in her hands. His whiskers scratched against her palms as she looked him in the eyes. "We've saved hundreds of folks already, and weren't none of 'em our clansmen. A year ago, you couldn't have got more than five Tuckers in the whole clan to care for someone not their own. You changed that, Omar. Changed it for them, changed it for me. I don't want any more dead Greenbriers. Do you want any more dead Tuckers?"

Omar's eyes focused somewhat. "It ain't up to me."

"That ain't what I asked."

"I... no. But how?"

"Trust me, Omar. I'm a neurocaster. I can stop the unbreds. Then we can stop the shooting."

"Those unbreds flanking the Tuckers are the only chance my clan has to win this fight. If you don't—"

"*Trust me.*"

"I can't betray my clan."

"I won't betray you." Ella stood and stretched out a hand to help Omar up.

Omar scowled at her hand, his brow furrowing in that grim way of his. But he clapped his scarred hand to hers in a firm grip and righted himself.

"Let's go," Ella said as Omar retrieved his matchet and the far-off pops and thumps of firearms crackled like corn in a kettle. "No time to waste."

The two started at a jog that became a run as they crested the hill, with Omar soon outpacing Ella with his longer legs and surer footing. By now, the battle had started in earnest, and soon, they could hear shouting between the shots.

A mountain rose way on up past the downward slope where the Tuckers seemed to be gathering. The Tuckers had pushed into a tangle of trenches and earthworks that wove through the woods, pushing right up to the edge of an empty killzone, on the other side of which they could see the shadowy silhouettes of the Greenbriers hunkering for scant cover. And coming in from the opposite direction, already skirmishing with the Tucker rearguard, were scores of pigmen.

The two of them ran downhill again, veering off towards the unbreds. Once in range, Omar primed his rifle and took aim. A bullhusker crashed through the brush a mere fifty paces out and to their right just then, roaring towards the Tucker line.

Ella had no sooner thrown out a hand towards the giant beast than the bullhusker recoiled as if scorched by a searing brand and fled back the way it had come. She turned to the other creatures with the look of a workmaid completing distasteful drudgery and sent them on their way as well. These unbreds had no real master anymore, and they would have been no match for Ella even if they did. She heard Omar whistle in low admiration before charging into the gap left by the retreating unbreds. Ella followed after.

They found a solitary figure wandering in the thinning woods a stretch ahead of them. When Ella closed the span, she made out Arnold Brody's form leaning up against a tree and ran up to him. His face stood out pale as he clutched a bleeding forearm. "How'd you two get through the unbreds? Where'd they go?" he asked, his eyes darting behind them, likely searching for signs of the unbred onslaught that had inexplicably vanished.

"It doesn't matter right now, Arnold. Are you all right? What happened?"

"Musketball took me right in the arm. Had to get out of the action for a bit. I'll be okay, 'cept it hurts like the dickens."

"Mr. Brody, we have to call off the attack. Omar and me—"

"Don't need to stop on my account. I—ouch—I think we'll get those Greenbriers good. They dug all these trenches, but we spooked 'em out. If we can get a couple guys up on the cliffs—can you send the message?"

She ran before he could finish giving her orders while Omar stayed behind to spin some useless yarn about how they had to pull the fighters away from the quarry because of the unbreds. The Tuckers were in the trenches—*there!* Tripping over tree, stone, and soil that might as well have been stone, she made her way to the front lines. She heard hoarse shouting, something about covering the Fillmores.

A bullet buzzed overhead, but she paid it no more mind than she would a junebug. Ella charged into the trenches like a madwoman, telling the Tuckers to stop, stop shooting, quit it. They either didn't hear her or ignored her. She found Job Brody and grabbed hold of his rifle, but the barrel was already scorching hot from the nitrogel.

"What's got into your head, girl? Get outta my way! I got Greenies to kill!" Job shouted as he pushed her back.

They wouldn't listen. Their blood was too hot.

On down the trenches, she saw where Omar had caught up again, and their eyes met. The thunder of a gun punctuated a cry of pain somewhere in the rocks and quarry tailings across from the trenches.

For the first time, she saw quiet despair on his face. Omar was right about the world, and Ella wrong, and she could see he took no pleasure in it. But his look of despair changed to one of horror as she made her decision.

She struggled to her feet and charged out of the trench, toward the Greenbriers.

"Ella, wait!" Omar called out, but she was too far away, or the noise of the firefight drowned him out, or she simply didn't listen. She flitted away, a nymph untouched by the cacophony. She skipped out of the reach of Job Brody, who'd leaned out of cover to pull her back.

"Ella, wait!" Omar shouted again to the deaf air, following the line of breastworks after her swiftly retreating form. But the fairy was gone. Where the trenches met the mouth of the quarry, a stray bullet struck the rock face above his head and ricocheted in a whining whir. But rather than ducking, Omar stood fully upright, like a man startled from slumber in a strange place. "Ella, what are you doing?"

Ella wove through the rapidly thinning trees, gathering her skirts to keep from tripping.

Omar clawed his way past Tucker fighters in the trench. "Ella, come back!" he called, but she heeded nothing. She didn't heed anyone, not even the Tucker men nearby, shouting at her to get down, to get the hell out of the line of fire. Then there she was, at the treeline, a wide, bare expanse in front of her. She paused the space of one deep breath before she put one bold foot into the clearing.

Omar pulled himself out of the trench and scrambled forward to an oak beyond it. "Ella, wait! *Don't go out there!*" He didn't hear the shouts of the Tuckers saying the same thing, nor notice that they'd stopped shooting.

Ella took deliberate strides through the tall grass around her, heading for the woods on the other side where the Greenbriers crouched. She waved her arms, bidding the fighting to stop. Omar reached the edge of the clearing but dared no further. *"Ella, no! Come back!"*

Ella bit her lip as she strode into the face of the enemy fusillade.

Back in the woods, over the hill, her diary lay open on the ground where Omar had left it. The wind flipped the page.

*I asked God to take this cup from me at the beginning. It hurt. I had to pretend to care for him. To even be decent. But I'm not sure I'd give up this cup anymore, not for all the pigman teeth in the world. I've changed. It's not duty anymore. I'm not pretending anymore. I don't know how this will turn out, but I do know this: Omar Walking is a good man, and I love him.*

Ella made it halfway through the hardscrabble killing field. Three shots rang out simultaneously. One of them missed her, but the other two didn't. A spray of blood misted the air, and the thin dead grass of the meadow swallowed her whole.

Omar staggered as if drunk when Ella went down, one hand out-stretched to her resting place, his jaw slack in a silent moan.

In an instant, the great masquerade came crashing down. Now, there was just Omar: warrior, spy, traitor, wretch. He lurched out into the open, oblivious to the battle, his face numb. He couldn't see—only flashes.

Flash: blood.

Flash: Ella's smile.

Flash: blood.

Flash: Ella's eyes.

Flash: Ella's blood.

Omar gained momentum as his legs carried him noiselessly out into the field. The ringing in his ears swelled to a senseless tide as he drew closer to where she lay. There she was, not far ahead, the one living soul in this whole God-forsaken universe who had dared care for his worthless, wicked, self-serving hide, and he'd—he'd—

"Oh no, oh no, *oh no.*" He ran over to her and kneeled over her crumpled mass. Her eyes were closed, and her skin was pale where it wasn't covered in blood. There was so much blood everywhere. It was his fault—all his fault. He cradled her head in his arms. His chest and throat constricted like old cellophane tossed onto hot coals, squeezing out a cry like that of a wounded animal.

"No, no, no, no. No, Ella. *You're all right. You're all right. Please, be all right!*" he sobbed. "Oh, my darling, my darling, my sweet darling!"

From the Greenbrier line, a single thoughtless question rang out in the stunned stillness, clear as a bell. "Omar, what are you doing?"

And then everyone knew, and every loaded Tucker gun drew a bead on Omar's kneeling body. But no one fired a shot. The fighting, the shouting—everything had stopped but for the cries of the wounded and the weeping of Omar.

*Life is a tragedy. There is a terrible darkness in the world, but without it, how would we see the stars? Evil is a terrible thing, but I think the good stands out so much brighter against it. Some have said that we're only animals who dream of being angels. Others say we're angels that act like animals. Which is true? I suppose both are. Some lose themselves in the darkness and go blind; others keep their eyes fixed on the glimmers of hope. Do I really believe that love overcomes? Is faith a sign of strength, or a sign of weakness? And on the darkest of nights, when I hear a voice whisper to me, "Take heart, for I have overcome the world," do I really have the will to live and die for that voice?*

Omar didn't notice the first moan, but the second one made him start, choking him in the middle of a heaving sob. A soft murmur escaped Ella's barely parted lips. He lifted a hand to her mouth and felt a small gust of breath. He saw her chest move and felt her heartbeat. He held his breath as he examined her wounds for the first time. One shot had taken her in the chest—no, too high, too off-center to be a chest wound. She'd been shot in the shoulder. The other bullet had entered her left leg above the knee. Both wounds were bleeding profusely, but that meant—
She was still alive.
He looked up to the Greenbrier line a mere fifty paces away—far too close for the non-lethal wounds to be anything less than miraculous—or intentional. Sniffing like a child trying to put on a brave face, Omar tore scraps of cloth from his undershirt and her skirts with shaking hands. He had to stop the bleeding. "Somebody! Help!" he called to anyone who could hear. "Somebody please help me!"

No one moved on either side of the clearing. No man made the no-man's-land his own. Omar wadded a piece of cloth into a ball and pressed down on Ella's shoulder. Her moans rose in pitch and volume as she began to come to. "Ssh, ssh. I'm sorry, I'm sorry. I know it hurts."

He lifted his eyes to see a solitary man emerging from the woods on the Greenbrier side with no gun, no bow, no spear, no sword. The young man paused as if expecting the Tuckers to cut him down in a moment. Waiting and finding his body still unbroken, he continued forward. When he reached Omar and Ella, he kneeled down beside them.

"Ah, Vin, I knew you would come. Put pressure on her leg."

"Omar, I'm—I'm sorry, I—"

"Shut up and help me."

A voice spoke up from behind Omar. "You need to check the wounds." It was one of the Brodys. "Peel back her shirt and get that shift out of the way."

Another two Greenbriers came forward, and there were still no shots. They carried no weapons with them except for a knife they used to help cut away torn, bloody bits of fabric. The exposed wounds were stark travesties of mangled flesh, but the leg wound was the worse of the two. The ball had taken her a couple inches above the knee, and the blood poured out in swells in time with her pulse.

"Pack that hole in the shoulder," Cephas Finch said.

"Leg first. Tourniquet," a burly Greenbrier responded, removing the twine holding up his pants.

Omar helped loop the twine around Ella's thigh above the ragged hole. The Greenbrier helping him shoved a stick through the slack and started twisting.

"It hurts, Omar," Ella whimpered.

"I know." He held her hand and squeezed as they tightened the ligature.

By the time the bleeding stopped, Ella was screaming.

The Greenbrier named Vin ran back to fetch more help and some supplies. A couple more Tuckers ran on in to replace him.

"We got us a place not far back where we can do some quick fixin', once we get her there," Clyde McDaniel said.

"We've got more wounded back at our barricade."

"Well, bring 'em out; we'll make stretchers for 'em. Go on now, get some help," Clyde said to the younger Tucker when he hesitated.

The dam broke then. A dozen Tuckers came forward, and more than half that many Greenbriers, and not just to see Ella.

"God, how old's that wound?"

"Couple weeks."

"Don't you folks have a doctor?"

"He's dead. Y'all killed him."

"Oh."

"We got a doctor. We get some stretchers, we can get Doctor Bernhard to fix them all up."

"Nigel, let Doctor Bernhard know we're coming. And let Arnold know what's going on. And run on over to the Finches' place and see if you can't fetch us some carts. We'll see if we can't get folks back to town for surgery, or at least the Newells'. You know what? Get some other young legs to help you."

"I can go," a Greenbrier kid offered.

"No, no, son." Job Brody cleared his throat. "Wouldn't want one of ours to, uh, take a shot at you 'cause they didn't recognize you." He cleared his throat again. "Maybe Omar oughta—"

"I'm not leaving Ella," Omar said, still gripping her hand.

"How's she looking?"

"Puttin' pressure on the shoulder. We'll see about the leg later."

"Keep your guide arm steady, Omar," Vin said, laying a hand on his back. "We'll pull through this."

# Chapter 25: God and Sinners

W ord of what was coming on down the road had already reached the two female sentries at the gate of the Tucker clan when the first cartload of wounded rattled through, but the belief that their eyes told the truth didn't arrive until the second cart. Tuckers and Greenbriers lay side by side on stretchers while their brethren marched alongside them unarmed.

The Greenbrier wounded went first to the tent on the clan main, but they wouldn't last out a winter night there. Doctor Bernhard and his wife went to work, and most of that work involved amputating limbs. Bernhard called up a couple of his apprentices to help care for them, and Becky Brody as well once the demands grew too cumbersome.

Omar, however, they sent outside the tent. He'd collected himself enough to remain silent, and he paced around the clan main rather than resist calls for him to wait. Still, Tuckers and Greenbriers alike watched him as if he were a smoldering match placed too near the powder stores.

He paced through the rest of the day and on into the evening, his jaw clenched tight enough to chip teeth, listening to Ella moan, occasionally sob, and at one point, scream. He had to be held back then.

Omar wasn't the only one facing scrutiny. Greenbrier and Tucker fighters milled about with their heads hung low. The Tuckers who had not been in the battle gossiped and hissed, and the Tuckers who had were in no hurry to speak of what had happened, other than to say a cease-fire had been reached. The town Tuckers dared not ask the Greenbriers for clarification. Dozens of the Greenies milled about, smack-dab in the middle of the Tucker's town square, all unarmed, and nobody did a thing! In fact, Arnold Brody had forbidden any firearms on the clan main. Had the Tucker fighters lost their minds?

Perhaps the fighting men wondered the same thing. But they didn't do anything, and if they weren't going to do anything, then neither were the town guards and sentries, and if the guards and sentries weren't going to do anything, then the surviving tradesmen and their wives and sons and daughters weren't going to do anything either. Instead, the fighting men sat down. Some of them wept with gentle, hitching sobs, trembling hands hiding their faces in shame. Some of the Greenbriers did the same—some of them even alongside their enemies.

When evening came, Arnold Brody, the butcher, walked out of the surgery tent with a bandaged arm. "Who's your leader here?" he asked of the Greenbriers still assembled in the middle of the town.

One of the men, a great barrel-chested beast of a man, tentatively raised his hand, a meek gesture for someone as imposing as he.

Arnold walked up to him and introduced himself. "Arnold Brody. Butcher."

"Big Todd. New clan watchman."

"Doctor Bernhard is doing his best."

"How are they all doing?"

"Doctor expects most of them to live. We have... antibiotics. We're not worried about infection carrying them away. We'll see what the night holds. We'll put the wounded up indoors, in proper beds. Get them out of the cold, let 'em rest."

"Very well."

"There's something else."

"Yeah?"

"Well, things have changed. In ways I wasn't rightly expectin'."

The two of them beheld the sprawl of Tucker and Greenbrier fighters lying about, all going to great lengths not to meet the gaze of their enemies. "I reckon they have," Big Todd said.

"I'm one of the elders. Not a lot of us left. Normally, we would have had our schoolteacher speak with you, but he's dead. So, I reckon it's my job to speak for the clan."

"Speak, then."

Arnold sighed. "I'm tired. Our clan watchman is dead. Our reverend is dead. My kin is dead. My wife is dead. My friends are dead. The one who rose up to lead us is dead. Our crops were burned or carried away, most of our livestock slaughtered or stolen. Our meetinghouse was burned. We used to be angry, but now we're all tired and cold. It's been a long, sad winter, and I'm... I'm a butcher who's sick of the killing, wouldn't you know it. We all are. I don't know about you. I'm done. I ain't fighting no more." He unsheathed his matchet and tossed it aside.

The big Greenbrier said nothing for a moment. He looked to his own clansmen. "It's been a long spell of winter," he said finally. "Thirty years of it, since I was just a little boy. But I think springtime's come at last."

The two lifelong enemies shook hands. That night, the Tuckers shared with the Greenbrier war party from the stores brought in from the Ashburn deal.

When Mrs. Bernhard came out from the tent, she was directing a couple Tucker boys carrying a patient on a stretcher. Omar caught her and asked about Ella.

"She's alive, and she's awake," Mrs. Bernhard said, wiping her hands on a cloth as she watched the patient go to his lodgings for the night. "Looks like the bullet to her shoulder missed her collarbone. Just a flesh wound. It'll heal up pretty well, but—"

"But what?"

"Her leg had to go. The ball shattered her bone. No use trying to save it."

Omar contemplated the stack of severed, naked arms and legs in the wheelbarrow off to the side. A part of Ella was in that rotting mass somewhere. He turned to leave before the sickness in his heart spread to his stomach.

"There's one more thing, Mr. Walking."

"What?"

"When we'd finished the amputation, the first thing she asked for was to see you. I insisted she wait a few hours until the laudanum took the edge off. She's much calmer now."

Omar closed his eyes and inhaled deeply as if bracing himself for a plunge into cold water, then nodded.

"When you're done, we'll send her home to rest." Mrs. Bernhard swept the canvas cover of the tent back for Omar to enter.

The remaining wounded lay on cots, some of them still moaning. Ella lay at the far end. She smiled at the sight of Omar, and as he approached, she swung up into a sitting position. She gingerly favored her right leg, where her nightshirt had been pulled away from the bandaged stump.

Omar stopped short at the sight of Ella's maimed limb, clapping a hand over his mouth, fresh tears welling up in his eyes.

"Don't fret, Omar. I'll be okay," she said, still smiling through the pain in her leg and shoulder.

Omar choked down the bitter feeling that had clutched his throat and nodded. "I'm... sorry, Ella."

"I love you, Omar."

He turned away to wipe his leaking eyes.

"Has it been a while since you cried?" Ella asked.

"Not since..." He choked. "Not since my sister."

"No shame in it. Ah," Ella said, wincing at a particularly bad twinge before waving Omar off as he rushed to her side. "It's okay. The doctor gave me a nip of that poppy stuff. At least—at least I still got my pretty eyes, right?" She looked up at him and reached out with her hand, and he grasped it.

"It should have been me. I deserve to be shot."

"Deserve's got nothin' to do with it."

"I love you, Ella," he said, but his grip weakened.

"I know."

But Omar let go of her hand and left her. "You should rest up. See your family. Look to your kin," he said over his shoulder before he left the tent, having finally mastered himself.

He tried to ignore the whispers that followed him as he left the clan main, but he'd grown used to following whispers, and he felt their eyes. The people who would have killed him two years ago now stood staring.

Was he one of them? A Greenbrier? Or was he a drifter? Hadn't he been inked as a Tucker? But the Greenbriers treated him as one of their own. He could have done so much mischief; was that what Bill's powdershop accident had been all about? But he'd fought for the Tuckers, too; why'd he do that? He was a walking contradiction.

He could at least leave those questions unanswered, but he had to say something to the Hollands. He owed them that much.

He shuffled to front door like the stranger he was and knocked softly on it. Ella's stepmother opened the door. Her eyes were red. Clive and Margaret came running out without bothering with the strange formalities the grown-ups had taken up.

"Omar! What's going on? What are all those folks doing here? Is Ella gonna be all right?"

"I think so," Omar said, nearly whispering.

"Mr. Brody said they cut off her leg. Is it true?"

Omar nodded.

"Is the feud over?" Margaret asked, the weight of everything around her finally starting to strike home.

"I don't know."

"Will you stay?"

"I don't know."

"You..." Leah Holland said, blinking back tears. "You saved Margaret from the screevler... Why?"

Omar shook his head. "I know what you Tuckers think about us. But there are some things even Greenbriers wouldn't allow."

Phil Holland walked into the hallway, gave Omar a hard look, and walked away again.

"I came to get my things and offer my leave-taking," Omar explained. "I don't imagine Mr. Holland cares for a Greenbrier living next door."

"You'll have to tell Phil." Leah nodded to the workshop door. "Thank you," she added as he turned to seek out her husband.

Omar entered the workshop and closed the door behind him. Phil had placed himself across the workshop floor from Omar and was staring the Greenbrier down in the dim lantern light. Neither said anything; perhaps neither of them wanted to make the first move.

"The Greenbriers," Phil said at last, "killed my boy. I loved my son, probably too much. I swore I'd never let a Greenbrier go. And then somehow, God sees fit to put a Greenbrier right under my nose for a full year and have him fall in love with my daughter. Isn't that a fine howdy-do?"

Omar said nothing.

"You wanted *her*, didn't you? That's why you came back, isn't it? You went back to your clan and realized you'd rather be here, with her. And I would have trusted you with her, too." Phil took stock of Omar with a shrewd eye, smirking in a way that was both amused and accusing.

Omar said nothing.

"You saved my daughter. But you almost got her killed, too, and now she's a cripple. And I don't reckon you give a darn about all the rest of the Tuckers what got hurt, but you can bet she does. You happy about that?"

"Do I look happy?"

Phil sighed, relenting. "No. No, I'd always say you seemed to be about the most unhappy person I ever laid eyes on. Only time I saw any different was when you were with Ella or Amos, God rest his soul."

"I know it don't make a lick of difference," Omar said, "but I'm sorry. For everything."

"It don't make a difference," Phil said without heat, as if he were trying to bite but didn't have the venom left to make it sting. "After my boy died, I promised myself I'd kill every Greenbrier I ever met. But... I don't find myself as hasty to keep that promise. I feel... funny inside, you know? Probably from that screevler guttin' me. I... I ain't thinkin' straight." He scratched the back of his head, shuffling his feet now.

"Is there... something you're trying to get at?"

"I guess what I'm trying to say is... I forgive you, I reckon." Phil made a face, as if tasting something sour. "Go ahead and run along, now. We'll get this shop cleaned up tomorrow and get back to work."

"You ain't gonna fire me?"

"Why'd I want to do that? I said I forgave you, and unless the elders want to banish you again, I need the help around here. And if you're gonna end up my son-in-law, it won't do to have your clan come between us, will it? Go on, now, git, before my head catches up with all these crazy doin's lately." Phil shook his head in bewilderment. "My girl, falling for a Greenbrier..."

Omar turned to leave.

"Wait. One more thing." Phil stopped Omar at the door. "Just being curious, but—you wouldn't happen to know who it was killed my son? Would have been about three years ago, caught alone out in the woods just south of town?"

Omar turned back to face Phil. "That man?" he said. "He's dead."

# Chapter 26: Flowers Among the Ashes

The next day, the Tuckers directed the Greenbrier war party to the shallow graves they'd dug in the old town for the Greenbrier dead left behind from past raids. They had no parson, but nevertheless, they held a memorial service for the long-dead, as well as a funeral for the Tuckers and Greenbriers who didn't make it. Amos Taylor was among the names of the dead.

Omar said a prayer for their souls and for his own, but he wasn't sure God would hear any of them.

The Greenbriers left the next day with their walking wounded, while a few of the more serious cases remained to convalesce with their Tucker hosts. Omar remained with the Tuckers as well, helping Phil Holland silently in his shop. Routine was the only thing that could make sense of anything anymore.

Ella stayed in her room and asked every day to see Omar, and every day, he politely declined. When she left her room for exercise, he made sure he was out of the Holland home. Yet when Mrs. Bernhard or one of the apprentices came over to change her bandages, Omar stood outside her door every time, pacing and listening to her whimpers.

In the evenings, by the light of the stoked fireplace, Omar read Clive and Margaret bedtime stories. Eventually, Margaret took to holding Omar's hand when Ella had her checkups, and soon, Clive joined in as well.

In a week, the Greenbriers returned with a formal delegation to end the feud. They left their guns at the gate without being asked, and the surviving elders signed the truce as one, without a single voice against.

A part of the terms required an emissary from one of the clans to be in place at the other at all times, and for steady correspondence to pass between them. It was clear the Greenbriers were thinking of Omar, and the Tuckers agreed to the suggestion. In the end, Omar agreed to it as well.

So, another week after the Greenbrier delegation left, Omar left his apprenticeship to trace his way down the same path he'd taken home when the Tuckers first exiled him. This time, he left with whatever antibiotics the Tuckers had left to spare and a message for the Greenbriers written on American paper.

In the first morning past the halfway point, Omar shook off the winter chill, untied himself from his tree, and got back on the path. He was past the bottom of the dell, making his slow, winding way back up to the next hill, when he saw the silhouette of something that at first glance looked like a man.

It was a shadower, unmoving, staring down at him.

Omar unslung his rifle, looking about him for an unbred ambush, and saw nothing. The shadower didn't move as he lined up his shot.

Then, the shadower saluted him with a casual two-fingered wave.

Omar lowered his rifle, his mouth agape. "Amos?"

The shadower buried its head in its spindle-fingered hands, turned, and slumped over the crest of the hill, out of sight.

Omar finished his journey unmolested, but the sight of the weeping shadower stayed with him. Like so many other things, he knew it would stay with him forever.

Omar returned at the end of the month with a Greenbrier trade caravan, and again the next month. They came with food and medicines and building supplies. They saw to their own wounded, then went out to the farms and helped patch up some of the barns and fences and the eastern gate. Doctor Bernhard journeyed back with Omar to the Greenbrier clan to care for their sick and wounded for a spell.

Disputes arose, and old grudges surfaced again, but by late February, Ella was out of her room with a crutch, and the grievances shriveled to nothing in the face of her humble kindness. The elders first invited her to their meetings, then deferred to her judgment on certain cases, and soon, it was clear who would fill the void left by Sam Chambers.

Becky Brody was out on patrol east of town when she flagged down an incoming nomad caravan. It was a new one, come down from Sylvanian territory to scope out the new trade routes opening up. And they carried news from New Ashburn. It so happened to be a Tuesday, so before she delivered the news to the elders, Becky swung by the Holland home to see Sophie and Ella.

"*Mrs.* Puckett's baking soda?!" Sophie exclaimed when Becky showed her the small box of white powder with a custom-printed label. "Pa didn't waste any time."

"I don't reckon Melissa did, either. Listen to this." Becky dodged one of Sophie's toddling twins, unfolded a paper, and read, "'Make your bread and biscuits pop with this new formulation cooked up by the greatest minds in Appalachia. No fermentation needed. Use for baking, cleaning, stomach problems, bug repellent, and air freshener. Mrs. Puckett knows what you need in the house. Let her help you make it a home.'"

"Did *she* write that?" Sophie asked, mouth agape.

"Sure as heck Bill didn't," Ella said, scooping rotten spots out of potatoes as she sat at the kitchen table, her injured leg propped up on a cushioned chair.

"Ralph might coulda helped him."

"Ralph McDaniel? Didn't I hear tell he found himself a girl out in New Ashburn?" Sophie asked, heaving the other of her twins over her pregnant belly to nurse.

"Never mind all that. You won't guess who else is helping Bill."

Ella shrugged, hiding a grin with one hand. "I'm stumped."

"Ella, quit jokin' about your leg," Sophie said, then turned to Becky. "Who else—"

"Johnny Grierson."

"Mr. Grierson!" Ella plopped another diced potato in a pot to soak. "I thought he'd died."

"Believe me," Becky said, looking out the eastward window like she was trying to remember something important, "so did I."

"Wow." Ella whistled softly. "How are they—gettin' along?"

"Seems fine so far. Bill sent home a whole string of jaws for you, Sophie." Becky held out the tidy sum of money.

"Land's sakes! This keeps up, I'll never have to work a day in my life."

"That might just be what Bill's aiming for. He sent you this letter, too." Becky passed the note along and turned to Ella. "How's the leg?"

"Oh, that's neither here nor there."

"Are you going to keep these bad jokes up forever?"

"Maybe."

"Really, how are you doing?"

"I'm about at the point where the phantom pains bug me more than the actual wound itself, so long as I don't bump it into something. Good news is, I ain't stickin' my foot in my mouth as often."

Becky snorted and hid her face. When the moment passed and her grin eased, she asked, "What about Omar?"

Ella sighed. "I think he thinks he's got to earn forgiveness."

Becky nodded. "Good."

Surprise flashed across Ella's face. "Not good."

"I ain't saying we shouldn't forgive him, Ella. I'm saying it goes both ways. If a feller feels like forgiveness is owed him, why, that's just a step up from Bert Daly. Good folks know they ain't owed forgiveness."

"Fine, fine. But that goes for us, too."

"I know. That's what makes me nervous whenever the Greenbriers come around again. I've... killed myself a couple of them. Seems like the only thing keeping the feud from breaking out again is *everyone, everywhere*, electing not to pull the trigger *every moment*. It's a miracle we ain't cut each other's throats yet."

"And folks think God has abandoned us." Ella shook her head at the absurdity, as if God's benevolence were as plain as the sunrise.

"Aw, Papa's coming to visit this April," Sophie said, reading the letter with one hand as she switched out her twins. "Yeah, it says here he's hitched his horse alongside Melissa." She put the letter down as something dawned on her. "I'm gonna call her 'Mama.' Who'd have thunk?"

Becky leaned up against the kitchen doorway. "Who'd have thunk a lot of things? Just the other day, I saw some Greenbriers tossing around a bull's bladder with some Tucker kids, wouldn't you know it?"

"Did you see who won?"

"The Greenies. But I tell you, these Greenbriers don't know the first thing about sharpshooting, what with those ammo-wasting breechloaders. Come summertime, after we get our harvests wrapped up, I'm fixin' to get a shootin' competition put together. Show them upstarts how it's done."

"There's talk of throwing in with the Greenbriers and switching the mill on the river over to electric power," Ella said.

"You think it'll work?"

"Probably not; there's more to electricity than getting a wheel to spin. Maybe if we can borrow some know-how from New Ashburn, we can swing it. I'll still support it if the elders lean that a-way. For me, the important thing is finding a common aim for both the clans. When the good feelings go, I want our gathered need to keep us headed the same way. When Bill's nitrogel factory takes off, I aim to build a factory here and make fertilizer, and I want to hire Greenbriers to help build and work and manage it."

"But you'll own it?" Sophie asked.

"I don't care much who owns it. The important thing is getting some deal drawn up with the Greenbriers so as one of them can run things around here."

"I don't think Tuckers will cotton to that notion," Becky said.

"They would if it were Omar," Ella answered, her gaze far-off and determined. "And they would if I put my weight behind it,"—she looked down at her missing leg—"even if it isn't as much as it used to be."

Becky regarded Ella as if for the first time. "You knew Omar was a Greenbrier, didn't you? How long?"

Ella didn't answer right away. "A long time."

"Was this your plan?"

"I don't know if '*plan*' is the right word as much as—takin' the pickin's as they come."

Sophie laughed. "You ornery little weasel. You used to say you weren't at ease around boys."

"Once you learn to be at ease around a Greenbrier, you can be at ease around *anybody*."

Both Ella and Sophie laughed, but Becky only stared at Ella.

"What?" Ella asked.

"Nothing, it's just..." Becky shook her head. "I was one of your closest friends, and—"

"You still are."

"But I never thought you had this in you. I don't reckon anyone did."

Ella shrugged. "I didn't either. But what starts as a little uphill stream has a way of turning into a real gully-washer on down the line."

Epilogue

The green was returning to the pastures, and the trees and brush were fuzzy with blossoms and catkins when Omar finally returned from a trip to the Greenbrier clan. Rather than make camp for the night and finish the journey the next day, he pushed on into the night. The night watch let him in through the western gate, and rather than find his bunk in Bill Puckett's empty house, he slipped into the Hollands' home, lit a lantern, and went up to Ella's room.

Ella's face shone when she woke at a knock on her door to see the tall, brooding Greenbrier standing there at the far end of her room. "Omar!"

"Hey, Ella."

"It's been a while." She rubbed her eyes. "Is it the middle of the night?"

Omar turned his face toward the darkened window, embarrassed, and embarrassed for being embarrassed. "It's likely near morning. I couldn't sleep. I—wanted to see you."

Ella blushed, but then she saw the look on his face. "What's the matter?"

He didn't answer.

"Hey, buck up, feller! The feud's over. Omar, we did it. We won!"

"I can't do it."

Ella's smile melted. "What?"

"I can't make it up to you. And the weight of it is too heavy. I can't—I don't think I can live here after all I done."

"That ain't true."

"I don't deserve you, Ella. You know it better than anyone. What I done—"

Ella only smiled. "I won't tell anyone if you won't."

Omar looked away.

Ella sat up straighter, insistent now. "I ain't joking. Who's gonna point the finger at you?"

"How you think this is going to turn out, Ella? I marry you, and we start a happy family, and—"

"Yes."

"And I live my whole life knowing how much I hurt you? Are you just going to pretend it never happened? Are we going to live that lie?"

"If I say you haven't wronged me more than I could stand, that's the way it is. Ain't no lie. I love you, and if you think that's going to change so easy, you can go ahead and move a mountain while you're at it."

In that moment, even one-legged, Ella looked like she could stare down a bullhusker. He'd already seen her stare down the Pied Piper and make him blink. And yet those same wide eyes gazed on Omar with an innocence as untarnished as ever, still gleaming with a resilient vibrancy that warmed and chilled Omar to the core.

"I don't think I can forgive myself."

"Don't say that, Omar. Don't torture yourself."

"In another world, Ella, I would have been yours." He seized her hand, his eyes glistening.

"Would you break my heart because you didn't feel like you were worth saving?"

Omar said nothing.

"Omar," Ella said, trying to rise and stumbling, the outline of the stump of her leg showing under her nightshirt as she swung over the side of the bed, "I think there's a full moon outside, and the stars are so beautiful. But I can't get there to watch on my own. Won't you carry me, dear?"

Omar blinked. He shook off the evil spell.

She spoke to him not like a young sweetheart, but like a doting wife of many years—as if the struggles and pain of their pasts had only forged their bond into an even tougher metal. As if their yet-unknown children already lay tucked safely in bed, and the winter wheat would show a good harvest this year, and the scars on his hands and face were from honest work, and her missing leg was a mere nuisance. She spoke to him as if, when death finally came for them, it would be a relief—not from the pains of their arthritis and the weight of their many years, but because they would still, in some mysterious way, have their best days ahead of them. She spoke as if their loved ones, already gone before them, were not altogether lost, and might someday be found again. That future was already within reach, and all Omar had to do was grasp it.

He picked her up in his arms and carried her out of the room and down the stairs. Her hands wrapped around his sinewy neck and pulled him closer.

Together, they left the house, and there was no one and nothing there but the blooming trees to watch Omar walking Ella to the stars.

Together, they watched a new sun rise between the cleft of the distant eastern hills.

# About the author

Ethan Warrener grew up in Southwest Missouri, which resembles West Virginia if you *really* squint. If he's not writing or teaching, he's spending any extra free time with his wife and kids or playing too many video games. As you might expect from a Midwesterner, he's an occasional farmer, a regular churchgoer, and a huge metalhead. *The Tucker Clan Saga* took him about a third of his life to finish.

You can find out what he's up to and access exclusive content on his website: https://www.ethanwarrenerauthor.com/

# Acknowledgements

Being an indie author means relying on people even more than as one traditionally published. This trilogy took fourteen years to write, and the number of people I've gone to for advice, support, encouragement, editing, feedback, artwork, childcare, etc. numbers in the dozens. Thank you all.

I would like to thank Oren Eades, my editor, for his meticulous work and his enthusiasm for this project.

Thanks to both Erin Parrot and Marcus Siebert for their art skills and their patience with my repeated requests for edits.

Thanks to Mom for her proofreading skills; you saved me from an avalanche of tpyos.

Thanks to Mark Robertson for being a bro.

Thanks to Emily Beaver, Daniel Baird, and Jane Robertson for your insights on the story at various stages of development.

Thanks to my wife, Judith Beaver, without whom there wouldn't be a third book in a series I swore up and down would never be a trilogy. In case that many negatives in a sentence was confusing, that is both a sarcastic thank-you and a genuine one. Your commitment to excellence kept my writing standards high when I wanted to cut corners.

Thank you to... honestly, most folks in my life right now, from my family, to my friends, to my excellent coworkers, my neighbors, everyone. Thank you for being yourselves and opening my eyes to the rich tapestry that is humanity.

# Also by Ethan Warrener

*For Home and Hearth*

*For Peace and Purpose*